EX LIBRIS

BEST SELLERS

FROM READER'S DIGEST
CONDENSED BOOKS

THE READER'S DIGEST ASSOCIATION
Pleasantville, New York

Reader's Digest Condensed Books are published every two to three months at Pleasantville, N.Y.

CONTENTS

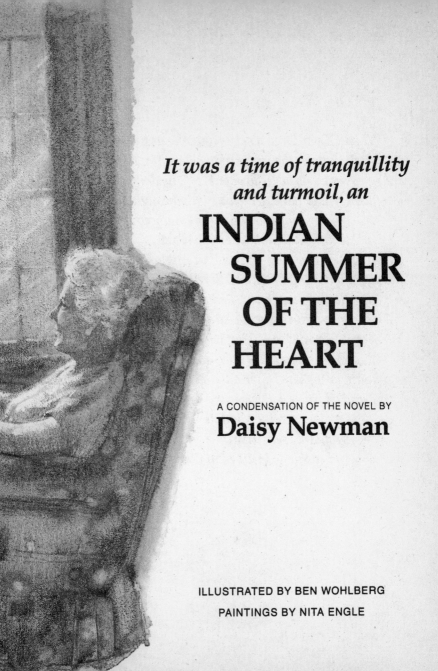

*It was a time of tranquillity
and turmoil, an*

INDIAN
SUMMER
OF THE
HEART

A CONDENSATION OF THE NOVEL BY
Daisy Newman

ILLUSTRATED BY BEN WOHLBERG

PAINTINGS BY NITA ENGLE

When Oliver Otis, a seventy-eight-year-old widower,
fell in love, the realization shook him to the core.
What was he to do about it? The daily silences
of his Quaker faith, which usually brought him insight,
failed to enlighten him now.
He longed to unburden his heart. . . . But his
daughter, Heather, far away in England, would never
understand. And Peter and Serenity Holland, who shared
his Rhode Island farm, had all they could cope with,
trying to build separate careers while caring for their
three-year-old son. That left Loveday Mead herself,
and Oliver dared not imagine her reaction. She was
a younger woman, after all—seventy-two, to be exact—
and a former college dean. What would she want
with a simple farmer?
A radiant, sensitive love story that celebrates
old-fashioned values in the modern world.

PART I: *Oliver*

CHAPTER ONE

IN THE summer of his seventy-ninth year Oliver Otis of Firbank Farm fell in love, not circumspectly, as an elderly widower might properly do to secure companionship and decent cooking, but wildly, without design, head over heels. The preposterous situation frightened Oliver. It was unseemly. *At thy age!* he reproached himself a dozen times a day.

He could think of little else.

Every morning, sitting quietly in his study, cultivating his spirit, as he always did before going out to cultivate the stony Rhode Island soil, Oliver reviewed his condition. And on First Days—Sundays—enveloped in the silence of the Friends Meeting at Kendal, he waited anxiously for insight. But the turmoil persisted. I'm ordinarily calm, Oliver argued with himself. How did my emotions get so out of control? He had told no one, naturally.

At times he suspected that Serenity and Peter Holland, who lived with him, had a tiny inkling. They seemed to regard him more tenderly these days, almost in sorrow, as if they feared that his judgment was impaired. For *their* sake, Oliver thought, I ought to explain; assure them that I'm not senile, only in love.

Yes, he'd tell them, but not right now. This was his time for solitude, for withdrawing into his secret self. Even in the harvest

7

season, when Oliver begrudged every moment he wasn't working outdoors, he still set this half hour aside, sitting quietly by the window in his study. It was a time to suspend preoccupation with those mundane matters the old Quakers used to refer to as "creaturely activity," a time to center down.

When his wife, Daphne, was alive, they had had their morning silence by the living-room fire in winter, while the dogs lay on the hearthrug. In summer they sat on the back porch in the old glider, holding hands. Sharing the silence in love had made it a joy. Now Oliver continued the practice by himself, although this solitary silence, more than anything else in his routine, revealed the depth of his loneliness.

Still, he welcomed the opportunity to relax and measure his life, face its inadequacies, fan the divine spark within him so that he might more clearly approximate the person he wished to be. But today he was restless, incapable of detaching himself from the thought of all he had to do.

The orchard—it was getting beyond him. Everything ripened at once. Serenity had been doing the preserving the past few seasons, but this year she was so busy that she didn't start till late at night, and she never quite finished all the canning and freezing. She ought not to be doing it. With a small child to care for, a husband, her studies, and all she did for Oliver, she had far too much on her shoulders.

Oliver tried to forget the orchard for a few minutes, to harvest what William Penn called the "fruits of solitude." But even more pressing this morning was his weekly letter to his daughter, Heather. That letter weighed on Oliver. He couldn't center down, he decided finally. So he switched to the chair by the typewriter table. After carefully spelling out Heather's name and London address on an aerogram, he got only as far as "Dear Heather"; then his thoughts wandered back to the Hollands. If he were to confide in them—admit to the state of his heart—mightn't his equanimity return?

I'll go and tell them right now, he resolved. *Quickly*, before they leave for the university. But he just sat in his chair, unable to stir. *In love!* Applied to himself, the condition sounded so amusing that he laughed out loud.

What would Heather say, though, if she knew? *She* wouldn't find it so amusing. Oliver loved his daughter dearly and he knew she loved him, but they seldom saw eye to eye. He faced the typewriter again. Under no circumstances would he mention the lady who had unaccountably invaded his heart.

"Eggplant's enormous now," he wrote instead, choosing a safe subject. "Thee knows how beautiful it is. Mother used to paint mounds, stacked along the side of the barn. Against that weathered red, the lustrous amethyst, highlighted in silver . . ."

Oliver had plenty of interesting items to report, and his letters to London always carried a full account of what was happening at Firbank. But now he felt guilty—he was holding out. And yet if I tell Heather, he argued with himself, even the miles of ocean between us won't temper the force of her reaction.

Whatever has got *into* you, Father? she would demand by return mail. You can't possibly be thinking of *marrying?* You were always so reasonable.

Marrying? he'd write back. *Me?* I'd never dreamed of such a thing. Till thee suggested it. How could thee suppose that a younger woman—seventy-two, to be exact, vivacious, independent, a former college dean—would want to marry *me?* It's simply that I'm—well—drawn to her.

That would send Heather into a panic. She would telephone. Transatlantic. I'm flying over *at once!* she would say.

But Heather wouldn't, of course, do anything of the sort. Oliver's imagination was running away with him. She might be a bit too solicitous sometimes, but she never criticized or said anything unkind. It was what she *wouldn't* say that Oliver really dreaded. In her usual way, she'd merely respond obliquely, inquiring, perhaps, about the Hollands, the implication being that with them to look after him and her own annual visits, what more did Oliver need? Not a wife, surely.

Indeed the Hollands were good to him—if anything a little more considerate now, sensing that he was troubled. And their little boy was one subject Oliver could write about to Heather without the fear that it would backfire. Having exhausted the eggplant, he went on. "I wish thee could see how fast Ross is growing. Catching on about the bathroom, too. *Finally!*"

Rereading what he had typed so far, Oliver wondered if even this was wise. In her last letter Heather had expressed anxiety concerning what she called her father's baby-sitting. Oliver had quickly reassured her. Serenity got Ross up in the morning and took him to nursery school before going to her classes at the university. Oliver simply called for him at noon, gave him lunch and put him down for his nap. Later they went out and gardened till Peter came home and took over. Really, it was nothing. Ross was such a companionable child.

Oliver hadn't added that his own nap was often postponed because Ross wanted to hold on to a knobby forefinger until sleep overtook him, and sometimes Oliver was so tired he fell asleep himself, sitting upright beside the bed. Heather would not have approved. Baby-spoiling is what she would have called it. She had brought up four children and considered herself an authority. Oliver preferred not to argue with her. Ross needed this security. When a little boy's mother is gone all day, *someone* has to . . .

This letter was becoming more and more difficult. Despairing, Oliver gazed out the window for inspiration. A cardinal was perched in the hemlock at the edge of the Firbank woods. Pleading with the bird not to fly away, so he could watch him instead of writing, Oliver thought of the Hollands again.

Why couldn't he bring himself to confide in Serenity and Peter? He trusted them as if they were his children. Each evening over supper they discussed the day's events together, its difficulties and satisfactions. When they had first come to Firbank five years ago, perplexed lovers themselves, they had confided in him. He and Daphne had been able to help them— Daphne especially. If only she might have lived to see them happily married a year later!

Now it was Oliver's turn to be perplexed, though in his case there was no thought of marriage. That was out of the question for a man who so loved his wife that when she died he felt as if he had suffered an amputation. Nor was he exactly a teenager, at the mercy of inexorable sexual pressures, as Serenity and Peter had been. Still, in a different way, wasn't he in need of help, too?

The cardinal had a mind of his own. Indifferent to Oliver's pleading, he took off. Unwilling to return to the typewriter, Oliver fixed his attention on the white window curtain that was ballooning like a sail in the breeze.

What was it that drew him to this stranger who, unannounced, had suddenly appeared at Firbank? No one could be more unlike Daphne. His wife had never tried to manage anybody, whereas this woman betrayed, in a well-bred yet overpowering way, how important it had been to her to wield authority in that little college of hers. Yet there was something in her eyes, in her manner, that seemed to contradict this, to cry out for a different fulfillment she'd missed. This hunger touched Oliver. He longed to share the vision he thought she glimpsed here, even as he craved the unaccountable joy it gave him to be in her presence.

An explosion in the driveway shattered the silence. It was only Peter's van, uncertain—as it was every morning—whether it wished to start. When it consented, Peter drove off for a day of teaching introductory astronomy, after having spent half the night in the observatory collecting data for his doctoral dissertation. Serenity came out now, pulling Ross with gentle firmness. There was a howl as she picked him up and buckled him into his car seat, and then they pulled away, too.

Sighing, Oliver covered the typewriter and pushed back his chair. He opened the door and started down the hall to the kitchen. It was too late to tell the Hollands now. They'd left.

The kitchen had its usual morning air of hurried departure. An eggy bib decorated the back of Ross's chair. A stream of orange juice ran down one side of the tablecloth. In the middle of the floor lay Peter's work shoes, like faithful dogs waiting for their master's return. The real dogs, Lion and Duffy, also waited—

beyond the screen door, vociferously requesting the pleasure of Oliver's company. "Just a minute," he called.

Carefully stepping around some scattered toys, Oliver pushed in the chairs and wiped the plastic tablecloth that was easier for Serenity to keep clean than the bare wood he and Daphne had loved. He missed polishing the walnut grain till it shone. He missed the pewter teapot, too, with its century-old nicks; the Hollands simply dragged a tea bag through a cup of water, leaving the bag to stain the saucer and dry up.

How different the house was now from the way Daphne and he had kept it—everything scrubbed and shining, with a sense of homely beauty and repose. Still, Oliver thought, it's a warm room. The people have gone, but their aura remains.

It was the aura of young people devoted to each other, to their child and to him, mixed with an atmosphere of breathless haste, of overburdened lives. They belonged to an age that expected every young man and woman to perform the duties of several persons simultaneously and with perfection.

Serenity had given Ross her wholehearted attention until his third birthday. Then she and Peter had decided that this was the year for her to enroll in graduate school. Now, Oliver observed that when she came home—tired, with dinner to prepare and mountains of books to study before morning—she scarcely had time and energy left to play with Ross. She was as devoted to him as before, but she had other commitments, too.

Not my business, he told himself. They must bring up their child as they see fit. But more and more Ross was becoming Oliver's child, looking to him for security and comfort, a bulwark against those baby-sitters who kept appearing. Ross was a sturdy little fellow and would grow up somehow. But Serenity and Peter, warmhearted, generous, conscientious, pressured beyond endurance—what was going to become of them?

Oliver regretted not having told them his secret before they left. Tonight he'd definitely tell them. But would they understand? To youngsters in their middle twenties, wouldn't it be inconceivable that a man of seventy-eight should fall in love—

practically at first sight? It might well strike them as ludicrous. Oliver had laughed at the idea himself, but he didn't think he could bear it if they were to laugh at him.

He would point out that people in their seventies were indeed capable of loving, and if two people love each other, he would exclaim, how can age matter? *If* they loved each other—ah, that was the real impediment.

Scrubbing the sink, he told himself sadly that what was driving him to the verge of despair was simply the conviction that his feeling wasn't reciprocated. How could it be, with her interests? he thought. They're entirely outside my range of knowledge. Those composers she's always talking about as if they're still living: the Mozarts, the Haydns, the Strausses. I love music, but with my background— She must find me very dull.

When the kitchen looked a little more shipshape, Oliver stood in the middle of the floor wondering which of his many jobs to tackle first. Before he knew it, twelve o'clock would be here. It would be time to pick up Ross. And, Oliver reminded himself, Austin Young had promised to come over this afternoon to help shock the field corn. Better sharpen the corn knife. He went to the back hall for his floppy white hat.

The woodshed opened off the back hall, and Oliver stopped at the door and looked inside. This had been Daphne's studio. Here she had painted those masterpieces that were now hanging in museums around the country. And here Oliver had found her that day four and a half years ago, when he brought in her tea. Her heart had stopped, but she was still holding her brush.

The big potbellied stove in the corner, which had made the woodshed so cozy, was cold now with the ashes of the last fire Oliver had built for her. No one used the room. Those ashes ought to be cleaned out, he told himself. But just standing there a moment, Oliver drew solace from what he saw within.

Daphne spoke to him. Her canvases, stacked against the walls, spoke with her voice: portraits of people they'd known, scenes of places they'd visited, and hundreds of vignettes of Firbank. There was the maple tree outside the window, painted at every season of the year: in the scarlet, gold and crimson glory of early autumn, shot through with vestiges of summer green; in the tracery of bare branches thrusting into the winter sky; in the first, delicate leafing-out of springtime. There were the wild flowers—lady's slippers, blue flags, marsh marigolds and violets. There was even a sketch of the kitchen table as they kept it in those days. A shaft of sunlight streaming in through the back door overlay the polished surface.

Oliver suddenly felt more peace than he'd known in weeks. Daphne would have understood.

OUTDOORS, it was a rare morning—there might not be another day so beautiful till next summer. Oliver started for the barn to get ready for shocking corn. But as he stepped out of the warm sunshine into the chilly interior, it came over him like a God-given leading that it was a sin not to celebrate this superb day. So he did an unheard-of thing—he turned on his heel, walked out of the barn and headed for Salt Pond. He, who was so conscientious, who cared for his land as if it were part of his family—he, Oliver Otis, ran away to sea!

The dogs were ecstatic. Young Lion, the retriever, loped ahead on his long legs; poor, affectionate little Duffy, the ailing thirteen-year-old fox terrier, could barely keep up with Oliver. By the time they reached the pond, Lion was already in the dory, but Duffy hesitated, looking over the edge of the dock. Formerly she had jumped in bravely, too. Now she stood there, anguished, lurching forward tentatively, then pulling back in fear. Oliver tucked her tightly under his arm as he stepped into the boat, not quite so springily himself as in earlier days, but ably enough. Untying the painter, he cast off, rowing slowly, leaving his cares ashore.

The pond was still, but Oliver could hear the surf crashing beyond the dunes. Exhilarated by the clear air, gliding over the glassy pond, he felt as soul-satisfied as the dogs appeared to be, curled up in the stern. Drifting lazily, he gave himself up to the delight of reliving the events of recent weeks.

That afternoon in early August when Serenity had brought home an unexpected guest— Oliver had been on the living-room floor, playing with Ross, when a handsome woman walked in. Soft creases in her face, deepening as she smiled, made no secret of her age. Neither did the white hair, cut short and simply combed. But she moved easily, and her open, unaffected manner gave the impression that she was younger than her years.

She had caught him in a most undignified position—propped on one elbow, his long legs outstretched, building a garage of blocks. He was adding the top row of blocks—a delicate operation—and thought he'd heard Peter's van and Serenity's car arriving. He hadn't bothered to get up. Then Serenity entered, accompanied not by Peter but by a woman, a stranger.

Oliver struggled to sit up, his jerky movements causing the garage to collapse with a crash, scattering the blocks across the room. He felt like a fool.

Ross was hilarious. "Thee busted it, 'cle Oliver!" he shouted gleefully. He dropped an armful of toy trucks on the ruins and ran to his mother.

But Serenity was bending over Oliver, holding out a helping hand, talking all the while. "Oliver, this is Mrs. Mead. I happened to be in the library when she came in, and I overheard her tell the new cataloguer that her ancestors were southern Rhode Island Quakers and she wanted to find out about them." Ross was tugging at Serenity's skirt, begging to be noticed. She placed her free hand on his head lovingly as she went on. "No one knows as much about Quakers as thee does, Oliver. So I asked Mrs. Mead to come home with me for supper."

Serenity bent to kiss Ross. Then, turning back to her guest, she asked, "By the way, what's your first name?"

"Loveday." It was enunciated slowly, distinctly, as if the owner were accustomed to having her name misheard.

Oliver caught his breath. *Loveday*—how absolutely beautiful! He'd heard it before—where, he couldn't recall.

"Quakers don't like titles," Serenity was explaining, fearing that the visitor might think it rude for her to demand a given

15

name on such short acquaintance. "When a Friend uses a person's whole name, he isn't being familiar. It's a mark of respect, just as it would be for someone else to say Mrs. Mead."

"Loveday," Oliver murmured under his breath, enchanted. Where had he heard it before? It eluded him. "An ancient name, isn't it?" he guessed.

The woman's face lit up. "You're the first person I ever met who knew that! Most people think, because they've never heard it, that it's a joke, corny. It's been a trial all my life. I nearly changed it."

"I think it's beautiful," Oliver assured her.

"Well, I know how it is when your name isn't common," Serenity exclaimed. "I have the same problem. Anyway, Loveday Mead, meet Oliver Otis."

Oliver shook the woman's outstretched hand. She smiled at him, as anyone would on being introduced. And yet to Oliver, distraught though he was, that smile conveyed more than politeness. It was an intimation.

Now, watching Firbank recede as he rowed across the pond, Oliver noticed the sea lavender. Masses of tiny, pale blue flowers covered the marsh like an azure haze. But his mind was still turned inward, conjuring up the smile with which Loveday Mead had acknowledged Serenity's introduction.

She had gone on to thank Oliver in advance for his assistance. "I'm spending some time in Boston and I thought before returning home to Kansas I'd drive down to Rhode Island and hunt up my ancestors. But the person I spoke to at the library didn't seem to know her way around. Luckily I was"—she laughed— "rescued."

"I knew thee could help," Serenity said to Oliver. Then she took Ross's hand and led him off to the kitchen.

Oliver was still flustered. "I'll be glad to assist thee—I mean, you—any way I can, Loveday Mead. Do sit down."

She settled immediately into the nearest chair, her elbows reposing on the arms, her hands in her lap. She looked at ease, happy to be relaxing.

But Oliver was shaken. She had chosen Daphne's chair. No one who came to Firbank these days ever chose it, remembering Daphne sitting there by the fire with the dogs at her feet. Not that Oliver wished it to be preserved inviolate—he abhorred sentimental rubbish like that. Yet as he settled himself in his own chair, he suddenly couldn't think of anything to say.

His visitor didn't seem to be expecting immediate conversation. She was looking around the room—at the shelves of books stacked clear to the ceiling, at Daphne's portrait of Grandmother Serenity over the mantel and at the paintings on the walls. "That sampler!" she exclaimed. "It must be at least a century old."

"Older. My grandmother made it at the age of eight. The date's in the lower left-hand corner—1842."

Loveday got up and went over to the wall where the sampler hung in a narrow gilt frame, and read aloud, " 'Walk cheerfully over the world, answering that of God in every one.' " The words of George Fox, so familiar to Quakers, were evidently new to her, for she read the text twice.

Oliver took this opportunity to recover his composure and take in her appearance, from the white blouse, open at the throat, to the blue skirt, which fell just over her knees. Even though she'd spent the past months in the city, her arms and legs were tanned. And she was wearing a wedding ring. Was her husband waiting for her in Boston? Oliver was curious.

She, it appeared, was curious, also. Was this his house? she inquired. Did the Hollands live with him? Or was it the other way around?

Oliver explained that Firbank Farm had come down to him from his grandmother Serenity Otis, the one whose portrait hung over the fireplace. "Actually she left Firbank to all her descendants, but I was the only one who was willing to farm. So it came to me, along with her red hair."

Loveday laughed, then sat down again.

"That's the color my hair used to be," Oliver amended quickly, so she wouldn't think he had illusions about his appearance. "The present Serenity and Ross and my daughter, Heather, got the Otis hair. Serenity is my cousin Edmund Ross's daughter."

"She's lovely-looking."

"Yes. Beautiful, not just in appearance but in spirit. Daphne and I were so surprised when she turned up five years ago. We'd been out of touch with Edmund—you know how these things happen in families—and Serenity came here because she and Peter thought they might like to have a Quaker wedding. They wanted to find out how to go about it. A year later they were married in Kendal Meeting. Peter had a fellowship for graduate study, and Serenity had a grant from the Museum of Contemporary Art to assist me with the book I was writing. And as they had no place to live, it seemed natural to invite them—"

"*You* wrote a book?" Loveday broke in.

He ignored the question. Did she think that because he was a farmer he couldn't write? "It seemed natural," Oliver repeated, "to invite them to make their home with me, since Serenity was working here and Peter could commute to the university. For their part, they offered to take over the housekeeping and some of the chores. We only expected to do this till my book was finished, but then Ross surprised them and they stayed. It's been four years now. I've had care and loving companionship. They've had a home they enjoy."

"And a built-in sitter."

"Oh, no! The little I do can't be classified that way. It's simply that one of the girls Serenity engaged to come in frightened Ross, so I begged to be allowed to take over."

"Well, whatever you call it, do continue," Loveday urged. "It's so important for a young mother to get out. I still remember how frustrated I was when the kids were small. I pined all day for adult conversation. It wasn't till my husband died and I entered graduate school, preparing to support my family, that I really felt fulfilled."

Oliver was shocked. "Fulfilled?" The word had escaped; he wanted to bite his tongue. How could a woman feel fulfilled by her husband's death?

"Yes," she said calmly, not perceiving his reaction. "I'd always wanted to teach. At the ripe age of forty I got my Ph.D. in European history."

"If Serenity keeps going," Oliver remarked, "she'll still be in her twenties when she gets her doctor's degree."

"So much the better. It's harder later, I can tell you. But I worked. And eventually I became dean of studies at William Allen White College in Emporia, Kansas." She said it modestly, not to impress him, merely to support her contention. "I always used to tell our women students to fight for their careers. Sounds disgustingly aggressive," she acknowledged, "but how else will they ever overcome masculine domination?"

She almost made Oliver feel guilty for being a man. And yet, hadn't Quakers always upheld the equality of the sexes?

"I do hope," she told him, "that the Hollands can stay with you till Serenity finishes her education."

"As far as I'm concerned, it would be ideal if they stayed forever," Oliver exclaimed. "Someday I'll have to give up farming. Who'll care for Firbank then? My only child lives in England, so by the terms of my grandmother's will, Serenity would be entitled to the place. But she wants to be an art historian and Peter's an astronomer. Farming's not for them."

"Naturally," Loveday said, crossing her legs.

They were the color of that honey from Mount Hymettus. Oliver thought of himself as a gentleman of the old school, though not stuffy and seldom critical of others—only demanding of himself the behavior that had been drilled into his generation. And now, thoroughly fascinated, he was unashamedly studying a strange woman's legs!

Suddenly he looked up with a start. The legs had changed position; their owner must be aware of his interest. Yes, she was watching him. He was miserably embarrassed.

"About your Quaker ancestors," he said quickly.

She seemed to have forgotten them. Leaning forward and appearing a trifle shy, she asked, "Why did you change a few minutes ago? You started to say thee to me and then . . ."

He explained that only a few old-fashioned Friends still used what they called plain language—the singular form in addressing one person. "These days, you see, it's become a language of intimacy, and we only use it among ourselves."

She leaned back again, looking downright disappointed.

"Your ancestors," he repeated. "What were their names?"

"Austell—Thomas, his son Isaac and his *twelve* children. Can't remember all their names," she confessed, laughing, "or which settled in Rhode Island and which were Quakers. But I do know one—David Austell—married out, as they called it. He migrated to Kansas in the 1850s. Mother used to tell me the frontier stories that were handed down to her, but I never paid much attention. It's strange, since I eventually became a historian. Now my daughter-in-law, Sara Ann, wants to know about these ancestors. She's making a family tree for my grandchildren. I can't believe Michael and Jed will ever want to look at a family tree. All they care about is baseball and television. But I don't want to ignore my daughter-in-law's wishes."

"Austell," Oliver murmured. "No, I can't place them."

"Thomas originally emigrated from the south of England—Somerset, I believe."

"My wife came from Yorkshire. She was a painter."

"Do you mean *Daphne* Otis? She was *your wife?* I've heard of her, of course."

"These paintings," Oliver said, waving his hand around the room, "were all done by her."

He hoped she would ask more about Daphne. But she didn't. Reluctantly he returned to the ancestors. "With a little patience, you might track down the Austells. In the early days Friends didn't keep membership lists. They figured anybody could spot a Quaker by his or her speech and dress. But they kept careful records of their meetings for business, and if your forebears were active in Kendal Meeting, they might be mentioned in one of the old minute books at the meetinghouse."

"Is Kendal Meetinghouse far from here?"

"Eight miles. I'd be glad to take you someday."

She looked at him eagerly. "*Would* you?"

CHAPTER TWO

ROWING lazily, lost in recollection, Oliver was carried by the current to the south shore of Salt Pond. Lion didn't wait for him to beach the boat but jumped out and splashed up the bank. Duffy gazed apprehensively over the side. "Soon as I get my sneakers off," Oliver promised, "I'll take thee ashore." These days, getting shod and unshod was proving increasingly difficult. Oliver's feet seemed to be getting farther from his arms.

At last he stood up, barefoot, and stepped into the warm water, with Duffy on his hip. The mud of the flats squished between his toes till he reached dry sand. Taking care not to crush the silver clumps of dusty miller, he climbed to the top of the dune and stood still, watching a flock of well-ordered sandpipers sweep by.

Before him spread a wide expanse of ocean. *The face of the deep,* he quoted to himself from Genesis, awed. As the waves rolled in from the horizon and broke along the sunny beach, the world seemed brand-new, just coming into being.

The beauty of the pond, the dunes and the ever changing ocean had nourished Oliver all his life. Yet now, thinking of Loveday, he found the world even more beautiful. Exuberant, he wanted to shout her name from the top of the dune. How she would enjoy standing here, she who came from landlocked Kansas! But of course she'd seen the ocean before, in other parts of the world. She had traveled widely.

On that first visit, when she was telling Oliver about her ancestors, she'd said, "Last year I went to Austria to see where my father's people came from. They were Protestants and during the Counter-Reformation they were severely persecuted. Finally, in 1733, the bishop of Salzburg expelled twenty thousand of them. Most fled to Germany, but a little band made its way to the New World. Johann and Katherl Klaus, my ancestors, found a haven in Georgia. Their descendants moved to Ohio, and later to Kansas, near the town of Emporia."

Oliver could no longer restrain his curiosity. "What about your

husband's family?" he asked. "You must include them in your family tree."

"Of course." Her face lost its animation. "But we never discussed genealogy and there's no one left to ask about it now. Anyway, as I was saying, I went to Austria. It's a beautiful country—snowcapped mountains, and lakes with tiny steamers. The best way to get around is on a sight-seeing tour. One of the places our bus stopped was Saint Gilgen, right on a lake, and we were taken to see the birthplace of Mozart's mother. It was a great surprise for me to learn that Mozart's sister had lived there, too, in the same house, after she married the local mayor."

Loveday seemed to be assuming that Oliver was familiar with the life of Mozart. Although he enjoyed the composer's music, Oliver knew nothing about his family.

"You see," Loveday was saying, "when I was a little girl, taking piano lessons, I was fascinated by the stories about Wolfgang Amadeus Mozart and his sister, Nannerl, touring together as children—he playing a tiny violin and she the clavier—going from court to court, dressed in gaudy clothes. But it had never occurred to me to wonder what became of Nannerl after she grew up, until one day when I went to the Mozart Museum in Salzburg and began to piece together a few facts. Talk about masculine domination! Nannerl was one of its worst victims."

Oliver felt guilty again.

"So," Loveday continued, "when I stood before the house where she'd lived, studying a bas-relief on the wall with heads of the mother and daughter, both looking so wistful . . ." Loveday paused, leaning forward. "Something happened to me. It was as if Nannerl reached down and touched me on the shoulder, begging me to tell the world that *she* was somebody, too—not only as a child prodigy but later. That's why I came east—to do research on her at Harvard."

She stopped, studying Oliver, as if to determine whether he was taking her seriously. Sensing that he was, she blurted out, "It's changed my whole life—that one short stop on a sight-seeing tour. All the plans I had for my retirement, all the things I'd been looking forward to doing—Nannerl crowded out everything."

Now it was Oliver who leaned forward. "And you're doing it? You're telling the world that this—what did you call her?—that she was *somebody?*"

"Yes. Her name was Nannerl. It's a nickname—she was baptized Maria Anna, and she married a baron, but all her life she was just known as Nannerl. How she must have suffered! A gifted artist pushed into domesticity merely because of her sex."

Loveday's readiness to respond to a cry for recognition was both touching and grand, Oliver thought. It had the authentic ring of what Quakers call a leading.

Suddenly Ross came running in. Hurling himself against Oliver's knee, he eyed the stranger warily. "What is it?" Oliver asked. "Was thee sent to call us in for supper?"

"No."

Sensing the child's anxiety that this might be yet another baby-sitter, Oliver took him on his lap to reassure him. He hoped Loveday would continue her narrative. But she showed no inclination to go on. Instead, she said, "It's charming, your plain language."

Oliver confided how happy he was that Serenity and Peter used it. Before they came to Firbank, he explained, they had never heard it spoken. "But it's the language in which they made their marriage promises, you see. And when they came to live here, they slipped naturally into responding in the way I spoke to them. It's especially gratifying to me because my daughter revolted against the plain language as soon as she went to school. The children laughed when they heard her speaking it, and she has never overcome her aversion."

"How contrary life is," Loveday murmured. "Your daughter has the right to say thee and thy, but doesn't care to, while I— It makes me wish that ancestor of mine hadn't married out!"

Standing on the dune, facing the ocean, Oliver recollected Loveday's expression as she had said this. There had been a hint of wistfulness in her voice that had gone straight to his heart.

He turned and started down the steep dune to the water's edge, where he lifted Duffy tenderly into the dory beside Lion. Then he pushed the boat clear of the beach and climbed in.

Still dreaming of Loveday's first visit, Oliver was scarcely conscious of reaching shore.

"Would you like to see a bit of Firbank?" he had asked her.

"Yes, indeed!"

"Me, too," Ross begged. Oliver stood up and took the little boy's hand, telling him to wait and let the lady go first.

At the door she stopped. Turning to him, she asked, smiling, "Won't you call me Loveday?"

Something went queer in Oliver's chest, like the sensation he used to have in swimming when he'd been underwater for what seemed like hours and surfaced at last.

"Maybe you'd rather use my nickname—Lowdy," she added.

"No!" Oliver declared vehemently. "I don't like nicknames, and I think your given name's beautiful."

She had appeared pleased. "It's really old, you know. It goes back to the Middle Ages. When serfs quarreled, the lord of the manor appointed a day on which they had to settle their dispute amicably—a day of love, they called it: *dies amoris*. In the beginning the name was given to girls born on that day. Then the origin was forgotten and girls were named Loveday who were born anytime."

Oliver walked back to the house along the path he had taken with her that day, remembering everything—the sun starting to go down, Ross skipping ahead with the dogs, all that he had told her: how he hoped she'd call him Oliver; how much bigger his garden used to be; how he had grown Christmas trees for his and Daphne's cash crop. Then he had pointed to the acres in the distance that he called the Vietnamese Forest, telling her about the experiment he had conducted in wartime for revitalizing ravaged soil.

"Those defoliation bombs!" he'd said. "Imagine killing the leaves on a tree. It's almost as sinful as killing a person. And we know now that those bombs *did* kill or harm people, too."

"I know," Loveday said sadly.

"There was no way I could stop the damage at the time. But I thought that if I could just find a method for restoring life to contaminated soil, then, when the war was over, we'd be able to go to Vietnam and replace all the trees and vegetation our chemicals had destroyed."

"Go to Vietnam? You were *going* there?"

"Why not? I assumed that after the war Friends would be sent over to repair as much as we could, just as Friends have done after the other wars. So I tried to simulate conditions in Vietnam in those acres you see over there—"

"Here in New England?" she cried. "But Vietnam's tropical."

"This is the only land I had to experiment with." He went on to explain how, after killing the vegetation in those acres, he tried various formulas till he found one that revitalized the soil, so that the seedlings he subsequently planted in it did grow. It had taken years of labor and failure, but in the end he triumphed. "Then," he concluded sadly, "after the war was over, I never had a chance to apply what I'd learned. None of us were allowed into Vietnam."

Loveday had looked as if his experience were as disappointing to her as it had been to him.

Now, six weeks later, the warmth of that sympathy filled Oliver with such joy that he forgot where he was until he reached the barn. He glanced at his watch. Eleven thirty! He must start for the nursery school right away, or Ross would be waiting for him, feeling abandoned and inconsolable.

But once on the Post Road in his ancient pickup, he caught himself thinking of Loveday again, recalling the morning he first took her to Kendal. He had stopped the truck a second in front of the meetinghouse before parking, to gauge her reaction. How would she take the plainness—the dove-gray clapboards, the clear windows? Would she love the simplicity, as he did?

"It's beautiful!" she'd exclaimed, and he was pleased.

They had climbed up into the gallery, where the minute books were stored in a sea chest, and sitting side by side had leafed through the old leather volumes, looking for some reference to Loveday's ancestors.

Deciphering the archaic eighteenth-century handwriting was slow work. It had required two more visits, and they had still found no record of early Friends named Austell. So she would have to come again! The weeks between her visits seemed endless, but they were bearable, compared with Oliver's fear that Loveday might actually discover what she was looking for. Then she'd have no reason for ever returning to Firbank. . . .

The thought was so devastating that Oliver failed to see an oncoming car until it was almost upon him. He just missed landing in a ditch as he swerved to avoid it. Realizing how narrowly he had escaped disaster, Oliver was mortified that he should nearly have an accident because he was dreaming about a woman. And not Daphne, but another woman—one so unlike his wife that it was almost as if Oliver had become another person. But I *feel* just the same! I *am* the same. Only, he thought wryly, only—I'm in love.

Did every woman bring out a different side of a man's character? This one sometimes seemed at war with herself, divided in mind and heart, though she spoke with such assurance that she probably wasn't aware of that part of herself which was totally different. Oliver believed he discerned it more clearly than she did, and it drew him inexorably to her.

Was it to reconcile the opposing forces in her nature that he longed to take Loveday in his arms? But she's not my wife! How can I feel that way about someone I scarcely know?

When he reached the school and stuck his head inside Ross's classroom, relief and joy sprang into the child's eyes. And Oliver, bending down to put his arm around the small waist, also felt relief and joy. The terror on the highway, the outrageous thoughts—surely these were just caused by some momentary aberration that would never come again.

On the way home he stopped with Ross at the cove to talk to the swans and the egret, as they did every noon. Then they had lunch, and Oliver put Ross down for his nap, settling himself beside the bed. Instantly a little hand grabbed his forefinger and held it fast.

Oliver felt blessedly calm now. He hadn't, after all, lost control on the highway. He was all right, and the truck wasn't damaged. Flexing his captive forefinger, which was growing numb, he thought with amusement that life would have been simpler if, as his joints aged, his feelings had, also. But he still craved the companionship of a charming woman.

Until Loveday appeared, his future had seemed predictable—a continuation (at best) of the present, with his powers slowly diminishing. Now, anything might happen. The possibility filled him with alarm. And yet it was invigorating, too. Disparate though they were, he and Loveday shared an essential quality. They were both what Friends called seekers—open to leadings of the spirit.

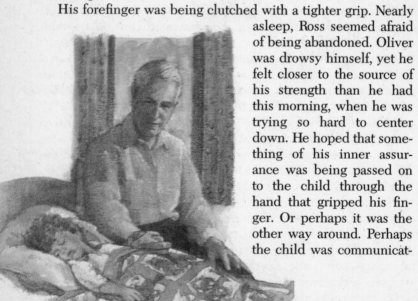

His forefinger was being clutched with a tighter grip. Nearly asleep, Ross seemed afraid of being abandoned. Oliver was drowsy himself, yet he felt closer to the source of his strength than he had this morning, when he was trying so hard to center down. He hoped that something of his inner assurance was being passed on to the child through the hand that gripped his finger. Or perhaps it was the other way around. Perhaps the child was communicating this to him. For Oliver's habitual reserve was melting away, demolishing his defenses, overcoming the fear of exposing his heart. Suddenly he couldn't wait till the Hollands came home. The desire to speak of Loveday became irrepressible.

"Ross," he asked in a low voice, "does thee remember Loveday Mead, who came to see us?"

Ross nodded sleepily. He was still holding the finger.

"Thee sees," Oliver whispered, hoping the child was awake enough to hear, "I love her."

BY THE time Oliver and Ross awoke from their nap, Austin Young was already in the barn, pulling that contraption they used to stack the sheaves—the corn horse—out from its place against the south wall.

There was something about Austin's shy smile that Oliver found touching; it belonged to a man who wished to be more outgoing than he was capable of. He and his wife, Judy, were active in the Friends Meeting. When Daphne died, it had been Austin who had quietly attended to things, picking up Serenity and Peter at the airport, bringing extra benches to the meeting-house so that the many people who came to honor Daphne could be seated at the Meeting of thanksgiving for her life.

Getting the corn horse out to the field was slow work, especially with Ross, who was determined to help but constantly in the way. "I planted less corn this year," Oliver told Austin. "Only a few rows. Beginning to know my limitations."

The two men went about the shocking in a unison born of having worked together often—gathering the stalks and tying them up without talking. For Oliver these bundles of corn were a link between him and all the husbandmen who had worked the land throughout the ages. The green shocks were beautiful, standing in rows, symmetrical, straight, yet each with a tilt and shape of its own. He wished Loveday were here to enjoy the sight. As for the johnnycake into which this corn would be made—she'd never taste it, for she'd be back home.

On her second visit, Loveday had reported to Oliver about

29

her research at Harvard on Nannerl Mozart. "She fell in love with a young tutor, Franz D'Yppold. And he loved her, too, only that domineering father, Leopold Mozart, wouldn't let her marry him. Franz's prospects of advancement were too modest. But Wolfgang cared deeply for his sister and urged her to leave Salzburg with Franz and come to Vienna, where Wolfgang had established himself as a composer, far from their father's domination. Instead of going, though, the obedient daughter meekly renounced Franz and later married a horrible man, much older, with a raft of unmusical children. This man, Baron von Berchthold zu Sonnenberg, suited Leopold because he was the mayor of Saint Gilgen and possessed a petty title. But the title didn't make Nannerl happy in her marriage."

Just recalling Loveday's outrage caused Oliver to ache for those star-crossed lovers of two centuries ago. Or was it actually Loveday who caused this ache? For he had a hunch that her own marriage had been anything but happy.

On later visits she had easily been prevailed upon to spend the night in Heather's old room, overlooking the pond. Oliver enjoyed the enthusiasm with which Loveday threw herself into the life at Firbank—naturally, as if she were a member of the family. She had helped Serenity with the preserving, shelling limas and canning tomatoes, chatting all the while, but not the way Kendal women usually did. These two discussed academic matters: Serenity's courses, her long-term aspirations, the prospects for her career. Listening to them, Oliver realized that this was what Serenity had been needing—someone besides Peter to talk to who understood the problems of young people.

Wrapped in his reverie of Loveday, Oliver realized with a start that he had been totally ignoring Austin—Austin, who'd been kind enough to come to help him at this time of year when, as a potato farmer, he had more to do himself than he could manage. With a twinge of conscience, Oliver tried to make amends as they walked back to the barn, caught up in a whirl with the dogs and Ross. "How's thy crop?" he asked. "Good?"

"Yup." There was a long pause.

Oliver hit on another topic of conversation. "How's Judy?"

Austin looked away. "Okay," he muttered. "I guess."

Oliver turned to him quickly, but Austin avoided his eyes. What did that mean—he *guessed?* Was there trouble?

Without facing him, Austin cried out in a desperate tone, "What do they want, anyway?"

"Who?"

"The women. I don't understand them. Seems everything I was brought up to think a good man's supposed to do is wrong now." Austin swung around and faced Oliver. "The hymn that I like to sing in the shower sometimes—'Dear Lord and Father of mankind'—you know it? Judy used to like it, too. Then, suddenly, real angry, she says she don't want to hear it no more. That word—mankind—should be persons, she says. But *persons* don't fit the tune, and the rhyme don't come out right. Can you change the words of a hymn we've sung so long?"

Oliver found it hard not to laugh. If John Greenleaf Whittier's poem, written over a hundred years ago, were to be revised, all the other Quaker writings would have to be rewritten, too.

Now Austin became so talkative that Oliver realized how upset he was. "The real trouble started," Austin explained, "because I called Judy my girl—always had called her that, loving like, for twenty years! Then, one day, it makes her mad. 'I'm not a girl,' she yells at me. 'I'm a woman, forty-eight years old. How'd you like for me to call you a boy?' I couldn't see what she was driving at. Sure, I'm not a boy. But I wouldn't want to call Judy my woman, like she was loose or something."

They entered the barn. Just then Serenity's little car came puffing up the drive. As Ross dashed off to meet his mother, Austin said slowly, "Judy's left me. Walked out."

"No!" Oliver exclaimed. He couldn't believe it.

"Yup. Gone to New York. Says she don't want to be a farmer's wife all her days, now the children are out from under."

All Oliver could think of to say was, "It's a hard life, thee knows, being a farmer's wife."

Austin waved this aside. "Never complained before," he argued bitterly. "Not even when she was taking care of Mom in her last illness. What started it all was this group she was going to in Providence. Kept saying she had to exercise *assertiveness.* But I was always good to her. Anything she wanted, if I could give it to her— What am I supposed to do, Oliver?" he implored. "Can't just sell out because she wants the city. What would I do in New York? Worked here on the farm all my life."

Oliver's heart reached out to him. "Give her time, Austin. She's entitled to her life, just as thee is to thine. But I'm sure Judy loves thee. Maybe when she's had time to consider, she'll come home. Thee mustn't reproach her then. Just rejoice and enfold her in thy love."

Austin shook his head. "She won't come back. She's proud."

Oliver moved a step closer to Austin and looked at him earnestly, hoping that in the companionship of silence, Austin would turn to his inward teacher for understanding. "Stay and have supper with us," Oliver urged after this quiet interval.

Austin shook his head again. "Got chores," he said. Turning away, he left the barn and climbed into his truck. But then he leaned out of the cab. "Reason I told you is, Judy's on that Yearly Meeting committee that gathers in Cambridge. With her not going, there won't be no representative from Kendal."

Austin drove off. Only then did Oliver feel the full weight of the Youngs' difficulty. Austin and Judy fell between two generations whose views on intimate relationships were poles apart. Their parents had been solid Quaker farm folk, who needed each other to survive. Their children, on the other hand, had experimented with what they called alternative life-styles, which were not necessarily based on the expectation of permanence. Caught between these two extremes, was it any wonder that Austin and Judy were in a muddle?

Love is a living being, Oliver reminded himself, and when it sickens and dies, we mourn. He wondered wistfully why Judy should choose to leave her spouse, while he, Oliver, who wanted nothing more than to be with his, had been deprived. Judy still might come back. Daphne never would.

Standing there in the dooryard amid the bronze and gold chrysanthemums that Daphne had painted year after year, Oliver reflected that a love characterized by lifelong constancy survives the bodies that contained it. There was no need to mourn for love such as he and Daphne had been blessed with: it was immortal.

But what, then, of this new awakening in him, this overpowering attraction to a woman with whom he couldn't hope to share such unity? And suppose by some miracle she were to reciprocate his feeling. Would this new love, flowering in the autumn of life, survive the winter?

CHAPTER THREE

SERENITY was upstairs, giving Ross his bath, when she heard Oliver enter the house. She rushed to the head of the stairs. "Oliver," she cried, waving a sheet of paper, "look!"

He saw at once that something momentous had happened; she ran down the stairs, leaving Ross, naked and plaintive, watching her from the landing. Oliver recognized the letterhead of the Museum of Contemporary Art on the paper in her hand.

"Here!" Serenity exclaimed, bubbling over with happiness. "Read this. It's from Aquila Chase."

Oliver fished in his breast pocket for his glasses and read the letter rapidly.

You will recall that at the time of Daphne Otis' death, a fund was established in her memory by various art lovers. This fund has been augmented by the proceeds from the sale of Oliver Otis' biography, which has enjoyed great success. Therefore the museum trustees have voted to earmark this income for the appointment of a curator to take charge of our Daphne Otis Collection.

Since you knew Daphne Otis well and contributed so greatly to the biography, it seems appropriate to offer the post to you before anyone else is considered. And in view of your special competence, the trustees are waiving the academic qualifications they

33

would ordinarily require. Could you come down to New York as soon as possible and discuss this?

If you need a place to stay, I can put you up.

Oliver, looking up at Serenity, saw his own joy reflected in her face. The letter was overflowing with good news—the esteem in which Daphne was still held, the success of Oliver's book, Serenity's incredibly wonderful opportunity.

"Isn't that something!" Serenity exclaimed. "Me, a first-year graduate student—they want *me* in that museum!"

Still on the landing, Ross was howling. Suddenly Oliver saw beyond the splendor that dazzled him when he first read the museum's offer. "What about Peter?" he murmured. "Won't he mind giving up his job? He was so happy to get it."

"For a chance like this?" Serenity cried. Then she turned gravely thoughtful, but only fleetingly. "I can't wait to tell him. He'll be so excited. Thee knows how Peter loves me."

SITTING at the round table in the cozy kitchen with Serenity and Peter on either side and Ross opposite, Oliver bent his head over the plastic cloth and silently gave thanks. Serenity was holding his right hand and Peter his left in their habitual clasp before breaking bread—the reassuring touch of fellow pilgrims traveling through life along a road that is sometimes obscure and invariably hazardous.

Still bowing his head, Oliver wondered what had happened while he was out in the chicken house collecting eggs. Peter had come home, and Serenity must have shown him the letter. How had he reacted to this threat to his future? For a man so young, Peter had attained a remarkable position at the university.

With an affectionate squeeze, they let Oliver's hands go, and he turned to look at Peter. His nice, friendly face looked preoccupied, and his bright yellow hair, of a length Oliver found pleasing, seemed to be parted in several places, as though he had just run his fingers through it in perplexity. Recalling how easygoing Peter had seemed when he first came to Firbank,

34

Oliver asked himself, not for the first time, why young people should be so overburdened these days.

But even with all the pressures, this was an unusually happy family. The parents were pursuing the careers of their choice. The child was a joy—affectionate, alert, content. That is, Oliver was obliged to add to himself, Ross is content as long as one of us is with him.

It was always a source of wonder and gratitude to Oliver that he should be included in this loving circle. As he started eating, he thought with emotion that this was the time he'd been looking forward to all day, the opportune moment when he would confide his secret to them. But before he could think of a way to lead up to the subject, Peter announced that he was in a hurry to get back to the observatory, and Serenity began to fret over an imminent exam. It hardly seemed the time for him to burden them with the state of his heart.

Savoring the delicious casserole Serenity had made, Oliver thought of Austin, alone at Periwinkle Farm, probably eating a can of hash in front of the television. Serenity and Peter would have to be told about Judy. They'd take it hard. The Youngs had been overseers at their wedding. Oliver put down his fork and in a low voice reported that Judy had left home.

Far from being the shock he had anticipated, the news elicited no comment at all. "I'm sure," Oliver added—someone had to say something—"that she'll return soon."

Serenity shook her head. "No. She's taken a year's lease on an apartment."

So Serenity and Peter knew! They hadn't told Oliver because they figured it would upset him. A year's lease! He *was* upset.

"Judy!" Serenity exclaimed, as if hit by an idea. "That's where I'll stay when I go to New York—at her apartment."

"Thee's *going?*" Peter asked incredulously.

"Of course! Thee thinks I'd turn down a chance to find out what they want me to do and how much they'll pay?"

"But is thee seriously thinking of taking the job?"

"How can I tell now? We'll talk it over—weigh your job

35

against mine. I'll go the first day thee's free to take care of Ross."

"I can't do that till vacation. I'm teaching every day."

"Vacation? They want me right away. Never mind. I'll take Ross with me, stop off in Neville and leave him with Mother and Daddy. They'll love it."

"Ross won't."

"No," Serenity admitted, frowning, "he won't. But if I didn't have to take him along, I guess I could stay overnight with Miss Chase. The director of the museum! A very successful woman. Who knows? Maybe someday I'll—"

"She doesn't have a child to look after," Peter pointed out, adding ruefully, "and a husband."

"Does thee think," Serenity demanded, "I can't look after my husband and child in New York as well as here?"

"Look, Rennie," Peter said, "I'm not going to stand in thy way. But I can't throw up my job." He leaned across the table and stretched out his arm to take Serenity's hand. "It's the first security we've had. Besides, Professor Evans counts on me. How can I just walk out?"

Ross was banging his empty bowl with a spoon. Letting Serenity's hand go, Peter got up and lifted the boy off his chair.

"Thee could take care of Ross," Serenity suggested, laughing. "Be the househusband." Peter let this pass. He sat down again with a contented son curled in the crook of his arm.

Oliver tried to think of some excuse to leave the table. The discussion was tearing him apart. The Hollands' dilemma might be more readily resolved without his presence. But they hadn't had dessert, and he didn't want to make matters worse by interjecting his own discomfort. It was a real impasse. Neither Peter nor Serenity was making an unreasonable demand, yet one of them would have to sacrifice a great opportunity. Could the strongest of marriages withstand such a tug-of-war? I must have trust, Oliver said to himself, trust that when they meditate on this together, they'll have a leading.

"Suppose after a few months thee decides thee doesn't like that setup?" Peter asked. "What then? We'll have nothing to live on. And Ross—what about him? He's used to the country, running around in safety everywhere."

"Kids grow up in the city, too," Serenity argued. Then she faltered. Evidently she hadn't considered the negative aspects of the offer. Now it was she who reached for Peter's hand. Instead of giving it to her, Peter pushed back his chair, walked around the table with Ross in his arms, plunked him on Serenity's lap and, squatting beside her, put his arms around them both. "Thee's right," he said. "It would be a mistake not to look into the offer. Thee go to New York. I'm sure Clara or Alice would help Oliver with Ross for a day or two. I'll be here at night."

Suddenly aware of Oliver and what their leaving Firbank would mean to him, Serenity turned to him and said softly, "If we go, thee'll be alone again." Her eyes filled with tears.

Oliver reached out and patted her shoulder. "I'll manage, same as before. Thee must do what's best for the three of you."

Peter was clearing the table. Putting Ross down, Serenity got up to fetch the dessert. On her way to the refrigerator, she stopped behind Oliver and kissed the top of his head.

" 'Be still and cool,' " he said, looking up at her. " 'Be still and cool in thy own mind and spirit from thy own thoughts.' "

"Say!" Peter exclaimed, standing there with a plate in each hand. "That's beautiful. Did thee make it up or is it a quote?"

Oliver went to the shelf above the hutch, where the devotional books were ranged, and took down George Fox's *Journal*. He went back to his chair and hunted for the page from which he'd quoted. Peter and Serenity sat down, too, leaving untouched the stewed pears she had dished out.

"Here it is," Oliver announced. " 'Be still and cool in thy own mind and spirit from thy own thoughts. Then thou wilt feel the principle of God to turn thy mind to, whereby thou wilt receive his strength and power from whence life comes, to allay all tempests—' "

The ring of the telephone interrupted the reading. Serenity hurried to the front hall to answer it. She stayed a long time.

Peter lingered at the table; he seemed to have forgotten that he had been in a hurry to leave. "Can't understand Judy," he was saying. "Always so concerned about the rights of minorities, so full of compassion for people she didn't even know. How could she treat her own husband like that? Wouldn't blame Austin"—he hesitated, as if he were afraid of shocking Oliver—"if he took up with someone else. What's a man to do? I mean, Austin's still young enough. Maybe at thy age—"

"*Even* at my age," Oliver assured him. "I sympathize with Austin. One never outgrows the wish to be loved."

"Funny," Peter observed, "the way things happen. The summer before Rennie and I were married, when I worked on Austin's farm, he kept telling me thee ought to sell out."

"*I* ought to? Sell *Firbank?*"

"Yes. He said the farm was getting too much for thee. And now, five years later, thee's doing fine, but Austin may have to sell out. If Judy insists on staying in New York, what else can he do?"

Trust steadfast Peter to believe that love would endure, whatever sacrifices it might require! He was looking at Oliver intently now. "I remember after Rennie'd been here the first time, she came back to college starry-eyed about thee and Daphne. Thee had given her thy grandmother's leather-bound copy of Woolman's *Journal* as a present. Does thee remember?"

Oliver remembered Serenity's first visit to Firbank very well. The Woolman passages he'd quoted to her at the time had contrasted sharply with the artificial world from which she came. The experience had shaken her.

"We read bits of the *Journal* aloud to each other at college," Peter said. "Thee'd told Rennie how thee and Daphne discovered it when you were first married, and how after reading it, the whole concept of thy future changed. Thee was going to take a job thee didn't like, just to make money so thee could write in thy spare time. You were eating sandwiches near the lighthouse at the mouth of the Connecticut River when Daphne asked why you couldn't stay at Firbank and run the farm."

Oliver laughed. "Yes, and I exclaimed, '*Me!* Farm?' Farming was the last thing I'd ever thought of doing."

They were both chuckling over this when Serenity returned from the telephone. "It's for thee," she told Oliver. "Loveday."

Like that she told him, as if it were just anybody calling him. Oliver jumped up with the alacrity of a young man. "Calling from *Kansas?*"

"Boston."

When he reached the telephone, Loveday's voice vibrated with excitement. "Rennie's just told me she's been offered a terrific job in New York. And to think she doesn't even have a master's degree! You must be delighted."

"Well, it's taken us all by surprise."

There was a pause. "I see," Loveday said. "I should have realized. Your life will be greatly altered if they leave Firbank."

"I'll manage. It's Peter and Ross who'll suffer, I'm afraid."

"But it's Rennie's turn, Oliver. High time she had a chance." Then Loveday changed the subject, her tone becoming absolutely jubilant. "Reason I called—something wonderful's happened. I'm going to write a book! I had to tell you."

She had to tell *him!*

"The way it came about," she continued, "I had lunch with one of my former students, who works in a publishing house here. When I told her about my research on Nannerl Mozart, she said the story ought to be written up. Of course, I can't be sure anyone will publish it. I have to write the book to find out."

While Oliver was felicitating Loveday on her enterprise, she changed the subject again. "I don't know if Rennie told you she's going to New York for an interview, and she's worried about Ross. She doesn't want you doing more for him than you already do, and Peter isn't cooperating."

"Peter can't stay home, Loveday. He's teaching. As a former dean, thee—I mean, you—should understand."

"Yes, I do. That's why I'm coming. *I'm* going to baby-sit."

"Oh!" That was all Oliver was capable of saying.

"Do you mind? It's just to help Rennie out."

"Mind?" he repeated stupidly. "I'm delighted." Then he felt obliged to add, "Ross is the one who'll mind."

"Oh, he may be a little sticky at first, but we'll get along."

Overcome with joy, Oliver had a boyish impulse to declare the full state of his heart to the faceless telephone. But Loveday was ringing off. She's coming, she's coming! he sang to himself as he hung up and hurried back to tell the Hollands, to tell them everything.

The kitchen was empty. Peter must have left for the observatory; footsteps overhead told Oliver that Serenity was tucking Ross in. No one was there to share his joy. But at the west window the setting sun shed tinges of splendor on the ruffled curtains, drawing Oliver outside to witness the ball of fire sinking into Little Narragansett Bay.

He walked down the path for a last glimpse of the pond. In the gathering dusk only the outlines of the dunes appeared, silhouetted against the red sky. But out at sea the lighthouses were already at work. Oliver visualized them, one by one: Fishers Island, Little Gull, Montauk in the west; Block Island to the south; Point Judith in the east. All his life he'd looked to them for comfort and direction. They could be counted on in fair weather or foul, in blizzards and haze, even in the fogs that often blanketed this coast. One might not be able to see the lights, but they were there.

No one to share his joy? How could he have thought that for an instant? Loveday was still in New England. Northeastward, beyond Point Judith, getting ready to come to Firbank! What more could he possibly wish for? Oliver turned and walked back up the path.

In the kitchen again, he switched on the light. Fox's *Journal* still lay on the table, surrounded by dirty dishes. Rolling up his sleeves, Oliver went to the sink, ran the hot water, then went over to the table to collect the dessert plates. But he couldn't resist picking up the *Journal* and putting on his glasses. As he scanned the pages, Oliver suddenly felt his heart soar. For his eye had lit on the name he'd been trying to remember—Hambly. Loveday Hambly! That's where he'd heard the name Loveday before—it belonged to one of Fox's earliest followers. When Fox was imprisoned during the Quaker persecution in the mid-seventeenth century, the news spread across Cornwall in western England. Instead of acting as a deterrent, it drew to the prison men and women who were longing for a religion they could truly believe in and who wanted to hear Fox speak. Among them was Loveday Hambly.

Forgetting the dishes, Oliver began to read, and her whole story came back to him—how her cows were taken away because she refused to pay tithes for the support of a clergy that did not speak to her condition; how she herself was imprisoned; how her home became the center of Quakerism in that part of England. Fox had written:

> About this time I was moved to give forth the following exhortation: Friends . . . Be patterns, be examples in all countries, places, islands, nations, wherever you come; that your carriage and life may preach among all sorts of people, and to them; then you will come to walk cheerfully over the world, answering that of God in every one; whereby in them ye may be a blessing, and make the witness of God in them to bless you.

"To walk cheerfully over the world . . ." This is no lighthearted stroll through life, Oliver thought, freshly aware of the sobering words. It's the ultimate demand on one's humanity. To speak not with words but with one's character; to uncover beneath ego-needs that divine spark which ignites all sorts of people— the unlovable as well as the lovely. And answering—uncovering the spark in oneself. To bless and thus be blessed.

The magnificent prose reverberating through his being, the discovery of that other Loveday, and above all, the prospect of the living Loveday's coming visit raised his spirits to heights they hadn't attained in years.

The moment he finished the dishes, Oliver went to his study. This morning he hadn't been able to think of anything to write to Heather. Now his thoughts came faster than his fingers could type. She would be very much interested in Serenity's job offer and all the changes it portended for Firbank.

She plans to spend two days in New York next week being interviewed. Peter has classes, so he can't take care of Ross, but a new friend of the family has generously offered to come and help. I hope Ross won't prove difficult. Thee knows how he hates being cared for by strangers.

Our friend has already been here a few times this summer. She is a widow, the retired dean of a college in Emporia, Kansas, who has been doing research at Harvard for a book she plans to write.

The aerogram was pretty well filled up by now. Oliver sent his love to Stephen and the children and signed off, neatly creasing the form. Then, just as he was on the point of licking the gummed flap, he added a postscript. "She's a charming woman, good company. When she's here, I feel whole, as I haven't felt since Mother went. Nothing to worry about, dear. Thee knows thy father isn't a foolish old man."

PART II: *Loveday*

CHAPTER FOUR

DRIVING to Firbank from Boston, Loveday remembered that about thirty miles south of Providence, between Perrytown and Kendal, a double row of maples lined the Post Road for six tenths of a mile. Just beyond the maples a road branched off on the left, zigzagging toward the upper end of Salt Pond. Little more than a sandy trail covered with broken scallop shells, it petered out in front of a rural mailbox marked FIRBANK FARM.

When the line of maples finally appeared and Loveday started to drive under the leafy arch, she caught her breath. She was proceeding under a shimmering canopy, with sunlight filtering through leaves of scarlet, gold and lemon yellow. The arch was a portal through which, on previous visits, she had passed into a world of unsuspected enchantment.

Jewels of leaves fell carelessly onto the hood of the car. Leaning out of the window, Loveday laughed as whirls of color, blowing past, almost touched her cheek. Then she reproached herself for letting her tires mash the red carpet, flecked with gold, that seemed to have been rolled out in welcome. The world she was entering, she thought happily, was unlike any she'd ever known, a world in which goodness took precedence over success, and gentleness prevailed.

At Firbank there was an almost palpable beauty. There was calm, not inactivity—the place was a beehive—and an awareness of unfailing security, though the doors were never locked. Yet the man who communicated all this was completely human, chock-full of idiosyncrasies, brimming over with humor and, at the same time, possessed of a self-knowledge that awed Loveday. Firbank was a revelation, the antithesis of the world she'd frantically pushed through during all her working life.

Returning to it had become almost an obsession with her, and she had sat in her apartment in Boston trying to think of some excuse to invite herself there again. When she finally did call Oliver on the pretext of sharing her news about the book, things had turned out far better than she'd expected. Rennie's predicament about Ross had given Loveday a perfect opening, and she had grabbed it. She'd go to Firbank and baby-sit!

But now that she was nearly there, Loveday wondered whether she would be up to taking care of a small boy. She was unusually well and energetic; still, there were days when aches and pains gripped her—nothing major, just enough to make her aware of her age. Furthermore, on her previous visits Ross had feared her. Would he take to her this time? Oliver adored him. If Loveday failed to win over the child, she'd lose Oliver's esteem.

And yet how much esteem was there to lose? Oliver was gracious, listening to her with that extraordinary interest, as if what she was saying mattered wholly to him. But he listened that way to everyone. Although he always looked at her with a warmth that in another man might have signified special affection, Loveday Mead knew that she really meant no more to Oliver Otis than anyone else. Besides, it wasn't Oliver, she assured herself, but the whole ambience of Firbank that attracted her—the red barn, the silo in back, the old white farmhouse.

Now, as she drew up beside the horse block and stopped the motor, she saw him standing in the doorway, tall and erect. All at once it dawned on her that with all its beauty, it wasn't Firbank that drew her back so forcefully. It was Oliver.

The realization proved so upsetting to Loveday that she lost her poise, and instead of returning Oliver's greeting as he ran down the steps and hurried toward her, she blurted out, "Where's Ross?" What a betrayal of anxiety!

Opening the car door and smiling down on her, Oliver answered, "He's upstairs with Serenity." Then, as he always did when Loveday arrived, Oliver said cordially, "Welcome to Firbank." He lifted her bag out of the car.

She found herself standing in the driveway, taking his outstretched hand and meeting his blue eyes, which were unmistakably joyful. She wanted to tell him about the splendor of the maples on the Post Road. Yet no words came. As he stood aside to let her enter the house, she wondered, What's the matter with me? I've always been self-possessed. Suddenly I'm acting like a teenager. Me—Dean Mead—shy and ill at ease! Then the gracious entrance hall enfolded her and she felt better.

Rennie was coming down the stairs, followed by Ross, who was humming happily, his red curls bobbing above the banister. Loveday glimpsed his face. Ethereal, she thought, and remembered her own children at his age.

Ross hadn't seen her yet, because his mother was ahead of him. As he reached the bottom, Loveday stepped forward and bent down to kiss him. Sudden fear stiffened the little body. He wriggled away and hid behind Rennie.

"Oh," Loveday murmured. "I shouldn't have rushed him."

"Are you the baby-sitter?" Ross asked tremulously.

Loveday laughed. "The baby-sitter? *Me?* Why, I'm just—" But hadn't she told Oliver on the telephone that she was coming to baby-sit? And he had told her frankly then that Ross would mind her coming, so it really couldn't surprise her now. What did shock her was Rennie's greeting.

"Hi," she said coldly. It sounded as if she wished Loveday hadn't come. Didn't Serenity want to go to New York, after all? On the telephone, she'd been dying to.

Usually Serenity carried Loveday's bag upstairs. But this afternoon she excused herself, saying she had to go down to Four Corners for gas; the station wouldn't be open when she left early in the morning. Oliver patted Rennie's shoulder and told her to take her time. He would see Loveday to her room.

"By the way," he added, "if thee should speak to Judy Young in New York, ask her whether she wishes to be replaced on the Yearly Meeting committee in Cambridge. If she does, then the Kendal Meeting will appoint someone else."

Rennie nodded, took Ross by the hand and started out the door. "Oh, and Serenity," Oliver called after her, "ask Judy whether she'd like me to come and see her."

This stopped Rennie. "Thee means thee'd go all the way to New York?"

"Why not? I can take the train. But I don't want to unless she'd like to see me. I keep thinking she must miss Friends."

Rennie looked touched. "I've been thinking that, too."

Carrying Loveday's bag, Oliver led the way upstairs and across the landing to the ell, explaining a bit breathlessly about the Youngs' situation. "Doesn't surprise me too much," he admitted. "Just before Austin's mother died, she told me how lovingly Judy took care of her. And Judy always said nursing gave her a feeling of doing something for someone in need, while much of what she did on the farm could just as well be done by a machine. So now she's left."

Instinctively Loveday sided with this Judy, whom she didn't even know. Why should anyone do meaningless work?

But Oliver seemed baffled. "What do you think Judy really wants? I thought you might know. I confess that to me the marriage would have seemed more important than anything."

"You men just can't understand how a woman feels."

It was clear from his expression that indeed Oliver couldn't understand. Loveday saw no point in prolonging the discussion.

She smiled to indicate that while they didn't agree, they were still friends.

The room he ushered her into was exactly the way she'd remembered it. The brass bedstead, the diminutive fireplace, the sketches covering the walls—of a little girl at six months, a year, and three or four. Oliver put her bag on the luggage rack and started to leave.

"Are these sketches of your daughter?" Loveday inquired.

"Yes. Daphne did them of Heather more than fifty years ago." Backing into the hall, Oliver added, "Heather paid us a lovely visit in July. I must be patient now till next summer."

"Does Heather resemble you?"

"Oh, no! She's good-looking."

So are you, Loveday almost exclaimed. But he already seemed uneasy. Was it improper of her to be detaining him in a bedroom? But she didn't want him to go.

"Well," Oliver conceded, "she's tall, like me, with the Otis hair—red and curly. But it's silver now. . . . Gracious! The window's open. I'd better shut it for you. It sticks."

He came in once more, and Loveday watched him struggle with the sash. From the back, she thought, one would never guess his age. But it was more than his beautiful carriage that distinguished him. It was his bearing, the combination of dignity and humility. To Loveday, these had always seemed mutually exclusive. In Oliver they were clearly intertwined.

Turning from the window, he suddenly looked at Loveday with a light in his eyes that she'd never seen before, as if he were about to come toward her and take her in his arms. Her heart lurched. But, of course, he did no such thing. It was just Loveday's crazy imagination. Instead, he walked right past her to the door. Then, as he was about to close it behind him, he said apologetically, "In the excitement of your arrival, I forgot to ask how your book is progressing."

Loveday looked at the floor. "Well, it really isn't a book yet. I don't quite know when to stop going to the library. It's a temptation just to go on and on with the research."

Oliver nodded. "I know. At some point one has to discipline oneself to begin writing." Seeming reluctant to leave, he added, "Anytime you're ready, come down. I'll be in the living room."

He started to go a third time, but now Loveday detained him. "Serenity doesn't seem pleased to see me. Has she changed her mind?"

"No, I'm sure she's grateful for your coming. But she's faced with a difficult decision and she hasn't had a clear leading. Maybe after the interview at the museum, she'll know better what her choice should be."

"I'll talk to her tonight," Loveday promised. "Give her a little push."

Oliver didn't seem to appreciate the offer. He changed the subject. "I've been thinking about your ancestors. Would you like to have another look at those minute books? We could go to the meetinghouse tomorrow while Ross is at nursery school."

Loveday didn't want to find anything there. That would remove the excuse for another visit. She changed the subject, too.

"Oliver," she pleaded, taking a step closer in her earnestness, "don't let Rennie miss this marvelous opportunity. A husband's job isn't more important than a wife's."

She expected him to dispute this, but to her surprise he answered calmly, "Only Serenity can be the judge of what's right. We who love her can best support her not by offering advice, but with our prayers, leaving her free to seek divine guidance."

Suppose she doesn't find it? Loveday thought. But before she could ask him that, he left. And this time he didn't return.

Standing in the middle of the floor, Loveday felt rejected. Why should Oliver restrain her from helping Rennie? Shouldn't a woman with her experience help a younger one to become more than just someone's wife and some child's mother? Oliver didn't seem to value Loveday much when it came to having an input into the Hollands' affairs.

Suddenly she noticed a yellow rose standing in a slender vase on the dressing table. She knew Oliver had put it there; he always did, when he expected her. Sniffing the delicate scent, she thought, How can I feel rejected?

Looking around the room now, Loveday was pleased to see that the pale blue bedspread, sprinkled with irises and daffodils, was still there. Though faded and worn, it had a charm one seldom saw in modern designs. In a way, she thought, this is more like home to me than the apartment in Boston or even— but how could this be?—than my house in Emporia.

On each visit here, she found a new selection of books on the bedside table. This time there was *The Journal of John Woolman.* So Oliver wanted to introduce her to his eighteenth-century hero. Beside it was a history—*Quakers in Boston.* She must read that when she went to bed. Then she caught sight of a fine binding and read the title with a start: *Daphne Otis, Her Life and Art.* Under it was the author's name, Otis. It's Oliver's book!

Loveday exclaimed to herself. He'd never shown it to her. But by placing it here unobtrusively, he had made it available. Part of her was eager to read it. Part of her didn't want to.

When Oliver spoke about his wife, Loveday felt uncomfortable; she guessed it was because of the unusual tenderness and pride in his voice. They made her a little jealous. Her husband, Bill, had cared for her as much as he had for anybody—she knew that. But he hadn't been capable of caring about her the way Oliver did about his wife. Maybe, too, Daphne's professional success roused some envy in Loveday. To be both cherished and famous—that was too much.

And Loveday had so wanted to be cherished! When she was young, affection and passion bubbled over in her. She had put everything into the marriage, trying to make something of herself so Bill would be proud of her. He didn't even notice. And when he knew he was dying, he showed less sorrow over being separated from her than from his dog.

She had resolved then never to risk surrendering her life again. It's not really that I'm jealous of Daphne, Loveday thought. I'm glad she had Oliver's love. What hurts is that Bill couldn't give me something like that. If he had, I would have been more content.

Oliver himself must be terribly lonely. Had he really been thinking of taking her in his arms? His old-fashioned code would never have permitted it. But had he been *thinking* of it?

After unpacking, Loveday ran a comb through her hair and started to leave the room. On second thought, she decided to change from her skirt and knit top to the dress she'd brought— her favorite, a soft blue-and-rose paisley print.

Loveday changed and left the room. Oliver must have been listening for her footsteps, because as she crossed the landing and came down the staircase, he was waiting for her below, his shining face uplifted. And now there was no mistaking his impulse. His arms were stretched wide to receive her.

She would go to him. Why not? What more did it imply than simple friendship? But before she reached the bottom step he caught himself. His arms fell to his sides.

THINGS were not the same at Firbank this time, even though dinner was preceded by the customary silence and ring of hands. The underlying unity, which had set the household apart, seemed to be missing. Rennie, appearing tense, briefed Loveday on Ross's schedule, and Peter, who was ordinarily a listener, talked all through the meal about variable stars and intergalactic space. Oliver's eyes kept wandering, and Ross whimpered in a monotone that Loveday found irritating.

She fixed her gaze on Peter to assure him that *she*, at least, was spellbound by his lecture. Actually she didn't understand a word. Relaxing for a second, she turned away.

Oliver was staring at her! Their eyes met. He quickly turned and concentrated on Peter.

With equal haste, Loveday spun to face Rennie. How troubled she looked! Loveday's heart went out to her. She must help her, must do what she could to stiffen that young backbone. Never mind what Oliver thought.

When the meal was finished, Rennie went to the old-fashioned sink and filled the dishpan. Oliver cleared the table, and Loveday followed, carrying a couple of plates, while Ross climbed onto Peter's back for the journey to bed. Horse and rider circled the kitchen, stopping first so Ross could shower his mother with kisses. Next he was carried to Oliver. He snuggled against the old man. But when they came to Loveday, Ross drew away.

"Don't you love me?" she asked with mock chagrin.

His eyes level with hers, Ross answered unequivocally, "No."

Loveday laughed as Peter hurried off with Ross. Her feelings weren't hurt. He was just a child. She was still laughing when Oliver startled her, saying he had to leave at once for Kendal. "A Called Meeting," he explained, adding anxiously that he was already late. "Peter's on duty at the observatory, and Rennie has to stay home with Ross. But will you come? May be a bit boring. . . ." He sounded eager but not insistent.

Loveday considered the invitation. If she went, there'd be no time to speak to Rennie, who was leaving for New York at dawn. She would be running out on a floundering younger sister.

Oliver went over to Rennie. " 'Be still and cool,' " he said, putting his arms around her. Rennie brightened instantly.

There was a bond between these two that Loveday was just beginning to appreciate. But she was annoyed. Still and cool! she thought scornfully. The worst possible advice. What Rennie needs is to be assertive and on fire.

Clearly Loveday must stay here and counteract Oliver's misguided efforts. So, when she found herself climbing into Oliver's pickup under a starlit sky, she wondered how it had come about. Her determination to do her duty had been canceled out by her desire to be with Oliver. "What's this you're taking me to?" she asked him.

"A Friends Meeting ordinarily convenes for the transaction of business once a month. But occasionally, such as now, there are urgent matters. I'm afraid you'll think our deliberations are maddeningly slow, but just as we seek guidance in our meetings for worship, we wait for it in our meetings for business, too."

"Business? What does business have to do with religion?"

"What else is religion but the business of our lives?" he said calmly. "It's not a Sunday pastime. As John Woolman put it so beautifully, 'To turn all the treasures we possess into the channel of universal love becomes the business of our lives.' "

Noble words, she thought. But what did they mean?

"The item for consideration tonight," Oliver said, as streetlights began to appear on the outskirts of Kendal, "is the disposition of a bequest. A beloved Friend, Melissa Gray, has left her home and estate to the Meeting. We are to use them for whatever purpose seems best."

Loveday was intrigued. "Think of all you can do with the money!" she cried.

But Oliver was far from jubilant. "The Meeting operates on a small budget. Suddenly it's affluent. It makes us uncomfortable."

They had arrived at the Friends Meetinghouse. Only glimmers of light shone through its tall windows as they left the truck and mounted the steps. Once inside, Loveday saw why—there was no electricity. The flickering oil lamps hanging between the windows were charming, she thought, but they gave barely enough illumination.

Oliver was running a finger along the bookshelves that lined a vestibule wall. He stopped at a small gray volume, which he removed and slipped into his coat pocket.

At the door of the meeting room he explained in a whisper that the chairperson—"clerk," he called her—was Clara Ludlow. She was a pretty, middle-aged woman. "The assistant clerk," Oliver added, "is Neil Hill. He runs a boatyard on the Kendal River." It pleased Loveday that a woman had the top post.

Oliver led the way to an empty bench. When they were seated, he closed his eyes, draining all expression from his face. He must be seeking that "leading" he kept harping on. The room was intensely quiet. Everyone in it seemed to be meditating.

Suddenly Oliver stood up, fished in his pocket for the book, and flipped through the pages till he found what he was looking for. Raising his head, he said clearly, "As we deliberate, let's consider some of our traditional advices." He began to read. " 'Take heed, dear Friends, to the promptings of love and truth in your hearts, which are the leadings of God.' " Oliver paused for a moment, as if to take heed himself, and then went on. " 'Use your abilities and possessions not as ends in themselves but as God's gifts entrusted to you. Share them with others.' "

That's what I was trying to do with Rennie, Loveday thought, aggrieved—share my abilities. And he wouldn't let me. His next words made her feel less smug.

" 'Use them in humility and with courtesy. Guard against the love of power; be considerate of the needs of others and respect their personalities.' "

Love of power! During the student demonstrations in the 1960s, one strident young hothead had accused Dean Mead of loving power. She'd dismissed the affront as unworthy of notice. But the injury must still be festering, or she wouldn't recall it now, after all these years. Was Oliver speaking to her?

He closed the book and sat down. A moment later the clerk began to speak.

"At a Called Meeting of Kendal Meeting of Friends, held at Kendal, Rhode Island, Tenth Month twenty-fifth, nineteen members are present. We also welcome Loveday Mead, a visitor at Firbank Farm."

Hearing her name, Loveday jumped. Friends were turning to her, smiling, enthusiastically taking her into their midst. She smiled back and turned to Oliver. He was looking at her with unmistakable pride. She was glad she'd come.

But he was right about the proceedings being boring. Well, not boring—exasperating. These people were so impractical; their whole idea seemed to be to get rid of that money as quickly as possible. Suggestions were made for selling the house, liquidating the assets and giving the proceeds to disadvantaged people all over the world. Loveday wanted to stand up and tell Friends to look out for themselves first. The discussion got still more unreal when a man near the front of the room rose. "Lucas Lang," Oliver whispered, "a teacher in the high school."

"How would we present the money?" Lucas asked. "Quaker service is never impersonal. We don't just send checks. Money is only part of a larger testimony—friendship, extended by human hands. Which of us is in a position to travel to Indochina or even across the United States? I'll only be comfortable disbursing this bequest where we can make personal contact."

After Lucas sat down, there was a long silence. Then a little old lady struggled to her feet. "I remember Daphne Otis telling about her work in France after the First World War," she began. "Daphne was part of a team stationed at the Swiss border to assist prisoners of war who were being repatriated; she carried bowls of soup to the people in the trains. And she always said it wasn't the nourishment that heartened them—most were too sick to eat—so much as the friendly words from strangers who

53

cared enough to come to them. I agree that we should only offer money where we can make a personal testimony of love."

After another silence, the clerk announced it was growing late and she believed it was the sense of the Meeting that no action be taken immediately. The assistant clerk read the minutes, there was a final period of silence, and then Oliver turned to Loveday and extended his right hand. Along the rows of benches, people were shaking hands with their neighbors.

Many Friends now crowded around Loveday. The woman who had chaired the meeting came up to her and held out her hand. "I'm Clara Ludlow. We were so pleased to have you with us tonight. Will you have dinner with John and me tomorrow?" She turned to Oliver and repeated the invitation. His smile conveyed his pleasure in accepting.

"Thank you," Loveday said. "You're all so cordial."

The intimacy generated by the silence seemed to have knit Friends together, so they lingered, chatting, in the aisles, in the vestibule. As Oliver and Loveday finally broke away, he took her arm companionably and led her toward the truck.

Opening the door of the cab for her, Oliver looked up at the starlit sky. "That universe Peter sees through the telescope," he observed. "I can't grasp it."

"Neither can I," Loveday confessed.

"But this canopy of stars," he said with emotion, "has spread beauty and poetry over me all my life. Its very mystery is a kind of knowledge. On a clear night, the few constellations I can identify are always in their proper places, waiting to greet me."

He got behind the wheel and they set off for Firbank.

CHAPTER FIVE

LOVEDAY woke early, then turned over and tried to doze off again. She'd had only four hours' sleep. Last evening, about to turn out the light, she'd picked up Oliver's book from the bedside table, just to glance at the reproductions of Daphne's paintings. Becoming completely absorbed, she had had no idea how late it was till the grandfather clock downstairs struck two. She had read the book from cover to cover. This morning, bits of the story kept running through her head, preventing her from going back to sleep. Finally she gave up and reached for the book to read certain passages again.

During World War I, while Daphne was in France nursing war prisoners, Oliver was in the States, being court-martialed and imprisoned for refusing to bear arms. In that war, there had been no exemption from military service for conscientious objectors. Prison! Loveday thought, appalled. *Oliver's been in prison.*

When he was released, Oliver went to France to help restore the war-ravaged farms. There he met Daphne. After he graduated from Harvard, they married and came to Firbank, where she painted the portrait of Serenity Otis, Oliver's grandmother, that established her reputation.

Skipping to the end of the book, Loveday reread Oliver's heartbreaking account of Daphne's stroke: how it paralyzed her right arm so she could no longer paint.

> Slowly, agonizingly, Daphne learned to use her left hand. But the zest for painting was gone. Then, one day, not quite a year before her death, a young cousin of mine, whom we had never seen, came to Firbank. Her name was Serenity—my grandmother's name, too.
>
> Daphne saw something in this young woman that stirred her—a promise. For the first time in three years, she felt moved to paint. This portrait was her last and unquestionably her greatest work. Known as *The Second Serenity*, it hangs today in the Museum of Contemporary Art in New York.

A portrait of Rennie! In that museum! Why hadn't anyone ever told Loveday? Oliver and the Hollands were too modest.

Oliver's book was more than just a biography. It was also the record of a rare marriage. Loveday had always assumed that marriage was first of all an arrangement for sexual fulfillment and secondly a division of labor. It was an accommodation. Two people carefully staked out their claims and traded off sacrifices.

But Daphne and Oliver seemed never to have staked out anything. They'd made no recognizable claims, demanded nothing. They were quite simply each other's servants, motivated by a devotion that transformed service into a glorious privilege. But I always thought being a servant was demeaning, Loveday said to herself, puzzled. Especially for a woman. Paradoxically, disregard of their own prerogatives appeared to have given Daphne and Oliver freedom. Was it their commitment to each other that freed them?

A wave of regret swept over Loveday. If only she'd grasped years ago what she was learning about life now. Here she was, seventy-three soon, and only just beginning to understand.

Coffee—that was what she needed. She would take it back to bed and sip, gradually coming to. But the kitchen here was downstairs, way at the back of the house, and it would mean passing Oliver's room, which was right at the head of the stairs. Still, she was supposed to be in charge today, wasn't she?

Crossing the landing in her robe and slippers, stepping gingerly to avoid making the floorboards squeak, Loveday saw with a shock that Oliver's door was open. Too late to turn back! Propped against pillows in a big, old-fashioned bed, Oliver was reading his Bible. When he raised his eyes, he was looking directly at her.

She felt fussed. She hadn't expected to be discovered sneaking downstairs, or to catch Oliver in bed. But he smiled unselfconsciously and wished her good morning.

"I opened my door so Ross can come in," he explained. "I hope you rested well."

"Not long enough. I read your book, cover to cover. It—well—involved me. You write beautifully."

"I loved writing about Daphne. It was like having her back." Once again, jealousy gripped Loveday. "I've been wanting to tell you about her," Oliver went on softly, "only you never seemed interested. You see, it's impossible to understand me without knowing Daphne, both her art and her personality."

"I've never heard of anything quite like your relationship,"

Loveday said. "Didn't it ever bother you that she became famous while you just—"

"Farmed? No. I rejoiced in her success. We weren't running a race to see who could beat the other. Why would a husband and wife do that?"

"We did. At least I—"

"Besides"—Oliver evidently hadn't heard her—"Daphne didn't paint for recognition. She always used to say that what she painted was never as beautiful as the vision she had in her mind. She painted simply to project that vision, just as I farmed for what Friends call 'unity with the creation.' " Closing the Bible, Oliver laid it on the stand by his bed.

Loveday was holding on to the banister with one hand, clutching her robe with the other. There was something dreamlike in this conversation between a man in blue pajamas and a woman in a dressing gown. It seemed unreal. And yet the old man propped against the pillows spoke with such genuine feeling that she knew it was not a dream. She had simply arrived by chance at a place where life was lived on a different plane.

"There was something else," he added. "It's not easy to talk about, but I'd like you to know." He looked down at the patchwork quilt a moment. "Every morning Daphne and I spent half an hour together, seeking direction silently, and yet of one mind. Why this meant so much to us, I can't explain. Every aspect of our love seemed sacred, so our reverence for each other merged imperceptibly into our reverence for God."

Listening more with her heart than her ears, Loveday didn't notice Ross coming up behind her on his little bare feet until he brushed past. " 'cle Oliver!" He dived into the big bed.

Loveday swung around and started down the stairs. "I'm going to make myself some coffee," she announced. But before she reached the second step Oliver called her. Turning back, she saw the self-consciousness in him that she had expected earlier.

"Would you care to join in the silence with me this morning?" he asked hesitantly. "After breakfast?"

"Me, too!" Ross cried.

"Thee, too," Oliver promised. Then he looked eagerly toward Loveday.

"Will it be like last night?" she asked. In the meetinghouse, what Oliver read had been troubling. She didn't want to be stirred up again.

"It's a time of retiring into our innermost selves, yet seeking divine light together. As the light reveals our shortcomings, tension may mount, but if this drives us to set things right, we eventually find peace."

She looked down at the landing. Finally she said, "I guess I'll join you. Would you like some coffee now?" she added quickly, looking up at him again.

"No, thank you. Ross and I are about to get up."

Suddenly aware of her responsibilities, Loveday started back to her room, forgetting the coffee. "I'll just get ready," she told Oliver. "Then I'll come back and dress Ross."

"No, you won't!" Ross shouted after her.

ALTHOUGH Loveday was determined to discharge her duties faithfully, she took longer than usual deciding what to wear. She finally settled on a skirt instead of slacks, and then went down to the kitchen. Ross was perched on a pile of telephone directories placed on top of a chair, and he was pushing a tiny car across the table. Oliver was reading the newspaper. He rose stiffly as Loveday entered.

"Sorry to be so long," she said. "I was going to dress Ross."

"He dresses himself. Looks it," Oliver added with a chuckle. Yet when Loveday promised to comb out the tousled curls at once, Oliver became unexpectedly severe. "We encourage independence," he declared.

Surely Oliver didn't intend to take the child to nursery school unkempt? Instinctively, looking around for help, Loveday asked, "Where's Peter?"

"He's left for the university."

Breakfast was ready, the table set with care. In the center, standing in a pewter mug, were a handful of marigolds, orange and russet, still glistening with dew. "Come and sit down," Oliver said.

On earlier visits the quaint silence that preceded meals at Firbank had made Loveday slightly uneasy, particularly the ring of hands—an embarrassingly sentimental gesture, she thought. This morning she eyed Ross anxiously. Without his parents to subdue him, would he keep still? He did. All the while, though, he peeked at Loveday solemnly. She realized that *he* was checking on *her*.

When breakfast was over, Loveday washed up and Oliver dried. Ross put away the silverware. Then the three of them moved into the living room, where the sun streamed through the bay window, illuminating the portrait of Oliver's grandmother— the focal point of the room. It was *Daphne's* painting! Her presence dominated everything here.

She's dead, but I can't get away from her, Loveday thought bitterly. Gives me the creeps.

Yet Loveday couldn't take her eyes off the picture. What fascinated her was its springtime mood. She knew it had been painted shortly before the first Serenity died at the age of eighty-three, but it radiated such zest that she could think only of youth.

Noticing Loveday's interest in the portrait, Oliver observed, "John Greenleaf Whittier, the Quaker poet, wrote about the Indian summer of the heart. That phrase always makes me think of Grandmother. In old age, she radiated the translucent atmosphere and mellow sunshine that dispel the frosts of autumn."

"What a beautiful phrase!" Loveday exclaimed. "How does it go again?"

> *"Years have passed on, and left their trace . . .*
> *Yet hath thy spirit left on me*
> *An impress Time has worn not out . . .*
> *The shadows melt, and fall apart,*
> *And, smiling through them, round us lies*
> *The warm light of our morning skies,—*
> *The Indian Summer of the heart!"*

Oliver excused himself for a minute, and Ross disappeared. Alone in the room, Loveday went over to the wall where two wedding certificates and an old lithograph hung side by side. She had read the certificates on an earlier visit. The left one belonged to the first Serenity and her husband, Edmund Otis; the one on the right was the Hollands'. Although separated by more than a hundred years, the wording of the two documents, all but the names and places, was almost identical.

The lithograph portrayed a Quaker wedding in the early nineteenth century. A young couple stood hand in hand, evidently promising to be "loving and faithful, so long as we both shall live." Both wore an expression of quiet elation. There was no minister. Older people sat behind the couple on raised benches. Most of the men wore broad-brimmed hats. All the women had bonnets.

Oliver returned. Seeing Loveday studying the lithograph, he came to join her. "Do you like it?"

"I find it very touching."

"So do I. It seems to me to portend that the occasion will sustain these two all their lives, in fair weather or foul. Originally it belonged to our Serenity's grandmother, who was the daughter of the first Serenity, the one over the mantel. But the daughter married out of the Society, and her son, Serenity's father, found the picture when he was disposing of her effects. He didn't have the heart to throw it away, yet it didn't fit in anywhere; so he put it on the third-floor landing of his house, where no one would be likely to notice. But something amazing happened. The picture caught our Serenity's fancy, and it made her curious about her heritage. So when she was thinking of getting married, she decided to find out what a Quaker wedding would be like. That's what impelled her to look us up."

"So this picture, which the father rejected, determined the direction of the daughter's life. How fantastic!" Loveday said. "Sounds like a novel!"

"A leading, I would call it."

Ross reappeared. He had combed his hair himself, slicking it down so zealously that drops of water trickled onto his forehead.

"You look very nice this morning," Loveday commented.

Ross gave her one of his radiant smiles—the first ever.

"Let's sit down," Oliver said. Loveday walked toward the couch. "Please sit in your usual place," Oliver begged, motioning to the upholstered chair in front of the hearth. "Our friends avoid it because it was Daphne's. But I like it to be used. When it's empty, I feel as though I'd suffered an amputation. With you there, I'm whole again."

With *me* there, Loveday thought in wonder. *Me!*

Oliver settled himself on the other side of the hearth, with the dogs at his feet. The liveliness left his face as he withdrew into the habitation of his spirit. Ross climbed onto his lap and rested his head against the old man's chest, playing quietly with the buttons of Oliver's shirt.

Peaceful, that's how they look, Loveday decided. She herself felt apprehensive. In her determination to relax, she clenched her hands, but her eyes wandered. From time to time Oliver stroked Ross's curls, his attention elsewhere, a long way off. He was centering down.

Even so, Loveday was aware of some inexplicable communication. The strange silence conveyed meaning never quite defined by words. A mystery. Ross was watching her again, and she gazed out the window, pretending not to notice. But she knew now that the unspoken communication wasn't only between herself and Oliver; it was a three-way thing.

She'd never had this communication with her own children. How could she? There'd been precious little leisure in Loveday's busy life, certainly none when the children were small. There was still less when Bill was sick, and later, when Loveday was struggling through graduate school and fighting for a foothold in the academic world. Too late now, she thought sadly. How could I have been so superficial? But even today, in her retirement, she would normally never think of sitting down like this early in the morning and just doing nothing.

Doing nothing? She was, Loveday suddenly discovered, very

occupied, engrossed in a kind of videotape passing through her head—more real than a dream, inexorable as memory. The image on it was of a young, attractive woman who was determined to have a career as well as a husband, the latter not to interfere with the former. But things didn't turn out that way.

William Junior's arrival was unplanned. She had had to give up her job. Will was still in diapers when Emily was born. By the time Toby came, Loveday was stir crazy.

She always thought she'd borne her frustration heroically. But now the videotape was alarming. On it she kept demanding her rights; her expression was chronically dissatisfied. Even while she did the proper things—cooked, cleaned, looked after the kids—she complained: Bill was free to go out and advance in his job; she was a captive. No wonder our marriage held so little joy, she thought, watching herself in horror.

Then Bill got sick, and nursing him was like having another baby—a big, irritable, terminally ill baby. Loveday felt cheated, not by him but by life. Why me? she heard herself ask. Her self-pity, viewed in this penetrating silence, was so shaming that Loveday tried desperately to recall some redeeming aspect of her marriage. We did have a satisfactory sex life, for a few years, anyhow. But the joy that still seems to illuminate Oliver—that we never knew.

A small sigh made her turn. Ross was sliding down from Oliver's lap. He started to play quietly with his toys on the rug.

Loveday closed her eyes, and Bill's shadowy image appeared on the tape in her mind, very different from the picture she had transmitted to the children, who'd scarcely been old enough to remember him. Their impressions of him had been created by her, after his death, unconsciously constructed to present herself as a woman victimized by male domination. But the tape denied this. It put her in a very poor light. Here was a genial man who hadn't been tough enough to cope with her complaints, who was already seriously ill. Could his slowly progressing illness have been the cause of what she considered his lack of feeling? Was it *she* who had failed *him?*

In agitation she clutched her left hand with her right, appalled by the confrontation with a self she wasn't willing to own, a petulant woman who nagged her sick husband and deceived her children. Was she exaggerating? She hadn't been that bad. Just the same, she wanted her children to know the truth.

I must go home, she thought miserably. I must go home and tell them the way it really was, that their father had actually been a much nicer person—

Opening her eyes with a start, Loveday found Oliver standing before her, reaching for both her hands. He stood holding them and looking down into her eyes in wonder and admiration. Suddenly Loveday felt full of possibility, with a treasure in her possession of which she was unaware, but which he recognized. If she were really such a bad woman, would a man like Oliver be gazing at her this way?

"You were right about the silence," she told him softly. "It didn't make me peaceful. It got me to thinking about things I'd never wanted to confront before—awful things."

"We all have regrets," he said. "But when we face ourselves in the silence, with companions who are also seeking guidance, we often find strength to begin anew. Beginning over is all that's asked of us."

"But it's too late."

"Never." His grip tightened in reassurance.

"Oliver," she confessed, wanting to be honest with him, "I didn't come here just to help Rennie. I wanted an excuse to return. That's why I called—hoping you'd invite me."

"Whatever brought you, I'm glad you came."

"There's something here that—I can't describe."

He smiled down on her warmly. "Perhaps you've discovered your Quaker ancestors after all—in yourself."

"Yes," she said. "Only now I have to go home. I never intended to stay so long."

"You're leaving? This morning?"

"Oh, no. I promised Rennie I'd stay till she gets back. Then I'll pack up my stuff in Boston and head home."

"To *Kansas?*" He looked stunned. "But," he argued, "you haven't completed the family tree for your daughter-in-law."

"Sara Ann will be disappointed, but I have to go."

Oliver's hands, which had been grasping hers so affectionately, suddenly released their grip.

CHAPTER SIX

ALL the way to Kendal, Loveday was beside herself. The peculiar mood that had enveloped her during the silence had vanished, but not before it betrayed her. What got into me? she wondered, aghast. What made me say I'm going home, when all I want is to be here? I could have written to the children. No need to *go*. Now I've burned my bridges. After telling Oliver that I'm leaving, I can't very well stay.

If only he'd try to dissuade her! She'd capitulate at once. But he said nothing till they reached the nursery school, and then he merely spoke to Ross. "Loveday Mead and I'll be close by, at the meetinghouse. Lunchtime, we'll pick thee up and drive to the cove to say hello to the swans." When Ross was safe inside the school, Oliver drove on.

In sunshine, the Friends Meetinghouse looked even more starkly unadorned than last night. But beautiful. In the bright October morning, the clear antique glass in the windows glinted violet and gold. The sky was a cloudless blue. The leaves of the trees that shaded the dove-gray walls of the old building were crimson, saffron and brittle russet.

As they mounted the steps, Loveday noticed a plaque beside the door saying that the meetinghouse was erected in 1829. "Oliver, that's the year Nannerl Mozart died—blind, alone, penniless. What memories she must have had! And regrets. . . ."

Oliver watched Loveday trace the date with her finger.

For a second Loveday was transported from Kendal to Vienna. "That was the time of the beginning of the waltz craze," she recalled as Oliver unlocked the meetinghouse door. "A young fiddler named Johann Strauss was composing catchy tunes that

set everyone dancing, even common people." Loveday giggled. "The man actually put his arm around the woman's waist. They gazed into each other's eyes and whispered secrets!"

Oliver smiled. "Quakers weren't allowed to dance at all then. My generation was the first to have that freedom. And while all that gaiety was going on in Vienna," Oliver reflected, "in this Rhode Island village a handful of farm folk built this simple house of worship, which still testifies to their faith."

How far apart we are, Loveday thought. Our inner landscapes are as far apart in feeling as in space.

"The old Quakers were ahead of their time in many respects," Oliver was saying. "But in music, no! Music was excluded from their lives, even from their worship. A member who happened to be present at a gathering where there was fiddling and dancing was termed guilty of disorderly walking."

"Disorderly . . ." Loveday was shocked, but amused. "Why?"

"It was thought to distract from the main business of life, which was the cultivation of the spirit. Inconceivable in this day and age, isn't it?"

The mustiness that greeted Loveday upstairs in the gallery was so familiar as to be almost welcoming. As she looked down to the room below, where she'd sat with Oliver last night, she was struck again by its austerity. No altar, no pulpit, just sunshine glowing on the plain pine benches. But there was a reverent aura about the simple whitewashed room, as if the aspirations experienced there still permeated it.

In a corner of the gallery Oliver was bending over a sea chest, lifting out huge leather-bound volumes and lining them up on a bench. "There," he said, puffing a little. "These are the minutes of the 1770s." He turned the tall, stiff pages carefully, stopping suddenly as he came to an item of interest. "Listen to this, recorded at the Yearly Meeting session held in Newport in 1774: 'Divers Friends in this Meeting manifesting a concern that the liberty of the Africans might be fully restored—' Think of it, 1774! Other Americans were fighting for their own liberty, while complacently owning slaves."

Loveday's eyes scanned the page as Oliver read the slanting script aloud. " 'That such laws may be made that tend to the abolition of slavery and to get such laws repealed as any way encourages it, we appoint these Friends to use their influence at the General Assembly of the Colony of Rhode Island or with members thereof: Thomas Hazard, Ezekiel Comstock, Stephen Hoxie, Isaac Austell—' Austell. Your forebear!"

Loveday turned to Oliver in disbelief. "Isaac Austell," he repeated. "There you are, Loveday." But far from gloating over his success, he sounded bereft.

Now Loveday possessed the information that she'd originally come to Kendal for, that she'd since hoped fervently wouldn't turn up. It was there on the page before her, plain as day. She was sunk.

"An ancestor to take pride in," Oliver was saying, "who labored to free the slaves nearly a century before most of his countrymen did anything about it." He smiled wryly. "You're going home with something glorious to tell your grandchildren."

Loveday tried to smile, too, but her face was frozen. Even if she hadn't already announced her departure, the discovery now demanded it. There could be no turning back.

AFTER that the whole scene became blurred. All the things that made Firbank so appealing were the same, but in her imagination Loveday was already in Kansas, looking back with bittersweet nostalgia on her idyllic New England experience. Yet in spite of her gloom she enjoyed the evening with the Ludlows.

John and Clara Ludlow lived very simply in a little New England saltbox. Everything in the house struck Loveday as having been chosen with unusual taste. Clara served a delicious meal with a minimum of fuss, while John talked to Oliver and Loveday. She was as impressed by him as she had been by Clara the previous evening. John was Ross's pediatrician, a good-looking man with a humorous twinkle and a gracious manner. But what Loveday would cherish most in her memory of that evening was the happiness Oliver appeared to feel because she was with him. And the Ludlows treated her as if she belonged, simply because she was Oliver's friend.

Back in Firbank, saying good night to her on the upstairs landing, Oliver again took both of Loveday's hands in his. Looking at her the way he had when she thought he was about to kiss her, he said, "Thy coming has enriched us all. We tend to get a little ingrown here." But he didn't kiss her.

Like a bad dream, the finality of her departure troubled Loveday's sleep all night. Packing her bag in the morning, she decided to leave right after Rennie returned. She'd have that talk with her first and then take off.

"The fair weather's still with us," Oliver announced at breakfast. "Indian summer, perfect for digging the last of the potatoes." Tongue in cheek, he inquired whether Ross would mind staying home from nursery school to help; the joyful reply was deafening. Loveday offered to go with them.

"Hard to believe, isn't it," Oliver commented when they stood in the field surveying the rows of dead plant tops, "that under those withered stalks there's a whole winter's sustenance for us? So many things are like that. We see only a surface desolation, not the riches waiting beneath for us to harvest."

They worked slowly, Oliver plunging the fork into the soil, then resting on it while Ross lifted each potato out of the ground with incredible care, laying it on the surface to dry. Loveday worked, too, but her back wasn't used to that kind of activity and she soon had to stop. It wasn't long before Oliver also had had enough.

Late that afternoon Rennie's car chugged up the lane. Ross rushed out of the house to greet his mother. Peter, just home from work, rushed out, too, looking no less eager, if somewhat apprehensive. The dogs bounded after him—Lion jumping on Rennie as she got out of the car, and almost knocking her over in his delight; Duffy limping, but wagging her stubby tail with consummate devotion.

Oliver and Loveday watched from the doorway. Beyond the

brick walk the three Hollands were locked in a passionate embrace, as if they could never get close enough to make up for the two-day separation. Loveday saw that the trio formed a compact unit. Did she really wish to see it disrupted over a job?

She had barged in where angels like Oliver kept out. She had acted as if Rennie were single, instead of recognizing her as an indispensable component of this ideal but fragile unit. No wonder Ross had regarded Loveday with suspicion! No wonder Rennie, who'd originally been so friendly, had become reserved.

Sickening fear gripped Loveday. Suppose the Hollands left Firbank and split up, even if only temporarily? It now became clear to her that it was her intervention in this family's affairs that threatened to destroy what she most wanted to preserve.

Turning to Oliver suddenly, she blurted out, "I'm going to rewrite my life! Even before I write Nannerl Mozart's." Oliver looked puzzled.

Before Loveday could explain—she wasn't sure just what she really meant—Peter, Rennie and Ross came trooping up the front steps, joy overflowing at their being together again. Rennie reached out to Oliver and Loveday. "Wow, it's good to be home! But it was wonderful in the museum. Aquila sends thee her best, Oliver. Now that I'm going to be a colleague, she wants me to call her by her first name. Loveday, thanks ever so much. You'll stay tonight, won't you?"

Loveday shook her head. "I'm leaving now."

"Not before we've had tea. The kettle's on," Oliver declared. "Loveday's planning to return to Kansas," he explained to the others. "Yesterday, looking through the Kendal Meeting minutes, we finally found a reference to one of her ancestors. She's eager to get home and tell her children. Now come in the kitchen, everyone. We want to hear about thy trip, Serenity."

While Ross climbed onto his telephone books and the others took seats at the kitchen table, Oliver brewed tea in an antique pewter pot. Setting it down beside the cake a neighbor had brought, Oliver asked Rennie, "Did thee speak to Judy?"

69

"Yes. She was very touched by thy offer to come, but she doesn't want thee making that long trip."

"How was the museum?" Loveday asked.

"Marvelous! I got so excited seeing Daphne's pictures hanging there. The museum owns some of her finest canvases."

"Thee's accepted the job?" Oliver inquired.

"Yes. Well, I said I'd let them know definitely after I've talked it over with Peter. But I don't see how we can *not* accept. I'll be earning more than he is now. We'll have to live with Mother and Daddy in the beginning, and I'll commute to New York."

"What about me?" Peter cried. "Thee expects *me* to live with thy folks? I'm not about to give up my job and this home to go live with them."

"Okay, then Ross and I'll come here weekends. I hope Mother won't mind taking care of him while I work. If so, there's a day-care center in Neville where I can leave him."

"Rennie! Thee wouldn't do that to Ross?" Peter exclaimed.

"Would thee leave him with me?" Oliver asked diffidently. "Since thee'd be coming weekends—"

"That's sweet of thee," Rennie said. "But a child his age needs his mother. Anyway, Peter and I haven't had a chance to discuss this yet."

"Well, I'm not going to let Ross be pushed around just for a little extra money," Peter declared, taking the child on his lap.

Rennie's blue eyes blazed. "It's not just the money! This is the chance of a lifetime for me." Turning to Oliver, making a noticeable effort to be calm, she changed the subject. "How did the Called Meeting go the other night?"

"We had a good session. There's a general sentiment that we should tie the disbursement in with personal service. I agree."

Peter asked, "What would thee like to see done, Oliver?"

Oliver thought carefully and then said, "Well, thee knows how many stranded walkers, cyclists, even motorists we take in every summer. They come for a pleasant stay at the beach, only to find at nightfall that there's no place to lay their heads. They've pitched tents in our woods, slept in the hayloft—even

70

on the living-room floor. What's needed here are simple, inexpensive accommodations for people of all ages. Sharing the natural beauty one is blessed with seems to me to be as great a spiritual service as one can render."

"Say," Peter cried, "that's a terrific idea! Melissa Gray's house is close to the beach. It could easily be converted into a hostel. There's a lot of land for camping. All of us in the Meeting could take turns being there and providing an evening meal. Afterward I'd take them out and show them the stars," he added. "Ross could come along. He'd have kids to play with there."

"That's just what he needs!" Rennie exclaimed.

Their enthusiasm made Oliver look happier than he'd seemed all day. "Sounds as though we'd benefit more from such an enterprise than the people we'd be doing it for," he said.

I wish I could be here, Loveday thought. Then she remembered she'd intended to leave as soon as Rennie came home. "I must be going," she said. "I'll just run up and get my bag."

"Let me get it," Rennie urged. "I can't stand these city clothes another minute." They walked to the front hall together.

This was the opportunity Loveday had been waiting for—to give Rennie the pep talk she'd planned ever since she heard about the job offer. But the talk didn't come off the way she'd rehearsed it. "I'm sorry," she said instead, surprised by her own words. "Sorry if I seemed to be pushing you. The young women at college needed to be encouraged to find fulfillment. I kept forgetting that you're older."

"That's okay," Rennie said. "I knew you meant well. But I do have to have space to figure things out for myself. I'm so glad, though, that I asked you to come home with me that day in the library, and I want to thank you for making Oliver happy. He's very lonely." Then she ran up the stairs.

I? Loveday thought. *I* make Oliver happy? *He* makes *me* happy. Dazed by Rennie's last words, she slipped into the living room and went over to where the sampler hung on the wall. She reread the text: "Walk cheerfully over the world. . . ." *I must remember that,* she thought, *when I'm back home.*

Rennie came down with Loveday's bag, and they went out-side together. Oliver, Peter and Ross were waiting in the drive-way. Fearful of breaking down, Loveday made short work of the good-bys. Yes, Oliver did look lonely, and there was a tragic finality in the way he closed her car door.

The motor was already running when, on an impulse, Love-day reached through the window, hoping for a last-minute sign of affection from Ross. "Will you kiss me?" she asked, laughing.

"No."

She should have let it go at that. "Don't you love me?"

He shook his head.

"Don't you?" Loveday pleaded, trying to sound jocular.

"No." Then Ross said gravely, " 'cle Oliver loves you."

The little wretch! Trying to embarrass her— Loveday drew back into the car, her cheeks burning.

Shouting above the roar of the engine, Ross repeated, " 'cle Oliver loves you!"

"Ross!" Serenity cried. "Don't say things like that."

"But he *told* me. 'cle Oliver told me."

Loveday stepped on the gas and sped down the lane.

PART III: *Oliver*

CHAPTER SEVEN

As LOVEDAY's car disappeared, Oliver stood in the driveway with the Hollands, still seeing in his mind's eye the consterna-tion in Loveday's face when Ross made his startling disclosure. What must she think of him, confiding in a child, yet never declaring himself to her? And what must Peter and Serenity think? They were looking reproachfully now at Ross, who appeared afraid and bewildered. Oliver turned in anguish and headed for the house. The child started after him.

"Come with us, Ross," Serenity called. "Daddy and I are walking down to get the mail." Peter whistled for the dogs.

Shut up in his study, Oliver collapsed into a chair by the

window. He felt exhausted. What must Loveday think of him? he asked himself once more. But how could he have declared himself to her? A declaration of love implied a proposal. And marriage wasn't what he'd had in mind that afternoon six weeks ago when, aching with loneliness, he had confided in the sleepy child. Marriage, he reminded himself, affects not only the man and woman who enter into it but their families as well. Why, he hadn't even told Heather yet.

Struggling with these thoughts, Oliver was suddenly interrupted by Ross, who burst in without knocking—something he never did. He was sobbing.

Oliver took him on his lap and held him tightly. "Don't cry," Oliver whispered soothingly, thinking that Peter and Serenity must have criticized him. "Thee didn't mean any harm."

"But she's hurt!"

"Maybe not. Loveday Mead is a sensible lady."

"Not her!" Ross wailed. "Duffy! Truck bop—bop—bopped Duffy."

Looking up, Oliver saw Serenity standing in the doorway, her face white. "Ross told thee?" she asked.

"Yes. Is it bad?"

Serenity was slow to answer. "It was instantaneous," she said finally. "Duffy couldn't have felt anything."

Instantaneous! So Duffy wasn't just hurt; she was dead. Oliver relaxed his hold on Ross and shrank into himself.

"I know how thee loved her," Serenity said softly. "We all did. But Oliver, that truck just missed"—she caught her breath in a repressed sob—"just missed Ross."

This roused Oliver from his misery. "*Ross?*"

"Yes. The truck came tearing down Salt Pond Road so fast that Ross and Lion would never have escaped if Peter hadn't seen the truck coming and grabbed Ross. Lion leaped after him. Duffy couldn't move quickly enough."

"Trucks have no business on that road. . . ." Oliver started to get up from his chair. His legs were like water.

"Sit still," Serenity said. "Peter's taking care of everything."

Again Oliver tried to stand and again he fell back, the room spinning. Was it a stroke? Perspiration broke out on his forehead.

"Oliver," Serenity said, alarmed, "should I call Dr. Liveek?"

"That won't be necessary," Oliver answered gruffly.

"I'll get thee a cup of tea. Come, Ross, Daddy needs thee."

Oliver's shirt was drenched with perspiration, and yet he was shivering. He tried moving his arms and legs. They worked. And he could speak. So it wasn't a stroke. Was it a heart attack?

Serenity returned and handed Oliver the tea. "Ross is helping Peter dig the grave. They're putting Duffy down near the orchard, under that big pine tree." She perched on the edge of Oliver's desk and said earnestly, "Ross didn't mean to stir up trouble, saying what he did to Loveday. Thee knows that, Oliver, doesn't thee? I can't imagine where he got the idea."

"I told him."

"Then it's true?"

"I'd been intending to tell thee and Peter all along, but somehow there never seemed to be a right time. I'm sorry."

Serenity smiled. "We suspected it. In fact, we were hoping—"

"You *were?*"

"Of course! Peter and I think it would be an ideal marriage."

Oliver jumped. *"Marriage?* What has that to do with it? She doesn't even know how I feel. At least she didn't till Ross—"

"Loveday's great!" Serenity exclaimed, disregarding this. "From the day I first brought her here, it was obvious she was interested in thee."

"I doubt that."

"She is. Can't thee tell? She's always wanting to come back."

"Not anymore. It was simply to find out about her ancestors."

"Thee doesn't know much about women, Oliver. Loveday may not know it herself, but she's gone on thee. She'll be back."

Unable to take this in, Oliver just stared at Serenity.

"Now," Serenity commanded, walking to the door, "thee take a nap. Later Peter'll help thee to thy room."

"No need for anything like that," Oliver cried after her indignantly. But sinking back, he knew it was a false boast.

74

AT SUPPERTIME OLIVER MANAGED to drag himself to the kitchen. As soon as he sat down, Lion was under the table, putting his head on Oliver's shoes.

"He's grieving," Peter said. "He and Duffy did the same thing when Daphne died. They just lay quietly at Oliver's feet."

When Serenity and Peter grasped Oliver's hands before beginning the meal, he recognized how deeply he was cherished and gave thanks. But he couldn't eat. Despite his earlier bluff, he was grateful when Peter offered to go upstairs with him.

When they reached his room, Oliver heaved a sigh of relief and sat down on the edge of his bed. He felt chilled.

Peter's friendly face was unnaturally grave as he squatted to untie Oliver's shoelaces. He cleared his throat nervously. "If what Ross told Loveday's a fact," he finally blurted out, pulling the right shoe off, "what's thee waiting for, Oliver? Is it because of us—that thee doesn't want us to feel crowded out? We're leaving anyhow, thee knows."

Oliver stared at him. "You're *leaving?* Then it's settled?"

"No. But we'll go. Rennie has her heart set on this thing."

"It's a wonderful opportunity," Oliver admitted feebly as the left shoe hit the floor.

"Believe me," Peter assured him, "I don't want to go away and I don't want to quit my job. But I'm not going to split up the family, even for part of the week. We all need each other. So, with us leaving, it'd be neat if thee had Loveday."

"But Peter, your leaving Firbank is no reason for me to marry. Heather's been urging me to come to England. She has a cozy retirement home all picked out, only an hour from London."

"Why go to some place like that when thee can be here? I'm not suggesting thee marry Loveday because thee's lonesome. It's because thee said thee loves her. What better reason?"

Oliver couldn't think of any.

"The way Loveday looks at thee—Rennie and I've both noticed it—we think, if thee'd propose, she'd be a pushover."

How the roles were reversed! He'd been afraid the Hollands would laugh at him. Instead they were driving him to a conclusion he hadn't yet envisaged. Even after Peter shut the door behind him, Oliver looked within himself fixedly, trying to understand. Propose! he thought incredulously. Then he turned out the light and snuggled under the covers.

DURING the weekend Oliver continued to feel listless. Serenity and Peter didn't conceal the fact that they were worried about him. Hadn't they better call Dr. Liveek?

Oliver refused. He had no pain, only this unusual malaise. With God's help, he would heal himself. He'd done it before.

"The Ashaways will pick Ross up after school today," Serenity said before departing on Monday morning. "But we don't like leaving thee alone. Sure thee doesn't want me to call Alice Hill and ask if she can come?"

Oliver was sitting at the kitchen table, eating an egg. "I'll be all right," he declared. "I don't want company. Too many letters to write." One to Heather, telling her everything, even Peter's fanciful suggestion. It wouldn't alarm her, now that Loveday had left forever. Maybe he'd write Loveday, too—inquire about the traffic on her drive back to Boston.

Serenity gave Oliver one last troubled glance and left. Ross followed her, looking over his shoulder with an almost paternal solicitude that was both amusing and touching.

When Oliver finished eating, he went to the hutch to get Fox's *Journal*. Sipping his tea, he opened the book and turned to the letter that Fox wrote to Lady Claypole when her mind was troubled. Daphne had marked parts of the letter that impressed her. After her death, these passages had sustained Oliver. Mightn't they restore him to his rightful mind now?

> Be still and cool in thy own mind and spirit from thy own thoughts, searching, seeking, desires, and imaginations, and be staid in the principle of God in thee.... This then is the word of the Lord God unto you all; do not look at these temptations, confusions, corruptions; but look at the light, which discovers them; and with the same light you will find grace and strength: there is the first step to peace.

Contemplating those words, Oliver was suddenly jolted by an impulse that felt like an authentic leading: instead of writing Loveday, why not telephone her?

What would I say? he wondered. Should I simply wish her a safe journey to Kansas—act as if nothing had happened? Oh, but something had! Remembering the look on her face as she drove off, Oliver's resolve hardened. He'd call and apologize—not deny what Ross had said (how could he?) but ask forgiveness for causing Loveday embarrassment.

Oliver almost lost his nerve as he dialed. Way off in Boston, the telephone began ringing. He counted anxiously—six, seven, eight, nine. But there was no answer. At noon Oliver tried again. No answer. After lunch he went to his study, followed by Lion, and settled himself by the window, intending to call every hour. But he promptly fell asleep.

It was late afternoon when Lion's barking woke him. Oliver blinked. John Ludlow was standing by his chair, looking down on him kindly. Then it dawned on him why John had come.

"So they sent for thee? They thought I needed a pediatrician, that I'm suffering from a disease of second childhood."

John didn't seem to understand. "Thee sick? No one told me. I'm sorry. I just came by to ask—"

"What?"

John's eyes twinkled. "First tell me what's ailing thee." When Oliver didn't answer, John demanded with the authority of a physician, "What ails thee, Oliver?"

"Nothing, really, just this sudden weakness. Could it be my heart? I feel no pain."

John reached for Oliver's pulse and drew his stethoscope out of his pocket. "Something upset thee?" he asked.

"My little fox terrier was run over—Duffy. Remember her?"

"Of course. I was wondering where she was."

"And the Hollands are leaving." Oliver didn't mention Loveday. "How's my heart?" he asked, when John finished listening.

"Fine. Thee might have a touch of this virus that's going around. Boston's riddled with it."

So it wasn't just in his mind! Oliver was relieved.

"That good-looking woman who came to the Called Meeting with thee and to our house the other evening—she came from Boston, didn't she? I've forgotten her name."

"Loveday. Means peacemaking."

"That's it! Was Loveday feeling all right?"

"First-rate. At least, she appeared so. But does thee suppose Loveday was suffering from that virus?"

John returned his stethoscope to his pocket. "She could have had such a light case that she didn't even know she had it and then communicated it to thee. Anyhow, whatever thy trouble was, thee's in good shape now." He turned the desk chair around and straddled it, facing Oliver. "Where's Ross?"

"At the Ashaways'. Peter will call for him on the way home. I wish I weren't failing Ross. He counts on me."

"Thee'll be up to taking care of him tomorrow."

"I hope so. Ross is frightened of strangers, thee knows."

"There's nothing wrong with Ross. It's our society—mothers having to go to work or simply finding more satisfaction outside the home, and putting a small child's needs second. When he's a little older, Ross will accept strangers like anyone else."

"He still has the radiance of early childhood. I hate to see that beautiful aura frightened out of him."

"As long as he has thee when his parents are absent, he'll be all right. But what's this about the Hollands leaving Firbank? I thought they loved it here. Has Peter been offered a job?"

"No, Serenity has. The Museum of Contemporary Art has asked her to be the first curator of the Daphne Otis Collection. It's an irresistible opportunity, so Peter's decided to give up his faculty appointment and they will move to New York."

"And thee? What will thee do?"

Oliver's answer came slowly. "Heather has always been keen on a retirement home she's found for me in England."

"Would thee like that?"

"No. I'd have more time with Heather, and that would be a joy. But I couldn't forsake Lion. Besides, this is my home. What

78

would I do with everything? Daphne's canvases, for instance—there are hundreds stacked in the woodshed."

"I see no reason why thee shouldn't stay here. With someone coming in a few hours a day to help, thee could manage. I happen to know that Judy Young's miserable in New York. Firbank might be just what she needs."

Oliver's spirits leaped. "It would be a real help to me to have Judy."

"Oh!" John exclaimed, slapping his forehead. "Speaking of Judy—that reminds me. Reason I came here today—Judy has sent in her resignation from the Yearly Meeting committee that's reviewing the queries read in meetings. We must appoint someone in her place, and I've been charged with asking whether thee'd be willing to finish out her term."

"There's no committee I'd rather serve on," Oliver confided. "Since we have no creed to keep us in line, we need the queries to remind us of our obligations as decent human beings."

John looked delighted. "I was hoping thee'd accept."

"That committee meets in Cambridge," Oliver suddenly remembered. "Does thee think I'll be up to traveling?"

"Three weeks from now? Of course! And you could stay overnight in that lovely guest room in the Friends Center, up at the top of the house, looking across the river to Boston."

"Yes. Daphne and I often stayed there."

"Do go, Oliver. Ross isn't the only one who has to adjust to shattering separations. What with the Hollands leaving and Duffy— Thee's had a few blows, too."

John had discharged his duty now, but he didn't get up to go. Suddenly Oliver felt an urge to confide in him. Looking away, he said softly, "The trouble *is* in my heart, John. But thee can't hear it with that contraption of thine."

He found it hard to go on. John waited, saying nothing. "Thee sees," Oliver said, after a long silence, "the past few months I've enjoyed Loveday's company. She's a seeker like us, though not aware of it quite; she's working to develop insight and the art of living in the presence of God. It was a joy being with her. Now

all that's over. She left on Friday under distressing circumstances. That's when I collapsed." Oliver now faced John.
"Thee understands—this is just for thee."

John looked touched by the confidence. "Thanks for telling
me," he said, standing up and stretching out his hand.

"Thy father," Oliver told him, taking it affectionately, "was
one of the best friends I ever had. Thee comes close thyself."

"In that case," John said, "maybe thee won't mind my saying
that if I was in thy place and saw a woman I took a shine to, I
wouldn't let her get away. I'd run after her!"

"Run? But Loveday's miles away. I've tried all day to reach
her on the telephone. She must have left for Kansas."

"Then," John said, grinning, "if thee can't run after her, thee'll
have to *mount up with wings as eagles.* But whichever means of
transportation thee's obliged to use, go!"

Later, after John had gone, Oliver wrote to Heather:

> The roles are reversed. All those committees on clearness I've
> served on, trying to make sure the couples who wished to be
> married under the care of our Meeting understood the promises
> they intended to make! And Peter and Serenity—how Mother and I
> tried to counsel them! Now *they're* counseling *me!* They're en-
> couraging me to ask the widow I mentioned in an earlier letter to
> take me in marriage.
>
> Thee mustn't think I've allowed myself to be persuaded. I've
> resisted the idea out of fear that I might be behaving like a foolish
> old man. But my unremitting desire to cherish and serve her have
> at last convinced me that it's right. I have no reason to think that
> she reciprocates my feeling. Still, it's time I declared myself.
>
> It goes without saying that thee and I must have unity before I
> proceed. I know it will be hard for thee to imagine my wanting
> anyone after the glorious life I had with Mother. But I believe this
> is the course I should take. We shall need to write freely to each
> other until we are both clear that it is. Not until I have that
> assurance shall I make the offer.
>
> My dear, dear daughter, nothing must ever be allowed to come
> between us. I hope thee'll write soon. Were thee to know the lady,
> thee'd love her, too.

CHAPTER EIGHT

THE Friends Center was nestled in a quiet corner in Longfellow Park in Cambridge. Of warm rose brick with white trim and a slate roof, it welcomed Oliver this November day as it had for over forty years. He had spent an anxious three weeks. He had been unable to reach Loveday in Boston by phone, and she had not contacted him. Nor was there any response yet from Heather. The mails were simply slower than he, in his eagerness, had allowed for.

As he mounted the steps of the center, the door opened. Ellen, the secretary, had spotted him through the window. "Oliver Otis! It's good to see you!" she exclaimed.

"Ellen!" He beamed down on this old friend and shook her hand. "I feel like Rip Van Winkle. How has thee been?"

Ellen wasn't a Friend, but she was so devoted to the Meeting that addressing her in the plain language came naturally. Oliver could remember when she and her mother had arrived here, refugees from Nazi Germany.

"I'm fine," Ellen replied. "But my mother had the flu. It's been bad this year."

"I had a touch myself." As he spoke, Oliver noticed a copper bowl on the hall table. Some Friend had made a breathtaking arrangement of wild flowers and grasses: golden yarrow, brown burdock, teasel, yellow-gray tansy—even dried they had a strong, woodsy smell. Sprigs of sea lavender gave the whole thing a cloudy, airy feeling. It so reminded Oliver of Daphne that it hurt. In winter the wild flowers and grasses had sat for Daphne, as people did for their portraits, linked to her in silent communion while she lightly touched the paper with color.

"Let me take you to your room." Before Oliver could protest, Ellen picked up his bag. He followed her up the stately staircase, still thinking of Daphne. Long before World War II they had come here together to help resettle refugees.

Ellen opened the door of the sunny guest room, put the bag on a stand and left. From the south window Oliver could look out over the Charles River to Boston. There were twin beds by the north window, which faced the center's lawn.

Daphne had invariably chosen the bed to the left. Oliver had always squeezed in with her, and they'd slept blissfully entwined all night, just as they did at home. The sight of that bed now triggered the most overwhelming longing, and to avoid looking at it, Oliver unpacked his bag. Carefully lifting out a loaf of corn bread that Serenity had baked for tonight's potluck supper, he recalled the day last January when he had taken the corn over to Perrytown to be ground into meal.

He didn't even know then that Loveday Mead existed. Next January, when it came time to go to Perrytown with the corn, where would they be, he and Loveday? She in Emporia? He at Firbank? Or both at Firbank? He simply couldn't imagine.

He took some committee documents out of his bag and sat down in an armchair to study them. But glancing up from a page, Oliver found himself looking directly at Daphne's old bed again. This time, however, instead of disturbing him, it gave him comfort. Daphne was there with him, taking his hand as she used to do when they lay together. But now she was leading him into the future. She was sending him on his way, unafflicted by regret. This was her legacy of love.

Feeling her dear presence, Oliver had an access of understanding that shook him; before he could marry again, he must enshrine Daphne in a much deeper recess of his heart, where her absence would no longer be such a sorrow. In this recess he could abide with her in the same love that had blessed him for over fifty years, but without the yearning for her that still beset him. Only by letting go this way would he be worthy of another wife. Until then he had no right to ask Loveday for her hand.

Without altering his feelings, he must reeducate his heart. Was he capable of doing this much for Loveday?

THERE were ten Friends on Oliver's committee. He knew only two, but they all welcomed him warmly. The contributions they had brought for supper were spread on the long oak table in the kitchen. Oliver added Serenity's loaf. He served himself and joined the others for a jolly meal, with joking and high spirits. When it was over, they all moved to the parlor.

Before beginning their work, they settled into a dedicating silence. Oliver felt conscience-stricken; his mind was wandering, he was unable to center down. But finally the clerk raised his head. The committee was about to get down to business.

"We're considering the ninth query," the clerk began. "This is how it reads now: 'Do you regard your possessions as given to you in trust, and do you part with them freely to meet the needs of others? With reverence for life and for the splendor of God's continuing creation, do you try to protect the natural environment and its creatures against pollution, abuse and harmful exploitation? Do you actively promote just distribution of the world's resources through frugality in your own life and through your support for social and economic practices which will sustain and enrich life for all?' "

"Too long," someone said. Oliver was inclined to agree, and someone suggested deleting "with reverence for life and for the splendor of God's continuing creation." A discussion ensued, and Oliver was trying to decide on his point of view when a young man put his head in the door.

"Oliver Otis?" Oliver rose to his feet. "Call for you on the pay phone," the man said, pointing to a cloakroom by the stairs.

Oliver found the receiver dangling from the wall. It was Serenity. "Has something happened?" Oliver asked.

"Well, yes. I just had a call from . . . from Loveday."

"*Loveday?*"

"Uh-huh. She's been sick. That's why we didn't hear from her. After leaving Firbank she went to New York, intending to stay two days, and she came down with the flu. A really bad case. Sounded to me like pneumonia."

"Pneumonia! Is she out of danger, Serenity?"

"Yes, she's okay. Got back to Boston this afternoon." Serenity hemmed. "Oliver . . . why doesn't thee phone Loveday?"

"I shall. I'll call right away."

After Oliver hung up, he fished in his pocket. Luckily he had a dime. He dropped it in the slot and dialed her number.

A moment later Loveday was saying hello.

In the narrow cloakroom, wedged between bulky coats, backpacks and folding chairs, Oliver tried to collect himself. "This," he finally managed to say, "is Oliver. How are you feeling, Loveday? Are you all right?"

"Yes, I'm fine now. Did Rennie tell you I had the flu?"

She sounded so beautiful, so entirely like herself, that all Oliver's longing came over him in a rush. But she sounded guarded, too, as if unsure how to respond to him. No wonder!

"I went to New York on the spur of the moment and was staying with friends when I suddenly got sick. It was embarrassing. I'd come for a couple of nights and stayed weeks. The Woman Who Came to Dinner, they called me, trying to laugh it off. The doctor says I must stay put for another week, but I'm cheating a bit—the children are anxious for me to get home, so I'm going on Monday. If I can get packed."

Should he extend his stay and help her pack, see her off? But Ross . . . Oliver had promised him he'd be back tomorrow.

"I didn't want to go home," she was saying, "without thanking you for helping me find out about Isaac Austell. He really is an ancestor to be proud of."

"Loveday," he asked, "may I come to see you?"

"*Tonight?* It's nearly ten. Why don't you wait till tomorrow?"

How could he? Evidently she found it easy. But he answered quickly, "That will be first-rate. We'll go out for lunch. What time shall I pick you up?"

She seemed to be thinking it over.

"I have a lot to tell you," Oliver added, hoping he wasn't pressing too hard. "And I'm leaving on the five-o'clock train."

"In that case," she said, "we'd better meet early. What about ten? I'd come to Cambridge, but I don't have that rented car anymore."

"Never mind," Oliver cried, elated. "I'll take a taxi."

"Do you know where Chestnut Street is, on Beacon Hill?"

There was a sudden burst of noise in the front hall. The committee must be adjourning. For the pleasure of conversing with Loveday, Oliver had neglected his duty. He should have waited till now to call her. But how could he have done that?

Someone put a hand on his arm and whispered, "Good night." Loveday was still talking. Oliver didn't like to ask her to repeat the directions, but he had no choice.

"I live at Eight Chestnut Street, near the corner of Walnut. Second house on the right as you face the Common."

"Next door to Friends House! I know well where that is."

"I'll see you, then."

"Good night, my dear," he murmured, forgetting himself.

"Good night, Oliver."

Aghast, he hung up. He'd called her "my dear." His knees were buckling. He had to get out of the stuffy cloakroom. He made his way to the bench in the front hall and sat down. Everyone had gone.

Tomorrow—tomorrow morning, he was going to see her! He hugged his happiness to himself, wishing he were home so he could rush to Serenity and Peter with his news. No, he thought, not even the dear Hollands could understand what I feel. Only Loveday—she is the one to share my joy.

HALF the night Oliver thought about the flowers he intended to bring Loveday. Choosing them would be an act of love in itself. But what would it be like when they met? What would they say? These thoughts went through his head while he should have been sleeping. Nevertheless, in the morning he was refreshed.

As he dressed, the light slanting through the north window made him aware of his fraying cuffs. He'd worn this suit every First Day for over twenty years, never thinking it was shabby. But to visit Loveday, he ought to be looking his best. On the way to Beacon Hill, he would stop at the Harvard Coop and see whether they had anything appropriate.

It was a magnificent day, cold but sunny. Oliver felt buoyed up as he left the Friends Center and stepped into a nearby flower shop. There he spotted a tall vase with sprigs of acacia—clusters of small, feathery golden balls—mimosa, Daphne used to call it. The florist held out a sprig to him.

"Yes. That's the very thing!" Oliver said. "What shall we put with it?"

"How about a little baby's breath and statice? The soft purple will go well with the gold. Surrounded by laurel . . ."

A few minutes later Oliver left the shop, elated, holding the bouquet with tender care. He walked to the Coop, around the corner. There, in the men's clothing department, he balanced the flowers in one hand while sliding the hangers along the racks with the other, glancing at his watch every few minutes and rapidly surveying the suits.

Suddenly his hand was arrested. "Beware of all enterprises that require new clothes" had popped into his head. Thoreau was challenging him. Was he thinking of buying a suit because he needed it, or was he trying to impress Loveday?

Troubled, he left the store, walked out onto Massachusetts Avenue and climbed into a taxi. Leaning back against the upholstery, he could barely contain his impatience to reach Loveday.

Once he arrived on Chestnut Street, Oliver was in another world. The handsome nineteenth-century brick mansions were of modest height, elegant in their Georgian simplicity, with the golden dome of the State House visible above the rooftops. A curving flight of steps led up to the door of number eight, which was overhung by a columned portico.

"Be still and cool," Oliver admonished himself as he entered the foyer and pressed the button marked MEAD. But he wasn't, not the least bit. He leaned against the outside door so it would open the moment the buzzer sounded.

Loveday's apartment was on the ground floor. Even before she opened her door, Oliver was there, waiting.

Suddenly, to his intense surprise, they were in each other's arms. How had this happened? The bouquet, which had been carefully held upright till now, was dangling down Loveday's back. Oliver would have been happy to remain that way forever, but Loveday quickly let go.

In the living room he handed her the flowers. "Oh, Oliver!" she exclaimed. "How beautiful! I'll take them home with me—they'll keep."

Her pleasure couldn't have been more gratifying.

"Sit down," she urged. "I'll just put them in water."

As she headed for the kitchen, the ease with which she moved made her seem young. In a moment she returned, carrying a vase with the flowers attractively arranged, placed it on a drop-leaf table and sat down across from him.

His heart was beating fast. Much as he'd thought about Loveday, now that he was with her he couldn't think of the appropriate things to say. He studied her face, afraid of what he might find. She seemed more self-possessed than she'd ever been at Firbank.

Suddenly she did an incredible thing: she burst out laughing! "Don't be so glum," she begged. "Let's forget the whole business with Ross. It did upset me, I admit, but I've put it out of my mind. Why don't you do the same? We only have a short time together. Let's enjoy it."

He saw the rightness of her plea. And yet he had to make amends. "Ross meant no harm. And in a moment of loneliness, I did confide in him, never dreaming he'd remember. In fact, I thought he was half asleep."

She ignored this. "How are things at home?" she asked.

He told her about the Hollands' plan to move to New York and how this troubled them. "But tell me about yourself, Loveday. I'm distressed to think you were so ill."

"I'm fine now. And Oliver, I have the most wonderful news! I've heard from Mary Day, my former student who's now an editor here in Boston. She says her department head is very interested in my book."

"That *is* wonderful!"

"Yes. They want me to come in and talk about it on Monday before I go home."

If only Oliver weren't obliged to leave this afternoon! They might have spent Sunday together. But Loveday wasn't urging him, and this one precious day was passing fast. It was already time to take her to lunch.

They walked out into the sunshine together, found a restaurant along the Common and were given a table by the window. When they were seated, Loveday opened the conversation. "How's Ross?"

"Doubly precious. We almost lost him."

"*Ross?*"

"Yes. A truck came racing down Salt Pond Road. Peter snatched Ross to the side just in time."

"Oliver! What happened? Was Ross hurt?"

"No, he's fine. But the dogs were with them and Duffy—"

"Oh, Oliver! You mean—"

"It was instantaneous. She was a dear little thing, Loveday."

"I know."

Her sympathy emboldened Oliver. He reached across the table and laid his hand on hers. "Loveday, please hear me out. There are some things I have to say. Will you let me?"

She looked at her plate. "I didn't mean to shut you up earlier," she said apologetically. "It's just been so painful. You see"—her self-possession vanished—"I care about you, too. But . . ."

The emotion that rose in Oliver then must have been apparent to her. "Until a few weeks ago," he said, "I never thought of marriage as a possibility at my age. I simply felt this high regard for you and acknowledged to myself that it was, indeed, love. Then lately I've been encouraged to think that I might dare ask you to consider marriage. But there are certain matters to be settled first."

He was almost silenced by her expression. He could tell she was at war with herself, being pulled in two directions. "I'm not proposing," he assured her. "Not yet. But I do look to a day when I shall talk to you about marriage."

It was out! His heart was racing. He leaned back, looking down into his lap. Loveday took a little notebook out of her purse, wrote on a page, then tore it out and handed it to him.

"That's my address in Kansas," she said. "I don't want you to think I'm running away from you. In fact, being with you at Firbank has been one of the greatest experiences of my life. But as long as you aren't proposing, I don't see why we can't just continue to be friends."

They said very little after that. What was there to say? Oliver paid the bill. He was planning to walk back to Chestnut Street with Loveday, but she explained that she had an errand to do and would leave him here. They stood outside on the pavement, inexplicably feeling closer than ever, now that they were parting, perhaps forever.

Oliver realized he hadn't been completely candid. He said hurriedly, "What stands in my way—partly—is the realization of how unfair it would be to ask anyone to marry me as long as I'm still grieving for Daphne. I must learn to love her without being so regretful."

"But Oliver, I don't see how you can do that until you have someone to take her place—not in your love, but in your life."

"Do you think so? Do you really think so?"

"I'm certain."

"Bless thee, Loveday," he said, reaching for her hands. "Thee has put great joy in an old man's life."

Still holding his hands, she lifted her face and kissed him.

It was a mercy that a taxi drew up just then, for Oliver was in danger of breaking down. That good-by kiss had undone him.

CHAPTER NINE

WHEN he reached the Friends Center and started upstairs, Oliver noticed that a three-by-five card taped to the newel-post bore his name.

"Oliver Otis," it said, "please call your home."

Now what? Something serious must have occurred. Standing once more in the stuffy cloakroom, he dialed, and counted the rings anxiously. When Serenity answered, he braced himself.

"Oliver, Heather phoned this morning. She called to say she's coming. Monday."

"Heather's coming? How wonderful!" But Oliver was unnerved. This was just what, months ago, he'd feared would happen if he wrote her about Loveday.

"Her plane gets into Boston at two o'clock," Serenity was saying. "She got thy letter, and she's worried about thee. She says getting married's a big step. We thought thee might like to stay over and meet her plane. Peter can drive up Monday afternoon and bring you both home, only he can't leave till five, so you'd better get supper there."

"But I promised Ross I'd come home today."

"That's okay. I'll explain it to him. He'll understand. And Oliver, if Loveday's still there when Heather arrives," Serenity went on, "why not have supper together, the three of you? Heather complained that she doesn't know anything about Loveday. So if she got to meet her . . ."

As soon as Serenity hung up, Oliver dialed Loveday's number. She was home! "Heather's coming," he announced, explaining that he was prolonging his stay.

"From London? Doesn't she usually visit in the summer?"

"Well—yes. But we have something to discuss," Oliver said lamely. "She's arriving Monday at two and Peter's picking us up that evening. Loveday, would you have supper with us? I'd like you to know Heather."

"That would be nice. But let's not go out. Please, bring her here—it'll be more relaxed."

Oliver felt pushy as he asked Loveday whether she had plans for tomorrow. Unfortunately, she would be busy in the afternoon—a neighbor had offered to help her pack. But would he like her to join him at Friends Meeting in the morning?

Would he! His spirits soared as he hung up the phone.

OLIVER had never considered himself worldly, so it shocked him to discover how much pleasure he took in a new suit—the first he'd ever bought by himself. He could no longer deny that he wanted to look his best for Loveday, so on Monday morning he went back to the Coop and selected one of pure wool, gray, as befitted an elderly Quaker, but with a herringbone weave that gave it quiet elegance. Loveday would approve. Even Heather might.

Waiting that afternoon at the airport gate where Heather would emerge, Oliver wondered how she would act when she met Loveday. Heather could be aloof to a degree that was downright discourteous. Then again, she might be the well-bred British matron, socially correct, secretly hostile. If Heather behaved either way, the supper would be a fiasco.

By the time the plane from London was announced, Oliver's apprehension had reached fever pitch, and he was overtaken by weariness. Then he saw Heather coming through customs, wedged in a mass of people, wearing a plum-colored coat and hat. Forgetting his fatigue, he rushed forward to embrace her.

"My dear," he murmured, "my dear." He held her tightly.

She kissed him but quickly backed off. "We're blocking traffic," she said. She looked tired, too. Oliver took her suitcase.

"Well, Father," Heather said when they were clear of the crowd, "how are you?" Before Oliver could answer, she added, "I tried writing you, but I just couldn't think what to say. I tore up three aerograms. So I decided to fly over. It's not a convenient time. Stephen's in Scotland on business. But—"

"How's Stephen? How are the children?"

"All in good form."

They reached the street and hailed a taxi. "Beacon Hill," Oliver told the driver. "Six Chestnut Street." He had arranged for them to have tea at the Beacon Hill Friends House, the student residence next door to Loveday's apartment.

"Where are you taking me? Aren't we going to Firbank?"

"Tonight. Peter's coming for us. Now we're having tea at the Quaker student house. This evening Loveday has invited us for supper."

"Loveday," Heather repeated, drawling the syllables. "What an odd name. You never mentioned it. I didn't have the foggiest notion what she's called till I rang up and Rennie told me."

"I'm sorry if I've worried thee," he said, patting her hand. "I had no thought of marrying until I wrote thee. At my age—"

"Yes," she broke in, suddenly showing her pent-up feelings. "If you were ten years younger, I could understand. But unless she's a schemer, what reason would any woman have for marrying an—"

"None, I'm afraid. Loveday doesn't seem inclined. Though till I ask her, I can't be sure. And till I know whether thee's comfortable, I don't feel free to ask her." Oliver glanced at Heather, hoping for some hint of approval, but she simply looked upset. He sighed. "Thy journey may have been in vain," he warned.

To his relief, the touchy conversation ended, for the taxi had arrived at Friends House, where they were welcomed by a smiling girl in blue jeans who introduced herself as Carol. She took their things and led them to the dining room. Places had been set for two at the end of a long table. After bringing in the tea and a platter of cookies, Carol disappeared.

Sitting beside Heather, Oliver noticed that her hair was almost white. He found it hard to grasp that his child was middle-aged. Wasn't it only yesterday that she was swinging from the branches of the apple trees, her red pigtails flying?

He took her hand in his, silently praying that with God's help they'd come to an understanding that wouldn't violate Heather's feelings or force him to repress his own.

"Oh, Father, thank you for the tea," she said after the second cup. "I feel ever so much better. This is a lovely place." She turned and studied him. "Isn't that a new suit?"

"My first since thy wedding. Does thee like it?"

"Very much."

"Well, I'm glad thee approves. I was a little afraid to trust my judgment. Mother and I always used to shop together."

"You're becoming independent," Heather observed, with what sounded like a touch of sarcasm. "I never did understand why you and Mother couldn't seem to do anything alone." She made a face. "You two were always so close."

In her fifties, Heather still hadn't lived down her adolescent notion that her parents had no room in their hearts for her because they were so wrapped up in each other! Oliver had never felt free to discuss this with her. Now he was resolved to do so.

"Heather," he began, squeezing her hand, "thee knows well that we loved thee as much as we loved each other."

"I know," she conceded grudgingly. "You were good parents. It was just the way I felt, and you and Mother were never able to convince me otherwise. Tell me," she said, changing the subject, "this woman—Loveday—is she anything like Mother?"

"Not at all! Mother had equanimity and a clear sense of purpose, while Loveday is at times torn by conflicting impulses."

"Sounds like a difficult person."

"Oh, no! She just hasn't quite found her niche yet."

"*At her age?* Didn't you say she's in her seventies?"

"*Early* seventies."

"What do you see in her?"

How could Oliver answer that? He twiddled his teacup, incapable of characterizing Loveday objectively. "Well, I simply fell in love, practically at first sight. I haven't been the same since."

"But I just can't understand. You used to be so reasonable."

Oliver ignored the reproach. "I'm convinced," he assured Heather, "that Loveday would blossom at Firbank."

"You always were selfless," Heather said. "That's why I came—to make sure you weren't overlooking your own welfare."

"I'm not. Loveday and I are both seekers. And her companionship makes me supremely happy. But in the past few days I've realized it wouldn't be fair to marry while I'm still grieving for Mother. So I may not be ready, though Loveday thinks I can't cease grieving till I have someone else to cherish."

"You seem to have discussed this with her pretty thoroughly. Well, I'm disappointed. With the Hollands leaving, I really counted on your coming to England."

Tears blurred Oliver's vision. So Heather hadn't come because she mistrusted his judgment. She'd come because she wanted him near her. He reached in his pocket for his handkerchief.

Noticing his emotion, she looked touched. "It will seem strange, having a stepmother. But all I want is to make sure that this Loveday won't take advantage of you."

"Thank thee, dear. When thee meets her, I believe thee'll feel easy. The real question is: Will she have me?"

Heather dropped her British speech and reverted to the slang of her New England youth. "Wanna bet?" she quipped.

LOVEDAY welcomed them with poise. "I'm glad I didn't miss your visit," she said to Heather, hanging up her coat. "I've heard so much about you." She led the way into the living room, scarcely looking at Oliver.

"So good of you to invite us, when you're just about to go on a journey," Heather murmured politely.

"Good of you to come. You must be tired. Jet lag . . ."

They were all nervous, Oliver decided. He waited for the women to be seated, then dropped into a lumpy armchair, feeling he was more of an observer than the cause of the whole odd confrontation. Heather was going on about the resemblance of Beacon Hill to certain parts of London. The superficiality of her tone bothered him. This was no time for small talk. It was important that Heather get to know Loveday.

"All these packing boxes!" Loveday was saying. "They're ready to be shipped home. The man was supposed to pick them up this afternoon, but he never came."

She was simply making conversation. Didn't she wish to be friends with Heather? Then gradually something dawned on Oliver: Loveday had guessed why Heather had come, and she was hurt.

"So you're flying west momentarily," Heather rattled on.

"Well, I *was*. But everything's changed suddenly. I'm flying east instead, as soon as I can get my reservation."

"East?" Oliver cried. "You don't mean to Europe?"

"Yes. I'm— Oh! Excuse me. Something seems to be burning."

Loveday flew to the kitchen, and soon returned carrying a

steaming casserole. As she carefully placed it on the card table by the living-room window, the tilt of her head expressed an assurance that revealed a new, highly attractive side of her character. But when they were seated around the table on tippy folding chairs, she seemed uncertain whether to suggest that they have the silent grace. Oliver took the initiative, reaching for her hand and Heather's, bowing his head.

Afterward, as he opened his eyes, he found Loveday looking at him intently, but it was hard to read her thoughts. *How could you do this to me?* Was that what she was asking him?

"What's this about your going to Europe?" he inquired, in a tone that was more testy than he meant it to be.

Loveday's face lit up. "The most wonderful thing happened today! You remember I had a lunch date with Mary Day? To my surprise, her boss came along, and we talked business. The upshot of it is, Oliver, the publishing house is sending me to Salzburg—paying my expenses. It's what they call an option. Not a contract—I hope to get that when my book is finished."

Heather looked impressed. "How long will you stay?"

"Well, the children won't like it if I'm not back by Christmas."

Oliver tried to tell Loveday he was pleased, but he didn't think he sounded very convincing. Austria was much farther from Firbank than Kansas, much too far.

"Do you have an address there?" he asked.

"No. I'll hunt up a room when I arrive. Last time I got my mail at the main post office. *Postlagernd*—general delivery—it's probably the best address."

Oliver wrote it down with care. Then, looking up, he saw Loveday silently pleading with him. What was she trying to say?

Aloud she said, "You're the one I have to thank for this, Oliver. You inspired me. My children thought I was wasting my time on a crackpot idea."

"I didn't do a thing," he protested, secretly flattered.

"Yes, you did," she insisted, giving him a smile that went right to his heart.

They were eating ice cream when the Hollands arrived.

95

Heather left the table and went to the door to meet them. Peter and Serenity greeted her affectionately. But Ross ran to Oliver. " 'cle Oliver!" he cried reproachfully. "Thee promised to come back tomorrow and thee didn't!"

Risking the collapse of the folding chair, Oliver reached out, drew the boy onto his lap and held him close.

"Come have some ice cream," Loveday said to the Hollands.

"No, thanks," Serenity answered. "We have to go right back. It's starting to snow, and Ross is dead tired. He and I weren't going to come, but he couldn't wait any longer to see Oliver."

"I missed thee, too," Oliver whispered to Ross, bending down to the little ear. "But Aunt Heather surprised us, thee sees. Will thee run over now and say hello to her?"

It was Oliver's last chance to have a word alone with Loveday, who had come back to the table. There was so much he wanted to say. How compress it into one final moment?

Turning to her, he said softly, "I'm sorry if I've ever caused you pain or annoyance. I never would give you a minute's distress, if I possibly could avoid it."

"Why can't we just go on being friends? It's been so beautiful. Why does it have to become complicated by outsiders?"

Ross returned and tried to climb on Oliver's lap again.

"Sit here, Ross," Loveday urged him, getting up. "I'll get you an ice-cream cone to eat in the car."

Peter was standing in the doorway. "Let's go, folks." Loveday reappeared with the cone and a handful of paper towels. Ross reached up and gave her a hug.

She was visibly touched. She was also plentifully smeared with ice cream. Oliver wished he could embrace Loveday, too. But there was no opportunity for a private farewell.

"Thank you for a delightful dinner," Heather said.

"I'm glad you came," Loveday told her. Then she took both of Heather's hands and looked directly into her eyes. "Enjoy your stay," she said reassuringly. "And don't worry. You have nothing to worry about. Believe me."

The click of Loveday's door closing behind them sent Oliver's mind spinning. The sidewalk was already slippery as he and Heather stepped into the street. He took her arm and lifted his face to let the snowflakes cool his cheeks.

"Well, Father," Heather said, "you were right. I needn't have come. I'm sorry for you, but she's obviously not interested in marriage. What a pity! She's charming. And so able."

PART IV: *Loveday*

CHAPTER TEN

THE bells of Salzburg transported Loveday into the eighteenth century. They rang hourly throughout the Old Town, but never in unison—too soon, too late, on pitch, off pitch—hurling a beautiful dissonance into the sky.

To capture the atmosphere she hoped to communicate in her book, she had rented a room on the street where Nannerl Mozart had lived after her husband died. It looked out onto the cobblestones of the Green Market and the casements of the Mozart children's birthplace. When the chatty landlady showed her the room, Loveday knew at once that she wouldn't be happy anywhere else.

But after a few days here, apart from the room and the bells, Salzburg seemed less attractive than on Loveday's previous visit, which had been in springtime. Now an icy wind blew down from the Alps, the fountains were boarded up, some of the museums and theaters were closed, and the churches looked streaky and stark in the cold rain. But the coffee and pastry were as fabulous as ever.

Loveday had formed the habit of going to the Residenzplatz every morning at eleven to hear the carillon. She would sit in the café there, always choosing a table near the same window. She was served by the same bald waiter, who usually exchanged a few words with her. She was so lonely that she looked forward to this chat with absurd eagerness.

But this morning the waiter was very busy, and hurried off

after taking her order. While Loveday waited to be served, she bowed her head, trying to draw in her scattered self, recalling the grace at Firbank—the unexpected current that electrified her as Oliver took her hand. But alone, she just felt numb.

The waiter arrived with a heavy tray. *"Bitte sehr,"* he said, setting down *Kremschnitten*—puff pastry with creamy filling—and coffee heaped with whipped cream. Then he rushed off.

Loveday sipped slowly. On account of the calories, she allowed herself only one coffee a day. As for the *Kremschnitten*—well, she wouldn't eat any lunch.

When she finished, she walked to the post office; she went there several times a day, hoping to find a letter from home. None had come so far, but there hadn't really been time yet for mail to arrive from the States. Still, she couldn't wait.

All those weeks that she'd stayed in Boston after she'd completed her research, hoping to be invited to Firbank again—she hadn't missed her children then. Now, all she thought of was hearing from them. No. All she really thought of was Oliver—of how wonderful it had been knowing him; how his touching confession of love had almost undone her.

She longed for his reassuring presence. She could picture him—his youthful bearing, the unusual aliveness of his expression. When he looked at her, his whole face crinkled into a rapturous smile. Ought she to write to him? Or would it be more fitting to indicate by her silence that the friendship had terminated as unexpectedly as it began? She didn't want it to end, though—ever. So shouldn't she at least send him a postcard? She might even write a letter, telling him about her work. Then when her book came out, she'd send him an autographed copy. He'd be impressed!

But *marriage!* What for? Wasn't she getting along fine on her own? With her first book she was starting a new career, one even more prestigious than the first. How could she think of settling down to domesticity in a little backwater, even one as charming as Firbank? And if she did, what would her children say? Emily, whose own marriage had been a disaster. And Toby—Loveday had never met the girl he was living with. Although he claimed to be crazy about her, he didn't seem to have the faith to make a commitment. Only Will, her eldest, was happily married.

Still, being with Oliver had been wonderful. Loveday had just never dreamed he'd fall in love with her. Well, she guessed she loved him, too, in an uninvolved way. He was attractive—very. That morning at Firbank, when she'd caught him sitting in that big old bed, reading his Bible, her feelings had been far from spiritual. He had roused something in her that she'd had to fight ever since.

She thought of those wedding certificates hanging on the wall at Firbank. Defining oneself in terms of a relationship rather than as an individual was a concept Loveday considered out of date. But had she been right to burn her bridges? "You have nothing to worry about," she'd assured Heather. Did she mean it? Or had she said it out of spite, because she was angry at Heather for coming to look her over?

She meant it. All the same, she did wish she could see Oliver. And it wasn't true that she was getting along fine. She was breaking down—she, who'd always been in command.

At the post office, there was no mail for her. She must go back to the room, settle down to work and forget.

BY THE following week, Loveday was writing her book in earnest. There still had been no word from home. One midnight she woke up sobbing. She must have dreamed—she couldn't remember. Her mind was blank, but her heart ached. For what?

The heavy eiderdown on her bed was oppressive. Loveday tossed it off. Now she was freezing, but she had nothing to cover herself with. The top sheet was fastened to the eiderdown. She got out of bed and found her coat. Lying down again, she pulled it up around her shoulders. Her feet stuck out, though, and she couldn't go back to sleep.

Yesterday had been Thanksgiving. It still is, Loveday suddenly realized. In Emporia it's only five o'clock. It's Thanksgiving and I'm not there. That must be what had made her cry.

Right now her family was eating turkey and cranberry sauce at Emily's house—with Will and Sara Ann, their two boys and Toby. Were Emily's daughters home? Or was this the year they spent the holidays with their father in Los Angeles?

She should have phoned. It would have cost a lot, speaking to each of them, but it would have been worth it. Why didn't she think of that before she went to bed? Should she dress and go out now? But where would she find a pay phone? They were in the post office, and it was closed. In fact, why wasn't Loveday in Emporia now, where she belonged? Hadn't she told Oliver the last time she was at Firbank that she must go home? As they sat in the silence that morning, it had seemed imperative that she go at once and tell her children how she had misrepresented their father to them all these years. Yet, when she had been unexpectedly offered this trip to Salzburg, she had put all that out of her mind, telling herself it could wait. But could it?

She might have an accident here and there'd be nobody to notify her children—she didn't know a soul. The only people who ever spoke to her were Frau Scheibl—her landlady—and the bald waiter. She might even die here. Then her children would never know what she'd intended to tell them. And Oliver would never know what had become of her.

He'd said something to Serenity the night before she went to New York for her job interview that had had the power of a charm. "Be still and cool." Be still and cool, she repeated, over and over. But without Oliver, it didn't work.

Morning came, the sun was shining, and it was market day in the street below. Standing at her window, Loveday watched the farmers erect their stalls and trestle tables. Huge red-and-white umbrellas sprang up; baskets of fruits and vegetables, pots of plants and flowers cluttered the cobblestones. Women were coming from all directions with their cloth shopping bags. One held a little boy by the hand, bundled up in an Alpine cloak. Loveday couldn't see his face, but he made her think of Ross.

Had the Hollands moved to New York yet? she wondered. If so, how was Ross taking the separation from Oliver? Loveday's heart went out to the little boy. Where had he had Thanksgiving dinner? Probably in Neville, with Rennie's parents.

In that case, Oliver was alone at Firbank, unless Heather had stayed to keep him company. Why was Loveday so angry with Heather? She evidently loved her father so much that when she thought he was threatened, she hastily flew across the ocean to try to protect him. What was wrong with that? And anyway, why dwell on it now? Loveday had work to do. She sat down at the table and looked over what she had written yesterday. Her manuscript was growing hefty.

> When the news of Mama's death—on July 3, 1778, in Paris—reached Salzburg, Nannerl had her hands full comforting Papa. Wolfgang needed money again and she sent it. Then the inexcusable happened: Wolfgang fell in love. Six months later he returned to Salzburg, brokenhearted. Nevertheless, he composed beautiful music that year: the Post Horn Serenade, the Sinfonia Concertante for violin and viola, the Concerto in E flat for two pianos.

Loveday remembered that Wolfgang had dedicated that concerto to Nannerl. But he hadn't invited her to play it with him at the first public performance in Vienna. He had chosen another young woman whom he didn't care for especially—simply because she was a better musician.

When Loveday had discovered this bit of information, it shattered her contention that Nannerl's gifts were underrated solely on account of her sex. The whole point of this book was to show the unfair treatment Nannerl received because she was a woman. But now that theory had collapsed.

In fact, the more Loveday learned about Nannerl, the more she realized Nannerl wasn't a very dynamic artist. Perhaps she didn't merit greater success. Her tragedy wasn't so much attributable to sex discrimination as to her inability to stand up to her tyrannical father—and, more important, to the fact that she was next of kin to a genius.

This was such a distressing discovery for Loveday that she almost considered abandoning the whole book. She had wanted to prove her theory. And now she found her theory didn't work. She realized she had never approached her subject as a historian.

Instead, she'd become a participant in Nannerl's story, living in it, just as she'd always lived in Mozart's music. The sufferings of these people had filled her with such pity and anger that she wept. Was it right for a historian to be so subjective?

She had let her anger about Nannerl slant the story. Why this anger? Why was she so bitter? If only Loveday could talk to Oliver now! She was losing her grip.

What she needed, Loveday decided, was her coffee. She left the house, passed the Franciscan Church and came to Saint Peter's. Then, on an impulse, she entered the cemetery and walked through the arcades, looking for Nannerl's grave marker among the monuments.

Nannerl hadn't planned to be buried at Saint Peter's; she had wished to rest beside her father, Leopold, and her daughter, Jeanette, in Saint Sebastian's churchyard. But three years before she died, something happened that outraged Nannerl. Her detested sister-in-law, Constanze, had remarried after Wolfgang's death and settled in Salzburg with her second husband, Georg von Nissen. Constanze hadn't even attended Mozart's funeral and had never visited his pauper's grave. But when Nissen died, she had him buried in the Mozart family plot at Saint Sebastian's. She erected a huge tombstone bearing Nissen's name and omitting Leopold's and Jeanette's. This had been too much for Nannerl. She asked to be buried elsewhere.

Now, among the markers, Loveday found Nannerl's modest wooden cross. Affixed to it was a small, weathered portrait of her holding a bunch of flowers. It had been painted shortly before she died at seventy-eight. Loveday was shocked by the contrast between this pathetic portrait and the stone bas-relief that she had seen at Saint Gilgen, from which Nannerl had looked down in the prime of life, demanding that the world be notified of its failure to appreciate her!

Loveday turned away, shivering. An icy wind swept through the cemetery as she hurried off to the comfort of her coffee.

On the fourth of December Loveday's landlady came to her room with a tall jar of wintry branches. "*Barbarazweige*," Frau Scheibl announced. "These twigs will bring you luck." It was Saint Barbara's Day—the saint who protected people in thunderstorms. On her day, Frau Scheibl explained, one must cut cherry branches and take them indoors. Then, if the branches bloomed by Christmas, Loveday would have good luck.

But by Christmas she'd no longer be here. "*Die Kinder*," Loveday explained. Her children wanted her home.

Frau Scheibl didn't conceal her disappointment. She'd thought Frau Mead was staying till spring, when she could rent the room easily to returning tourists. She started to leave, but then stopped at the door to observe that if Loveday would write the name of the man she loved on a card and tie it on a Barbara twig, she could count on being married within the year.

Loveday laughed. "Marry?" she cried, as the door closed. "I have no wish to." Still, the conversation had made her think of Oliver again.

It was almost noon the next day when Loveday thought about a letter from home—surely one had come by now. She put on her coat and set out for the post office.

Not since she arrived had Salzburg looked so enchanting. People were milling around Cathedral Square, patronizing the seasonal stalls. In passing, Loveday glanced at the displays: wreaths and garlands, and candles to hang on the tree; toys; colorful Advent calendars with little windows for impatient children to fold back, one each day, till Christmas.

Many of the things looked handmade. But it was the childlike faith of the women in shawls, purchasing the articles, that transfigured them. Their eyes seemed to be saying that these things were precious, that they would sanctify their homes.

At one stall there were gingerbread figures of Saint Nicholas, dressed as a bishop with miter and staff. His only resemblance to Santa Claus was a benign expression and a flowing beard iced in sugar. And unlike Santa Claus, he had a companion—a diabolic figure made of dried fruit. Loveday had never seen anything like it. The head was a fig, with currant eyes, a cherry tongue and curved horns—what they were made of, she couldn't guess. The trunk and legs were of prunes strung on wire, with toes turned up. This evil-looking creature carried a raisin chain and a twig for a switch. The devil? But what had he to do with Christmas? "*Was ist das?*" Loveday asked the old woman behind the counter.

"Krampus."

Seeing that Loveday was puzzled, the woman explained that on December 6 Saint Nicholas and Krampus went from house to house together, the saint bringing presents to the good children, the devil switching the bad ones and rattling his chain. Loveday was horrified. What kind of parents would let the devil in to scare their children? She hurried on.

But she couldn't resist glancing into one last stall. There, along with an assortment of carved animals, was a box no bigger than a matchbox, containing a Nativity scene. Against a typical Salzburg landscape were set tiny figures with hands and faces made of wax. Mother and Child, ox and ass, shepherds—all looked at Loveday with gentle, trusting eyes. And she looked back, unable to tear herself away. Maybe, she thought, if she took the little box back to her room, she'd be less lonely. It might even inspire her. She'd been having problems with her writing the past few days.

As she handed the money to a smiling girl dressed in a dirndl and embroidered sweater, Loveday asked herself why the little box seemed to mean so much to her. For even before she carried it off in its tissue wrapping, it had become essential to her, as if it were capable of working miracles.

She was crossing the square in front of the cathedral when all the bells struck noon at once—harmonizing, quarreling, captivating Loveday all over again. She stood still until the last one had sounded. Then she walked on, hearing the resonance that lingered in the air after the clappers came to rest—an aftertone far sweeter and more serene than the pealing turbulence.

At the *Postlagernd* window, she asked timidly if she had any mail. She was handed an envelope, and she turned it over. It was from Oliver! She couldn't control her impatience. Halfway to the door, she tore open the envelope. It was a long letter, which began:

My very dear friend,
Thee will, I trust, not take it amiss if I address thee in the plain language. The request I am making is so intimate that the form of address intended for the world seems quite inappropriate.
I can now ask thee with all my heart to become my wife. . . .

Loveday's fingers shook as she refolded the letter and stumbled out of the post office; she wanted to read it in the privacy of her room. But she hardly knew where she was going. Her vision was blurred by tears. No, she kept crying to herself. No, Oliver, I can't. How can I follow in Daphne's footsteps?

It was freezing in the room when she got there. Standing by the window, she took out the letter and read again, her heart pounding:

I can now ask thee with all my heart to become my wife. This, thee surely knows, has long been my desire. I felt constrained from asking thee earlier by the need to make certain that we would truly be joined to our families. On my side, way has now opened. Heather returned to London, assuring me she would be in accord. But she's convinced that such an able woman as thee would never want an old codger like me! I fear she may be right. Only my strong leading compels me to ask thee, anyhow.
At our age, time is very precious. Otherwise, I would not have mentioned the matter until thee finished thy book. At the moment, all I ask is that thee stop here on thy return from Austria. Together, we could talk over the questions we shall have to consider before thee can decide. Thee could then discuss them with thy children.

Discuss a proposal of marriage with her children? Indeed not! Suppose they disapproved? Would she pay any attention? But why was Loveday even asking herself that, when she didn't intend to marry, anyway? She must simply write and tell Oliver it was better for her not to come to Firbank, that she was flying right through to Kansas. Her mind was made up. But her heart ached as she read on.

> I've been out in the field the past few days, husking the corn that was still standing and carrying it to the barn. Slow work. I miss Ross. He used to "help."

So the Hollands have already left, Loveday thought, troubled.

> I am prepared to make any adjustments within my power that might contribute toward thy happiness. I hope I am not pressing too hard. Just knowing I might have a visit from thee would sustain me during the agony of waiting.

But Loveday mustn't visit Oliver. If she did, she wouldn't be able to resist him. His love would enfold her and she'd never be free again.

> All I have to offer, dear Loveday, is a heart filled with love and regard for thee.
>
> Thy,
Oliver

MOST of the night Loveday had lain awake, regretting what she'd written to Oliver—that she had a commitment to her book, that, anyhow, marriage was out of the question, that she'd better not visit him, and so on. She had taken the letter to the post office at once.

Returning at dusk, she sobbed in the street, telling herself she had just thrown away the most precious gift she'd ever been offered. What would Frau Scheibl say, Loveday wondered, if she knew that even without tying a card on a cherry branch, Loveday had received a proposal? But luck isn't what I need, she thought. A leading—that's the only thing that will help me.

In the morning she tried to work, but still feeling distraught, she went out for coffee. On the way she passed the cathedral, and went in. The lofty interior awed Loveday, with the painting of the Resurrection on the high altar, the inlaid marble floor, and the huge font resting on ancient copper lions. Except for the verger, she seemed to be alone in this vast edifice. If only Oliver were here to share the silence with her! When she shared it with him, the better of those warring selves inside her seemed to win. She was suddenly overwhelmed with longing for him.

Suppose she had let her feelings run away with her; suppose she'd accepted his invitation to go to Firbank and talk things over. Could she ever live up to his exalted concept of marriage? He had invited Loveday to enter into a relationship that her life experience hadn't prepared her for. Unprepared and scared—that's why she'd said no.

But Oliver was no fool. And he was ready to take her as she was, convinced that she would grow into such a relationship. If he believed in her, shouldn't she believe in herself?

Growing took time, though. One couldn't change direction overnight. But time was the one thing she and Oliver didn't have much of. "At our age," he'd written, "time is very precious." It was now or never, all or nothing.

Assuming she had said yes—how much time could they reasonably expect to enjoy together? Oliver was seventy-eight. The infirmities of age might make themselves felt any day. Would she be willing, if necessary, to nurse a sick husband again? But Oliver was in excellent health, Loveday reminded herself. *She* might go to pieces first.

She tried to center down, to quiet her emotions, to open her mind to the order and beauty of this place. But the cathedral made her homesick for the Friends Meetinghouse in Kendal, as plain as this was ornate. The feeling she had, however, sitting here in the silence, was the same. Not peaceful—though she did feel more relaxed and hopeful—but confident of finding her way, of having it "open," as Oliver would say.

Yes, she realized now, she would gladly have cared for him, in sickness or in health. She would gladly have offered him that treasure he seemed to think she possessed. If only she'd waited to answer his letter, her answer might have been different.

The comforting silence was suddenly shattered. The bells of

Salzburg were sounding the hour. Loveday had been in the cathedral a long time. What would her children think? she wondered, as she walked out and crossed the square. Oliver was right. Unless they were comfortable with her decision, she'd have to give it up. What decision? Hadn't she already said no?

As she rounded a corner, she bumped into a black figure. A chimney sweep? No. He didn't have a top hat, just horns, and his tongue was so long it hung down over his chin. He rattled a chain in her face, frightening her. Krampus! Of course, she thought with a start. Today was December 6. Loveday had collided with the devil!

She was relieved when Krampus passed by. But she couldn't take her eyes off him. Halfway down the block, he was joined by a man in a bishop's miter, carrying a staff. Saint Nicholas! In the dim light, he looked like a gingerbread man. Then Loveday saw that in every window, children were peeking through the curtains, waiting.

Saint Nicholas turned, smiled at Loveday over his shoulder and waved. She waved back, but he was already going on, drawing her after him. She followed, gaining on him till she could hear his boots hitting the cobblestones and echoing in her heart: *Now* or *never, all* or *nothing.*

Suddenly she realized that Saint Nicholas was leading her to the post office, the one place where she could telephone. Why had she waited so long when time was so precious? She knew Oliver's number. She just didn't know what she was going to say to him.

She went inside, placed the call and waited for it to go through. Way off in Firbank the phone was ringing. In a minute she would hear his voice! But it was Serenity who answered. "Loveday! Where are you?"

"In Austria. Please let me speak to Oliver."

"He's not home. He's back in Cambridge for that committee. We just came to pick up some books. Loveday, guess what! Peter's got a fabulous job in New York, working with research satellites!"

"That's wonderful. I'm so glad. Listen, I'm calling because I mailed a letter to Oliver yesterday and I wish I hadn't. I don't want him to open it, just to throw it away. Will you tell him?"

"Loveday, this isn't a very good connection. Did you say throw the letter away? Oliver wouldn't do that."

"Please, Serenity, tell him to. I don't want him to read it. And something else. Tell Oliver I'll fly to Boston as soon as I can get a reservation. I'll rent a car and drive straight to Firbank."

"Oh, Loveday, he'll be *so* happy!"

"I've got to hang up now, Serenity, or I'll run out of money."

Loveday walked out of the post office into the cool of the evening and inhaled the pure Alpine air. It was as if she'd been holding her breath all her life and could let it out at last.

She wasn't breaking down, after all. She was breaking out— out of that dark place she'd locked herself into years ago, with her unexamined theories about prerogatives, her need to direct others, when she didn't know how to run her own life. She was breaking out into the light. In the nick of time, Oliver had given her a second chance.

PART V: *Oliver and Loveday*

CHAPTER ELEVEN

HER coming to Firbank had made Oliver so happy that at times he wondered whether he could bear such intense emotion. Even when she had gone, after three beautiful days, the ecstasy persisted. And he was still glowing with it now as he went out to cut the Christmas tree. Tramping over a thin crust of snow between rows of white spruce, Oliver thought of Loveday—how she had unexpectedly appeared in the dooryard.

He hadn't heard the car coming up the lane, for he was out back, filling the bird feeders. When he suddenly saw her running toward him like a young girl, he rushed to meet her and caught her in his arms, almost knocking over the can of birdseed in his excitement. Through her coat he felt the spontaneity with which she nestled against him as he held her tightly. In this moment, he thought, we've become joined.

All that would follow—including the Meeting for worship in which they actually entered upon marriage—would be but a confirmation of the fact that Loveday Mead and Oliver Otis had taken each other for as long as they both should live.

In the living room, she took the chair she'd always chosen and leaned forward anxiously. "Did you get my letter?"

"No. Not yet."

She appeared relieved. "You think you know me, but you really don't," she said. "Sometimes I say things without thinking them through. It's as if there were two people inside of me, pulling in opposite directions. When I first got your proposal, my reaction was that I couldn't possibly marry, and I just dashed off that letter. But as soon as I'd mailed it, I wished I hadn't. Please understand. It takes time to get used to something so amazing as your love." She looked at Oliver anxiously. "Can you put up with someone like that? There'll be times when you'll find me impossible."

He went over to her and reached for her hands. "There'll be times when *thee'll* find *me* impossible."

Tears rolled down her cheeks. He took out his handkerchief and dabbed her face. "There," he whispered, as if she were a child. Then he bent and kissed her.

Later, at supper, he asked the question weighing on him. How would her children take to the idea of her remarrying?

"I really don't know. They're so used to having me around. But you're right, if they aren't content, it would be a mistake."

"I'm glad thee agrees," he'd told her. "Most people would say children's wishes are irrelevant. But how can there be harmony in the world if even parents and children disregard one another? It may take time for thy children to understand. If thee thinks their seeing me would help, I'll fly out. Oh, Loveday, thee makes me so happy! If thee shouldn't come back—"

"I'll come," she promised. "Whatever happens, I'll come."

"Thee must have found it hard to leave Salzburg."

"No, I got fed up with Nannerl. I found out she was a weak, self-centered person, without much talent. I'm thinking of giving up the book altogether."

Oliver was conscience-stricken. He had ruined Loveday's book by proposing before it was completed. He should have waited. "Think it over," he begged.

Loveday's letter from Salzburg arrived the next day. He handed it to her unopened. "Go ahead, read it," she said, handing it back. "You may as well know the worst about me."

He took the letter to the fireplace and dropped it on a smoldering log.

Oliver finally decided to cut a seven-year-old spruce for Christmas. Dragging it home in the snow, he remembered the presents Loveday had brought back from Salzburg. As soon as the tree was up, he'd put them under it.

She had explained that they were for the Hollands—an embroidered blouse for Serenity and a jaunty Austrian hat for Peter. "I realize," she'd said, laughing, "Peter never wears a hat, but I couldn't resist it."

Then she unwrapped a tiny package and showed Oliver the beautifully made box containing the Nativity scene. "This is for Ross," she said. "I fell in love with it in the Advent market and kept it on my worktable to cheer me when I was feeling low."

"Ross will be delighted!" Oliver exclaimed. "And if it has the power to cheer, it's just what he needs. He's finding life in a New York apartment very hard. No place to play. For six months his bed was dry. Now, even in the daytime . . ."

Loveday looked troubled. "That's hard on Serenity."

"Yes, she shows the strain. Thee sees, when they moved, Peter was planning to take care of Ross. Now, with his new job, they've had to make all kinds of stopgap baby-sitter arrangements. And each time they come here, the situation seems to have deteriorated. I think Serenity is beginning to regret having chosen what seemed best for her rather than what was best for them all."

Loveday set the Nativity box on the coffee table. "Oliver, I hunted and hunted for something you'd like, but nothing was good enough. So all I've brought you," she said gravely, "is myself, my whole self."

Overjoyed, he put his arm around her and drew her to the couch, so they could sit close together. "It's all I wish for," he assured her.

"I'm not the same person I was when I left," she said softly, resting her head on his shoulder. "Maybe you think at our age people can't change. But I have."

"I know," he whispered. "I saw it the moment thee arrived."

"In Salzburg I went through an awful time. A lot of my old notions were shaken up. I'm still sorting them out."

Oliver realized that he had changed, too. As he'd told Heather, he hadn't been the same since Loveday's first visit. When he had lost Daphne, he'd lost a certain buoyancy. He remained convinced of God's goodness, he still rejoiced in the return of each season and the fellowship of his friends, but his feelings seemed muffled.

Now life was coursing through him again. It was the transforming power of love! Perhaps that was why the practical matters Oliver had meant to discuss with Loveday slipped his mind until she had been about to go.

"I've saved a little," he told her, sticking his head through the open window of her car. "If inflation doesn't erode it, this should provide for thy needs, in case I— Firbank would be thine as long as thee lives, but after that, it would have to go to Serenity. Grandmother left it to all her descendants."

Loveday waved the whole subject aside. "I wouldn't need money. I have a pension. As for Firbank—naturally, it has to stay in the family. Anyway, what makes you think you would go first? Why worry about those things now? I have to convince the children. If I do, then we'll take our chances. But Oliver, whatever happens, just remember"—she craned her neck to kiss him—"I love thee."

It wasn't until she had disappeared down the lane that Oliver recalled another thing he had meant to ask her: under what auspices she wished to be married. That is, he reminded himself, assuming that the way opens.

For the present, it was rapture enough that she loved him, that she'd declared it in the plain language. She must feel, too, that they were already joined.

The night Loveday reached Emporia, her family congregated at Emily's house for dinner, all except Emily's daughters, who were away at college. Toby was there, looking very happy to see her, though a little drawn. Was his love affair getting him down? And there were Will and Sara Ann, with Michael and Jed, who even kissed their grandmother.

As soon as they were seated at the dinner table, Loveday announced solemnly that she was thinking of marrying a man called Oliver Otis, who lived at Firbank Farm in Rhode Island. No one said anything.

Loveday talked on with enthusiasm, describing what a lovable man Oliver was, how vigorous and enterprising. "And handsome," she couldn't resist adding. Then she told them about the Hollands.

Still no one spoke. "That part of Rhode Island is much like this—farming country," she continued. "Only, it has the ocean and sand dunes."

"I suppose Oliver's retired," Toby said.

"No. He still farms, just fewer acres."

Toby looked surprised. He was probably thinking it strange that his scholarly mother should fall for a farmer.

"He's published a book," she added. "About his first wife, Daphne Otis, one of the foremost artists in America."

They all looked blank.

"How long have you known him?" Will asked, frowning, obviously disapproving. "Seems like a whirlwind courtship."

"I suppose. But at our age—he's seventy-eight—time is precious. At first I couldn't imagine marrying again. But then I realized how much he's come to mean to me. Before going ahead, though, I want to be sure that you all are satisfied."

"A wedding!" Emily sang out, beginning to enjoy the idea. "What fun! Everybody in town will want to come."

She made it sound like a carnival. But no one had given Loveday the assurance she craved. When they were all seated in the living room after dinner, Sara Ann asked, "Will you be married in church?"

Loveday thought of Kendal Meetinghouse, with the sea gulls flying over the ridgepole; of the Hollands, Ludlows and Hills, worshipping quietly in the unadorned room. In their presence, before God, she and Oliver would make their promises to each other. Everyone would sign the certificate.

"Oliver's a Quaker," she explained, "like our ancestors. I'd like to be married in his Meeting. I hope you'll all come."

"You mean to Rhode Island?" Emily cried. "Why doesn't he come to Emporia? That's the usual way. The groom goes to the bride's hometown. There's a Quaker church here; I've seen it in the paper. Why do we all have to traipse east?"

"Lay off of Mom, Emily," Toby urged. "Naturally we'll go. If Mom really wants to marry this man . . ."

"Do I have to give you away?" Will asked, as if he'd rather die.

"A Quaker woman is her own person," Loveday told them. "She gives herself to the groom and he gives himself to her. They don't need a minister or any attendants. Everyone present is a participant, even the children."

Loveday was relieved when it was time to say good night. Walking into her own house after all these months, she felt how good it was to be home. When she had snuggled down gratefully in her bed, she wondered if she really wanted to leave again, to sleep in another strange bed? In Oliver's? After all these years, it would require adjusting to share a bed. And yet, to fall asleep curled up against him, with his arm around her . . .

In the morning Loveday got out her Bible; she'd scarcely looked at it since college. She must get in the habit of reading it. She tried to center down, but her eyes traveled around to the furniture, the pictures, the rugs. Once the children were in accord with her marrying, she must dispose of everything here.

They wouldn't want much of it. What would she do with the rest? She couldn't cart it to Firbank.

It was too hard, centering down alone. She needed Oliver to share the experience with her. That morning at Firbank, when they had settled into a silence with Ross, she had had what amounted to a revelation—the discovery that she had misrepresented their father to her children. She had resolved then to go home and tell them the facts. But now she was here, and she still hadn't told them. She was so wrapped up in herself that she had disregarded them completely. The next time they were all together she would right this wrong.

But how was she going to say something so damaging to her self-esteem? What would they think of her? Communication at so serious a level had never been very good between them. Had she always been this way with her children? she asked herself, as she put the Bible back on the shelf. Had she always been too absorbed in herself to come to know them at a level that would have made it easier now to set the record straight?

Loveday didn't see the children again till Christmas Eve at Will and Sara Ann's. Their house had a festive air. The troubling tension Loveday had felt when she first spoke to her children about Oliver seemed to have eased. But there was no reference to what Loveday thought of as the only gift she wanted for Christmas. Were they hoping the whole thing would blow over?

After dinner they all gathered around the piano and sang a few carols: "Silent Night" and "O Little Town of Bethlehem." Sara Ann played the piano, and Jed tried his trombone but mercifully gave up after a few earsplitting notes.

Loveday thought of Salzburg, of its captivating bells and dear Saint Nicholas—how in some inexplicable way the thump of his boots—*now* or *never*, *all* or *nothing*—had led her to follow what her heart wanted her to do all along. Suddenly she was reminded again of her unfinished business. She must tell the children about their father. Could she face it without breaking down?

As soon as things were quiet, she began. "One morning at Firbank, we had one of those Quaker silences, Oliver, Ross and

I. The silence sometimes results in what Oliver calls a leading—a whole new perspective on life." She looked down at her fingers, which were contracting and stretching in agitation. "That morning I realized that—"

She couldn't go on. She glanced at her children, imploring them for help. They were listening, waiting. "I realized," she finally managed to say, "that Daddy was a much nicer man than the one I used to talk to you about." And Loveday started to cry, sitting there surrounded by her children on Christmas Eve. "I wanted you to know," she sobbed.

They said nothing. But she felt their love enfold her, as it had all along, even when they refused to respond in the way she desired, though she hadn't understood that till this minute. They weren't giving up their mother lightly. They valued her. She couldn't tell them how thankful she was. She just cried.

Toby took her home. By the time they arrived, she had herself under control. She switched on the light in the living room and collapsed into an armchair. Toby stood looking down at her.

"All this stuff," she told him, waving her hand. "What'll I do with it? If I really go to Firbank— I don't know how to even start taking the house apart. It'll take forever."

"Mom, why don't you leave everything, lock the door and just go? We'll keep an eye on the place. You're in no shape to deal with moving. Getting married's enough to handle."

"But you all don't want me to," Loveday wailed.

"It's not that. We just feel that you're not acting like yourself. You were always in charge. And now you're asking us for our consent. It's like something's come over you."

"I guess it has. I've—what you'd call—fallen in love."

"That's just it. That's why we're worried. You were always so independent. We thought you were down on marriage—that you felt cheated when we were kids, because you couldn't get out and do things like Daddy. Now you want to go clear across the country and live on a farm with a man you barely know. And you make him sound—well—sort of odd."

"Quakers are," Loveday admitted, smiling a little. "They're

called a Peculiar People. Maybe he's a little more than most. Else why would he have fallen for me?"

"Well, you seem to be taking an awful lot on faith."

"Isn't that what marriage should be—an act of faith? I wish I'd made you all feel that when you were young, instead of what you say I did. How can I convince you now, so you won't have all these objections?"

"I have no objections, except that I hate to see you go so far away. But if you're sure you'll be happy, I'm satisfied. I think Will's the only one who objects. He wants to size up the guy."

"Oliver said he'd come if I needed him. Maybe I should ask him to. But if he doesn't pass muster, that would be cruel."

"No, don't do that. Will says he's the head of the family and it's up to him to be sure you aren't getting into something weird. He wants to case Firbank, says he'll take a few days off and drive you out, so you'll have your car there."

"You mean Will's going to do all that for me?"

"Yes. Soon as he can get away. Sometime after New Year."

New Year, Loveday thought with gratitude. A new beginning! A new life. But how could she make up to her children for her early failures? How could she awaken in them what Oliver had evoked in her?

"Just leave everything here, Mom," Toby urged again, moving toward the door. "Then, if things don't work out after you're married, you can come back."

"Toby, how can they not work out? Oliver is the most wonderful man."

"Sure, but he's old. So, if something happens, you can always return."

Toby was right. But if she and Oliver were given only a short time together, what a benediction on her life it still would be!

"We'll take our chances," she declared. "Oh, Toby, I wish you'd have faith." She kissed him, fighting back the tears. Then she said something she'd never said before, though she knew she should have, long ago. "Will you bring your girl, Jean, here for supper tomorrow?"

CHAPTER TWELVE

IT WAS on a Friday near the end of January that Loveday finally returned to Firbank. Will drove her car, scarcely speaking. Loveday almost felt she was traveling with a stranger instead of her firstborn.

Oliver, bundled up in a parka and stocking cap, was on the front step as they drove in. He greeted Loveday with restraint and reached out to Will with such cordiality that she wondered how Will could resist it.

"The Hollands are due any minute," he announced. "Coming to see thee, Loveday. They left New York at noon." His way of addressing her seemed to startle Will, though she had tried to prepare him for the plain language.

Will deposited Loveday's things in the ell. Her belongings filled the little room, and there were still more in the car. Where was she going to put everything? she thought. Assuming Will was settling into the top-floor guest room, she hurriedly went downstairs, hoping to get in a word alone with Oliver. She'd scarcely spoken to him yet, though the way he had looked at her, words weren't necessary.

But Will was already in the kitchen, watching Oliver make tea. There was an array of food on the counter, presumably for supper—a large casserole, two pies, a beautiful braided bread. Who had done all that? Friends, Loveday realized.

She noticed that the plastic cloth had been removed from the table, and Will was rubbing his finger over the polished wood surface, examining the grain. "What's this?" he asked Oliver. "Walnut?"

"Yes."

That was about the extent of the conversation. Will was sizing up his host, whose hand seemed a little unsteady as he poured the tea. Loveday thought of Heather's coming to Beacon Hill. Now it was Oliver's turn to be looked over.

The tension was broken by the arrival of Serenity and Ross.

The child rushed to Oliver, then to his toy box. His happiness in being back was touching.

"Where's Peter?" Oliver asked.

"He's just taking Judy Young over to Periwinkle Farm. We brought her with us from New York."

Oliver showed surprise. "Does thee think she might stay?"

"Don't get your hopes up," Serenity cautioned. "I worked on her. Their children are home this weekend. It'll give Austin a chance to express regret, if that's what he feels. But knowing Austin, I can't imagine him expressing anything."

Will was whispering to Loveday. "Doesn't he have a television set here? Can't see one anywhere."

Loveday shook her head. Had Oliver flunked already?

When Peter arrived, things went better. He and Oliver, with Ross between them, took Will out to see the farm before it got too dark. Loveday and Serenity stayed behind to set the table.

Later, as they all sat down to dinner, Loveday recalled how supercilious she had been about the Quaker grace when she first came, and she wondered how Will would take it. But peeking at him during the silence, she thought he was more reverent than she had been.

The only person Will seemed to talk to at supper was Ross. He told him about Michael and Jed, about the Little League, and how the family suffered while Jed practiced the trombone, illustrating this with sound effects, which Loveday considered too realistic. But Ross laughed so hard he nearly fell off the chair.

"Tell me about your jobs," Loveday asked Serenity and Peter.

"I love mine," Serenity answered. "If it weren't for Ross . . ."

"I've no complaints," Peter added. "The research satellite firm I'm in is just starting, and even junior staff like me know what's going on at the top. That's nice. We're both lucky, only Ross . . ."

Peter and Serenity exchanged glances.

There was something in the way they looked at each other that jolted Loveday—a unity she'd never witnessed in a marriage. These two young people liked their work, but it wasn't what fulfilled them. Their oneness with each other and with Ross took precedence over everything. Do I have what it takes to make that kind of marriage? Loveday asked herself anxiously. I love Oliver, but can I ever be that giving?

After dinner the men washed the dishes. As Loveday followed Serenity into the living room, she recalled how assertive Serenity had been when she first returned from New York after her interview, all fired up over the job offer. Loveday had identified with her completely. But the woman who had looked at Peter that way a few minutes ago had changed.

"You're going to love living here," Serenity said as she and Loveday sat down by the fire. She spoke as if it were a foregone conclusion. "Peter and I miss the country and the community, the Meeting, our friends. We don't know people in New York. We've been invited places, but we don't have much time to socialize and we hate dragging Ross out at night."

Loveday's heart went out to Serenity. The beautiful young woman, who had looked uncommonly serene only a few months ago, was drawn and troubled now.

Suddenly Serenity said, "I know this is going to disappoint you, because you were so keen to have me take the job, but I'm not sure I'm going to stay. I come home tired after a day's work and riding the subway in rush hour, with dinner to get and the laundry, and there's Ross, who's been waiting for me all day. When we went, we thought Peter was making the sacrifice, so I could have a career. But it's turned out it's Ross. I don't want that." She broke down.

Loveday went over and put her arm around her. "I'm sorry, Serenity," she said. "I was so stupid, urging you to take the job. I never stopped to consider what it would do to your family. You wouldn't believe how I regret sounding off. I've changed."

"I know," Serenity said, wiping her eyes. "You used to call me Rennie and now you say Serenity, like Oliver."

"Until you can work things out, would you leave Ross with us? He loves Oliver, and he won't have him forever."

Serenity looked startled. "Thanks," she said. "It's sweet of you to offer. I'll speak to Peter. Now I'm going to put Ross to bed." She started for the door, then stopped, her expression thoughtful. "But I couldn't come home and not find Ross there."

When the men came in, Loveday took Will around the living room, showing him Daphne's portrait of the first Serenity, and the sampler, trying to explain the meaning of the words. They didn't interest him. Only the two wedding certificates attracted his attention. He read the words under his breath. " 'And Peter Holland, taking Serenity Ross by the hand, did, on this solemn occasion, declare that he took her to be his wife, promising, with divine assistance, to be unto her a loving and faithful husband as long as they both should live; and thereupon Serenity Ross did in like manner declare that she took him—' Phew!"

They all sat down, and Oliver attempted to draw Will out—inquiring about his work and the farming conditions around Emporia. Little by little, Will began to talk. But just when he was loosening up, the telephone began to ring, interrupting them again and again.

"Sorry," Oliver said, coming back after the third call. "It's all about the Friends Hostel."

"When do you expect to open?" Peter asked.

"In June, we hope." Oliver turned to Will and explained. "A nice old house, close to the beach, was left to our Friends Meeting. At first we intended to turn it into a place where city people, coming here to enjoy the swimming, could spend the night simply and inexpensively. Now the scope has broadened."

"How?" Loveday asked. "Last I heard, that was the plan."

"Well, with the cutting back of government funds for social programs, many people here are experiencing hardship. Some welfare allowances are so reduced that the recipients have to choose between housing and eating. On top of that, people are being released from prisons and mental institutions who have no home to go to and little prospect of finding work. We're not equipped to help them on a long-term basis. But we care. And we can provide shelter for a few homeless people until better arrangements can be made."

"That's a huge undertaking!" Loveday exclaimed.

"Yes, but it seems the only right thing to do."

Loveday noticed Will listening intently, staring at Oliver with what she took to be admiration. But soon after that, when they said good night, Will didn't even refer to the matter that was uppermost in Loveday's mind.

The next morning, as Loveday was getting ready to take Will to the airport in Providence, he still had given her no reason to think he felt easy about her marrying.

"Want to come along?" she asked Oliver.

He must have realized it would be better if she and Will went alone, and he declined. Then, while Will stood on the doorstep shaking Oliver's hand, he asked, "When's the wedding?"

Oliver looked as if he were having trouble maintaining his composure. "We don't know," he said. "First we want to be sure thee and thy sister and brother feel comfortable about my running off with thy mother. I promise to take good care of her."

Will nodded. "It's okay," he muttered.

Loveday understood. This was his way of expressing approval. She threw her arms around his neck and kissed him.

He looked at her affectionately, a little embarrassed. "Can I bring Sara Ann and the kids?"

"Of course!" Oliver exclaimed. "We want all of you—all. Plenty of room in Kendal to put everyone up. As for the date— we can't set it till we pass Meeting. That takes several months."

"Why so long?"

"The Meeting appoints a committee on clearness, usually two men and two women, who try to make sure that nothing is likely to interfere with the success of the marriage."

"What kind of people are they?" Loveday asked, sounding anxious. "Marriage counselors?"

"Oh, no, just Friends who seem to understand the art of a good marriage. Then when they report back to the Meeting that all is satisfactory, a committee of overseers is named to see that the wedding is conducted with reverence and simplicity. Only then can a date be set."

"Wow!" Will exclaimed, grinning. "If I'd had to go through all that to marry Sara Ann, I'd have stayed single. I'm sure glad that Quaker ancestor of ours married out."

HEATHER, Oliver thought, as he watched Loveday leave with Will. I must write at once and tell her. He went to his study, but instead of sitting down at the typewriter he flopped into the armchair, suddenly overcome with fatigue. Then a tiny, squeaky whistle drew his eyes to the door. Ross was standing there. Oliver called him in and drew him close.

"Ross, remember how I told thee long ago that I loved Loveday? And thee told her one time, when she was driving away?"

Ross frowned with what seemed to be a twinge of conscience.

"It was kind of thee to do that for me. And I want to tell thee something surprising: Loveday loves me, too! Isn't that wonderful? So we're going to be married. Will thee come to our wedding?"

Ross nodded gravely.

"That's good! We wouldn't think of being married without thee. Thy parents haven't heard the good news yet. Will thee run and tell them?"

Ross flew out of the room, and came back bringing Serenity and Peter. "We were so hoping," Serenity said, hugging Oliver. Then she turned to Ross. "Let's make a paper chain to decorate Loveday's chair at lunch. Thee go and find the colored paper."

The child rushed out the door. "Last evening," Serenity told Oliver, "Loveday asked me if we'd like to leave Ross here till we can make a better arrangement for him. Peter and I talked about it till late last night. But I've decided instead to resign from the museum. We can live on Peter's salary, even in New York. When Ross is in school all day, then I'll go back to work."

"Is thee sure thee won't regret it, Rennie?" Peter asked. "Thee wants a career so badly."

"I'm not giving it up, only postponing it to give Ross the care he needs. It's the best arrangement for the whole family."

Oliver looked sympathetically from one to the other. "After

you and Will had gone upstairs last evening, Loveday and I discussed something, too. I asked her to tell me candidly how she would feel, should you ever wish to come back to Firbank."

Oliver was surprised by the intentness with which they seemed to await his next words. He hadn't realized how much they needed the assurance he was about to give them.

"I don't think I'm overstating when I say that Loveday would welcome you as warmly as I would. This will always be your home, no matter where your work may take you. If I should predecease Loveday, I wish her to continue living here as long as she chooses. But she has indicated that her children would want her to return to Emporia. In any event, thee, Serenity, will inherit Firbank. Thy great-grandmother left it to all her descendants, and thee's the only one who's shown an interest in it."

Serenity hugged Oliver again. "We're so happy about Loveday," she said. "And now I'm going to see what Ross is up to."

"And I must write to Heather," said Oliver.

"Why doesn't thee phone?" Peter asked, following Serenity to the door. "This is a pretty special occasion."

"Thee's right." Oliver went to the telephone at once.

"What a relief!" Heather exclaimed, when she heard Oliver's voice and he told her his news. "I was sure something terrible had happened or you wouldn't be ringing up. Of course, we'll all come."

"I'm so glad, Heather darling," Oliver said. "Even though we're separated by great distance, I want us to be a united family."

When Loveday returned from the airport and they sat down to lunch, Oliver thought it was impossible to tell whether she or Ross derived greater pleasure from the garlanded chair. She looked radiant.

"Let me show thee something," Oliver said to her after the meal, leading the way to the woodshed. He had lit a fire in the potbellied stove.

"How cozy and cheerful!" Loveday exclaimed.

"Since Daphne died, I've never made a fire here. I knew I should clean out the stove, but something held me back. Now I realize I was waiting for this day, keeping a bed of ashes to build a new fire on. I hope thee'll make this thy study."

Daphne's canvases, easel and paints had been removed. In their place were two cretonne-covered armchairs. A little old-fashioned desk stood by the window.

"My grandfather made this for my grandmother," Oliver said,

running his hand over the top of the desk. "She treasured it. I thought thee might enjoy pressing it into service again."

"Oh, Oliver!" Loveday exclaimed. "It's lovely."

"Thee will, at least, look over thy manuscript, won't thee? Perhaps thee'll change thy mind about finishing it."

She looked at him shyly. "If I heard thee read it, I might be inspired again. Will spoke of it, too, this morning. He said they were all proud of me. When I left Emporia, he thought it a crackpot idea. I don't understand what made the change."

Oliver took Loveday in his arms. "Thee," he whispered, "thee made the change. Shall we write our letter to Kendal Meeting, requesting to be married under its care?" He stepped back, holding her at arm's length, so that he could look into her eyes. " 'Do you recognize marriage as a sacred, loving, and permanent relationship, requiring mutual consideration and adjustments?' That's the query we shall be asked to answer in our own minds. I feel quite clear about it. Does thee?"

"I do." They kissed solemnly and again Oliver had the conviction that they already belonged to each other.

But something was still troubling Loveday. "I— Oliver, when I was in Emporia, Toby told me the children felt they took second place with me when they were little. It made them mistrustful of marriage. Can I ever make it up to them?"

"I don't know," he said. "But offspring aren't all that love begets. Hope, understanding, sympathy—we're not too old to beget these. When thy children come and feel our love, maybe . . ."

Loveday's face lit up. "It may be happening already! Toby brought Jean—the girl he's living with—to my house one evening. I'd never met her. She's lovely—just right for Toby. But he's had this stop in his mind about getting married. He told her about us that night, and for some reason the thought of two old people being in love stirred her. 'It gives one hope,' she said. And Toby agreed. Oh, Oliver, wouldn't it be wonderful if our love turned out to mean something to them?"

"I think that's the crucial test of love—whether it generates new life in others."

THE DAYS THAT FOLLOWED were supremely happy. From breakfast until they kissed good night and retired to their rooms, Oliver and Loveday savored the joy of being together. Every morning he lit a fire in the woodshed stove, so Loveday would be comfortable while she worked on her book. Her interest in it seemed to be returning.

One afternoon a letter came from Heather, addressed to Loveday. It was a touching expression of her approval. "I wanted Father to come and live near me," she wrote, "but he would have been sad, so far from Firbank. After the Hollands left, I worried terribly. Now I know he's in good hands. Bless you, Loveday, for making him happy."

On First Day, when they were driving to Kendal, Oliver confided to Loveday that nothing had been so painful after Daphne's death as going to Meeting alone. "Now," he rejoiced, "I have thee." Still thinking of Daphne as they sat in the deepening silence, he realized how much more reconciled he had become. He could think of her now without aching.

THE next evening John Ludlow called to say that the nominating committee had proposed four members for the committee on clearness. Before asking these Friends to serve, he wanted to know if Oliver and Loveday would be comfortable with them.

"There's Neil and Alice Hill," he said. "And the other two are Austin and Judy Young. I expect this will come as a surprise."

"It's unusual to ask Friends whose marriage is in trouble. But thanks, anyhow, John. I'll speak to Loveday and let thee know."

Loveday found the Quaker process baffling. "I thought these were going to be people who had a satisfactory marriage. I know Austin. I haven't met Judy."

"She's a good woman. She put up cheerfully with him until she became a feminist. Then she left."

"Why should a woman put up with an impossible husband?"

"*Thee* promised to. Has thee changed thy mind?"

Loveday burst out laughing. "I can't. We've written the letter!"

"Austin's good, too," Oliver argued, becoming serious, "only he's not very perceptive. I wish we could help him and Judy."

Loveday put her arms around him. "Maybe when the Youngs are around us, they—" Her last words were cut off by a kiss.

On Saturday they drove over to the Hills' house, on the Kendal River, where they were to meet with the committee on clearness. Oliver thought Loveday seemed withdrawn. Did she look on this meeting as an inquisition? Or as just a joke? Oliver struggled with himself, feeling obliged to face this, yet afraid to ask Loveday whether she had any doubts.

She said nothing as they drew up at the Hills'. The Youngs had already arrived. Earlier that day Peter had dropped Serenity and Ross at Firbank, then driven Judy, who had again come with them from New York, on to Periwinkle Farm.

"I invited her to stay here, if she preferred not going to her own house," Serenity had told Oliver. "But she said she didn't mind. Living there didn't mean she had to act like Austin's wife. Anyway, they're talking, and at the last minute she decided to bring most of her stuff from the city. She says she'll stay home till she decides what she wants to do."

"That's wonderful news!" But Oliver's first impression of Judy when he saw her was that she had aged. Or was it the city veneer—those high heels and the loss of country color in her cheeks? He introduced Loveday, and they exchanged a few words. Austin was standing across the room, looking glum.

Oliver then drew Loveday to the window to show her the view of Little Narragansett Bay, at the mouth of the river. She still seemed apprehensive. "These are our friends," he whispered, pleading with her to understand. "They're not here to pass judgment, only to join in our search for truth, to make us sensitive to problems we may not have faced. Actually we've pretty well covered the ground ourselves, doesn't thee think?"

"I guess so."

How would she respond when Friends asked those probing questions that it was their duty to bring up at this point? Oliver wondered. Would her replies be halfhearted? It had never occurred to him that they would have the slightest difficulty in convincing Friends of their clearness for marriage. But now he was uncertain. "Be still and cool," he murmured, trying to encourage himself. Loveday heard him, and a wonderful change came over her. She smiled and patted his sleeve.

They turned back to the room. Everyone looked at them expectantly. Judy seemed pleased when Oliver took the chair beside her. Neil Hill offered Loveday the armchair. As everyone settled into silence, Oliver couldn't recall ever having quoted those words for Loveday. Yet hearing them, she had become her old self. They had worked like a charm. Puzzled, he gave thanks.

"Seems funny," Neil said, breaking the silence, "to be counseling thee, Oliver, when thee's done that for us all these years. I don't know where to begin, except to say we're here to help you two forestall any possible difficulties."

Oliver glanced at Loveday. She looked relaxed. To his surprise, it was taciturn Austin who began the discussion. "What about property? Firbank and all. Have you made your wills?"

Oliver explained that marriage would change nothing as far as property was concerned. Loveday's would go to her children, and his to Heather, apart from Firbank.

Judy waved this question aside impatiently. "What happens after they die isn't important. It's how they're going to live together that we should be concentrating on."

Austin looked slapped down.

"You've both lived alone so long," Alice Hill said thoughtfully. "Are you prepared to share your innermost feelings?"

"Yes," Judy said. "That's what I want to ask, too. Without communication at a deeper level, a marriage is no good."

"We're communicating," Loveday said, sounding more assured than she had all day. "Maybe not as well as we shall when we're married. I never experienced the Quaker silence before I came to Firbank, but it's made me more sensitive."

Oliver stared at the Hills' rag rug. His conscience hurt. Loveday didn't know the depth of his reserve.

"Men think," Judy muttered bitterly, "that they don't have to show their feelings. Wives are there just to do things for them."

Oliver turned to her gratefully. "Thank thee for the warning."

Alice had another question, this one just for Loveday. "I understand thee's writing a book. Isn't it going to be difficult to pursue thy career and devote thyself to Oliver, too?"

"Oliver's first in my life now," Loveday said. "I've written my editor, explaining that I will be delayed submitting my manuscript." She laughed. "Anyhow, I have to have something to do while Oliver's poring over those seed catalogues."

For a moment there were no more questions. Then Austin suddenly asked, "What'll you do when you have a fight?"

The Hills looked amused. They seemed to consider this improbable. But while supposedly counseling Oliver and Loveday, the Youngs seemed to be talking to each other, airing their grievances. Maybe this had been the nominating committee's wish when it chose them.

"That's a question we've never considered," Oliver told Austin. "I'll tell thee what I hope I'd do: take Loveday in my arms and let her feel I love her. Then I'd ask her to sit down and talk. But every few sentences, I'd find some way of reminding her that I want to make her happy."

Austin was listening to him intently.

"What we do," Neil said, grinning at Alice, "is we go out in the boat and sail up and down the river. It's so beautiful—how can anyone stay mad? I'll be holding the tiller and Alice will be sitting opposite in the cockpit, and suddenly we'll begin to laugh at each other. Then we know it's all over. Well . . . as far as I'm concerned, Oliver and Loveday are clear for marriage."

The other members of the committee agreed.

CHAPTER THIRTEEN

AT THEIR Meeting for business in March, Kendal Friends appointed a Meeting for worship on the twenty-first to solemnize the marriage of Oliver Otis and Loveday Mead. John and Clara Ludlow and Peter and Serenity Holland were named overseers.

For Oliver this was a busy season. He began sowing seeds in the hotbed—lettuce and beets, most of the annuals. He brought his bulb plants into the house, along with branches of fruit trees and flowering shrubs. Inside, he assured Loveday, the buds would be forced and the flowers would proclaim the beauty of spring by the time the guests arrived.

Serenity and Ross came first. "We're going to have a baby!" Ross shouted, before he was even out of the car.

"First-rate!" Oliver shouted back with all his might.

Ross helped him fill the kindling box and remove remnants of hay from the flower beds. Now that his mother was home full time, he was a happy little boy. But Serenity looked peaked. She confided to Loveday that the first weeks of pregnancy were rough. Still, she insisted on giving a hand with the cooking.

Then Heather and Stephen and their children had to be met at the airport. They filled the whole of Firbank's top floor. After meeting Heather's husband, Loveday thought she understood Heather better. He was gracious but reserved. Their children had beautiful manners. They were also brimming with fun, and Heather kept assuring Loveday that this was the happiest of occasions for her.

Nevertheless, Loveday was nervous. How would her children fit in here? What would Heather make of Emily? As for Emily's sophisticated daughters— And Michael's and Jed's manners!

Loveday needn't have worried. Oliver's joy in welcoming his future stepchildren and stepgrandchildren was contagious. Everyone was eager to meet everyone else. Differences were discussed with humor. Heather's and Emily's children took pleasure in mimicking one another's accents.

It was one glorious house party. Loveday wasn't allowed to do a thing. Oliver devoted himself so wholeheartedly to the guests that Loveday feared he was overdoing. Then the Friends Hostel demanded his attention; it had been broken into during the night. But Oliver seemed equal to it all.

It was Loveday who became exhausted. She had to retreat to the ell. Resting on the spread with the irises and daffodils, she reflected happily that her children were discovering Firbank, as she had—the beauty, the tranquillity, the unusual caring. And at the center of it all, the wonderful man who was reaching out to them with a love they'd never known.

On the day of the wedding, when it was almost time to leave for the meetinghouse, Oliver drew Loveday into his study and shut the door. He was wearing the suit he'd bought before he visited her on Beacon Hill.

Taking both her hands, he looked searchingly into her eyes. "Loveday Mead, does thee truly wish to marry me?"

"Yes." Why had she ever hesitated? "With all my heart."

"Will thee allow me to remove thy old wedding ring? In just a little while, I'll put another one in its place." Without waiting for permission, Oliver took off the band Bill had put on Loveday's finger all those years ago. He kissed the finger reverently and backed away to admire her. "Thee looks lovely."

She glanced down at her dress, a soft challis with little white flowers on a delphinium ground. Oliver had fallen in love with it when he spied it through a shopwindow. Now he did something he'd never done before; he reached out and caressed the material where it curved over Loveday's breasts.

She grasped his hands and pressed them to her. "After today," she whispered, "we won't have to be proper anymore." The embrace with which he responded conveyed his passionate impatience.

"Gracious!" Oliver said now, noticing the time. "We must go."

From his desk he took a corsage he'd made for Loveday of Firbank blossoms—apple, forsythia, scilla and downy shadbush. His boyish eagerness as he waited to see how she liked the corsage was as much an evidence of spring, Loveday thought, as the flowers. He, too, was burgeoning with new life.

Can *I* have made him so happy? Loveday asked herself, awed. And she found herself praying, even before the wedding, praying she might be worthy of his trust and the gift she was about to receive.

When they reached the meetinghouse, they lingered in the

vestibule, greeting their guests. Inside, the people who'd already arrived were establishing the hush that would sanctify their union.

A small table stood in one corner. On it lay the wedding certificate, which Oliver and Loveday would sign after they'd made their promises—she with her new name! Oliver took her arm. "Let's go in," he said.

SITTING on the narrow marriage bench, facing the Meeting, Oliver dedicated himself to Loveday, praying that he might possess the insight and selflessness to be a loving and understanding husband. The sun streamed through the south windows, lighting the faces of friends and loved ones, giving the room an air of ethereal joy. On every sill stood a slender vase containing a daisy and a daffodil, set off by the dark red buds of a maple branch, announcing the arrival of spring.

Looking at the sea of faces before him, Oliver was touched by the number of Kendal folk who had never been here before, yet had come to wish him well. And in the front row Heather and her family filled a bench. Oliver let his eyes rest a second on each one, hoping to transmit his thankfulness. Their coming from England was a magnificent wedding gift. But he felt concerned about Heather. She'd been charming all week, assuring him that she was pleased with the outcome of events. And yet Oliver knew that she was finding it painful to accept his love for another woman.

He glanced sideways at Serenity and Peter, whom he thought of as his children, too. Grandchildren, he corrected himself. What they feel like, though, is contemporaries. How troubled they look! Turning, he hunted for Ross, who'd been told in advance that as overseers his parents would be sitting next to Oliver, while he would have to sit with the Youngs. Spying the top of his bright head, between Judy and Austin near the aisle, Oliver thought he seemed content.

But Judy and Austin—Oliver's heart went out to them. Their faces showed the struggle they were going through. What must they be feeling, attending his wedding, recalling their own! Carried away by his happiness, he thought how little it would take for them to recapture the magic that drew them together originally. No, it would take a great deal. They would, with God's help, have to recognize that marriage requires mutual consideration and adjustments.

Loveday's children and grandchildren were sitting across the way. Will and Sara Ann looked very solemn. Michael and Jed were fidgeting, finding the unaccustomed quiet tedious. Emily and her girls gave the impression that they felt a little out of place. But Toby seemed absolutely transported.

Although Oliver had resolved to be a good father to all three of Loveday's children, Toby was the one who particularly appealed to him. When the news had come about the damage to the hostel, it was Toby who offered to go and take care of things.

"Thank thee," Oliver had answered. "But Peter's already gone. When thee comes this summer, the hostel should be in running order."

Toby's face lit up. "Could I come? But—" He looked embarrassed. "I mightn't be by myself. I've been thinking, if Mom can get married, why not— Would that be okay? You and Jean would hit it off great." Then he added quickly, "I'm not sure yet. Don't say anything to Mom."

How happy this news would make her! Oliver thought.

Now it was time for Oliver and Loveday to declare their promises. They stood up and faced each other. Oliver's heart was racing; Loveday appeared serene. Taking her right hand, looking at her with his whole spirit, Oliver said clearly, "In the presence of God and these friends, I take thee, Loveday, to be my wife"—overcome with emotion, he had to stop and catch his breath—"promising with divine assistance to be unto thee . . ."

When he had finished, she gave him her promise, speaking more softly but with assurance.

Oliver took the ring from Peter and placed it on Loveday's finger. The look she gave him then brought tears to his eyes. He thought, If she's ever impatient with me or a bit thoughtless, I'll remember this moment. I'll forget everything but this bond of perfectness. They kissed and sat down. Loveday reached for Oliver's hand.

Planning the wedding, they'd decided that Heather should have the honor of reading the certificate. Michael and Jed were to carry it in on the little table. Oliver nodded to them now, and at his signal they stomped forward with the table and slammed it down.

Oliver and Loveday signed their names. Heather walked up to the table, took the certificate and began to read it to the witnesses, her hands shaking. " 'Whereas,' " she read in a low voice, " 'Oliver Otis of Firbank Farm . . .' "

Oliver wasn't thinking of the words but of Heather herself as she read, " 'And Loveday Austell Mead of Emporia, Kansas, having declared their intentions of marriage with each other . . .' "

Her voice was unsteady, but she persisted bravely. " 'And Oliver Otis, taking Loveday Mead by the hand, did, on this solemn occasion, declare that he took her to be his wife. . . .' "

To publicly proclaim an event she regretted, even while rejoicing with her father—what devotion to him this bespoke! When she had finished, Heather put the certificate down and returned to her place in the front row. The boys removed the table, and the Meeting settled into silence again.

Suddenly a throaty explosion warned Oliver that someone who was terrified by the prospect was about to speak. Glancing around, Oliver couldn't believe his eyes. It was Austin! But Austin never spoke in Meeting. Now that he was on his feet, he didn't seem to know what he wanted to say. He looked around helplessly. Then he blurted out, "Live and learn," and hastily sat down.

Before Oliver had a chance to figure out what this meant, titters drew his attention to the other side of the room. Over by the window Michael and Jed were nudging each other and shaking with giggles. Then Oliver saw why: while Austin was on his feet, Ross had quietly slid out behind him and escaped into the aisle. He was heading straight for Oliver, and he climbed up on the narrow bench beside him. Squeezing in, he grinned happily.

Not in the least ruffled, Oliver moved closer to Loveday and, putting his arm around Ross, returned to his meditation. But now it was clouded by anxiety. The child's unexpected move reminded him of what Peter had said to him early this morning. Oliver had taken him into the study, opened a little box and handed him the wedding ring.

"Will thee take care of this and give it to me at the appointed time? Otherwise I'll forget which pocket it's in and Loveday will be standing there waiting, while I turn out my loose change onto the meetinghouse floor."

Peter had laughed and tucked the ring in his pocket.

Then Oliver thanked him for taking care of the damage at the hostel. "We've been careless," he said. "Property like that ought not to be left uninhabited. If we could just find the right people to live there—"

"What about the Hollands?" Peter asked, smiling diffidently.

"Why, Peter! Thee can't be giving up thy job."

"I didn't want to bother thee now, when thee's so busy and it's such a happy time. But last week the firm I work for was offered a multimillion-dollar contract to use its satellites for spying. I don't think I can live with that, Oliver. And Rennie feels the same way." Now Peter looked downright frightened. "Thing is, she's pregnant."

"I know."

"Is it irresponsible to throw up the job now?"

Oliver said nothing. Peter must decide himself.

"If we just had a place to stay while I'm hunting for something else, it wouldn't be so risky. With the baby coming— We were feeling so good about that. Now it's scary."

"Loveday and I would welcome you back anytime. Thee and Serenity know that. But it would be a real help to the Meeting if you were to take care of the hostel."

"And to us. From the first, we were excited about the project. We'd be happier living in the country. But the main thing is, our children would know that we were willing to sacrifice our security in order to uphold what we believe."

Now, remembering Peter's dilemma, in the silence of the Meeting, it struck Oliver that nothing would bring the Hollands so much clarity as the child sitting beside him. He stood up and with a reassuring smile lifted Ross onto the neighboring bench, where he was joyfully received. A noticeable change had come over Peter and was reflected in Serenity's lovely face. Could they have made their decision to leave New York in the past few minutes? They seemed at peace.

Greatly relieved, Oliver sat down again, and as Loveday gave him an approving smile, Serenity rose to speak.

"Listening to Oliver and Loveday make their promises," she began slowly, facing the people before her but holding Ross's hand, "I couldn't help thinking about when Peter and I were on that narrow bench, saying the same thing. I didn't come from a religious home, as Peter did," she confided, "so when we first talked about being married in Meeting, I had trouble with the words 'in the presence of God.' How could I say that, when I didn't know what God is? Peter argued that I was taking him on faith, so why not God?" She paused and took a deep breath. "I was scared, too, of that awful phrase, 'as long as we both shall live.' So many couples were breaking up. Peter told me one had to promise that on faith, too.

"My parents wanted me to have a big snazzy wedding," she continued, laughing nervously. "I wanted to be married here. I'd just discovered Firbank and Oliver and"—she lowered her voice—"Daphne. This is where the great-grandmother I was named for got married. So my parents finally gave in. I crowed to Peter, 'And they lived happily ever after!' I thought we'd never again have to face anything as bad as that struggle with my parents. Little did I know!"

A wave of sympathetic amusement rippled over the room.

"I was just a kid," Serenity went on. "I didn't know the first thing about life. I couldn't understand why Oliver told me that while we'd won the freedom to make our own decisions, it would depend on what we did with that freedom. I remember his saying, 'Firbank will help. The pond and the dunes and the ocean will counsel you.' Well, they did. But mostly it was Oliver."

She turned toward him and he felt her affection reaching out.

"Thanks to Oliver," Serenity was saying now, "Peter and I are making decisions as a family, and I know we couldn't do it without divine assistance. Because doing what you feel is right sometimes means taking big risks. You don't know how it'll work out. You may not even be able to feed your children. Taking risks is leaving the outcome to God."

Looking as if she might break down any minute, Serenity said, "I think it's even more wonderful for old people—who know how rough life can be—to make this commitment. Oliver often quotes a verse about the Indian summer of the heart. He says it makes him think of my great-grandmother Serenity. I didn't know her. It makes me think of Oliver and Loveday." She turned to them with a radiant smile, although there were tears in her eyes. Then she sat down.

Barely able to contain his joy, Oliver said to himself, My whole life has been a continuum of love.

He had been just a little boy like Ross when his mother died and his grandmother took him into her love. She made Firbank home for him. When the time came, she passed him on to Daphne. Now Daphne was passing him on to Loveday.

We may not have many years, he conceded to himself, as he and Loveday walked jubilantly out of the meetinghouse together, while the guests lingered in the silence a few minutes longer. But love isn't measured by time. It may be the only thing in the universe that lives forever.

An Afternoon with Daisy Newman

She greeted me with a smile at the door of her white clapboard house in Lincoln, Massachusetts. I stepped into an atmosphere of warmth and beauty evocative of Firbank Farm: arrangements of spring flowers, lustrous wood surfaces, and colorful fabrics on chairs and windows. Above the fireplace were two originals of the illustrations that appeared in the Condensed Books edition of *I Take Thee, Serenity*, her previous

novel, which was also set in the fictional Quaker community of Kendal.

A table was set for tea. As we sat down to it, Mrs. Newman talked about her life today. Like Oliver Otis in *Indian Summer of the Heart*, she is seventy-nine years old, with an energy that belies her age. Once a week, she said, a group of Quaker writers meets at her house to discuss their work. On Sundays she goes to meeting in Cambridge, usually with friends, but driving by herself if no one else is going.

After tea, Mrs. Newman took me to her book-lined study. A straight-backed wooden chair was drawn up to a small table and a 1943 electric typewriter. On the walls was a gallery of photographs: her late husband, two children, several grandchildren, and many old friends, including a courtly Quaker who inspired the character of Oliver Otis. She turned to the subject of her books: "What challenges me today is the despair young people everywhere are voicing at the fear of nuclear annihilation. It's taking away all hope. They aren't having as many children, they aren't working as hard in school. But if the world isn't blown up, what kind of life will they be prepared for? Religion can give them hope and real values to live by. I also think the different generations have much to offer each other. And so do men and women, though some tend to forget that these days. In my writing I try to interpret them all to each other."

Clearly, she and Oliver have that in common, too.

—M.D.T.

Illustrated by Frank Morris

A winning day at Ascot:
cheers, toasts . . . and terrible revenge

Banker

A CONDENSATION OF THE NOVEL BY
Dick Francis

"It's a beautiful day for racing," young banker Tim Ekaterin remarks at the Royal Ascot meeting. Seated in a flower-filled box, enjoying strawberries, champagne and the company of elegant guests, Tim finds the afternoon a delight. Especially when a spectacular colt named Sandcastle makes Tim and his friends all winners.

But the end of the splendid day holds a grim surprise: one of the guests is assaulted by a young man with a knife, and only Tim's quick thinking averts tragedy.

What had happened? Who was the assailant? Not until months later, when a horse breeder applies to Tim's bank for a multimillion-dollar loan to buy the wondrous Sandcastle, does Tim begin to find the answers. As his routine credit investigations lead him deep into the racetrack world, he discovers that fraud and murder can be as much a part of racing as swift horses, lucky bets and glittering boxes at Ascot.

The First Year
May

GORDON Michaels stood in the fountain with all his clothes on.

"Good Lord," Alec said. "What is he doing?"

"Who?"

"Your boss. Standing in the fountain."

I crossed to the window and stared down two floors to the ornamental fountain in the forecourt of the Paul Ekaterin merchant bank. Down to where three entwining plumes of water rose gracefully into the air and fell in a glittering circular curtain. To where, in the bowl, calf-deep, stood Gordon in his navy pinstriped suit . . . in his white shirt and sober silk tie . . . in his charcoal socks and black shoes . . . in his gold cuff links and onyx ring . . . in his polished City persona . . . soaking wet.

I whisked straight out of the deep-carpeted office, through the fire doors, down the flights of gritty stone staircase and across the marbled expanse of entrance hall. The uniformed man at the security desk was staring toward the wide glass front doors with his fillings showing, and two arriving visitors were looking stunned. I rushed past them into the open air.

"Gordon!" I said.

His eyes were open. Beads of water ran down his forehead from his dripping hair and caught here and there on his lashes. He looked at me unblinkingly with earnest vagueness, as if he were not at all sure who I was.

"Get into the fountain," he said.

"Er . . . why, exactly?"

"They don't like water."

"Who don't?"

"All those people. Those people with white faces. They don't like water. You'll be all right if you're wet."

His voice sounded rational enough for me to wonder wildly whether this were not after all a joke. "Come out of there, Gordon," I said uneasily.

"No, no. They're waiting for me. Send for the police. Tell them to come and take them all away."

"But *who*, Gordon?"

"All those people, of course. Those people with white faces." His head slowly turned from side to side, his eyes focused as if at a throng closely surrounding the whole fountain. Instinctively I, too, looked from side to side, but all I could see were the stone walls of Ekaterin's, with heads appearing disbelievingly at the windows, and I saw Henry Shipton, the chairman of the bank, striding briskly across the forecourt toward us.

"Now, Gordon, my dear chap," the chairman said, coming to a purposeful halt at my side. "What's all this about?"

"He's having hallucinations," I said.

The chairman's gaze flicked to my face and back to Gordon, and Gordon seriously advised him to get into the fountain, because the people with white faces couldn't reach him there.

"Do something, Tim," the chairman said, so I stepped into the fountain and took Gordon's arm.

"Come on," I said. "If we're wet, they won't touch us. We don't have to stay in the water."

"Oh. All right. If you're sure."

"Yes, I'm sure."

He nodded and, with only slight pressure from my arm, stepped over the knee-high coping onto the paving stones of the forecourt. I held on to him firmly and hoped to heaven that the people with white faces would keep their distance.

The chairman's concern was deep and genuine, as he and Gordon were firm and longtime friends. They were both in their fifties, at the top of their powers and comfortably rich.

"I think," the chairman said, casting a glance at the inhabited windows, "that we should go indoors. To the boardroom."

He took Gordon Michaels by his other sodden sleeve, and

between us one of the steadiest banking brains in London walked obediently across the entrance hall to the elevator.

On our floor the chairman's personal assistant came hurrying along the corridor, and the chairman told him not to let anyone disturb us; and Gordon and I in our wet shoes sloshed across the green carpet to the boardroom. Gordon consented to sit in one of the leather armchairs, while I removed his jacket and shirt. The chairman asked if the people with white faces were still there.

"Of course," Gordon said, looking around. "They're sitting in all the chairs round the table. And standing behind them."

"What are they wearing?" the chairman asked.

"White suits, of course. With black buttons. Down the front, three big black buttons."

"Clowns!" I exclaimed. "White-faced clowns."

"Oh no," Gordon said. "They're not clowns. They're not funny."

"I think we should take him home," said the chairman. "He's clearly not violent, and I see no benefit in calling in a doctor here. I'll ring Judith and warn her, poor girl. I'll drive him in my car, and I'd appreciate it, Tim, if you'd come along."

"Certainly." I went off to find a blanket, and the chairman's assistant produced a red one with FIRE written across one corner. With this wrapped snugly around his shoulders, Gordon allowed himself to be conveyed to the car, where the chairman slid behind the wheel and drove his two damp passengers southward through the fair May morning.

Henry Shipton, chairman of Paul Ekaterin Ltd., was a big-framed man whose natural bulk was kept short of obesity by raw carrots, mineral water and willpower. I admired him. One had to. During his twenty-year stint Paul Ekaterin Ltd. had grown so successful, it was accepted worldwide with respect. I could easily measure the spread of public recognition of the bank's name, since it was mine also: Timothy Ekaterin, great-grandson of Paul, the founder. People always expected me to have the fortune to match, which I hadn't.

Gordon lived, it transpired, in leafy splendor on Clapham Common, in a late Victorian house surrounded by head-high garden walls. There were cream-painted wooden gates, and a short gravel driveway between tidy lawns.

Judith Michaels erupted from her front door as the car rolled up, and the first thing she said, aiming it between Henry Shipton and me, was, "I'll throttle that bloody doctor." Then, "Come along, love, we'll get you tucked into bed in no time."

She put sheltering arms around the red blanket as her husband stumbled out of the car, and said to the chairman and me, "Now you lambs go into the kitchen—there's some coffee in the pot—and I'll be down in a sec. Come on, Gordon, my dear love." She helped him inside and up a paneled staircase.

Judith Michaels, somewhere in her later thirties, considerably younger than her husband, was a brown-haired woman in whom the life-force flowed strongly and with whom I could easily have fallen in love. I'd met her several times before and had been conscious each time of the warmth and glamour that were as normal to her as breathing. Whether I in return held the slightest attraction for her I didn't know and hadn't tried to find out, as entangling oneself with one's boss's wife was hardly best for one's prospects. With these thoughts, I hoped, decently hidden, I went with Henry Shipton into the friendly kitchen and drank coffee.

"A great girl, Judith," the chairman said with feeling, and I looked at him in rueful surprise and agreed.

She came to join us after a while, seeming more annoyed than worried. "Gordon says there are people with white faces sitting all round the room. It's infuriating. I'm so angry I could *spit*."

The chairman and I looked bewildered.

"Oh. I suppose I'll have to tell you," she said, observing us. She took a deep breath. "Gordon hates anyone to know, but he's got mild Parkinson's disease. Not bad enough for him to have to stop working, but his left hand shakes a bit now and then. I don't expect you've noticed. He tries not to let people see."

We blankly shook our heads.

"Our regular doctor's just retired, and this new man has taken Gordon off the old pills, which were fine as far as I could see, and put him on some new ones. As of the day before yesterday. So when I rang him now in an absolute *panic* he said not to worry, this new drug quite often causes hallucinations—it's just a matter of getting the dosage right. I tell you, I could kill him!"

Both Henry Shipton and I, however, were feeling markedly relieved. "You mean," the chairman asked, "that this will all just wear off?"

She nodded. "That bloody doctor said Gordon should stop taking the pills and he would be perfectly normal in thirty-six hours. I *ask* you! And after that, he's got to start taking them again, but only half the amount, and see what happens." She suddenly sobbed, twice, and wiped crossly at her eyes.

After a sympathetic pause the chairman said, "Did the doctor say how long it would take to get the dosage right?"

She looked at him with a defeated grimace. "He said it might take as much as six weeks to get Gordon thoroughly stabilized. He said each patient was different, but that if we would persevere, it would be the best drug for Gordon in the long run."

HENRY Shipton drove me pensively back to the City, as Londoners refer to the financial district. "I think," he said, "that we'll say in the office that Gordon felt flu coming on and took some pills which proved hallucinatory. No need to mention Parkinson's disease, if he doesn't wish it."

"I'll say nothing," I assured him.

The chairman grunted and lapsed into silence. It wasn't until we were a mile from the bank that he spoke again. "You've been in Gordon's confidence for two years now, haven't you?"

"Nearly three," I murmured, nodding.

"Can you hold the fort until he returns?"

It would be dishonest to say that the possibility of this offer hadn't been in my mind since approximately ten fifteen that morning, so I accepted it less with excitement than relief.

There was no rigid hierarchy in Ekaterin's. To be "in so-and-so's confidence" meant one would normally be on course for more responsibility, but unlike the other thirty-two-year-olds in the firm, I lived under the severe disadvantage of my name. The board of directors, afraid of accusations of nepotism, made me double-earn every step.

"Thank you," I said neutrally.

He smiled a shade. "Consult, whenever you need help."

I nodded. His words weren't meant as disparagement. Communication between people and between departments was an absolute priority in Henry Shipton's book; it was he who had swept away a host of small offices to form opened-up expanses. He himself sat always at a fairly opulent desk in a room that contained eight similar, all within easy earshot of each other.

As Ekaterin's was a merchant bank, one never actually saw any money. There were no tellers, no clerks, no counters, no deposits, no withdrawals and hardly any checkbooks.

There were three main departments, each on its own floor of the building. Corporate Finance acted for major clients on mergers, takeovers and the raising of capital. Banking, which was my area, loaned money to enterprise and industry. And Investment Management, the oldest and largest department, aimed at producing the best possible returns from the vast investment funds of charities, companies, trusts and trade unions.

The lives of all the three hundred and fifty people who worked for Ekaterin's were devoted to making money work, to the manufacture of business and jobs. It wasn't a bad thing to be convinced of the worth of what one did, and there was a tough basic harmony in the place.

When the chairman and I returned to the hive he was pounced upon immediately by a worried figure from Corporate Finance. Upstairs, in Banking, Alec was giggling into his blotter.

Alec, my own age, suffered, professionally speaking, from an uncontrollable bent for frivolity. It brightened up the office no end, but as court jesters seldom made it to the throne, his career path was observably sideways and erratic.

He had scattered freckles on cream-pale skin; a high forehead, a mat of tight tow-colored curls, and alert blue eyes that looked out from behind gold-framed spectacles. He was liked on sight by almost everybody, and it was only gradually that one came to wonder whether the examiner who had awarded him a first in law at Oxford had been suffering from critical blindness.

"What's up?" I said, instinctively smiling to match the giggles.

"We've been leaked." Alec tapped the paper that lay on his desk. "This came out an hour ago," he said with mischievous pleasure. He lifted up the paper, and all was explained.

There had recently appeared a slim publication called *What's Going On Where It Shouldn't*, a descendant of the flood of investigative journalism spawned by Watergate. The publication had fast caught the country's attention and was reportedly read avidly by the police.

"What does it say?" I asked; as who wouldn't?

"It says that someone at Ekaterin's has been selling inside information about a takeover."

"Let's see," I said, and took the paper from his hand.

The piece, headed merely "Tut-tut," started by explaining that in merchant banks it was possible for a manager of investment funds to learn at an early stage about a takeover being organized by his colleagues. The shares of a company about to be taken over were likely to rise in value. If one could buy them at a low price before even a rumor of takeover started, the gain could be huge, so it was strictly illegal for an investment manager to act on this private knowledge. The article asked:

> However, what's going on in the merchant bank of Paul Ekaterin Ltd.? Three times in the past year, takeovers managed by this prestigious firm have been scooped by vigorous buying beforehand of the shares concerned. We are informed that someone within Ekaterin's has been selling the golden news, either for straight cash or a slice of the action.

"It's a guess," I said flatly. "There are absolutely no facts."

"A bucket of cold water," Alec complained, "is a sunny day compared with you."

"Do you *want* it to be true?" I asked curiously.

"Livens the place up a bit."

There, I thought, was the difference between Alec and me. For me the place was alive all the time, even though when I'd first gone there eight years earlier it had been unwillingly. My mother had been bankrupt then, her flat stripped by the bailiffs of everything except a telephone and a bed, and her bankruptcy had allowed my uncle to apply his blackmailing pressure.

"I'll clear her debts and arrange an allowance for her if you come and work in the bank," Uncle Freddie told me.

"But I don't want to."

"Give it three months. If you hate it after that, I'll let you go."

So I'd gone with mulish rebellion to tread the path of my great-grandfather, my grandfather and my uncle, and within three months you'd have had to prize me loose with a crowbar. All the teenage scorn I'd felt for "moneygrubbing," all the negative attitudes bequeathed by my failure of a father, all had melted into comprehension, interest and finally delight. I was now as addicted to the art of money management as any junkie.

"Who do you think did it?" Alec said.

"If anyone did. The article doesn't even say which takeovers they mean, let alone give figures."

True or not, though, the story in *What's Going On* was bad for the bank. Clients would back away fast if they couldn't trust us. Henry Shipton called an emergency meeting in the boardroom, and ripples of unease spread outward from there. By going-home time practically everyone in the building had read the bombshell.

The article had one good effect: it almost totally deflected speculation from Gordon Michaels; I had to explain to only two people about his "flu" and pills. When the very reputation of the bank was being rocked, who cared about a director taking a dip in the fountain?

ON THE following day I found that filling Gordon's job was no lighthearted matter. Until then he had gradually given me power of decision over loans up to certain amounts, but anything larger was in his own domain entirely. For him a ceiling hardly existed, except that with loans involving millions of pounds it was normal to consult with others on the board.

These consultations tended to stretch over lunch, which the directors mostly ate together in a private dining room. It was Gordon's habit to look at his watch at five to one and take himself amiably off in the direction of tomato juice and roast lamb. He would return an hour later with his mind clarified and made up. I'd been lent Gordon's job but not his seat on the board, so I was without the benefit of the lunches.

Once Gordon had said to me that in this job one's nerve either toughened or broke, and I understood what he meant when I faced a task that lay on his desk: a request for financial backing for a series of animated cartoon films.

It would be too easy to turn it down . . . and perhaps miss Peanuts or Mickey Mouse. I picked·up the telephone and invited the hopeful cartoonist to bring his proposals to the bank.

June

GORDON telephoned three weeks later, sounding thoroughly fit and well. I glanced across to where his desk stood neat and tidy; all the paper action was now on my own. "Judith and I wanted to thank you . . ." he was saying.

"Really no need," I said. "How are you?"

"Wasting time. It's ridiculous. Anyway . . . we've been offered a half share in a box at Ascot next Thursday. Would you like to come?"

"I'd love it," I said. "But—"

"No buts," he interrupted. "If you'd like to, Henry will fix it. He's coming himself. He agreed you'd earned a day off."

"I'd like to, very much."

"If you haven't a morning coat, don't worry. We're not in the royal enclosure."

"If you're wearing one . . . I inherited my father's."

"Ah. Good. Yes, then. One o'clock Thursday, for lunch. Very pleased you can come." He disconnected with a click.

I wondered how much he remembered about the white faces. Maybe at the races he would tell me. Maybe not.

Going to the races wasn't something I did very often nowadays, although as a child I'd spent countless afternoons waiting around the lines while my mother, in pleasurable agony, backed her dozens of hunches and bankers and third strings and lost money by the ton.

"I've won!" she would announce radiantly to all about her, waving a winning ticket, and the bunch of losses on the same race would be thrown away.

My father at the same time would be standing drinks in the bar, an openhanded lush with more good nature than sense. They would take me home at the end of the day, giggling happily together in a hired chauffeur-driven Rolls, and I never questioned but that this contented affluence was built on rock.

I had been their only child and they'd given me a very good childhood, to the extent that there were holidays on yachts on warm seas and Christmases in the Alps. The villain of those days was my uncle, who descended on us occasionally to utter dire warnings about the need for his brother (my father) to find a job.

My father, however, couldn't shape up to moneygrubbing. He never tired of his life of aimless ease, and if he earned no one's respect, few detested him either. A weak, friendly, unintelligent man. Not bad as a father. Not good at much else.

He dropped dead of a heart attack when I was nineteen, and it was then that the point of the dire warnings became apparent. We had lived on the capital inherited from Grandfather, and there wasn't a great deal left. Enough to see me through college, enough to bring Mother a small income for life, but not enough to finance her manner of betting.

In twenty-five years, it seemed, my mother had gambled away the best part of half a million pounds; all gone on horses, fast and slow. It might well have turned me against racing, but I remembered how much she and Father had enjoyed themselves. Who was to say that it was a fortune ill spent?

After talking to Gordon, I shuffled together a bunch of papers and went upstairs to see Val Fisher, head of Banking. A short man, very smooth and charming, with nerves like ice.

"Can I consult?" I said. "It's a cartoonist."

Val waved hospitably. "Pull up a chair." I sat down and spread out some of the papers, explaining about the wholly levelheaded artist I had spent three hours with two weeks earlier.

"He's been turned down by his own bank and by three other firms like ourselves," I said. "He's got no realizable assets, no security. If we financed him, it would be out of faith."

"Background?" he asked.

"Pretty solid. Son of a sales manager. Respected at art school as an original talent—I talked to the principal. For the past two years he's worked for a studio making animated commercials. They say he's good at the job, and they don't want to lose him."

"How old?"

"Twenty-four."

Val gave me an "oh-ho-ho" look and said, "What's he asking?"

"A studio. Funds to employ ten copying artists, with the expectation that it will be a year before any films are completed and can expect to make money. These sheets set out the figures."

Val made a face over the pages. "Why haven't you already turned him down?" he asked finally.

"Um," I said. "Look at his drawings." I spread out the rest of the papers—a riotously colored progression of pages that established two characters and told a funny story. I watched Val's sophisticated world-weary face as he inspected them; saw the awakening interest, heard the laugh.

"Exactly," I said.

"Hmph." He leaned back in his chair. "I don't know. It's too much like aiming at the moon with a bow and arrow."

"They might watch those films one day on space shuttles," I said mildly, and he gave me a fast amused glance.

"Leave the drawings here, will you?" he said. "I'll have a word with Henry at lunch." I guessed in a swift, uncomfortable moment of insight that what they would discuss would be not the cartoonist but the reliability of my judgment.

At four thirty my interoffice telephone rang. "Come up and collect your papers," said Val. "Henry says this decision is to be yours alone. So sink or swim, it's up to you."

ONE'S first exposure to the Royal Ascot meeting was either a matter of surprised delight or of puritanical disapproval. Either the spirits lifted to the sight of emerald grass, massed flowers and elegantly dressed men and women, or one despised the frivolity, the shame of champagne and strawberries while some in the world starved.

I belonged, without doubt, to the hedonists, both by upbringing and inclination. So it was with pleasure that I walked through the gates in my father's resurrected finery and made my way through the smiling throng to the high-up box.

"Welcome to the charade," Gordon said cheerfully, handing me a bubbling glass; and "Isn't this *fun!*" Judith exclaimed, humming with excitement in yellow silk.

"It's great," I said, and Gordon, looking sunburned and healthy, introduced me to the owner of the box. "Dissdale, this is Tim Ekaterin. Works in the bank. Tim—Dissdale Smith."

We shook hands. His was plump and warm, like his face. "Delighted," he said. "Met my wife? Bettina, darling, say hello to Tim." He put an arm around the thin waist of a girl less than half his age, whose clinging white, black-dotted dress was cut low. There was also a wide black hat and a practiced smile.

"Hello," she said. "So glad you could come."

The box was mostly filled by a dining table laid with twelve places for lunch, and masses of pink flowers lent an air of opulence. The end wall was of windows and a glass door, with steps going down to a viewing balcony.

Henry Shipton and his wife were standing at the door to the balcony. Henry lifted his glass to me in a gesture of acknowledgment; Lorna, as ever, looked as if faults were being found.

Lorna Shipton was a tall, overassured woman from whom disdain flowed outward like a tide. It was, I supposed, inevitable that I was placed next to her at lunch.

More guests arrived, Dissdale and Bettina greeting them with whoops and kisses. Dissdale decided there would be less crush if everyone sat down, and so took his place at the head of the table, with Gordon, his back to the windows, at the foot.

Laughter, chatter, the study of race cards, the refilling of glasses; Judith with yellow silk roses on her hat, and Lorna telling me that my morning coat looked a size too small.

"It's a beautiful day for racing," I said.

"You should be working. Your uncle Freddie won't like it. I'm certain that when he bailed you out he made it a condition that you and your mother should stay away from racecourses."

Uncle Freddie, former vice-chairman, now retired, still owned enough of the bank to make his unseen presence felt. Henry, however, his ear attuned across the table, said pleasantly, "Freddie knows Tim is here, my dear. Gordon and I obtained dispensation, so to speak." He gave me a glimmer of a smile.

"Oh," his wife said. I saw Judith trying not to laugh.

Dissdale's last guest arrived at that point, as if with a flourish of trumpets, a man making an entrance. Dissdale leaped to his feet and pumped him warmly by the hand.

"This is Calder Jackson, everybody," Dissdale said down the table. "You know, the miracle worker. Brings dying horses back to life. You must have seen him on television."

"Ah yes," Gordon responded. "Of course." But he raised his eyebrows in a question to me, and I fractionally shook my head.

Calder Jackson was a man with a head of hair that was designed to be noticed. He had a lot of dark curls going attractively gray, and a beard growing in a narrow fringe from his ears around the line of his jaw. From in front his face was circled with curls; from the side he looked as if he were wearing a helmet.

The girl sitting on my right was ecstatic. "How *divine* to meet you. One has heard so *much*. Do tell us your secret."

Calder Jackson eyed her blandly. "There's no secret, my dear. None at all. Just good food, good care and a few age-old herbal remedies. And, of course . . . the laying on of hands."

"But *how*?" asked the girl. "How do you do that to horses?"

"I just . . . touch them." He smiled disarmingly. "And then sometimes I feel them quiver, and I know the healing force is going from me into them."

"Can you do it infallibly?" Henry asked politely, and I noted that he'd let no implication of doubt sound in his voice: Henry, whose gullibility could be measured in micrograms if at all.

Calder Jackson slowly shook his head. "If I have the horse long enough, it usually happens. But sadly, not always."

"How fascinating," Judith said, and earned another of those kind, bland smiles. Charlatan or not, I thought, Calder Jackson had the mix just right: an arresting appearance, a modest demeanor, no promise of success.

"Can you heal people too?" I asked.

He turned my way with civility. "Whatever gift I have is especially for horses. I have no feeling that I can heal humans."

I nodded and saw Dissdale basking in the success of having hooked his celebrity. He told us that two of Calder's ex-patients were running that afternoon. "Isn't that right, Calder?"

The curly head nodded. "Cretonne, in the first race, used to break blood vessels, and Molyneaux, in the fifth, came to me with infected wounds. I feel they are my friends now."

"Are they going to win, Calder?" Dissdale asked roguishly.

The healer smiled forgivingly. "If they're fast enough."

Everyone laughed. Dissdale stood and was refilling glasses when the door from the corridor tentatively opened.

Any hopes I might have had that Gordon would supply a Bettina type for my benefit were immediately dashed. The lady who appeared and whom Judith greeted with a kiss on the cheek was nearer forty than twenty-five and more angular than lissome. She wore a pink linen suit and a beige straw hat.

Judith introduced the newcomer: Penelope Warner—Pen—a good friend of hers and Gordon's. Pen Warner sat down and made small talk with Henry and Lorna. I half listened and took in a few details, such as no rings on the fingers, no polish on the nails, no artifice in the voice. Worthy, I thought. Well intentioned, slightly boring. Probably runs the church.

A waitress appeared with lunch, during which Calder Jackson could be heard extolling the virtues of watercress for its iron content and garlic for the treatment of fever. "Of course, in humans," he was saying, "garlic is a lifesaver in whooping cough. You make poultices and bind them on the bottoms of the feet of a child at night, and in the morning you'll smell the garlic on the child's breath and the cough will abate."

I saw Pen Warner lift her head to listen, and thought I'd been wrong about her. I had missed the worldliness of the eyes, the long, sad knowledge of human frailty. A magistrate, perhaps?

Judith leaned across the table and said teasingly, "Tim, can't you forget you're a banker, even at the races?"

"What?" I said.

"You look at everyone as if you're working out just how much you can lend them without risk."

"I'd lend you my soul," I said.

"For me to pay back with interest?"

"To pay in love and kisses."

Harmless stuff, as frivolous as her hat. Henry, sitting next to her, said in the same vein, "You're second in the line, Tim. I've a first option, eh, Judith?"

She pulled his hand affectionately and glowed a little, and Calder Jackson's voice came through with, "The herb comfrey mends fractures in half the normal time. It is miraculous."

There was a good deal of speculation all around the table about a three-year-old colt called Sandcastle that had won the Two Thousand Guineas six weeks earlier and was hot favorite for the King Edward VII stakes, due to be run that afternoon. Dissdale had seen Sandcastle at Newmarket and was enthusiastic. "He positively eats up the ground."

"He was good as a two-year-old," Henry said, nodding.

"Glory, yes," Dissdale said fervently, and then spread his arms wide and laughed. "He's my banker. Okay, we've got a roomful of bankers. But Sandcastle is where I'm putting my money today. He simply can't be beaten."

By the coffee-brandy-cigar stage, people were dashing out to back their hopes in the first race. I wandered out onto the balcony to watch the queen's procession trotting like a fairy tale up the green course. "Isn't it *splendid*," said Judith's voice at my shoulder, and I glanced into the smiling eyes. "Gordon's gone to bet, so I thought I'd take the opportunity . . . We're really grateful to you for what you did that dreadful day."

I shook my head. "I did nothing, believe me."

"Well, that's half the point. You *said* nothing. In the bank, I mean. Henry says there hasn't been a whisper."

"Do you want to go down and see the horses?" I asked.

"Yes. It's lovely up here, but too far from life."

We went down to the paddock and watched the horses walk around the ring. Judith smelled nice. Stop it, I told myself.

"There's Cretonne," I said, pointing, "the horse Calder Jackson said he cured. The jockey in bright pink."

"Are you going to back it?" she asked.

"If you like."

She nodded, and we queued up to make the wager. All around us the Ascot crowd swirled, a feast to the eye in the sunshine.

"What are you thinking?" Judith said. "So solemnly."

"That on a day like this, one could fall in love."

"Yes, one could." She was reading her race card overintently. "But should one?"

After a pause I said, "No, I don't think so."

"Nor do I." She looked up with a serious smile. "I've known you six years."

"I haven't been faithful," I said.

She laughed and the moment passed, but the declaration had quite plainly been made and in a way accepted.

The horses cantered to the start, and I said, by way of conversation, "Who is Dissdale Smith?"

"He's in the motor trade. He loves to make a splash, but I don't think he's doing as well as he pretends."

From where we stood we couldn't see much of the race, only a head-on view of the horses as they came up to the winning post. When the leader proved to carry bright pink, Judith caught hold of my arm. "Tim, that's Cretonne. We've won!"

"Bully for Calder Jackson."

"You don't trust him," she said. "I could see it in all your faces, yours and Henry's and Gordon's. You all have the same way of peering into people's souls."

I smiled. "That sounds disgusting."

"I've been married to Gordon for nine years."

There was again a sudden moment of stillness. Then she shook her head slightly, and I thought that with a woman so straightforwardly intelligent I could have been content forever.

Escorting one's host's wife to the paddock was an expected civility, so it was with a benign eye that Gordon greeted our return. Looking at his unsuspecting friendliness, I was both glad and sorry that he had nothing to worry about.

The whole party crowded the box's balcony for the big race. Dissdale said he had staked his all on his banker, Sandcastle; and although he said it with a laugh, I saw the tremor in his hands. He's in too deep, I thought.

The rest of us, fired by Dissdale's confidence, happily clutched tickets doubling Sandcastle every which way. I found myself standing next to Calder Jackson.

"Do you gamble?" I asked, for something to say.

"Only on certainties."

I glanced across at Dissdale, who was faintly sweating. "And is Sandcastle a certainty?"

He shook his head. "No racing bet's a certainty. The horse might feel ill. Might be kicked at the start." He stopped with apparent finality, but as the crowd watched Sandcastle canter to the post, he said almost with awe, "That's a superb horse."

My place at the great man's side was taken by Bettina, who said, "Dear Calder, come to the front, where you can see better." She gave me a photogenic little smile and pulled her captive after her.

In a buzz that rose to a roar the runners covered their mile-and-a-half journey. In scarlet and white, Sandcastle was making no show at all, to universal groans, and lay only fifth as the field swept around the last bend. Bang goes the banker that can't lose.

Dissdale, unable to watch, collapsed weakly onto a chair.

"Sandcastle making his move . . ." the commentator's voice warbled over the loudspeakers. The scarlet-and-white colors had moved to the outside. The big, rangy colt was eating up his ground. Sandcastle still had three horses ahead. He was flying, though, and I found the sight of his fluid valor immensely exciting. I hauled Dissdale to his feet.

"Look," I shouted in his ear. "Watch. Your banker's going to win. He's a marvel. He's a dream."

Dissdale turned with a gaping mouth to stare in the direction of the winning post and saw Sandcastle going like a javelin, free now of the others, aiming straight for the prize.

"He's won," Dissdale's mouth said slackly. I helped him up into the box. His skin was gray and damp and he was stumbling.

"Sit down," I said, pulling out the nearest chair. He fell into it and stretched out a trembling hand to the champagne.

"Oh Lord," he said. "I'll never do that again."

"Do what?"

He gave me a flickering glance and said, "All on one throw."

All. "He's my banker," he'd said before. He surely couldn't, I thought, have meant *all* his money; yet not much else could have produced such physical symptoms.

Everyone piled back into the box with ballooning jollity. We had all backed Sandcastle, thanks to Dissdale.

In a while Henry offered to take Judith to the paddock. To my relief Gordon invited Lorna, which left me with the mystery lady, Pen Warner. "Would you like to go down?" I asked.

"Yes, indeed." She said little more until we had negotiated the elevators and escalators and emerged into the paddock. We stood watching the horses, and she told me that she lived down the road from Judith, in another house fronting the common. "I've lived there all my life, long before Judith came."

"Are you a magistrate?" I asked.

She looked startled. "No, I'm not. What an odd thing to ask."

"But you do do good in the world."

She was puzzled. "What makes you say so?"

"I don't know. The way you look." I smiled to take away any seriousness and said, "Shall we choose a horse and bet?"

"What about Burnt Marshmallow?"

She liked the name, she said, so we stopped at a window and invested some of the winnings from Sandcastle.

On our way back to the box we passed Calder Jackson, who was surrounded by respectful listeners. We slowed to hear.

"Comfrey is miraculous," he was saying. "It knits bones in half the time you'd expect."

"He said all that upstairs," I said.

Pen Warner nodded, faintly smiling. "Good, sound herbal medicine," she said. "You can't fault him. Comfrey contains allantoin, a well-known cell proliferant."

"Does it? I mean, do you know about it?"

"Mm. I don't know whether you'd think I do good in the world, but basically I dole out pills. I'm a pharmacist."

I suppose I was in a way disappointed, and she sensed it.

"Well," she sighed. "We can't all be glamorous."

We reached the box to find Judith and Henry there. "I told Tim I'm a pharmacist," Pen said. "He thinks it's boring."

I started to protest, when Judith interrupted.

"She's not just *a* pharmacist," she said. "She owns her own place, and half the medics in London recommend her. You're talking to a walking gold mine."

Dissdale's friends returned before I could reply, and shortly Gordon and Lorna crowded in. The race began, and because it was a time out of reality, Burnt Marshmallow romped home by three lengths.

The rest of the afternoon slid fast away. Henry at some point found himself alone on the balcony beside me. "How's your cartoonist?" he said genially. "Are we staking him or not?"

"Well, I got him to bring in more drawings. And his paints."

"His *paints?*"

"Yes. I thought if I could see him work, I'd know. So I took him into the interview room and asked him to paint the outline of a cartoon film while I watched; and he did it, there and then. Twenty-five outline sketches in bright color, all in an hour. Same characters, different story, terrifically funny."

"So you've decided?"

"Yes." With a sense of burning bridges I said, "To go ahead."

"All right." Henry seemed unalarmed. "Keep me informed."

AT THE end of that splendid afternoon the whole party descended together to ground level and made its way to the exit gate that opened onto the main road. Across the road was the car park. Calder was just ahead of me, the helmet curls bent kindly over Bettina, thanking her and Dissdale. Dissdale, incoherent with joy over his winnings, patted Calder on the shoulder and invited him over to "my place" for the weekend.

Henry and Gordon were fiddling in their pockets for car keys, and Judith, Lorna and Pen were talking to each other. It seemed to be only I who saw what was about to happen.

We were all out on the pavement, waiting to cross the road. All talking, busy; except me.

A boy dressed in jeans stood nearby, watchful and still. I noticed first the fixed, burning intent in the dark eyes, and then, with incredulity, the knife in his hand. I had to guess at whom he was staring, and there was no time even to shout a warning. He moved across the pavement with stunning speed.

I jumped without thinking. The steel was almost in Calder's stomach when I deflected it. I grabbed the boy's wrist, hitting him with my body in a flying tackle, and he fell beneath me.

He writhed under me, all muscle and fury, and I could feel him trying to get space enough to upend the knife. I pressed down onto him solidly with all my weight, saying, "Don't do it, don't do it, you bloody fool"; and I was saying it *for his sake*, which seemed crazy to me, even at the time. He was trying to do me great harm, and all I thought about was the trouble he'd be in if he succeeded.

We were both panting, but I was stronger and I could have held him there for a good while longer but for the two police-men who had seen the melee—seen, as they supposed, a man in morning dress attacking a pedestrian. With peremptory strength they hauled me off, though I resisted with all my might.

The boy comprehended the situation in a flash. He rolled over onto his feet, crouched for a split second, then slithered through the crowd at the gates and disappeared inside the racecourse.

By this time Henry, Gordon, Lorna, Judith and Pen were standing around in an anxious circle, and Calder was looking dazed and fingering a slit in the waistband of his trousers. I had stopped struggling with the policemen, but they wouldn't let go. And they seemed to have no thought of chasing the boy.

Finally I said to them, "Listen, that boy was trying to stab Calder Jackson. All I did was stop him. What do you think that knife's doing on the pavement?"

The policemen looked down to where it had fallen. Eight inches of sharp steel kitchen knife with a black handle.

They relinquished their hold, and I brushed the dirt off the knees of my father's suit and straightened my tie. I grinned at Judith. It all seemed a ridiculous mixture of death and bathos.

The aftermath took half the evening for Calder and me and was boring in the extreme: police station, hard chairs, coffee in plastic cups.

No, I'd never seen the boy before.

Yes, I was sure the boy had been aiming at Calder specifically.

Yes, he was only a boy. About sixteen, probably.

Yes, I would know him again.

Calder, wholly mystified, repeated over and over that he had no idea who could want to kill him. The police persisted. Most people knew their murderers, they said, particularly when, as in this case, the prospective killer was purposefully waiting for his victim. The boy might have known him, Calder said, because of his television appearances, but Calder had *not* known *him*.

Eventually we both left the building, Calder saying, "Er, Tim. Thanks are in order. I don't know what to say."

"Say nothing," I said. "I did it without thinking."

I had taken it for granted that everyone else would be long gone, but they had all waited, standing in a group by some cars and talking to three or four strangers.

Our party made a fuss over Calder. The strangers turned out to be gentlemen of the press and to my horror they produced notebooks and a camera and wrote down everything anyone said; which was why for a short time afterward I suffered from public notoriety as the man who had saved Calder Jackson's life.

No one seemed to speculate about his assailant's setting out for a second try.

October

GORDON was back at work with his faintly trembling left hand usually out of sight and unnoticeable. He had returned in July, had thanked me briskly for my stopgapping and had taken all major decisions off my desk and back to his.

One day in October, however, three whirlwind things happened more or less simultaneously. The cartoonist telephoned; *What's Going On Where It Shouldn't* landed with a thud throughout the City; and Uncle Freddie descended on Ekaterin's for a tour of inspection. To begin with, the three events were unconnected, but by the end of the day they were entwined.

I heard the cartoonist's opening remarks with a sinking heart. "I've engaged three extra animators and I need five more. And I'll need an increased loan to pay them all."

"Wait," I said.

He went right on. "I also need more space, and there's an empty warehouse next door. I've signed a lease for it and told them you'll be advancing the money—"

"*Stop*," I said, thinking wildly that I'd be licking stamps for a living as soon as Henry heard.

"Listen," the cartoonist was saying. "We all worked like mad and finished one twelve-minute film. And we did rough cuts of three others. And I've sold them."

"You've what?"

"Sold them." He laughed with excitement. "That agent you sent me to, he's fixed the sale and the contract. All I have to do is sign. Worldwide distribution, that's what they're talking about. But we've got to make twenty films a year from now on, not seven, like I had planned. And that could be just the start. I can't believe it. But I need a lot more money. Is it all right?"

"Yes," I said weakly. "It's all right."

"Thanks," he said. "Thanks, Tim Ekaterin, God bless your darling bank."

I put the receiver down and ran a hand over my head.

"Trouble?" Gordon asked, watching.

"Well, no." A laugh rose in my throat. "I backed a winner." I told him about the cartoonist and showed him the first drawings, which were still stowed in my desk.

"Wasn't that application on my desk?" he said, wrinkling his forehead in an effort to remember. "Just before . . . ?"

I thought back. "Yes, it probably was."

"Mm. Isn't he too young, or something?"

"That sort of talent strikes at birth."

He gave me a brief look and handed the drawings back. "Well," he said. "Good luck to him."

THE NEWS THAT UNCLE FREDDIE had been spotted in the building rippled through every department and stiffened many a slouching backbone. If true to form, he would visit Investment Management in the morning and attend a board meeting; then after lunch he would put his head into Corporate Finance, and end with a march through Banking. On the way, by some telepathic process of his own, he would learn what moved the bank's collective mind.

He had already arrived when the copies of *What's Going On* hit the office. As usual, Alec had slipped out to buy the six copies that the bank officially sanctioned. He delivered one copy to each floor, keeping ours to read first himself. Normal office life continued for perhaps five minutes after he opened the paper. Then he shot to his feet as if he'd been stung.

"Our leaker is at it again."

"What?" Gordon said.

"You'd better read it." He took the paper across to Gordon, whose look of foreboding turned slowly to anger.

"Disgraceful," Gordon said, and passed the paper to me. Under a heading of "Dinky Dirty Doings" it said:

It is perhaps not well known to readers that in many a merchant bank two thirds of the annual profits come from interest on loans. Investment and trust management and corporate finance departments are the public faces and glamour machines of these very private banks. But belowstairs, so to speak, lies the tail that wags the dog, the secretive banking department, which quietly lends from its own deep coffers and rakes in vast profits in the shape of interest at rates they can set to suit themselves.

Who in Paul Ekaterin Ltd. has been lending himself small fortunes from these coffers at *five* percent? Who in Paul Ekaterin Ltd. has set up private companies that are *not* carrying on the business for which the money has ostensibly been loaned? The man in the street (poor slob) would be delighted to get unlimited cash from Paul Ekaterin Ltd. at five percent.

Don't bankers have a fun time?

I looked up from the page and across at Alec.

"I wonder who's had his hand in the cookie jar?" he said, and he was, predictably, grinning.

"If you believe it," I said. "It had a dig at us before, remember? Back in May? And no one came up with any answers then. This column today is just as unspecific."

Gordon, however, said thoughtfully, "It's perfectly possible to set up a company and lend it money. All it takes is paperwork." He stood up, took the paper and went along to see one of his almost equal colleagues. Spreading consternation, I thought.

The morning had limped down almost to lunchtime when Henry's secretary came to tell me I was wanted on the top floor. Uncle Freddie, I thought. He's read the rag and in some way he'll make it out to be my fault. With a gusty sigh I took the lift to face the old warrior.

He was talking to Henry in the hallway. Both of them at six feet three topped me by inches. Life would never have been so ominous, I thought, if Uncle Freddie had been small.

"Tim," Henry said when he saw me. "Go along to the small conference room, will you?"

I nodded and made my way to the room next to the boardroom, where a copy of *What's Going On* lay on the polished table. My uncle came into the room with Henry and sat down, waving Henry and me to seats.

"What do you think?" Henry said to me, fingering the paper. "*Who* do you think?"

"It might not be anyone. There's not a single concrete detail. Same as last time."

Henry said, "Gordon tells me you can find out, Tim, how many concerns are borrowing from us at five percent. There can't be many. A few from when interest rates were low. If there are more recent ones, could you spot them?"

"I'll look," I said.

We both knew the search would take days and might produce no results. The fraud, if it existed, could have been going on for decades.

"Anyway," Henry said, "that isn't primarily why we asked you up here."

"No," grunted my uncle. "Time you were a director."

"Er . . . what?" I said.

"A director. A director," he said impatiently. "Fellow who sits on the board. Never heard of them, I suppose."

"But . . ." I looked at Henry, who was smiling and nodding.

"Don't you want to, then?" demanded my uncle.

"Yes, I do."

"Good. I've had my eye on you since you were eight. You told me then how much you would have if you saved a pound a month at four percent compound interest for forty years. Checked your figures. You'd inherited the gift, all right." He nodded. "I despaired of you at times. Thought you might be ruined by your parents. But I knew the gift was there."

I was pretty well speechless.

"We all agree," Henry said. "The whole board was unanimous at our meeting this morning that it's time another Ekaterin took his proper place."

"Would you," I said slowly, "have given me a directorship if my name had been Joe Bloggs?"

Henry said levelly, "Probably not this very day. But soon, I promise you, yes. You're almost thirty-three, after all, and I was on the board here at thirty-four."

He stood up and shook my hand. "Your appointment officially starts in a week, on the first of November. We will welcome you then to the boardroom, and afterward to lunch."

They must have seen the depth of my pleasure, and they themselves looked satisfied.

Gordon met me at the elevator and we went down. "They've been dithering about it ever since you took over from me when I was ill, and did okay. So I told them this morning about your news from the cartoonist. Some of them said it was just luck. I told them you'd been lucky too often for it to be a coincidence."

I WENT diffidently a week later to the induction and to the first lunch with the board, and I soon got used to the change of company and to the higher level of information.

There were usually from ten to fifteen directors at lunch. The food itself was no great feast, though perfectly presented. "Always lamb on Wednesdays," Gordon said at the buffet table as he took two lean cutlets. "Chicken on Tuesdays, beef Wellington most Thursdays." Each day there was a clear soup before and fruit and cheese after. Alcohol if one chose, but most of them didn't. Quite a change, all of it, from a sandwich at my desk.

They were all polite about my failure to discover "paper" companies to which the bank had been lending at five percent. I had spent several days in the computer room, checking through lists, but couldn't spot any companies that looked suspicious. Val and Henry shared my view that the rumor in *What's Going On* originated from malice and not fact. In any case, the rumpus was soon forgotten.

November

VAL Fisher said at lunch one day, "I've received a fairly odd request. Chap wants five million pounds to buy a racehorse."

Everyone at the table laughed except Val himself.

"What horse?" Henry said.

"Something called Sandcastle."

Henry, Gordon and I all looked at Val with sharpened attention, almost with eagerness.

"Mean something to you three, does it?" he said, turning his head from one to the other of us.

Henry nodded. "That day we went to Ascot. Sandcastle ran and won. A stunning performance. Beautiful."

Gordon said, "The man whose box we were in saved his whole business on that race."

"Yes, well," Val said. "About Sandcastle. He won the Two Thousand Guineas and the King Edward VII stakes at Royal Ascot. Also the Champion stakes at Newmarket last month. He could race next year as a four-year-old, but if he flopped, his value would be less than it is now. So our prospective client wants to buy him and put him to stud."

The rest of the directors were listening interestedly. A stallion made a change from chemicals, electronics and oil.

"Who is the client?" Gordon asked.

"A man called Oliver Knowles. Owns a stud farm. He wants to buy, the present owner is willing to sell. All they need is the cash." Val smiled. "Same old story."

"What's your view?" Henry said.

Val shrugged his well-tailored shoulders. "If it interests you at all, we could ask Tim to do a preliminary look-see. He has a long acquaintance, shall we say, with racing."

"What do you think?" Henry asked me.

"I'll certainly do it if you like."

Someone complained that merchant banks of our stature should not be associated with the turf.

"Our own dear queen," said someone else, "is associated with the turf. Knows the *Stud Book* well, they say."

Henry nodded to me. "Go ahead, Tim. And let us know."

DURING the next few days I telephoned around for information about Oliver Knowles, in the normal investigative preliminaries to any loan. I was told he was a sane, sober man of forty-one with a stud farm in Hertfordshire. There were three stallions there with ample provision for visiting mares, and he owned the one hundred and fifty acres outright, having inherited them from his father.

His local bank manager said that occasional fair-sized loans had so far been paid off as scheduled and that Mr. Knowles's business sense could be commended.

When I called a racing acquaintance of mine he said, "Oliver Knowles? I'll ask around," and an hour later came back with the news. "He seems to be a good guy, but his wife's just run off with a Canadian. Otherwise, the story is that he's as honest as any horse breeder, which you can take as you find it."

I told Gordon I was getting nothing but green lights, and at lunch I repeated the news to Henry. He looked around the table, collecting a few nods and a few frowns.

"Of course, we couldn't carry it all ourselves," Val said. "And it's not something we could take to our usual sources. They'd think us crackers."

Henry nodded. "I know a few people here or there who might come in. But two and a half million, I think, is all we should consider ourselves. Three at the outside."

"I don't approve," a dissenting director said. "It's madness. Suppose the horse broke its leg?"

"Insurance," Henry said mildly.

Into a small silence I said, "If you felt like going into it further, I could get some expert views on Sandcastle's breeding, and arrange blood and fertility tests. And I think someone like Val should go and meet Oliver Knowles and look at his place."

"Mm," Henry said. "What do you think, Val?"

Val Fisher smoothed a hand over his face. "Tim should go. All I know about horses is that they eat grass."

The dissenting director almost rose to his feet with the urgency of his feelings. "Look," he said. "All this is ridiculous. How can we possibly finance a *horse?*"

"Well, now," Henry answered. "The breeding of Thoroughbreds is big business. Look upon it as an industry like any other. We gamble here on shipbuilders, motors, textiles, you name it, and all of those can go bust. And none of them," he finished with a near grin, "can procreate in their own image."

I THOUGHT it prudent to bone up on the finances of horse breeding before going to see Oliver Knowles.

I didn't know anyone who knew much on the subject, but a friend told me that Ursula Young was the person who could put me right. "She's a bloodstock agent. Very sharp. She says she'll tell you anything you want—only if you want to see her this week, it will have to be at Doncaster races on Saturday."

I went to Doncaster by train and met the lady at the racecourse. She was waiting, as arranged, by the entrance to the Members' Club, and she swept me off to a table in a bar.

She was fifty, tough, good-looking, dogmatic and inclined to treat me as a child. She also gave me a patient and invaluable lecture on the economics of owning a stallion.

"Now, say you own a horse that's won the Derby and you want to capitalize on it. You judge what you think you can get for the horse, then you divide that by forty and try to sell each of the forty shares at that price."

"Why forty shares?" I asked.

"Because a stallion covers forty mares in a season. Forty is just about average—physically, I mean. Some can do more, but others get exhausted. Now, let's say you have a mare and you've worked out that if you mate her with a certain stallion, you might get a top-class foal; you try to get one of those forty places. The places are called nominations, and everyone who owns a share automatically has a nomination to the stallion every year. The mating season lasts roughly from February to June. Follow?"

"Gasping," I said.

She smiled. "But say you've got a nomination and no mare to

send to the stallion, then you sell your nomination to someone who *has* a mare. After three years the nominations may vary in price, and in fact are often auctioned, but for the first three years the price is fixed."

"Why?"

"Because for three years no one knows whether the progeny are going to be winners or not. The gestation period is eleven months, and the first crop of foals don't race until they're two. That means that the stallion has stood for three seasons, and covered a hundred and twenty mares, before the crunch."

"Right."

"So to fix the stud fee for the first three years, you divide the price of the stallion by one hundred and twenty. That's the fee charged for the stallion to cover a mare. That's the sum you receive if you sell your nomination."

I blinked. "That means," I said, "that if you sell your nomination for three years, you have recovered the total amount of your original investment?"

"That's right."

"And after that, every time, every year you sell your nomination, it's clear profit?"

"Yes. But taxed, of course."

"And how long does that go on?"

"Ten to fifteen years. Depends on the stallion's potency."

"But that's—"

"Yes," she said. "One of the best investments on earth."

We were on the point of standing up to leave when a man whose head one could never forget came into the bar.

"Calder Jackson!" I exclaimed.

Ursula casually looked. "So it is."

"Do you know him?" I asked.

"Everyone does. He's part of the scene."

She got to her feet and I with her, thanking her for her help. We made our way toward the door, a path, I saw, that would take us close to Calder. I wondered fleetingly whether he would remember me.

"Hello, Ursula," Calder said. "Bitter cold day."

"Calder." She nodded acknowledgment.

His gaze slid to my face, dismissed it; then he did a classic double take. "Tim," he said incredulously. "Tim . . . Ekaterin!"

I nodded.

He said to Ursula, "Tim, here, saved my life."

She was surprised until he explained. "I read about the attempt, of course," she said.

"Did you ever hear any more from the police?" I asked him.

He shook his curly head. "No, I didn't."

"How's the healing?" I said. "The tingling touch."

His eyes flashed briefly, as if he found the question flippant, but he answered civilly. "Rewarding. Heartwarming."

"Is your yard full, Calder?" Ursula asked.

"Always a vacancy if needed," he replied hopefully.

"One of my clients has a two-year-old which looks ill and half dead all the time, to the despair of the trainer."

"I have great success with that sort of general debility."

Ursula wrinkled her forehead, undecided. "My client feels Ian Pargetter would think her disloyal if she sent you her colt. He's been treating him for weeks without success."

Calder smiled reassuringly. "Ian Pargetter and I are on good terms, I promise you. He's even persuaded owners to send me their horses. Then we talk each case over and act in agreement."

"Is Ian Pargetter a vet?" I asked.

"Yes," Ursula replied. "One of a group practice in Newmarket. Many trainers swear by him."

"Just ask him, Ursula," Calder said. "Ian will tell you he doesn't mind owners sending me their horses. At least he trusts me not to make the patient worse." It was said as a joke, and we smiled. Then Ursula and I walked on, and behind us we could hear Calder politely answering another of the everlasting questions. "Yes," he was saying. "My favorite remedy for a prolonged cough in horses is licorice root boiled with figs."

The door closed behind us and shut him off.

"You'd think he'd tire of explaining his methods," I said.

Ursula said, "Calder depends on television, public relations and medical success, roughly in that order. He owns a yard outside Newmarket with about thirty boxes, and there's no doubt that horses do seem to leave his yard in a lot better health than when they went in."

"I've heard he's brought dying horses back to life."

"Hmph," she said. "Dying is a relative term when it doesn't end in death."

Ursula Young went off about her business, and I went back to London on the train. Sunday afternoon I drove off to Hertfordshire in search of Oliver Knowles.

HE LIVED in a stark hundred-year-old red brick house, which to my taste could have been softened by trailing creeper. Blurred outlines, however, were not in Oliver Knowles's soul: a crisp tidiness prevailed in every corner of his spread.

His land was divided into paddocks, each bordered by an immaculate white rail fence. There was a scattering of mares and foals in the paddocks, mostly heads down to the grass, sniffing out the last tender shoots of the dying year. The day was cold, with a muted sun dipping already toward distant hills.

Oliver Knowles opened his front door, proving to be a pleasant, lean man with a polite manner of authority.

"Mr. Ekaterin?" He shook hands, smiling. "I must confess I expected someone older."

I said, "I report back," to reassure him, and he invited me in.

Predictably the interior was also tidy. The furniture was antique, well polished, and the carpets venerably from Persia. He led me into a sitting room that was also office, the walls covered with framed photographs of horses, the windows looking out onto an archway that led into an extensive stable yard.

"Boxes for mares," he said, following my eyes. "Beyond them, the foaling boxes. Would you care to look round?"

"Very much," I said.

"Come along, then." He led me to the back of the house, collecting a cap and jacket and a black retriever from a mudroom on the way. "Go on, Squibs, old fellow," he said, watching his dog squeeze ecstatically through the door, and we walked out to the stable arch, with Squibs's nose down to the gravel.

"It's our quietest time of year," Oliver Knowles said. "We have our own mares here, of course, and quite a few boarders. Then we have the foals born to the mares this past spring, and the three stallions. Total of seventy-eight at the moment."

"And next spring," I said, "the mares coming to your stallions will arrive?"

"That's right." He nodded. "They come here a month or five weeks before they're due to give birth to the foals they're already carrying, so as to be near the stallion within the month following. They have to foal here, because the foals would be too delicate to travel straight after birth."

"And how long do they stay here?"

"About three months altogether, by which time we hope the mare is safely in foal again."

"There isn't much pause, then," I said, "between ... er ..."

He glanced at me with amusement. "Mares come into use nine days after foaling, but we think this a bit too soon for breeding. The estrus—heat, you would call it—lasts six days; then there's an interval of fifteen days, and the mare comes into use again for six days. This time we breed her. We try to have the mare covered two or three times while she's in heat, for the best chance of getting her in foal."

He led me briskly across the first big oblong yard, where long, dark equine heads peered inquisitively over half-open stable doors, and through a passage on the far side leading to two more yards. Beyond the last yard rose a fair-sized barn with a row of windows just below its roof.

"Breeding shed," Oliver Knowles said. Then we went along to another stable yard, this time of only six boxes, with feed room and tack room alongside. "Stallions," Knowles said.

Almost immediately three heads appeared over the half doors, three sets of dark, liquid eyes turning inquisitively on us.

"Rotaboy," my host said, walking to the first head and producing two carrots. The black lips whiffled over the outstretched palm and sucked them in. Knowles patted the horse's neck.

"He'll be twenty next year," he said.

He walked along to the next box and repeated the carrot routine. "This one is Diarist, rising sixteen."

At the third box he said, "This is Parakeet," and delivered his treats. "Parakeet turns twelve on January first. You can see why I need new blood here. Rotaboy has been an outstanding stallion, but he's old. Diarist and Parakeet produce winners, but none of them absolutely top rank. The *prestige* of a stud farm, quite apart from its income, depends on the drawing power of its stallions."

Oliver Knowles began to walk me back to the house. "This place is expensive to run," he said. "It makes a profit and I live comfortably, but if I am ever to achieve more, I must have more capital, in the shape of a world-class stallion."

"Which brings us," I said, "to Sandcastle."

He nodded. "If I acquired Sandcastle, this stud farm would immediately be more widely known and more highly regarded."

The big yard nearest the house had come to life, with horses being moved about and several lads carrying feed scoops, hay nets and buckets of water. Squibs, his tail madly wagging, went in a straight line toward a stocky man, who bent to fondle his black ears.

"That's Nigel, my stud groom," Oliver Knowles said. "If I can expand this place, I'll uprate him to stud manager; give him more standing with the customers. Come and meet him."

We reached Nigel, who was about my age, with light brown hair and bushy eyebrows. I was introduced merely as "a friend."

"Any problems?" Knowles then asked the groom.

"Nothing except the mare with the discharge."

His manner toward his employer was confident, and I had the strong impression it was Nigel's personality that suited Oliver Knowles as much as his skill with mares. Knowles was not a man, I judged, to surround himself with awkward, unpredictable characters.

I wondered idly about the wife who had "run off with a Canadian," and at that moment a horse trotted into the yard with a young woman aboard. A girl, I amended, as she kicked her feet from the stirrups and slid from the horse to the ground. A noticeably curved young girl in jeans and heavy sweater, with her dark hair tied in a ponytail. She led her horse into one of the boxes and then emerged to join us.

"My daughter," Oliver Knowles said. He gave her an indulgent smile, while looking as if his thoughts were elsewhere. Then he excused himself, stepping toward a mare that was being led past.

"Ginnie," the girl said, holding out her hand. "Are you the reason we didn't go out to the lunch party?"

"I don't know," I said. "I wouldn't think so."

"Oh, I would," she said. "Pa really doesn't like parties. He uses any old excuse not to go." She gave me an impish smile, and I wondered how old she was. As if reading my mind, she said, "I'm fifteen."

"Everyone has to go through it," I said.

Her eyes widened. "Did you hate it?"

I nodded. "Insecurity, self-consciousness . . . Terrible."

Coming back, Knowles overheard, and looked surprised. "Ginnie isn't self-conscious, are you, Ginnie?"

She looked from him to me and didn't answer. Knowles said he ought to go and see the mare with the discharge, and we all set off along one of the paths between the white-railed paddocks. I could hear Ginnie telling Nigel that school this term was a dreadful drag owing to the new headmistress' being a health fiend and making them all go jogging.

The mare proved to be in one of the paddocks at the boundary of the farm, and while Oliver Knowles and Nigel inspected her, I spent my time looking past the last set of white rails to the fields beyond.

The contrast to the Knowles fields was dramatic. Instead of extreme tidiness, a haphazard disorder; instead of brick stable yards, a ramshackle collection of wooden boxes.

Ginnie followed my gaze. "That's the Watcherley place, a hospital for sick horses," she said. "I used to go over there a lot, but almost all the patients have gone. Have you ever heard of it?"

I shook my head.

"It's pretty well known. Or at least it was until that razzmatazz man Calder Jackson stole the show. Mind you, the Watcherleys were no great shakes, I suppose, but the place was *cozy*, you know, and all the horses went home blooming, or most of them. But Calder Jackson, you see, is the *in* thing, with all those chat shows on television, and the Watcherleys got elbowed out."

Her father, listening to the last of these remarks, added his own view. "The Watcherleys have no business sense."

"I don't suppose they have a son about sixteen who hates Calder Jackson for ruining his parents' business?" I asked.

Ginnie shook her head. "They've never had any children," she said. "They just lavish all their love on animals."

It would have been too neat, I thought, if Calder Jackson's would-be assassin had been a Watcherley son.

Ginnie went off then to see to the horse she'd been riding, and Nigel to finish his inspections, leaving Knowles and me to return to the sitting room—office from which we'd started.

I'd come armed with sets of figures to cover the interest payable, should the loan for Sandcastle be approved. But I found that Oliver Knowles had been there before me.

"I'm used to repaying fairly substantial bank loans," he said. "This new venture is, of course, huge by comparison, but if I didn't feel it was within my scope, I wouldn't be contemplating it." He gave me a brief smile. "I'm not a nut case, you know."

"One can see," I said. I told him that the maximum length of an Ekaterin loan would be five years. "That means," I said, "that you'd have to receive almost eight million in that five years, even allowing for diminishing interest as you pay off some of the loan every year. It's a great deal of money."

"I understand," he said. "But even so, and even with the ridiculously high insurance premiums on a horse like Sandcastle, I'd be able to repay the loan in five years."

He spread out sheets of neatly written calculations. "A stallion fee of forty thousand pounds will cover it. His racing record justifies that figure, and I've checked carefully into the breeding of Sandcastle himself. There is no trace of hereditary illness or undesirable tendencies. He comes from a blue-blooded line of winners." He gave me a photocopied genealogical table. "I wouldn't expect you to advance a loan without getting an expert opinion. Please take this with you." He also gave me copies of his figures, and I packed everything into my briefcase.

Ginnie suddenly came into the office with an anxious air. "Dad, you won't forget about me going back to school?"

"Oh, all right." He looked at his watch. "Half an hour, then."

Ginnie looked relieved, though I clearly sensed his suppressed irritation. "My wife always did the school run," he said as the door closed behind his daughter. He shrugged. "She's away indefinitely."

"I'm sorry," I said.

"Can't be helped. Ginnie comes home on four Sundays a term. She's not yet used to her mother being gone."

"She's a nice girl," I said.

He gave me a glance in which I read both love for his daughter and a blindness to her needs. "I don't suppose," he said thought-fully, "that you pass anywhere near High Wycombe on your way home?"

"Well," I said obligingly. "I could."

I consequently drove Ginnie back to her school, listening on the way to her views on the new headmistress' compulsory jogging program ("All our bosoms flopping up and down, abso-lutely *disgusting* to look at") and to her opinion of Nigel ("Dad thinks the sun shines on him, and I daresay he is pretty good with the mares, but what the lads get up to behind his back is nobody's business. They smoke in the feed sheds, with all that hay around") and to her outlook on life in general ("I can't wait to get out of school uniform and out of dormitories and stop being bossed around. Why has everything *changed?* I used to be happy, or at least I wasn't unhappy, and no, it isn't because of Mum going away, as she was never a lovey-dovey sort of mother, always telling me to eat with my mouth shut and so on . . . and you must be bored silly hearing all this").

"No," I said truthfully. "I'm not bored."

"I'm not even *beautiful,*" she said despairingly. "I'll never look pale and bony and interesting."

I glanced at the still rounded child-woman face, at the peach-bloom skin and the worried eyes. "Practically no one is beautiful at fifteen," I said. "But if it's of any comfort to you, you do look as if you may be beautiful in a year or two, or at least not unbear-ably ugly."

She sat in uncharacteristic silence for a distance and then said, "Why did you come today? I mean, who are you?"

"I'm a sort of financial adviser. I work in a bank."

"Oh." She sounded slightly disappointed but made no further comment. Soon after that, she gave me prosaic and accurate directions to the school.

"Thanks for the lift," she said, shaking hands politely as we stood beside the car.

"A pleasure."

"And thanks . . ." She hesitated. "Thanks anyway."

I nodded, and she half ran to join a group of girls going into a building. Nice child, I thought, pointing the car homeward. Her future a clean stretch of sand waiting for footprints.

December

IT MADE the headlines in *Sporting Life* and turned up as the lead story on the racing pages of all the other dailies. SANDCASTLE TO GO TO STUD, SANDCASTLE TO STAY IN BRITAIN, SANDCASTLE BOUGHT PRIVATELY FOR HUGE SUM.

"Well," Henry said at lunch, tapping his copy of *Sporting Life*, "not many of our loans make so much splash. If one of the foals runs in the Derby, we'll take a party from the office." He added musingly, "Forty foals. Surely one of them might be Derby material."

"Er," I said, from newfound knowledge. "Forty foals is stretching it. Thirty-five would be pretty good."

Henry showed mild alarm. "Does that mean that five or six fees will have to be returned?"

I shook my head. "For a horse of Sandcastle's stature the fee is all up front. Payable for services rendered, regardless of results. That's in Britain, of course, and Europe. In America they have the system of no foal, no fee, even for the top stallions."

Henry relaxed, leaning back in his chair and smiling. "You've certainly learned a lot, Tim, since this all started."

"It's absorbing."

He nodded. "I know it isn't usual, but how do you feel about keeping an eye on the bank's money at close quarters? Would Knowles object to your dropping in from time to time?"

"I shouldn't think so. Not out of general interest."

"Good. Bring us progress reports, then. I must say I've never been as impressed with any horse as I was that day with Sandcastle."

Henry's enthusiasm had led in the end to Ekaterin's advancing three of the five-million-pound price to Oliver Knowles, with private individuals subscribing the other two. The tests had been excellent, the sale had been made, and Sandcastle was already standing in the yard in Hertfordshire alongside Rotaboy, Diarist and Parakeet.

DECEMBER was marching along toward Christmas, with trees twinkling all over London, and on an impulse I sent a Christmas card to Calder Jackson, wishing him well. Almost by return post

I received a missive asking if I would be interested in looking around his place sometime. If so, would I telephone. I did, and we made a date for the following Sunday.

I told Gordon I was going. We were working on a loan of nine and a half million for five days to a competitor, a matter of little more than a few telephone calls and a promise. My hair had almost ceased to rise at the size and speed of such deals.

Then Gordon asked me what I'd be doing at Christmas.

"Nothing much," I said.

"Judith and I wondered if you'd care to stay with us. Come on Christmas Eve, stay for a few days? Although I daresay you wouldn't find us too exciting."

Was it wise, I wondered, to spend a few days with Judith, when a few *hours* at Ascot had tempted acutely?

Most unwise. But I said, "I'd like to. Very much."

"Good," Gordon said. "Judith will be pleased." He went back to work, and I thought about Judith wanting me to visit. Because if she hadn't wanted it, I wouldn't have been asked.

CALDER Jackson's place at Newmarket, seen that next Sunday morning, was a gem of public relations. The yard had been cosmetically planted with central grass and a graceful tree, and brightly painted flower tubs stood outside the horse boxes. To one side was a small building painted glossy white, with a large red cross on the door, and underneath it the single word SURGERY.

Beyond the yard and the surgery stood Calder's house. I parked on a stretch of asphalt and walked over to ring the bell. The door was opened by a manservant in a white coat.

"This way, sir," he said when I gave my name.

Interesting to see the dramatic haircut in its home setting, which was Olde Worlde cottage on a grand scale: a huge room with oak rafters, a stone floor, a brick fireplace with burning logs. Calder advanced with a broad smile. "Tim!" he exclaimed, shaking hands vigorously. "This is a pleasure, indeed it is."

"Been looking forward to it," I said.

"Come along to the fire. How about a drink? And this is a friend of mine." He waved toward a second man. "Ian Pargetter."

The stranger and I nodded to each other, and the name tumbled over in my mind as one I'd heard before.

Calder Jackson clinked bottles and glasses and upon consultation gave me a Scotch of noble proportions.

"And for you, Ian," he said. "A further tincture?"

Oh yes, I thought. The vet. Ian Pargetter, the vet who didn't mind consorting with unlicensed practitioners. He held out his glass. "A small one, then, Calder. I must be off."

He was about forty, I judged—large and reliable-looking, with sandy, graying hair and a heavy mustache. Calder explained that it was I who had deflected the knife aimed at him at Ascot, and Ian Pargetter made predictable responses about luck, fast reactions, and who could have wanted to kill Calder?

"That was altogether a memorable day," Calder said, and I agreed with him. "We all won a packet on Sandcastle," he went on. "Pity he's going to stud so soon."

I smiled. "Maybe we'll win on his sons."

Ian Pargetter finished his drink at a gulp and said he'd be going. "Let me know how that pony fares, Calder."

"Yes, of course." Calder moved with him to the door and returned rubbing his hands together, saying that although it was cold outside, I might care to look around before his other guests arrived for lunch. Accordingly we went out to the yard, where Calder moved from box to box, giving me a brief résumé of the illness and prospects of each patient.

"This pony came yesterday, a prize show pony supposedly, and look at it. Dull eyes, rough coat, it's had diarrhea for weeks. I'm their last resort, they say." He smiled. "Can't think why they don't send me sick horses as a *first* resort."

We went on down the row. "Here's a star three-day-eventer. Came to me with blood in the urine, intractable to antibiotics. Now he's fine. I'm sure the trouble is cured."

He pointed to another box. "There's a colt who's been here two months and is only just responding. His owners were in despair, and so was I, privately, but then three days ago when I was in his box I could feel the force flowing down my arms and into him, and the next day he was mending."

He spoke with a far more natural fluency on his home ground and less as if reciting from a script, but still I felt the same reservations about the healing touch that I had at Ascot.

"Is there anything you can't treat?" I asked.

"Yes. There are some things, like advanced laminitis."

"You've lost me," I said.

"So sorry. Well, laminitis is a condition of the feet where the bone eventually begins to crumble, and horses in the end can't bear the pain of standing up. They lie down, and horses can't live for more than a few days lying down." He spoke with regret. "And there's coryne, a frightful bacterial infection which is deadly to foals. It induces a sort of pneumonia. Terribly contagious."

"Isn't there a vaccine?" I said.

"Very little research is done into equine diseases, chiefly because of the cost, but also because horses are so large and can't be kept in a laboratory for any controlled series of tests."

We proceeded on our rounds and came at length to a box with an open door. "We're giving this one sun treatment," Calder said, and looking inside, I saw a youth adjusting the angle of an ultraviolet lamp mounted on the wall. At first glimpse I thought he was the boy who had tried to attack Calder.

I opened my mouth . . . and shut it again.

He wasn't the boy, although he was of the same height, same build, same general coloring.

Calder saw my reaction and smiled. "For a split second, when I saw that boy move toward me at Ascot, I thought it was Jason here too. But it wasn't, of course. Jason wouldn't want to kill me, would you, Jason?"

"No, sir," he said stolidly.

"Jason is my right-hand man," said Calder heartily.

The right-hand man maintained an impassive countenance.

"Mind your eyes with that lamp," Calder said. "Where are your glasses?"

Jason fished into the pocket of his shirt and put on some ultra-dark sunshades. Where there had already been a lack of expression, there was now no way at all of guessing Jason's thoughts.

We moved off to the last box in the yard, the only empty one. "Emergency bed," Calder said jokingly.

I asked how much he charged for his patients, and he replied easily, without apology, "Twice the usual fees."

"*Twice?*"

"Yes. If I charged less, I'd be swamped by all those last resort people, and I simply haven't the time or the spiritual resources to take more cases than I do."

He gestured toward the surgery as we approached it. "My drugstore!" He produced a key to unlock the door. "There's nothing dangerous or illegal in here, of course, but one has to protect against vandals. So sad, don't you think?"

The surgery, which had no windows, was basically a large brick hut. The inside walls were painted white, and the floor was tiled in red. There were antiseptic-looking glass-fronted cabinets along the two end walls, and a wide workbench with drawers underneath along the wall facing the door. On the bench, a delicate-looking set of scales, a mortar and pestle and a pair of fine rubber gloves; behind the glass of the cabinets, rows of bottles and boxes. Along the wall that contained the door stood a refrigerator, a stove and a sink.

Calder pointed vaguely toward the cabinets. "In there I keep the herbs in pill and powder form. Comfrey, myrrh, sarsaparilla, fo-ti-tieng, things like that."

"What do they do?"

He ran through them obligingly. "Comfrey knits bones and heals wounds, myrrh is good for diarrhea and rheumatism, sarsaparilla increases physical strength, fo-ti-tieng is a revitalizing tonic."

The air in the windowless room was fresh and smelled faintly fragrant. As if to account for it, Calder started showing me the contents of the drawers. "I keep seeds here," he said. Three drawers contained opaque plastic bags fastened by clips. "Sunflower seeds for vitamins, phosphorous and calcium. Pumpkin seeds for vigor. Sesame seeds for general health."

He opened a deep drawer full of larger bags. "In these are hops, left after beermaking. They're packed with good things. I use them as one ingredient of my special decoction, my concentrated tonic."

"Do you make it on the stove?" I asked.

"Like a chef," he said. He opened the refrigerator door and I looked inside. Nearly the whole space was taken with gallon-sized plastic containers full of a brownish liquid. "We mix it in a bran mash, warmed of course, and the horses thrive."

I was definitely impressed. "How do you get the horses to take pills?" I said.

"In an apple usually. We scoop out half the core, put in the tablet or capsule and replace the plug. Incidentally, I make most of my own pills, and I fill the capsules myself." He opened another drawer under the workbench, lifted out a wooden box and raised the lid. "This contains the makings."

I looked down at a whole array of brass dies, each a small square with a pill-sized cavity in its center. The cavities varied from tiny to extra large, and from round to oblong.

"It's an antique," he said with a touch of pride. "Early Victorian. Dates from when pills were always made by hand. You put the required drug in powder form into whatever size cavity you want and compress it with the rod that matches it." He lifted one of a series of short brass rods from its rack and fitted its end into one of the cavities, tamping it up and down.

"Neat," I said with positive pleasure.

"Of course, capsules are quicker and more modern." He briefly showed me the empty tops and bottoms of a host of gelatin capsules of varying sizes.

He closed his gem of a pillmaking box and returned it to its drawer, then cast an eye around the place to make sure everything was tidy. With a nod of satisfaction he opened the door. Switching off the lights, he locked the door behind us.

A car was just rolling to a stop on the asphalt, and two figures emerged from it: Dissdale Smith and his delectable Bettina.

"Hello, hello," said Dissdale, striding across with ready hand. "Calder's been showing you all his treasures, eh?" I shook the hand. "Calder's proud of his achievements here."

"With good reason," I said civilly.

Bettina drifted slowly to join us, a delight in high-heeled boots and cuddling fur, dark hair falling glossily to her shoulders.

Calder took us all into the sitting room of his house and distributed drinks. Four more guests arrived—a married couple with their two twentyish daughters—and the occasion became an enjoyable lunch party.

Everyone left around three, and I drove back to London wondering if the herbs of antiquity held secrets we'd almost willfully lost.

"Caffeine," Calder had been saying toward the end, "is a get-up-and-go stimulant, tremendously useful. Good for asthma. A lifesaver after shock. And now in America they're casting caffeine as a villain and are busy taking it out of everything it's naturally *in*. You might as well take the alcohol out of bread."

"But Calder dear," Bettina said. "There's no alcohol in bread."

He looked at her kindly. "If you mix yeast with water and sugar, you get alcohol and carbon dioxide, which is the gas that makes bread dough rise. Simple chemistry, my dear girl. Bread is the staff of life, and alcohol is good for you."

There had been jokes and lifted glasses, and I could have listened to Calder for hours.

The Christmas party at Gordon Michaels' home was in a way an echo, because Judith's apothecary friend, Pen Warner, was in attendance. I got to like her very much, which Judith may or may not have intended.

"Do you remember Burnt Marshmallow at Ascot?" Pen said. "I bought a painting with my winnings."

"I spent mine on riotous living."

"Oh?" She looked me up and down. "You haven't the air."

"What do I have the air of?" I asked curiously.

"Of intelligent laziness and boring virtue."

"All wrong," I said.

She had appeared at the Michaels' house in a long, festive caftan, with mood to match, and during the evening the four of us ate quail with our fingers, and roasted chestnuts, and played a board game with childish gusto. On all levels the evening proved harmonious and fun.

Judith kissed me good night on the cheek. Gordon gave me a smile and a wave, and I went to bed down the hall from them and spent an hour before sleep deliberately not thinking about Judith—or not much.

After breakfast Judith and Gordon went to church. Pray for me, I said, and set out for a walk on the common. A surreptitious inspection, made that morning, of the brightly wrapped gifts waiting around the base of the Michaels' Christmas tree had revealed one from Pen addressed to me, and now I walked across the grass, wondering what to do about one for her. As often happens, a solution came quite by chance.

A small boy was out there with his father, flying a kite. It was a brilliant Chinese dragon with butterfly wings and frilly tail, and I stopped to watch. "That's fun," I remarked.

The father said, "There's no satisfying this one. I give him a kite, and he says he wants roller skates."

"Will you sell it to me?" I asked. "Buy the roller skates instead?" I explained my need for an instant present.

Parent and child consulted and the deal was done. I bore the trophy home, wondering what the sober pharmacist would think of such a thing. But when she unwrapped it (from gold paper cadged from Judith) she pronounced herself enchanted, and off we all went to the common to watch her fly it.

The whole day was happy. I hadn't had so good a Christmas since I was a child. I told them so, and kissed Judith uninhibitedly under the mistletoe, which Gordon didn't seem to mind.

ON THE morning after Christmas Day, I drove Judith across London to Hampstead to put flowers on her mother's grave.

"I always go. She died on the day after Christmas when I was twelve. It's the only way I have of remembering her, but Gordon thinks I'm sentimental and doesn't like coming."

"Nothing wrong with sentiment," I said.

I wasn't sure whether Judith knew that I lived in Hampstead in the upstairs half of a friend's house, and I said nothing about it until we were walking slowly out of the cemetery. Then I said neutrally, "My flat's only half a mile from here. This part of London is home ground."

After a few steps she said, "I knew you lived somewhere here." We reached the cemetery gates and paused. I was infinitely conscious of her nearness. She looked into my eyes and said, "Gordon knows you live here, also."

"And does he know how I feel?" I asked.

"I don't know. He hasn't said."

I wanted very much to go that last half mile. My body tingled, and I found myself clenching my back teeth.

"What are you thinking?" she said.

"For heaven's sake, you know very well what I'm thinking . . . and we're going back to Clapham right this minute."

She sighed. "Yes, I suppose we must."

"What do you mean, you suppose?"

"Well . . . I mean, yes, we must. I'm sorry. . . . For a moment I was tempted."

"As at Ascot?" I said.

She nodded. "As at Ascot."

"Only here and now," I said, "we have the place and the time and the opportunity to do something about it. And what we're going to do is . . . nothing." It came out as half a question, half a statement, but we walked down the road to where I'd parked the car, and I drove carefully and slowly all the way to Clapham.

At her house, we went indoors in a sort of deprived companionship, and I realized when I saw Gordon's smiling face that I couldn't have returned there if it had been in any other way.

Later, at lunch, I told them all about my visit to Calder. Pen was acutely interested and said she'd dearly like to know what was in the decoction in the refrigerator.

"What's a decoction?" Judith asked.

"A preparation boiled with water. If you dissolve things in alcohol, that's a tincture."

Gordon was laughing. "Have some tincture of grape." He poured wine into our glasses. "Do you honestly believe, Tim, that Calder cures horses by touch?"

"I'm sure *he* believes it." I reflected. "And he wouldn't be able to set his prices so high if he didn't get real results."

"Do the herbs come extra?" Pen said.

"I didn't ask. Would you expect them to?"

"Well, some of the ones you mentioned are fairly exotic. Fo-ti-tieng, which is *Hydrocotyle asiatica minor*, only grows in the tropical jungles of the Far East. Giving things like that to horses would be wildly expensive."

"I didn't know pharmacists were so clued up on herbs," I said.

"A lot of chemist's shops don't sell nonprescripton herbal remedies, but I do," she explained, "and honestly, for a stack of people they seem to work."

The four of us spent a comfortable afternoon and evening together, and at bedtime I walked Pen to her house.

"You're going home tomorrow, aren't you?" she said.

I nodded. "In the morning."

"It's been great fun." She fished out her keys and fitted one in the lock. "Would you like to come in?"

"No. I'll just walk for a bit."

She opened the door and paused there. "Good-by for this time, though I guess if Judith can stand it, I'll be seeing you at her house again."

"Stand what?" I asked.

She kissed me on the cheek. "Believe it or not, the herb known as passionflower is good for insomnia." Her grin shone out like the Cheshire cat's as she stepped inside her house.

The Second Year
February

IAN Pargetter was murdered at about one in the morning on February 1. I learned about his death from Calder when I telephoned later that day to thank him, very belatedly, for the lunch and to invite him for a reciprocal dinner in London.

"Who?" he said vaguely when I announced myself. "Oh, Tim. Look, I can't talk now, I'm simply distracted, a friend of mine's been killed and I can't think of anything else."

"I'm so sorry," I said inadequately.

"Yes. Ian Pargetter, but I don't suppose you know . . ."

I remembered at once. "I met him at your house."

"Did you? Oh yes. I'm so upset I can't concentrate. Look, ring me another time. . . . Tim, so sorry."

I thought at the time that he meant Ian Pargetter had been killed in some sort of accident, and it was only the next day when I saw a newspaper that I realized the difference. The report said:

> Ian Pargetter, well-known Newmarket veterinary surgeon, was found dead in his home yesterday morning. Police suspect foul play. They state that Pargetter suffered head injuries and that certain supplies of drugs appear to be missing. The vet is survived by his wife and three young daughters, all of whom were away from home at the time.

I found Pargetter's death most disturbing; and if I felt so unsettled about a near stranger, how, I wondered, did anyone ever recover from the murder of someone one knew well and loved?

BECAUSE OF ASCOT AND SANDCASTLE my long-dormant interest in racecourses seemed thoroughly reawakened, and on four Saturday afternoons that winter I'd gone to various tracks to watch the jumpers. Ursula Young, the bloodstock agent, had become a familiar acquaintance, and it was from her that I learned more about Ian Pargetter and his death.

"Drink?" I suggested one day at Kempton.

She looked at her watch and agreed on a quick one.

"Now tell me," she said, yelling in my ear over the din of a packed bar, "when you asked all those questions about stallion shares, was it for Sandcastle?"

I smiled without actually answering, and Ursula bent her head toward mine. "A wow-sized coup for Oliver Knowles."

"Do you know him?"

"Yes. He had a snooty wife, who left him for some Canadian millionaire; maybe he's aiming for the big time just to show her. She was a real pain and I hope he makes it."

She drank half her whiskey, and I said it was a shame about Ian Pargetter and that I'd met him once at Calder's house.

She grimaced. "He'd been out all evening saving the life of a colt with colic. He went home well after midnight, and they reckon whoever killed him was already in the house. He was hit on the back of the head with a brass lamp. Unpremeditated. *Stupid.*" She looked moved. "Such a waste. He was a good vet, everyone liked him. And all the police found missing were his case of instruments and a few drugs. Nothing worth killing for." She looked down into her glass. "I liked Ian."

"I think Calder Jackson feels much as you do," I said.

She glanced up, her good-looking fiftyish face full of general concern. "Calder will miss Ian terribly. There aren't that many vets around who'd treat a faith healer as a colleague. Ian had no professional jealousy. Very rare. Very good man."

Two weeks later, with Oliver Knowles's warm approval, I paid another visit to his farm in Hertfordshire, and although it was still winter, the atmosphere of the place had fundamentally changed. Where before there had been quiet near hibernation, there was now a wakeful bustle and eagerness; a crowd of mares with big bellies moved slowly across the paddocks.

To me the birth of animals seemed a wonder and a joy; to Knowles it meant constant worry. "I suppose," he said, walking me into the first big yard, "I hadn't mentally prepared myself for the value of the foals now being born here." He gestured at the patient heads looking over the half doors. "These mares have been to the top stallions. They're carrying fabulous bloodlines." He smiled ruefully. "I didn't realize the anxiety they would bring. We've always done our best for the foals, of course, but if one died, it wasn't a tragedy. With this lot . . ."

As we walked along a row of boxes he told me the breeding of each mare and of the sire of the foal she carried. To my ears it sounded as if every Derby and Oaks winner for half a century had had a hand in the coming generation.

"I had no trouble selling Sandcastle's nominations," he said. "Not even at forty thousand pounds a throw. I could even choose, to some extent, which mares to accept."

It was earlier in the day than my last visit—eleven in the morning—and more lads than before were to be seen mucking out the boxes and carrying feed and water.

"I've had to take on extra hands," Oliver Knowles said matter-of-factly. "Temporarily, for the season. I do it every spring. I keep the good ones on for the whole year, if they'll stay, of course."

We strolled into the second yard, where Nigel could be seen peering over a half door into a box.

"You know Nigel? He's now my stud manager," Oliver said.

Nigel withdrew his head from the box. "Floradora's eating again," he announced to Oliver, sounding relieved. "And Patta-cake is still in labor. I'm just going back there."

"We'll come along," Oliver said, and we walked down the path into the foaling yard. The box to which Nigel led us was larger than normal and thickly laid with straw.

"She started about midnight," Oliver said. "She's just lazy, eh, girl?" He patted the brown rump. "Same thing every year."

We hovered for a few minutes, but there was no change in Pattacake. Nigel, running knowledgeable hands over the shape under her ribs, said she'd be another hour, perhaps, and Oliver and I went on to the stallion yard.

In the last yard, there he was, the gilt-edged Sandcastle, looking over his door like any other horse.

One couldn't tell, I thought. True, there was a poise to the well-shaped head, and an interested eye and alertly pricked ears, but nothing to announce that this was the marvelous creature I'd seen at Ascot. No one ever again, I reflected, would see that arrowlike gallop, that sublime valor; it seemed a shame.

A worker was sweeping scatterings of peat off the concrete in front of the stallions' boxes. "Lenny," Oliver said. "You can take Sandcastle down to the small paddock opposite Parakeet."

"Yes, sir."

Lenny was middle-aged—small, leathery and obviously of long experience. He disappeared into a doorway and reappeared carrying a length of rope, which he clipped onto Sandcastle's halter. Every equine resident wore a halter with a metal plate stapled to it bearing the horse's name. Shuffle all the mares together without their halters, I thought, and one could breed the wrong mare to the wrong stallion and never know it.

Lenny opened Sandcastle's door and led him out, and one could see the sleek muscles in all their strength, the tugging sinews, the springlike joints. The colt pranced on the hard apron, tossing his magnificent head.

"Full of himself," Oliver explained. "He doesn't get the exercise he used to."

We stepped to one side to avoid the restless hindquarters as Lenny led him out of the yard, the long bay legs stalking in powerful strides.

We walked on, then stopped for Oliver to give two carrots and a pat each to Rotaboy and Diarist, so we didn't see the calamity. We heard a yell and the thud of fast hoofs, and Oliver went white as we ran to the disaster.

Lenny lay against one of the white-painted posts of the small paddock's rail fence, dazedly trying to pull himself up. Sandcastle, loose and excited, had found his way into one of the paths between the paddocks and was bolting at top speed.

Nigel stood in shock by the open gate.

"Get going! Get the Land-Rover," Oliver shouted to him. "I'll get the car. He can get out on the road that way through the Watcherleys'." He and Nigel ran off in different directions, and I, ignorant of how best to catch fleeing horses, simply set off in Sandcastle's wake.

He disappeared behind a distant hedge bordering the Watcherleys' farm. I ran across a thistly field and reached the Watcherleys' yard, to find Ginnie walking toward me.

"What is it?" she said. "Is one of the mares out?"

"Sandcastle."

"Oh no!" It was a cry of despair. "The road!" She turned away, already running, and I ran after her; out of the Watcherleys' yard and down the drive to the dangerous outside world, where a car could kill a horse without even trying.

"We'll never catch him," Ginnie said as we reached the road. "We don't know which way he went." She was in great distress: eyes flooding, tears on her cheeks. "Where's Dad?"

"He's gone to get the car. Nigel's in the Land-Rover."

"I heard a horse gallop through the Watcherleys'," she said. "I was in one of the boxes with a foal. I never thought . . ."

A speeding car passed in front of us, followed closely by two others doing at least sixty miles an hour. "Let's go this way," I said, pointing to the left.

Ginnie shook her head sharply. "Dad and Nigel will be on the road. But there's a track over there." She pointed slantwise across the road. "He might just have made it. And there's a bit of a hill, so even if he isn't up there, we might be able to see him from the top." She was off again, and I fell in beside her. Sandcastle was insured—I'd vetted the policy myself—but Oliver's prestige wasn't.

The track was muddy and slippery from recent rain, and there were a great many hoofprints, some looking new. I asked Ginnie pantingly if any of them could be Sandcastle's.

"Oh." She stopped running suddenly. "Yes. Of course. He hasn't got shoes on yet. The blacksmith came yesterday. He's going to make leather pads for under his new shoes. . . ." She peered at the ground dubiously, then pointed. "Those new marks might be his. . . ." She began running again up the track, impelled now by hope as well as horror, fit after all that compulsory jogging. I ran with her.

The track curved through the bushes and opened suddenly into a wider place where grass grew in patches beside the rutted mud, and there stood Sandcastle, head high, nostrils twitching, a creature of power and beauty and majesty.

Ginnie stopped and caught my arm fiercely.

"Don't move," she said. "I'll do it. You stay here."

I nodded, respecting her experience. The animal looked ready to bolt at the slightest untimely movement. He's frightened, I thought. He's out here, lost, not knowing where to go.

Ginnie walked toward him, making crooning noises and holding out her hand palm upward, an offering hand with nothing to offer. "Come on, boy," she said. "There's a good boy."

The horse trembled as he watched her. The rope hung down from his halter, its free end curling on the ground. I wondered whether Ginnie would be able to control the colt if she caught him, where Lenny with all his strength had let him go.

She came to within a foot of the horse's nose, her open left hand still held upward, bringing her right hand up slowly under his chin and reaching for the halter. But at the last second Sandcastle would have none of it. He wheeled away with a squeal, knocking Ginnie to her knees; laid back his ears and accelerated in my direction. Past me lay the open track, downhill again to the slaughtering main road.

Without thinking of anything much, I jumped, not out of his way but at his flying head, my fingers missing the halter and fastening around the rope.

He nearly tore my arms out of their sockets and all the skin from my palms. He yanked me off my feet and pulled me through the mud, bumping me with shoulder and knee. All the same, I clung with both hands to the rope, and shortly, more by weight than skill, I hauled him off the track and into the bushes.

Clumsily I wound the rope around a stump of branch, and that was roughly that. Sandcastle stood tossing his head and quivering but no longer trying for full stampede.

Ginnie appeared around the curve in the track, looking more distraught than ever. When she saw me she stumbled and half fell and came up to me, uninhibitedly crying.

"Oh, I'm so glad, so glad, and you should never do that, you can be killed, you should never do it." She leaned against me and like a child wiped her eyes on my sleeve.

"Well," I said pragmatically. "What do we do with him now?"

We decided, upon consideration, that Sandcastle and I should stay where we were, and Ginnie should go for her father.

While she was gone I made an inventory of damage, but there was nothing broken. I made a ball of my handkerchief in my right palm, which was bleeding slightly, and thought that one of these days a habit of launching oneself at things like fleeing stallions and boys with knives might prove to be unwise.

Oliver, Ginnie, Nigel and Lenny all appeared in the Land-Rover, gears grinding and wheels spinning in the mud. Sandcastle, to their obvious relief, was upon inspection pronounced sound, and Oliver told me forcefully that *no one* should *ever*, repeat *ever*, try to stop a bolting horse in that way.

"I'm sorry," I said.

"Never do it again," he said. "And thanks." He paused and swallowed. "Thanks for taking care of my investment."

I nodded and put my arm around Ginnie's shoulders, which seemed to disconcert her horribly. "Oh dear, you must think me so silly, crying like that."

I said, "All's well now, you know; it really is."

I naturally believed what I said, but I was wrong.

April

CALDER Jackson came to dinner with me while he was staying in London to attend a conference. I met him in a restaurant and immediately sensed a difference in him. Heads turned and voices whispered as we walked to our table, but because of television this would have happened anyway. Yet now, I thought, Calder really enjoyed it. He had become, even to himself, the great man. I wondered what had altered him, and it turned out to be the thing I would have least expected: Ian Pargetter's death.

Over a plate of smoked salmon Calder apologized for the abrupt way he'd brushed me off on the telephone on that disturbing night, and I said it was most understandable.

"Fact is," he said, "I was afraid my whole business would collapse. Ian's partners, you know, never approved of me."

"And it hasn't worked out that way?"

"Remarkably not. Amazing." We were both aware that diners nearby were almost visibly tuned to his distinctive voice. He put a forkful of smoked salmon in his mouth and made appreciative noises. "My yard's still full. People have faith, you know."

"Did they ever find out who killed Pargetter?"

He looked regretful. "I asked one of his partners the other day, and he said no one seemed to be asking questions anymore. He was quite upset. And so am I. Finding his murderer won't bring Ian back, but all the same one wants to *know*."

"Tell me about your work," I said, changing the subject. "I find it very interesting." I also found it one of the few things to talk about; there was still no drift toward an easy friendship.

Calder ate more smoked salmon while he thought. "I've just had a colt," he said at last, "who started bleeding into his mouth and down his nose and went on and on doing it."

"And did you discover what was wrong?" I asked.

"Oh no. It wasn't necessary. I laid my hands on him on three succeeding days, and the bleeding stopped."

The adjacent tables were fascinated, as indeed was I.

"Did you give him herbs?" I asked.

"Certainly. The one thing you can't do with herbs is *harm*. With medicines one has to be careful because of their power and their side effects, but I can give a horse all the herbal remedies I can think of, hoping one will hit the target, and it quite often does. It may be hopelessly unscientific, but if a trained vet can't tell what's wrong with a horse, how can I?"

I smiled with undiluted pleasure. "Have some wine," I said.

He nodded the helmet of curls, and the movement I made toward the bottle in its ice bucket was instantly forestalled by a waiter, who poured almost reverently into the healer's glass.

With the roast beef I asked after Dissdale and Bettina, and heard that while Dissdale had been away on business for ten days, Bettina had gotten a small part in a movie. Dissdale hadn't known whether to be pleased or not.

Over crepes suzette I asked about his yard in general, and how was the right-hand man Jason in particular.

Calder shrugged. "He's left. They come and go, you know."

"And you don't fear that he'd take your knowledge with him?"

He looked amused. "He didn't know much. I'd hand Jason an herb pill and tell him which horse to give it to."

We finished amiably enough with coffee and brandy, and sat for a final few minutes in mutual appraisal: two people utterly different but bonded by one tenth of a second on a pavement in Ascot. I smiled at him slowly and got a smile in return, but all surface, no depth, a mirror exactly of my own feelings.

IN THE office, things were slowly changing. Alec seemed restless, as if his job no longer held him enthralled.

"It's all right for you," he said once. "You've the gift. I can't tell a gold mine from a pomegranate at five paces, and it's taken me all these years to know it."

"But you're a conjurer," I said. "You can rattle up outside money faster than anyone."

"Gift of the old gab, you mean. But I'll never make a director, let's face it, and I have this feeling that time's just slipping away."

I hoped he would stay: he was the yeast of the office. As for myself, I had grown accustomed to being on the board, and Gordon now treated me unreservedly as an equal. His hair had grown a little grayer. His right hand now trembled also, and his handwriting had grown smaller through his efforts to control his fingers. In the brain department he remained energetic, but physically he was slowing down.

I had seen Judith only once since Christmas, in the office at a retirement party given for the head of Corporate Finance.

"How are you?" she said amid the throng, holding a glass of wine and smelling of violets.

"Fine. And you?"

"Fine."

She was wearing blue, with diamonds in her ears. I looked at her with absolute and unhappy love. "I was thinking," I said. "When it's warmer, could I take you and Gordon, and Pen if she'd like it, out somewhere one Sunday?"

She took longer than normal politeness to answer, and I understood all the unspoken things, but finally she said, "Yes. We'd all like it. I'd like it very much."

Henry approached then and said, "Tim, you go and leave me to talk to this gorgeous girl." He put his arm around her shoulders and swept her off, and we had no more moments alone.

From day to day when she wasn't around I didn't precisely suffer: her absence caused more of a faint background ache. And when I saw Gordon daily in the office I felt no constant envy. I

197

the good, clever man he was. Loving Judith was
and pain, delight and deprivation.
the office I said to Gordon, "Did Judith mention
take you both somewhere—and Pen Warner—as a
Christmas?"

"Yes, I believe she did."

"Easter Monday, perhaps?"

He liked the idea and reported the next day that Judith had
asked Pen, and everyone was pleased.

I CONSEQUENTLY collected Gordon and Judith and Pen at eight
thirty on Easter bank holiday morning. I was taking them to
Calder's yard, to the utter fascination of Pen. "But don't tell him
I'm a pharmacist," she said. "He might clam up if he knew he
had an informed audience."

Calder greeted us expansively and gave us coffee in the huge
oak-beamed sitting room, where the memory of Ian Pargetter
hovered peripherally by the fireplace. "Delighted to see you
again," Calder said to me, peering at the others as if trying to
conjure a memory to fit their faces. He knew, of course, who
they were by name, but Ascot was ten months since. "Ah yes,"
he said to Judith with relief. "Yellow hat with roses."

She laughed. "Well done."

We set off on the grand tour. The patients in the boxes were all
different, but their ailments seemed the same as on my first visit.
"This one came here five weeks ago with severe muscular
weakness and no appetite. He goes home tomorrow, strong and
thriving." Calder patted the glossy brown neck. "His owner
thought he was dying. It's really satisfying to be able to help."

Gordon said civilly that it must be.

Calder moved us along. "This mare came two or three days
ago in great discomfort with blood in her urine. She's responding well, I'm glad to say."

"What was causing the bleeding?" Pen asked.

Calder shook his head. "I don't know. Her vet diagnosed
crystalluria, which means crystals in the urine. He didn't know
what was causing it, but every antibiotic he gave failed to work."

"And you're treating her with herbs?" Gordon asked.

"With everything I can think of. And, of course, with hands."

"I don't suppose you'd ever let anyone watch?" Judith said.

"My dear lady, for you, anything. But you'd see nothing. And it would be terribly boring. I might even be *unable* if someone was standing there waiting." Judith smiled understandingly and the tour continued, ending as before in the surgery.

Pen stood looking about sociably and then wandered over to the glass-fronted cabinets to peer inside.

Calder pulled out his pillmaker and demonstrated it.

"It's beautiful," Judith said. "Do you use it much?"

"All the time. Any herbalist worth the name makes his own pills and potions."

"Tim said you had a universal magic potion in the fridge."

Calder obligingly opened the refrigerator door, revealing the brown-filled plastic containers, as before.

Pen bent down to pick up a pink pill lying on the floor and put it without comment on the bench.

"It's so kind of you to show us everything," Judith said. "I'll watch your television appearances with more fervor than ever."

Calder responded to her warmly, as all men did, and asked us into the house again for a drink before we left. Gordon, however, was showing signs of fatigue, so we thanked Calder enthusiastically and climbed into the car.

"Come back any time you like, Tim," he said. He waved, and I waved back as I drove away.

"Isn't he amazing?" Judith said. "I must say, Tim, I do understand why you're impressed."

Gordon grunted and said yes, Calder was impressive. It was Pen who expressed some reservations.

"I'm not saying he doesn't do a great deal of good for the horses. But I don't honestly think he does it all with herbs."

"How do you mean?" Judith asked.

"I found a pill on the floor, and it was no herb, it was plain straightforward warfarin."

"That may be plain to you," Judith said. "But not to me."

Pen smiled. "Warfarin is an anticoagulant. Makes the blood less likely to clot and block up the veins and arteries."

Gordon said, "How can you tell it was warfarin?"

"I handle it every day. I know the dosages, the sizes, the colors, the manufacturers' marks."

"Do you mean," I said interestedly, "that if you saw fifty different pills laid out in a row, you could identify the lot?"

"Probably. If they all came from major drug companies." She thought a moment. "Something else in those cupboards wasn't strictly herbal. He had some bags of potassium sulfate."

"Isn't potassium sulfate a fertilizer?" Judith asked.

"Yes, but potassium's just as essential to animals as to plants," Pen said. "It may well be an ingredient in that secret brew."

The place I'd chosen to have lunch proved disappointing, but the mood of my guests forgave all.

"You remember," Gordon said thoughtfully over coffee, "that you told us on the way to Newmarket that Calder was worried about his business when that vet was killed?"

"Yes," I said. "He was, at the time."

"Isn't it possible," Gordon said, "that the vet was letting Calder have regular official medicines, like warfarin, and Calder thought his supplies would dry up when the vet died?"

We all thought about that, and Pen nodded. "He must have found another willing source."

"But," I protested, "would vets really do that?"

"They're not brilliantly paid. Nothing to stop one from passing on a few pills to Calder in return for a fat untaxed fee."

The supposition seemed to deflate the pleasure of the morning slightly, but the afternoon's visit to Oliver Knowles's stud farm saved the day. We found the whole place flooded with foals and mares and activity.

"How *beautiful*," Judith said, looking away over the white-railed paddocks with their colonies of mothers and babies.

Oliver Knowles was as welcoming as Calder, and told Gordon that he would never be out of his debt of gratitude to the bank, however soon he paid off his loan.

The anxiety I had seen in him on my February visit had disappeared. Oliver was again the capable and decisive executive I had first met. The foals had done well, I gathered; not one from the mares coming to Sandcastle had been lost. And Sandcastle had proved potent and fertile, Oliver told me, and was a dream of a stallion.

"I'm so glad," I said, and meant it from the bottom of my banking heart.

With his dog, Squibs, at his heels, Oliver showed us through the yards, where the mucking out and feeding was in full swing. "A stud farm is not like a racing stable," he explained. "One lad here can look after far more than three horses, because they don't have to be ridden. So a lad does a particular section of boxes, regardless of which animals are in them."

In the foaling yard we came across Nigel and Ginnie. She ran across to me when she saw me and gave me a great hug. She tucked her arm into mine and said, "Come and look at the newest foal. It was born only twenty minutes ago." After introductions everyone went to look at the foal over the half door: a glistening little creature, all long nose, huge eyes and folded legs, already making an effort to stand up. The dam, on her feet, alternately bent her head to the foal and looked up at us warily.

"This mare will now come to Sandcastle," Oliver said.

"And will that foal win the Derby?" Gordon asked, smiling.

Oliver smiled in return. "You never know. He'll have the breeding." He breathed deeply, expanding his chest. "I've never been able to say anything like that before this year. No foal born or conceived here has in the past won a classic. But now . . ." He gestured widely with his arm. "It's a whole new world."

We left the foal and Oliver then led us on to the heart of the place, to the stallions.

We all gazed with proper awe at the head of Sandcastle, which swam into view from the shadows of his box. He held himself almost imperiously, as if his new role had basically changed his character; and perhaps it had. There was a quality of arrogance now, a certainty of his own supremacy.

"He's splendid!" Gordon exclaimed.

Oliver gave Sandcastle the usual two carrots and a pat, and we went on to where Lenny was mucking out Diarist next door. "We have two lads looking after the stallions full time," Oliver said. "Lenny, here, and another much trusted man, Don. And Nigel feeds them."

"Do you need much security?" Pen asked.

"Some," he said, nodding. "We've had the yard wired for sound, so either Nigel or I, when we're in our houses, can hear if there are any irregular noises."

We began after a while to walk back to the house, and later, fortified by tea, scones and whiskey, we set off slowly back to Clapham. When we reached the tall gates by the common I went in with them for supper, as already arranged, but everyone was tired from the long day and I didn't stay late. Judith came out to the car to see me off.

We didn't really talk. I held her in my arms, her head on my shoulder, my head on hers, close in the dark night. "A great day," she said, and I said, "Mm," and kissed her very briefly.

I got into the car and drove away.

October

SUMMER had come, summer had gone, sodden, cold and unloved. Only with the autumn, far too late, had days of sunshine returned, and it was on a bright golden Saturday that I took the train to Newbury to see the races.

Ursula Young was there, standing near the weighing room, when I walked in from the station. "Hello," she said. "Haven't seen you for ages. How's the moneylending?"

"Profitable," I said.

She laughed. "I'm supposed to meet a client. Time for a quick sandwich, though. Are you on?"

I was on, and bought her and myself a thin slice of tasteless white meat between two thick, tasteless slices of soggy bread. We chewed in joyless accord.

"How's trade with you?" I said.

"Fair. The cream of the yearlings are going for huge prices because they've cost so much to produce—stallion fees and keeping the mare and foal to start with, vets' fees and all the rest. On the whole, my sort of clients settle for second, third or fourth rank, and many a good horse, mind you, has come from the bargain counter."

I smiled at the automatic sales pitch. "Talking of vets," I said. "Is the Pargetter murder still unsolved?"

She nodded regretfully. "I was talking to his wife in Newmarket last week. We met in the street. She said she asked the police recently if they were still even trying, and they assured her they were, but she doesn't believe it. It's been so long, almost nine months. She's very depressed, it's dreadful."

"Have a whiskey," I suggested. "Cheer you up."

Over the drink she told me about the client she was meeting, a small-time trainer of steeplechasers. "He's such a fool," she said. "He makes hasty decisions, acts on impulse, and then when things go wrong he feels cheated and gets angry."

When we went outside, the trainer spotted Ursula from a short distance away and pounced on her. He was a short, wiry, intense man of about forty with a porkpie hat above a weather-beaten face. "There you are," he said. "I've been looking all over. I wanted you to see him before he's saddled."

Ursula gave me an apologetic look and departed for the pre-parade ring, where the horses for the first race were being led around by their lads before going off to the saddling boxes. I didn't follow, but climbed onto the steps of the main parade ring. The last of the field to appear was accompanied by the porkpie hat and Ursula, and I looked up the horse in the race card. Zoomalong, five-year-old gelding, trained by F. Barnet.

I didn't see Ursula or F. Barnet during the race, but Zoomalong zoomed along quite nicely to finish third, and I walked down from the stands toward the unsaddling enclosure.

Several people were there, including F. Barnet, who was still talking to Ursula about his now sweating charge. Ursula nodded, her eyes raking the gelding from stem to stern.

"This is Fred Barnet," she said when I came up. "And his wife, Susan." A motherly person in blue. "And their son, Ricky." A tall, dark-haired boy, pleasant-faced.

I had shaken hands with the older Barnets and was just taking the son's hand when Ursula said my name in her clear voice.

The boy's hand jumped in mine as if my flesh had burned him. I was astonished, and then I looked more closely at the suddenly frightened dark eyes, at the stiffening of the body; I wouldn't have known him if he hadn't reacted in that way.

"What's the matter, Ricky?" his mother said.

"Nothing," he said hoarsely, and looked around for escape. I knew exactly who he was now.

"What do you think, then, Ursula?" Fred Barnet demanded, returning to the business in hand. "Will you buy him?"

Ursula said she would have to consult her client.

"But he was third," Barnet insisted. "A good third. . . ."

To the son, under cover of his father's hard sell, I quietly said, "I want to talk to you. If you run away, I'll telephone the police."

He gave me a sick look and stood still.

"We'll walk down the course together to watch the next race," I said. "We won't be interrupted there."

It was easy enough for him to drop back unnoticed from his parents, who were still concentrating on Ursula, and he came with me through the gate. We walked down toward the last fence, and he told me why he'd tried to kill Calder Jackson.

"It doesn't seem real now," he said explosively. "I never thought I'd see you again. The papers said you worked in a bank."

"So I do. And I go racing. Go on," I said.

He made a convulsive gesture of despair. "All right. But if I tell you, you won't tell *them*, will you, not Mum and Dad?"

From his troubled face it was clear that it wasn't my telling the police he minded but my telling his parents.

"Just get on with it," I said.

"Well, we had this horse. Dad had bought it as a yearling, and it turned out to be good. Indian Silk it was called."

"Indian Silk . . . didn't that win at Cheltenham this year?"

He nodded. "The Gold Cup. The very top." The voice was bitter with a sort of stifled anger.

"Doesn't he still belong to your father?"

"No. He doesn't." More bitterness, very sharp. "Two years ago this month, when Indian Silk was five, like, he won the Hermitage chase very easily here at Newbury, and everyone was tipping him for the Gold Cup *last* year, though Dad was saying he was still on the young side and to give him time. See, Dad was that proud of that horse. The best he'd ever trained, and his own, not someone else's.

"Well, then Indian Silk got sick. Nothing you could put your finger on, he just lost his speed. He couldn't gallop properly, couldn't even beat the other horses in Dad's yard that he'd been running rings round all year. And the vet couldn't find out what was wrong with him."

We reached the last fence and stood there on the rough grass beside the course. "I was studying for exams at school," Ricky said, "and I had a lot of homework and didn't take much notice of Indian Silk. I suppose I thought the horse just had the virus and would get better. But he got slowly worse, and one day Mum was crying." He stopped suddenly and then went on. "You'll think it funny, but that upset me something awful."

"I don't think it funny," I said.

"Well, it got so that Indian Silk was so weak he could barely walk down the road and Dad was in real despair, and then some guy telephoned and offered to buy him."

"To buy a sick horse?" I said, surprised.

"Well, the man said he knew Indian Silk couldn't race anymore, but he'd like to give him a good home in a nice field for as long as necessary. It meant that Dad wouldn't have the expense of any more vets' bills, and Mum wouldn't have to think of him going to the knackers for dogmeat. So they let him go."

The horses for the second race came out onto the course and galloped down past us, the jockeys' colors bright in the sun.

"Then what?" I said.

"Nothing happened for weeks, and we were getting over it when someone told Dad that Indian Silk was back in training and looking fine. He couldn't believe it."

"When was that?" I asked.

"Last year, just before . . . before Ascot. My exams were actually coming up then," he said. "And I mean, they were important, they were going to affect my whole life, see?"

I nodded.

"Then Dad found out that the man who'd bought Indian Silk hadn't put him in any field; he'd sent him to Calder Jackson."

"Ah," I said.

"And there was this man saying Calder Jackson had the gift of healing and had simply touched Indian Silk and made him well. I ask you. So then Dad was in a frightful state, because Mum had once suggested he should send the horse to Calder Jackson while he was so bad, and Dad had said don't be so ridiculous, it was all a lot of rubbish. And now he and Mum were having rows, and she was crying again."

He gulped for air, the story now pouring out almost faster than he could speak. "And I wasn't getting any work done with it all going on. I took the first exam and just sat there and couldn't do it, and I knew I'd failed. . . . Then there was Calder Jackson one evening talking on television, saying he'd got a friend of his to buy a dying horse, because the people who owned it would just have let it die because they didn't believe in healers, and I knew he was talking about Indian Silk. He said he was going to Ascot that Thursday. . . . And there was Dad screaming that Calder Jackson had stolen the horse away, it was all a filthy swindle, and it all got so that I hated Calder Jackson so much that I couldn't think straight, and I just wanted to *kill* him."

The bedrock words were out, and the flood suddenly stopped, leaving their echo on the October air.

"And did you fail your exams?" I asked after a moment.

"Yeah. Most of them. But I took them again at Christmas and got good passes." He shook his head. "I was glad, even that night right after Ascot, that you'd stopped me stabbing him. I mean, I'd've thrown my whole life away. And all for nothing, because Dad wasn't going to get the horse back whatever I did."

The horses set off on their steeplechase and came down the course like a multicolored wave. As they neared us the ground trembled from the thud of the hoofs, the air rang with the curses of jockeys, and the effort and the speed filled eyes and ears and mind. Then they were gone, leaving silence.

"Who is it who owns Indian Silk?" I asked.

"A Mr. Chacksworth, comes from Birmingham," Ricky answered. "But it wasn't him that bought him from Dad. He bought him later, when he was all right again."

"Who bought the horse from your father?" I said.

"I never met him. His name was Smith. A funny first name."

"Could it have been *Dissdale* Smith?" I asked, surprised.

"Yeah. That sounds like it. He was a dead liar, you know, all that talk about nice fields."

"Who tells the truth," I said, "when buying or selling horses?"

"Are you going to tell Mum and Dad about me?"

"Perhaps they should know," I said.

"No!" His agitation rose quickly. "They've had so much trouble, and I would have made it so much worse if you hadn't stopped me. The only good thing was, I did learn that you can't put things right by killing people."

After a long pause I said, "All right. I won't tell them." Heaven help me, I thought, if he ever attacks anyone again.

To MY great delight the cartoonist came up trumps, his twenty animated films being shown on television every weeknight for a month. The nation sat up and giggled, and the cartoonist telephoned breathlessly to ask for a bigger loan.

"Do you *realize*," he said, "that they'll take as many films as I can make? No limit. They said to just go on making them for years and years."

"I'm very glad," I said sincerely.

"You gave me faith in myself," he said. "I'd been turned down so often I was getting depressed, but when you lent me the money it was like being uncorked. The ideas just rushed out."

"It's terrific," I said.

"It sure is. Brother, life's amazing." He put down his receiver and left me smiling into space.

"The cartoonist?" Gordon said.

I nodded. "Going up like a rocket."

"Congratulations." There was warmth and genuine pleasure in his voice. Such a generous man, I thought; so impossible to do him harm.

These days his illness seemed no worse. In the office one day he said, "How about coming over to lunch on Sunday? Judith was saying it's ages since she saw you."

"I'd love to."

"Pen's coming, Judith said."

"Great," I said positively. "Lovely."

Gordon nodded contentedly and said it was a shame we couldn't have a repeat of last Christmas, but he and Judith were going this year to visit relatives in Edinburgh, a visit long promised. So I would be dutiful, I thought, and spend Christmas with my mother in Jersey. And I would sadden her as usual by bringing no girl friend.

"*Why*, my love," she'd said to me once, "do you take out these perfectly presentable girls and never marry them?"

"There's always something about them I don't want to spend my life with."

"You're too choosy."

"I expect so," I'd said, smiling, and told her that one day I'd find the perfect girl to love forever. It hadn't occurred to me even fleetingly that when I found her she would be married to someone else.

SUNDAY came, I went to Clapham, and over lunch I said I'd seen the boy who had tried to kill Calder. They reacted as I'd expected, Gordon saying, "You've told the police, of course."

I shook my head and told them all about Ricky Barnet and Indian Silk and the pressure that led to the try at stabbing. "I don't think he'll do anything like that again."

"Fancy it being Dissdale who bought Indian Silk," Pen said. "Especially as he was saying he was short of cash."

"Mm," I said. "But after Calder had cured the horse, Dissdale sold it again and made a handsome profit, I gather."

"Ironic, the whole thing," Pen said, and we went on discussing it desultorily over coffee.

I stayed until six, then drove back to Hampstead in the usual post-Judith state, half fulfilled, half starved.

NOT long after that lunch I traveled again to Oliver Knowles's stud farm. Ginnie was home from school, and it was she who set off with me through the yards.

"Did you know we had a hundred and fifty-two mares here all at the same time, back in May?" she said.

"That's a lot," I said, impressed.

"They had a hundred and fourteen foals, and only one mare died. That's a terrific record."

"Your father's very skilled."

The whole atmosphere of the place was back to where I'd known it first, to the slow, chill months of gestation. Ginnie walked me to the stallion yard, where the curiosity of the residents brought their heads out when they heard our footsteps. Ginnie gave them carrots from her pocket, and Sandcastle graciously allowed her to stroke his nose.

I said, "What are you going to do when you leave school?"

She patted Sandcastle's neck. "Help Dad. I love the foals. Watching them grow. I never want to do anything else."

We left the stallions and walked between the paddocks with their foals and dams, along the path to the Watcherleys'. The neighboring place, whose ramshackle state I'd only glimpsed on my pursuit of the runaway, was now almost as neat as Oliver's spread, with much fresh paint in evidence.

"The Watcherleys are pretty lucky," Ginnie said. "Dad can't bear mess, so he's doing up their place *and* employing them to look after the animals in this yard. Maggie was telling me just last week that she would be everlastingly thankful that Calder Jackson stole their business."

"He hardly stole it," I said mildly.

"Well, did better at it, if you want to be pedantic."

We went into a few boxes, where Ginnie handed out the last of the carrots and fondled both mares and foals. She looked at peace and where she belonged, all growing pains suspended.

The Third Year
April

I was at my desk, reading a letter from a tomato grower asking for more time to repay his loan, when my telephone rang. I slowly picked up the receiver.

"Oliver Knowles," the voice said. "Is that you, Tim?"

"Hello," I replied warmly. "Everything going well?"

"No." The word was sickeningly abrupt.

"What's the matter?"

"Can you come down here today?" he asked, not directly answering. "Or tomorrow?"

"Tomorrow afternoon, if you like. If it's bank business."

"Yes, it is." The anxiety in his voice was plain.

"What's the trouble?" I asked. "Is Sandcastle all right?"

"I'll tell you when you come," he said.

He wouldn't say any more and left me with the dead receiver in my hand and some horrid question marks in my mind.

When I reached the stud farm the next day Oliver came out to meet me, and there were new deep lines on his face.

"Come in," he said, clasping my hand. "I'm seriously worried. I don't know what to do."

He led the way through the house to the sitting room–office and gestured me to a chair. "Read this," he said, and gave me a letter dated April 21.

Dear Oliver,
    I'm sorry to tell you that the Sandcastle foal out of my mare Spiral Binding has been born with a half of one ear missing. It's a filly, by the way, and I daresay it won't affect her speed, but her looks are ruined.
    So sad.

Yours,
Jane

"Is that very bad?" I asked, frowning.
He wordlessly handed me another letter. It said in part:

    My mare Girandette gave birth to a nice colt foal, but unfortunately he died at six days. A postmortem revealed that he had malformed heart valves. . . .

"And now this," Oliver said, and handed me a third.
The heading was that of a highly regarded and well-known stud farm, the letter briefly impersonal.

Dear Sir,
    Filly foal born March 31st to Poppingcorn.
    Sire: Sandcastle.
    Deformed foot, near fore.
    Put down.

I gave him back the letters and with growing misgiving asked, "How common are these malformations?"
Oliver said intensely, "They happen occasionally. But those letters aren't all. I've had two telephone calls. Two other foals have died of holes in the heart. That's five with something wrong with them." He stared at me. "And what about the other thirty-five? Suppose there are more. . . ."
There was a long, fraught pause in which the enormity of the position sank coldly into my banking consciousness.
The telephone rang suddenly, making us both jump.
"You answer it," he said. "Please."
I opened my mouth to protest, but then picked up the receiver.
"Is that Oliver Knowles?" a voice said.
"No. I'm his assistant."

"Oh. Then please give him a message. Tell him Patrick O'Marr rang him from Limballow, Ireland, about a foal born here three weeks ago. I thought I'd better tell Mr. Knowles we've had to put it down. Are you listening?"

"Yes," I said, feeling hollow.

"The poor little fellow was born with a sort of curled-in hoof. We had it x-rayed, and the lower pastern bone and the coffin bone were fused and tiny. The vet said there was no chance of them developing properly, and the little colt would never be able to walk, let alone race. A beautiful little fella, too, in all other ways."

"I'm very sorry," I said. "And thank you for letting us know."

I put the receiver down slowly, and Oliver said dully, "Another one? Not another one."

I nodded and told him what Patrick O'Marr had said.

"That's six," Oliver said starkly. "What am I going to do?"

"Get out Sandcastle's insurance policy."

He looked blank. "No, I mean about the mares. We have all the mares here who've come this year to Sandcastle, and nearly all of them have already been covered. I mean, there's another crop already growing, and suppose all of those . . ."

"The first thing," I said again, "is to look at that policy."

He went to a file and pulled out the needed document, a many-paged affair, which I read carefully from start to finish.

There were many definitions of the word accident, with stipulations about the number of veterinary surgeons who had to be consulted before Sandcastle could be humanely destroyed, for any reason whatsoever. There were stipulations about fractures, and about muscle, nerve and tendon troubles that would not be considered grounds for destruction.

Aside from these restrictions, the horse was insured against death from any natural causes whatsoever, against accidental death occurring while the horse was free (gross negligence being a disqualifying condition), against death by fire should the stable be consumed, and against death caused maliciously by human hand. He was insured against malicious or accidental castration, against infertility or impotence. In fact he was insured against every foreseeable disaster except one. He was not insured against being put out of business because of congenital abnormalities among his progeny.

211

I looked up at Oliver and my expression deepened his despair.

"I'm not insured, am I," he said.

"I don't know."

"I think you do." He was shaking. "When the policy was drawn up, six people, including myself and two vets besides the insurers themselves, tried to think of every possible contingency. And now the one thing that has happened is something we never imagined—a whole crop of deformed foals."

My skin felt clammy. Three million pounds of the bank's money and two million subscribed by private people were tied up in the horse. But the disaster that would mean just a painful financial setback for the lenders would mean total ruin for Oliver Knowles. If Sandcastle couldn't generate income, Oliver would lose his farm, his horses, everything he possessed.

I shook myself and said, "The first thing to do is nothing. Wait to hear if any more of the foals are . . . wrong. And I will consult with the other directors at Ekaterin's and see what can be done in the way of providing more time for your repayments while we look into other possibilities."

He looked bewildered. "What possibilities?"

"Well, of having Sandcastle tested. If the original tests of his fertility weren't thorough enough, for instance, it might be possible to show that his sperm had always been defective in some way, and then the insurance policy would protect you."

"And the mares?" Oliver said.

I shook my head. "In fairness to their owners you'll have to say that Sandcastle's off-color."

"And repay their fees," he said gloomily. "He covered two today. I haven't mentioned any of this to Nigel. I couldn't."

"So how many does that leave, er, uncovered?"

He consulted a list, fumbling slightly. "One that hasn't foaled yet, and four others."

Thirty-five more mares, I thought numbly, could be carrying that seed.

"The mare that hasn't yet foaled," Oliver said flatly, "was bred to Sandcastle last year."

I stared. "You mean one of his foals will be born *here?*"

"Yes." He rubbed his hand over his face. "Any day."

There were footsteps outside the door and Ginnie came in.

Her face lit up when she saw me. "Hello! How lovely. I didn't know you were coming."

I stood up to give her a customarily enthusiastic greeting, but she sensed something was wrong. "What's the matter?" She looked into my eyes and then at her father. "What's happened?"

"Nothing," he said.

"Dad, you're lying." She turned again to me. "Tell me. I can see something bad has happened. I'm not a child anymore."

"I thought you'd be at school," I said.

"I left at the end of last term. There was no point going back when all I'm interested in is here."

She looked far more assured, as if the school days had been a chrysallis and she were now the imago, flying free. "What is it?" she said. "What's happened?"

Oliver made a gesture of despair. "You'll have to know." He swallowed. "Some of Sandcastle's foals aren't perfect."

He showed her the letters and she went slowly pale. "Oh Dad, no. No. It can't be. Not Sandcastle."

She buried her face against my chest. I put my arms around her and kissed her hair and comforted her as best I could.

I WENT to the office on the following morning, Friday, and told Gordon the outcome of my visit to Oliver. He said, "Oh no," several times, and his hands trembled unnoticed on his desk in his overriding concern. "The first thing is to tell Val and Henry," he said finally. "Though what any of us can do is a puzzle."

Henry and Val were dismayed and told the other directors at lunch. The man who had been against the project from the beginning gave me a furious dressing down over the grilled sole. "Anyone could foresee," he said caustically, "that such a scatter-brained scheme would blow up in our faces. It's only because of your stupidity that the bank is facing this loss."

There were a few uncomfortable murmurs around the table, but Henry said with unruffled geniality, "We are all to blame, if blame there is, and it's unfair to call Tim stupid for not foreseeing something that escaped the imaginations of all the experts who drew up the insurance policy."

When everyone had rather silently stood up to drift back to work Henry asked me, "What will you do next?"

"I'm going down to the farm for the weekend," I said, "to go through the financial situation. Add up the figures."

"Let us know the full state of affairs on Monday," Henry said.

THE following day was miserable. Oliver and Ginnie walked about like automatons, and lunch, Ginnie's version, consisted of eggs boiled too hard and potato chips.

Toward four o'clock they both went out into the yards for evening stables, and I began adding the columns of figures I'd drawn up from Oliver's records. When I'd finished, the tally was appalling. It meant that Oliver could be bankrupt, in debt for the rest of his life. I wondered how I would ever tell them. In fact I didn't tell Ginnie, only Oliver, who sat with his head in his hands, despair in every line of his body.

"It's hopeless," he said.

"Not yet," I said encouragingly. "There are still the tests to be done on Sandcastle."

"It's such a long shot." He sighed. "But I'll do it. I'll ask the Equine Research Establishment at Newmarket to look at him."

I said tentatively, "I suppose it couldn't be anything as simple as something he'd *eaten?* Last year, of course."

He shook his head. "I thought of that. All the other stallions had the same food, and none of the others' foals are affected. Nigel feeds the stallions himself and we're always careful."

"Paint—something like that? Something new in the boxes, when you put in all the security? Something he could chew?"

He again shook his head. "I've been over it and over it. There's nothing in Sandcastle's box that wasn't in the others."

"Could an allergy have such an effect?"

"I've never heard of anything like that. I'll ask the research people, though. I'll ring them on Monday."

He got up to pour us both a drink. "It's good to have you here," he said. "A sort of net over the bottomless pit."

We had our supper, left in the refrigerator by Oliver's part-time housekeeper, and Ginnie went straight to bed, saying she would be up at two and out with Nigel in the foaling yard.

"She goes most nights," Oliver said. "She and Nigel make a good team. He says she's a great help."

We ourselves went to bed fairly early, and I awoke in the large high-ceilinged guest room while it was still dark. I got out of bed and went to the window, which looked out over the yards. There was no visible activity, and my watch showed four thirty. I wondered if Ginnie would mind if I joined her in the foaling yard, and got dressed and went.

They were all there, Nigel and Oliver as well as Ginnie, all in one open-doored box, where a mare lay on her side on the straw. Oliver turned as I approached.

"This is Plus Factor," he said. "In foal to Sandcastle."

His voice was calm and so was Ginnie's manner, and I guessed he still hadn't told Nigel about the deformities. There was hope, too, in their faces, as if they were sure that this one, after all, would be perfect.

"Here we go," Nigel said quietly.

The mare gave a grunt and her swelling sides heaved. A half-transparent membrane with a hoof showing within it appeared, followed very rapidly by the long, slim head and the whole foal, flopping out onto the straw, the membrane breaking open, new life beginning with the first fluttering gasp of the lungs.

"Is he all right?" Oliver said, bending down, the anxiety raw.

"Sure," Nigel said. "Just his foreleg's doubled over. . . ."

He knelt beside the foal and stretched out both hands gently to straighten the bent leg. He picked it up . . . and froze.

The leg wasn't bent. It ended in a stump at the knee.

Ginnie gave a choking sob and turned abruptly toward the open door. She took one rocky step and then another, and then was running, running from the unimaginable, running from the hopeless little creature on the straw.

I went after her. I found her in one of the paths not far off, sobbing beside a post. "Ginnie," I said.

She turned and clung to me fiercely, her body shaking from the sobs, my arms tightly around her. We stood like that until finally she could speak.

"It's one thing knowing it in theory," she said. "But *seeing* it. That's different."

"Yes," I said.

"And it means"—she took gulps of air, trying for control—"it means, doesn't it, that we'll lose our farm?"

"I don't know yet. If there's a way to save it, we'll find it."

She wiped her eyes on her handkerchief, and we went slowly back to the foaling yard. Nobody was there. I looked inside Plus Factor's box, looked at the mare standing there without the foal and wondered if she felt any sense of loss.

"Dad and Nigel have taken him, haven't they?" Ginnie said.

"Yes."

She nodded, accepting that. Death to her was part of life, as to every child brought up close to animals. We went back to the house while the sky lightened in the east to the new day.

SUNDAY. The work of the place went on. Oliver telephoned to various owners of the mares who had come to the other three stallions, reporting the birth of foals alive and well. He sounded strong, competent. One could almost see the steel creeping back, hour by hour, into his battered spirit.

Ginnie—showered, breakfasted—went off to the Watcherleys' and came back smiling; the resilience of youth. "Both of the mares we've got there are better from their infections," she reported, "and Maggie says she's heard Calder Jackson's not doing so well; his yard's half empty. Cheers Maggie up no end." After lunch she slept on the sofa, looking childlike and peaceful, and only when she awoke did the night's pain roll back.

"Oh dear." The slow tears came. "I was dreaming it was all right. That the foal was a dream, only a dream."

I went with her out into the yards, where the evening muck carrying and feeding were going on. Ginnie visited the mares, talking cheerfully to the lads while they bent to their chores.

"Hi, Danny. How's her hoof today?"

"Hello, Shane. Looks as if she'll foal any day now."

"Evening, Sammy. Is she eating now okay?"

The lads answered her straightforwardly and with respect. I looked back as we left the first big yard for the second, and for a moment took one of the lads to be Ricky Barnet.

"Who's that?" I said to Ginnie.

She followed my gaze to where the lad walked across to the yard tap, swinging an empty bucket and eating an apple.

"Shane. Why?"

"He reminded me of someone I knew."

"He's all right. They all are, when Nigel's looking."

We went on to the foaling yard, where a lad greeted as Dave was installing a heavy, slow-walking mare in one of the boxes.

"Nigel says she'll foal tonight," he told Ginnie.

"He's usually right."

We went on to the stallions, where Lenny and Don were washing down Diarist in the center of the yard.

"Mind his feet," Lenny said. "He's in one of his moods."

We came finally to Sandcastle, and Ginnie gave him a carrot. Her lips were compressed. "He can't help it, I suppose," she said, sighing. "But I do wish he'd never won any races."

We went back to the house, and soon Oliver was announcing briskly that it was time for whiskey, time for supper; time for anything perhaps but thinking.

Ginnie decided after supper that she felt too restless to go to bed early and would go for a walk instead.

"Do you want me to come?" I asked.

"No. I'm all right. I just thought I'd go out. Look at the stars." She kissed her father's forehead, and pulled on a cardigan. "You'll probably find me in the foaling yard if you want me."

He nodded to her fondly but absentmindedly, and with a small wave to me she went away. Oliver asked me how soon I thought the bank would decide on his fate, and we talked for an hour about his daunting prospects.

Shortly before ten there came a hammering on the back door.

"Whoever's that?" Oliver frowned and went to find out.

I didn't hear the opening words, but only the goose-pimpling urgency in the rising voice.

"She's where?" Oliver said loudly, in alarm. "Where?"

I went quickly into the hallway. One of the lads stood in the open doorway, panting for breath, wide-eyed and scared.

Oliver glanced at me over his shoulder, already on the move. "Sammy says Ginnie's lying on the ground unconscious."

The lad turned and ran off, with Oliver following and me close behind. And the lad's breathlessness, I soon found, was owing to Ginnie's being on the far side of the farm, down beyond Nigel's bungalow, near the gate to the lower road.

We arrived there still running, and found Ginnie lying on her side on the asphalt surface, with another of the lads on his knees beside her, dim figures in weak moonlight.

"What happened, what happened?" Oliver was saying.

"Sammy and I found her," the kneeling lad, Dave, said. "We were on our way back from the pub. She's coming round, sir."

Ginnie in fact moved slightly and said, "Dad."

"Yes, Ginnie, I'm here." He picked up her hand and patted it. "We'll soon get you right."

"Dad," Ginnie said, mumbling. "Dad."

"Yes, I'm here."

"Dad."

"She isn't hearing you," I said worriedly.

He turned to me. "Get an ambulance. Telephone from Nigel's house."

I stood up to go, but the breathless lad said, "Nigel's out. I tried there. There's no one. It's all locked."

"I'll go back to the house."

I ran as fast on the way back and had to fight to control my breath to make my words intelligible on the telephone. Then I fetched the quilt off my bed and ran back and found everything much as I'd left it. "How is she?" I said.

Oliver tucked the quilt around his daughter as best he could. "She keeps saying things. Just sounds, not words."

"Da . . ." Ginnie said. Her eyelids trembled, slightly open.

"Ginnie," Oliver said urgently. "This is Dad."

Her lips moved in a mumbling, unformed murmur. The eyes looked at nothing, unfocused.

"Oh God," Oliver said. "What's happened to her?"

The ambulance came, lights flashing, with two brisk men in uniform, who lifted Ginnie onto a stretcher. Oliver fetched the Land-Rover and we set off. The journey seemed endless, but we finally arrived at a huge hospital. Oliver parked and we went into the brightly lit emergency area, where we saw Ginnie being wheeled into a curtained cubicle.

A nurse told us to sit on some nearby chairs while she fetched a doctor. The place was empty, quiet, all readiness but no bustle.

A doctor came in a white coat—young, black-haired, wearily rubbing his eyes with forefinger and thumb. He went into the cubicle with the nurse, and for about a minute Oliver clasped and unclasped his fingers. Then the doctor's voice reached us clearly from behind the curtains. "She's dead."

Oliver was on his feet, bounding across the floor, pulling back the curtains with a frantic sweep of the arm.

"She's not dead. She was talking. Moving. She's not dead."

In dread I followed him. She couldn't be dead, not like that, not so fast. She *couldn't* be.

The doctor straightened up from bending over her. "I am sorry," he said. "Very sorry. She is gone."

"No!" Oliver said in agony. "You're wrong!"

The young doctor said gently, "There is no pulse. No heartbeat. No contraction of the pupils. She has been gone for perhaps ten minutes. There is nothing to be done."

"But *why?*" Oliver said. "She was talking."

The doctor looked at Ginnie, lying on her back, eyes closed, brown hair falling about her head. "Her skull is fractured," he said. "If she was talking, she died on the way here. With head injuries it can be like that. I'm sorry."

Suddenly an ambulance's siren wailed outside. "Traffic accident," someone shouted, and the doctor said, "I must go."

The nurse handed me a flat white plastic bottle she was holding. "You may as well take this," she said. "It was tucked into the waistband of her skirt."

She started to cover Ginnie with a sheet, but Oliver stopped her. "I'll do it," he said. "I want to be with her."

The nurse nodded, and she and I left the cubicle.

I sat drearily on a chair, waiting for Oliver. The white plastic bottle had a label on it saying SHAMPOO. I put it into my jacket pocket and wondered if it was just through overwork that the doctor hadn't asked how Ginnie's skull had been fractured.

THE next day the police came, with a truly awful series of questions, forms and officialdom. It appeared that the area was being plagued by a stalker of young girls, who jumped out of bushes, knocked them unconscious and sexually assaulted them.

"Not Ginnie . . ." Oliver protested in deepening horror.

The most senior of the policemen, Detective Chief Inspector Wyfold, shook his head. "It would appear not. We can't discount, though, that it was the same man and that he was frightened off by your grooms. When young girls are knocked unconscious at night, it's most often a sexual attack."

219

"But she was on my own land," Oliver said, disbelieving.

The policeman shrugged. "She could have talked to someone over the gate. Someone walking along the road. We'll need detailed statements from all your grooms, though it seems they weren't in their quarters but down at the village, in the pubs."

Through the day he came and went, and reappeared again with more questions. Sometime in the morning one of the lads came to the house and asked what to do about a mare who was having difficulty foaling, and Lenny arrived wanting to know when to take Rotaboy to the breeding pen. They stood awkwardly, saying they were so shocked, so sorry about Ginnie.

"Where's Nigel?" Oliver said.

They hadn't seen him that morning, they said.

"Didn't you try his house?"

"He isn't there. The door's locked and he didn't answer."

Oliver frowned and said to me, "There's a key to his bungalow over there on the board. Would you go and look?"

"Sure," I said. I walked down there with Lenny. I rang the doorbell and banged on the knocker without result. I fitted the key in the lock, opened the door, went in.

Curtains were drawn across the windows. I switched on a light and walked into the sitting room, where papers, clothes and dirty cups were strewn haphazardly.

There was no sign of Nigel. I looked into the kitchen and the bathroom. The last door in the hall led into the bedroom . . . and there he was, face down, fully clothed, lying on the bed. Lenny, behind me, took two paces back.

I went to Nigel and felt his neck behind the ear. Felt the pulse going like a steam hammer. His breath would have anesthetized a crocodile, and on the floor beside him lay an empty gin bottle. "He's drunk," I said. "Just drunk."

We went back into the sitting room, where I used Nigel's telephone to call Oliver. "He's flat out. I can't wake him."

After a brief silence Oliver said dully, "Tell Lenny to take Rotaboy to the breeding shed. And Tim, would you mind helping me here in the office?"

"Coming straight back."

The disjointed, terrible day wore on. I telephoned Gordon at the bank and Judith also, to pass on the heartbreak, and I took

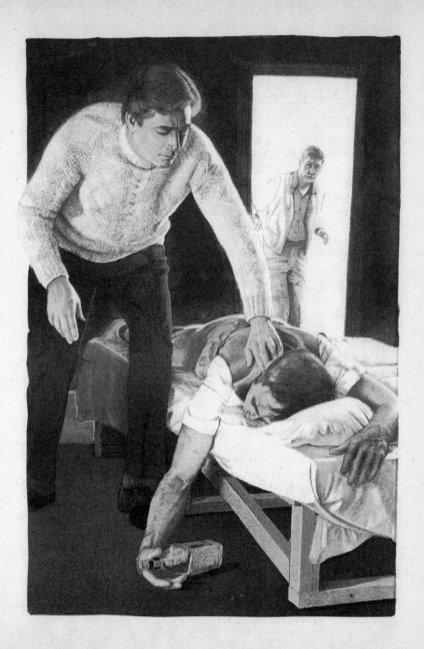

countless incoming messages as the news spread. At about two, Oliver and I ate some eggs, not tasting them, in the kitchen. He said finally, "I suppose I should have told Ginnie's mother last night." His face twisted. "My wife, in Canada . . ." He swallowed. "I'll call her now."

I left him alone to that wretched task and took myself upstairs to wash and shave. Taking my jacket off, I came across the plastic bottle in my pocket. An odd thing, I thought, for Ginnie to tuck into her waistband. The white label saying SHAMPOO had been handwritten and stuck on top of the bottle's original label, quite a bit of which still showed around the edges.

"Instructions," part of the underneath label said. "Shake well. Rub well into dog's coat and leave for ten or fifteen minutes before rinsing." At the bottom were the words, "Manufactured by Eagle, Inc., Michigan, U.S.A. List number 29931."

The bottle was full. I put it on the shelf and thought about it as I lay for a while on the bed. Shampoo for dogs.

I got up and went down to the kitchen, and in a high cupboard found an empty screw-top glass jar. I took it upstairs, and over the washbasin I shook the plastic bottle, then unscrewed the cap and carefully poured more than half the shampoo, a green liquid, into the jar. Then I stowed the jar in my bag, and when I went downstairs again, I took the plastic bottle with me.

"Ginnie had it?" Oliver said dully, squinting at it. "What for?"

"The nurse at the hospital said it was tucked into the waistband of her skirt."

A smile flickered. "She always did that when she was little. Books, bits of string, anything. To keep her hands free, she said. It all used to slip down into her little knickers, and there would be a whole shower of things when we undressed her." His face went hopelessly bleak at this memory. "I can't believe it, you know," he said. "I keep thinking she'll walk through the door." He paused. "My wife says she'll be here tomorrow morning."

Chief Inspector Wyfold turned up again at that point, and we gave him the shampoo bottle. He picked the bottle up by its cap and said to Oliver, "Do you have a dog?"

"Yes."

"Would this be what you usually use to wash him?"

"I really don't know. I don't wash him. The lads do."

Wyfold produced a paper bag from his pocket and put the bottle inside it. "Who has handled this, besides yourselves?"

"I suppose the nurse at the hospital . . . and Ginnie," I said.

"And it spent from last night until now in your pocket?" He shrugged. "Hopeless for prints, I should think, but we'll try."

He went away, and Oliver said he had better go out into the yards for his evening rounds. I went along, and when we reached the foaling yard, Nigel, resurrected, was there. His stocky figure leaned against the doorpost of an open box, as if without its support he would collapse, and the face he slowly turned toward us was unshaved.

"Sorry," he said. "Heard about Ginnie. Very sorry." I wasn't sure whether he was sympathizing with Oliver or apologizing for the drunkenness. "A policeman came asking if I'd killed her. As if I would." He put a shaky hand on his head. "I feel rotten. My own fault. Deserve it."

Oliver and I walked on to the stallions, and I asked if Nigel often got drunk. Oliver hadn't shown much surprise.

"Very seldom," Oliver said. "I don't like it, but he's so good with the mares that I overlook it."

He gave carrots to all four stallions but scarcely glanced at Sandcastle, as if he could no longer bear the sight.

"I'll try the research people tomorrow," he said. "Forgot about it today."

From the stallions he went past Nigel's bungalow toward the lower gate, to stand for a while at the place where Ginnie had been found the night before. In a drained voice he said, "Do you think she could have talked to someone out there?"

"She might have, I suppose."

"Yes." He turned to go. "It's all so *senseless*. And unreal."

Exhaustion finally overtook him after dinner and he went gray-faced to bed, but I went out again for restoration: for a look at the stars, as Ginnie had said. Thinking of Ginnie, I walked slowly along the path between the paddocks and stopped eventually at the place where I'd held her in racking distress the previous morning. The birth of the deformed foal seemed so long ago, yet it had been only yesterday—the morning of the last day of Ginnie's life.

I thought about that day. I thought of her tears and her courage, and of the waste of so much goodness. The engulfing, stupefying sense of loss that had hovered all day swamped my brain until it wanted to burst.

I had loved her more than I'd known, loved her as a brother. I'd thought of her young life once as being a clear stretch of sand waiting for footprints, and now there would be none.

"Oh *Ginnie*," I said aloud. "Little Ginnie . . . come back."

But my voice fled away in the darkness, and there was no answer.

May

FOR the next two weeks I worked on Oliver's financial chaos at my desk in the bank, and at a special board meeting I argued the case for giving him time before we foreclosed. I asked for three months and got him two, which was what I wanted.

I telephoned Oliver and told him. "For two months you don't have to make any interest or capital repayments, but this is only temporary. I'm afraid that if we can't find a solution to Sandcastle's problem, the prognosis is not good."

"I understand," he said, his voice sounding calm. "I haven't much hope, but thank you for the respite—I will at least be able to finish the programs for the other stallions, and keep all the foals here until they're old enough to travel."

The news of Sandcastle's disgrace, so far only a murmur here and there, broke with a screech, predictably, in *What's Going On Where It Shouldn't*:

> Build not your house on sand. Stake not your banking house on a Sandcastle. Three million pounds advanced by a certain prestigious merchant bank for the purchase of the stallion Sandcastle now look like being washed away by the tide. Sadly, the investment has produced faulty stock, or in plain language, several deformed foals. Speculation abounds as to what the bank can do to minimize its losses.

"It's a mess," Henry said gloomily at lunch, and even the dissenting director had run out of insults.

"Have they found out who killed Knowles's daughter?" Val Fisher asked me.

"No," I said, shaking my head.

"Such a sadness for him, on top of the other."

There were murmurs of sympathy, and I didn't think I'd spoil it by telling them what the police thought of Oliver's lads.

"Inspector Wyfold," Oliver had said on the telephone, "more or less told me I was asking for trouble, having a young girl on the place with all those lads. Some were drunk that night, so one of Wyfold's theories is that one of them jumped her and Dave and Sammy interrupted him. Alternatively, Nigel did it. Alternatively, some stranger walking down the road did it."

The police had found no weapon. The forensic surgeon said that there had been a single, very heavy blow to the base of the head. The apparent semiconsciousness had been illusory: parts of her brain would have functioned, but she would not have been aware of anything at all.

Oliver said his wife had gone back to Canada. Ginnie's death seemed not to have brought mother and father together, but to have made the separation complete.

"The dog shampoo?" Oliver repeated, when I asked. "Wyfold says that's just what it was, they checked it. He thinks Ginnie may have seen it lying in the road and picked it up, or that she got into conversation at the gate with a man who gave her the shampoo as a come-on and then killed her."

"I suppose it's possible," I said doubtfully.

"Wyfold says that particular shampoo isn't on sale in England, it's American. There's no way of tracing how it got here. And the fingerprints were no use; all a blur except a few of yours and mine."

THERE came a fine May day in the office when Alec opened a window to let in some fresh air. The fresh air duly entered and blew papers off our desks. We all left our chairs to retrieve our scattered work, and during my search for page three of a long proposal I received a severe shock in the shape of a pale blue sheet off a memo pad. There were words penciled on it and crossed out with a wavy line, with other words underneath.

"Build your castle not on sand" was crossed out, and underneath was written, "Build not your house on sand. Stake not your banking house on a Sandcastle."

"What's that?" Alec said quickly. "Let's see."

I shook my head, and when order was restored in the office I said, "Come along to the interview room. Right now."

We went into the only room on our floor where any real privacy was possible and I said, "This is your handwriting. Did you write the article in *What's Going On?*"

He gave a theatrical sigh. "It's a fair guess."

"And the others," I said. "Those other leaks, was that you?"

The blue eyes gleamed unrepentantly at me from behind the gold rims. "Yes, all right, the stories did come from me. I wrote them myself, like that one." He pointed to the memo paper in my hand. "And don't give me any lectures on disloyalty, because none of them did us any harm. Did us good, if anything."

"Alec . . ."

"Just think, Tim, what did those pieces really do?" he said. "They stirred everyone up, sure, but *because* of what I wrote we've now got much better security checks than we had before."

I listened to him openmouthed.

"All the checking and changing we've done to make us safer against frauds, that was because of what I wrote. And the Corporate Finance boys now keep their mouths zipped up like suitcases so as not to spill the beans to the investment managers. I did *good*, not harm."

"And this piece about Sandcastle. What good has that done?"

He half grinned. "Too soon to say."

I looked at the damaging scrap of paper in my hand and shook my head.

"You're going to say," Alec said calmly, "that I'll have to go."

"Don't you *care?*" I said in frustration.

He smiled. "I don't know. I'll miss *you*, and that's a fact. But as for the job, well, it's not my whole life, like it is yours."

"But what will you do?"

He gave a full cherubic smile. "*What's Going On*," he said, "has offered me a full-time job." He looked at my shattered expression. "I've written quite a bit for them, actually. They get masses of information in, but they need someone to evaluate it all properly, and there aren't many merchant bankers looking for that sort of job."

"No," I said dryly. "I can imagine."

"I'll resign from here," he said. "Make it easier."

"You're a fool!" I said explosively, feeling the loss of him acutely. "The office will be bloody dull without you."

He pointed to the piece of memo paper. "I'll send you pin-pricks now and then. You won't forget me. Not a chance."

AT MY request, Oliver had mailed me a list of all the breeders who had sent their mares to Sandcastle the previous year, and I spent two or three evenings telephoning them, asking after those foals we didn't know about. The final count came to:

Five foals born outwardly perfect but dead within two weeks because of internal abnormalities.

One foal born with one eye. (Put down.)

Five foals born with deformed legs. (All put down.)

Three foals born with part of one or both ears missing. (All still living.)

One foal born with no tail. (Still living.)

Two foals born with malformed mouths. (Both put down.)

One foal born with a deformed head. (Died at once.)

Apart from this horrifying tally, four mares who had been sent home as in foal had subsequently "slipped" and were now barren. One mare failed to conceive at all; three mares had not yet foaled, and fourteen mares had produced live, healthy foals with no defects of any sort.

I showed the list to Gordon and Henry, who went silent for a while, as if in mourning.

"There may be more to come," I said. "Oliver says thirty mares covered by Sandcastle this year are definitely in foal. Some of those may be all right . . . and some may not."

Henry shook his head regretfully. "Such a shame. Quite apart from the financial loss, a tragedy in racing terms."

OLIVER said on the telephone one morning, "Tim, I need to talk to you. Someone has offered to buy Sandcastle."

I sat in a mild state of shock. At last I said, "What for?"

"He says to put him back into training. I suppose it's possible. Sandcastle's only five. I suppose he could be fit to race by August or September, and he might still win next year."

"Good heavens."

"He's offering twenty-five thousand pounds."

"Um," I said. "Is that good or bad?"

"Realistically, it's as much as he's worth. He wants an answer fairly soon, because the longer the delay, the less time there is for training and racing this season."

"Where is he?" I said. "Sandcastle, I mean."

"Still being tested in Newmarket. But they haven't found any answers, and I think they want me to take him away."

"Are you sure this is a bona fide offer and not just a crank?"

"I've talked to him on the telephone, and to me he sounds genuine. Would you like to meet him?"

"Perhaps, yes."

We fixed a date for the following Saturday morning, and almost as an afterthought I asked the potential buyer's name.

"Smith," Oliver said. "A Mr. Dissdale Smith."

I WENT to Hertfordshire with a host of question marks in my mind, but it was Dissdale, as it happened, who had the deeper astonishment. He drove up while I was still outside Oliver's house, and the first thing he said was, "Hello, Tim, what a surprise, didn't know you knew Oliver Knowles."

Oliver looked from one of us to the other. "You know each other already?"

Dissdale said, "How do you mean, already?"

"Tim's my banker," Oliver said in puzzlement. "It was his bank, Ekaterin's, that put up the money for Sandcastle."

Dissdale stared at me in stunned amazement.

"Let's go indoors," Oliver said. "There's coffee ready." He led the way inside and to his sitting room—office.

Oliver had had four weeks by now in that house without Ginnie, but it was my first visit back, and I felt her presence to such an extent that to start with I listened to Dissdale with only surface attention.

"It might be better to geld him," he was saying. "There are some good prizes, particularly overseas, for geldings."

"It's too soon," I said, "to talk of that."

"Tim, face facts," Dissdale said expansively. "That horse is a walking bomb. I'm making an offer for him because I'm a bit of a gambler, and I have a soft spot for him because of his winning so much for me that day at Ascot. You remember, don't you?"

"I remember. It was partly because of that day," I said, "that Ekaterin's loaned the money for him. When the request came in from Oliver, it was because Henry Shipton—our chairman, if you recall—and Gordon and I had all seen the horse in action that we seriously considered the proposition."

Dissdale nodded his comprehension. "I'm sorry it's your bank that's been hit so hard."

"Dissdale," I said neutrally. "Did the idea of buying Sandcastle come from your profitable caper with Indian Silk?"

His face fell again into shock. "What . . ."

I said, "Didn't you buy Indian Silk for a pittance because he seemed to be dying, and then send him to Calder?"

"Well . . ."

"And didn't Calder cure him? And then you sold him again, but well this time, and since then Indian Silk's won the Cheltenham Gold Cup? Isn't that right?"

Dissdale raised a plump hand, palm upward. "Yes, there's no secret, that's what happened."

"Mm." I smiled at him benignly. "Calder said on television, didn't he, that buying Indian Silk was his idea originally, so I'm wondering if buying Sandcastle is his idea too."

Dissdale looked at me doubtfully. "Well, yes," he said, deciding to confide. "But it's my money, of course."

"And, um, if you do buy Sandcastle, will you send him along to Calder, too, like Indian Silk?"

"Calder said he could give him a quick pepping up to get him fit quickly for racing, yes."

Oliver, having listened restlessly up to this point, said, "Calder Jackson can't do anything for Sandcastle that I can't."

Both Dissdale and I looked at Oliver, hearing the orthodox view ringing out with conviction.

"I've been thinking about Indian Silk," I said to Dissdale. "Didn't you tell Fred Barnet, when you offered him a rock-bottom price, that all you were doing was providing a dying horse with a nice, quiet end in some gentle field?"

"Well, Tim," he said knowingly. "You know how it is. You buy for the best price you can. And I didn't cheat Fred Barnet; he could have sent his horse to Calder the same as I did."

I nodded. "So now, be honest, Dissdale. Is twenty-five thousand pounds for Sandcastle the same sort of bargain?"

There was a shade of dismay on his face. "Tim, it's a fair offer, anyone will tell you."

"I think my board of directors may invite other bids," I said. "If Sandcastle is to be sold, we must recoup all we can."

The dismay faded. "That's fair," he said. "As long as you'll come back to me if anyone tops me."

"Sure. An auction, by telephone. When we're ready."

"Don't wait too long. Time's money, you know."

Oliver took the empty coffee cup that Dissdale still held and asked if he would like to see the horse he wanted to buy.

"But isn't he in Newmarket?" Dissdale said.

"No, he's here. Came back yesterday."

"Oh. Then yes, of course, yes, I'd like to see him."

We went on the old familiar walk through the yards to the stallion yard, where the four heads appeared in curiosity.

The stay in Newmarket hadn't done Sandcastle much good, I thought. He looked tired and dull, barely arching his neck to lift his nose over the half door.

"Is that Sandcastle?" Dissdale said, sounding disappointed.

"He's had a taxing three weeks," Oliver said. "All he needs is some good food and fresh air."

"And Calder's magic touch," Dissdale said. "Most of all."

When Dissdale had driven away, Oliver asked me what I thought, and I said, "If Dissdale's offering twenty-five thousand, he's certainly reckoning to make much more than that. What we need to do is guess what scheme he has in mind."

Oliver was perplexed. "How can we possibly guess?"

"Well, suppose Dissdale acts to a pattern, which people so often do. He told Fred Barnet he was putting Indian Silk out to grass, which was untrue; he intended to send him to Calder and with luck put him back into training. He told *you* he was planning to put Sandcastle back into training, so suppose he *doesn't* do that. And he suggested gelding, so I'd expect gelding to be furthest from his mind." I reflected. "Do you know what I might do if I wanted to have a real gamble with Sandcastle?"

"What?"

"It sounds pretty crazy," I said, "but with Calder's reputation, it might just work. Suppose you could buy for a pittance a stallion whose perfect foals would be likely to win races."

"But no one would risk—"

"Suppose," I interrupted, "there was nearly a forty or fifty percent chance, going on this year's figures, that you'd get a perfect foal. Suppose Dissdale offered Sandcastle as a sire at say a thousand pounds, the fee payable only if the foal was born perfect and lived a month."

Oliver simply stared.

"Say Sandcastle's perfect progeny do win races, as indeed they should. There are fourteen so far this year, don't forget. Say that in the passage of time his good foals prove to be worth the risk. And Sandcastle stands in Calder's yard, with Calder's skill on the line. Isn't there a chance that over the years Dissdale's investment would provide a nice, steady return for both Dissdale and Calder?"

Oliver looked at his feet for a while and then said, "There's something you'd better know, Tim. Come with me."

He set off toward the Watcherleys' and would say nothing more on the way. "Over here," he said when we arrived in the Watcherleys' yard, leading me to a box. "Look at that."

I looked where directed—at a mare with a colt foal suckling.

"He was born three days ago," Oliver said. "I do so wish Ginnie had seen him."

"Why that one, especially?"

"The mare is one of my own. And that foal is Sandcastle's."

It was my turn to stare. I looked from Oliver to the foal and back again. "There's nothing wrong with him," I said.

"That's right."

"But . . ."

Oliver smiled twistedly. "The mare was staying here at the Watcherleys' because the foal she had then was ailing, but she herself was all right. I had planned to breed her to Diarist, but I was looking at her one day when she'd been in season awhile and on impulse I told Nigel to fetch Sandcastle, and we mated them there and then. The foal's the result."

"He should be worth quite a bit," I said.

"I don't think so," Oliver said. "And that's the flaw in your reasoning. It's not just the racing potential that raises prices at auction, it's the chance of breeding. And no one could be sure, breeding from Sandcastle's stock, that the genetic trouble wouldn't crop up forevermore."

We stood for a while in silence. I looked at his calm, strong face—the captain whose ship was sinking.

"I'd try anything, you know, to save you," I said.

"And to save the bank's money?"

"That too."

"I wish you could, but time's running out."

The date for bringing in the liquidators had been set, the lawyers were closing in. The respite I'd gained for him was trickling away.

We walked back to the house, Oliver patting the mares as they came to the fences. He looked away over the white-painted rails to the long line of the roofs of his yards. "I try not to mind," he said levelly. "But I don't quite know how to bear it."

WHEN I reached home that evening my telephone was ringing. I answered it, and on the other end was Judith.

"I just came in," I said. "I went to see Oliver."

"The poor, poor man." Judith had been very much distressed over Oliver. "Well, anyway," she went on. "Pen has had a reply from America about the shampoo you asked her to check. Are you still interested?"

"Yes, certainly."

"Then Gordon and I wondered if you'd come here for the day tomorrow, and Pen will show you the letter."

"I'll be there," I said fervently.

I was at Clapham before noon the next day, and Pen, over coffee, produced the letter from the drug company.

"I sent them a sample of what you gave me in that little glass jar," she said. "And, as you asked, I had some of the rest analyzed here. And it's just shampoo, as it says."

I looked over the letter. It said:

Dear Miss Warner:
    The shampoo in question is our "Bannitch," formulated especially for dogs suffering from various skin troubles, including eczema. We enclose the list of active ingredients and excipients, as requested.

"What are excipients?" I asked.

"The things you put in with the active drug for various reasons," she said. "Like chalk for bulk in pills."

I read the list: " 'Excipients: bentonite, ethylene glycol monostearate, citric acid, sodium phosphate, glyceryl monoricinoleate, perfume. Active ingredients: captan, amphoteric, selenium.' "

Pen explained. "Bentonite is a thickening agent. Ethylene glycol monostearate is a wax, to add bulk. Citric acid is to make the whole mixture acid, not alkaline, and sodium phosphate is to keep the acidity level constant. Glyceryl monoricinoleate is a soap, and perfume is there to make the dog smell nice."

"How do you know so much?" Gordon asked, marveling.

Pen just smiled. She pointed to the column of active ingredients. "Captan and amphoteric are both drugs for killing fungi on the skin, and selenium is also antifungal and is used in shampoos to cure dandruff." She stopped and looked at me doubtfully. "I did tell you not to hope too much."

"What did you expect, Tim?" Gordon asked.

"It wasn't so much expect as hope," I said regretfully.

"Of what?"

"Well, here was Ginnie with the shampoo, and the farm was in such trouble, and it seemed to me just possible that she had somehow discovered that something in the bottle was significant." I looked at Pen. "I suppose what I was looking for was something that could have been put into Sandcastle's food that affected his reproductive organs."

Gordon said, "Is that possible, Pen?"

"I don't know. I've never heard of anything like that. But I'll go and get a book or two. And we'll look up the ingredients, just in case. But honestly, don't *hope*."

She went home, leaving the three of us feeling subdued. For me this had been the last possibility.

Pen came back in half an hour with a thick tome and a piece of paper. "I've been reading," she said. "Sorry to be so long." She looked down at the paper she carried. "This is another analysis report I got on the shampoo from a British lab. Same ingredients, though written in the opposite order, with selenium put at the top, which means that that's the predominant drug."

She began turning the pages of her large pharmacological

233

book. "Here we are," she said. "Toxicity of minerals. Selenium . . . selenium . . . It says selenium is poisonous if taken internally, though it can be beneficial on the skin."

"What is selenium?" Judith asked.

"It's an element," Pen said. "Like potassium and sodium."

She read on, and then it seemed to me that she totally stopped breathing. She looked at me, her eyes wide and dark.

"What is it?" I said.

"Read it." She gave me the heavy book.

I read, " 'Selenium is absorbed easily from the intestines and affects every part of the body. Selenium is teratogenic.' What does teratogenic mean?" I asked.

"It means," Pen said, "that it produces deformed offspring."

"*What!*" I exclaimed. "You don't mean . . ."

Pen was shaking her head. "No. It couldn't affect Sandcastle's reproductive organs. It would simply poison his system. Teratogens have nothing to do with males."

"Then what . . . ?"

"They act on the developing embryo," she said. "You could get deformed foals if you fed selenium *to the mares.*"

AFTER lunch I telephoned Oliver. "Sit down," I said.

"What's the matter?" He sounded immediately anxious.

"Do you know what teratogenic means?" I said.

"Yes, of course. With mares one always has to be careful."

"Well, there was a teratogenic drug in the bottle of dog shampoo that Ginnie had."

"*What?*" His voice rose an octave on the word. "That could mean . . . that could mean . . ."

"Yes," I said. "It could mean that Sandcastle was always breeding good and true and could return to gold-mine status."

I could hear Oliver's heavily disturbed breathing.

"No, Tim," he said after a pause. "No. If shampoo had gotten into a batch of feed, all the mares who ate it would have been affected, not just those covered by Sandcastle."

"If the shampoo got into the feed accidentally, yes. If it was given deliberately, no. It is possible to give teratogenic substances to mares?"

"Yes."

"But horses wouldn't drink shampoo."

"No."

"So how would you give it to them and when?"

"I don't know *how*. They'd spit it out. But *when* would be a few days after conception, when the body tube is forming in the embryo. Then teratogens would do a lot of damage."

"Do you mean," I said, "that giving a mare selenium just *once* would ensure a deformed foal?"

"Giving a mare what?"

"Sorry. Selenium. A drug for treating dandruff."

"Good heavens." He rallied toward his normal self. "I suppose it would depend on the strength of the dose and its timing. Perhaps three or four doses. No one could really *know*, because there wouldn't have been any research."

"No," I agreed. "But supposing that in this instance someone got the dosage and the timing right, and also found a way of making the shampoo palatable, then *who was it?*"

There was a long silence. "I don't know," he said finally. "Theoretically it could have been me, Ginnie, Nigel, the Watcherleys, or any of the lads who were here last year. It would have to be someone who could come and go here all the time."

"And someone who knew which mares to pick," I said. "Would that knowledge be easy to come by?"

"Easy!" he said explosively. "It is positively thrust at everyone on the place. There are lists in all the feed rooms and in the breeding pen itself saying which mares are to be bred to which stallion. Everyone is supposed to double-check the lists all the time so that mistakes aren't made."

"And all the horses wear halters with their names on."

"Yes, that's right. An essential precaution."

All made easy, I thought, for someone intending mischief toward particular mares and not to any others.

"Your own Sandcastle foal," I said. "He's perfect. It may be because on the lists your mare was down for Diarist."

"Tim!"

"Look after that colt," I said. "And look after Sandcastle."

"I will," he said fervently.

"And Oliver, is that lad called Shane still with you?"

"No, he's gone. And so have Dave and Sammy."

"Then could you send me a list of the names and addresses of all the people who worked for you the last two years?"

"I'll do it straightaway."

"If Dissdale Smith should telephone you, pressing for an answer, just say the bank is still deliberating. And Oliver, I think it would be best to keep this new possibility to ourselves, until we can prove whether or not it's true."

"Dear God," he said fearfully. "I hope it is."

THAT evening I talked to Pen, asking if she knew any way to get the selenium out of the shampoo.

"I'll work on it," she said. "I'll ask a few friends."

"And Pen, could you or your friends make a guess as to how much shampoo you'd need to provide enough selenium to give a teratogenic dose to a mare?"

"We'll certainly try, dearest Tim."

On Thursday she sent a message asking me to come to her house after work. I went, and she opened her door smiling.

"Like a drink?" she said.

"Well, yes, but . . ."

"First things first." She poured a whiskey for me and a Cinzano for herself. "Now I'll tell you what we've managed. We started from the premise that if someone had to use shampoo as the source of selenium, then that person didn't have direct access to poisonous chemicals, and he also wouldn't have sophisticated machinery available for separating one ingredient from another—a centrifuge, for instance. Okay so far?"

I nodded.

"What we needed was a *simple* method of separating ingredients, something anyone could do anywhere. So we let the shampoo drip through a coffee filter, which is after all specifically designed to retain very fine solids while letting liquids through easily."

"Yes," I said. "Highly logical."

Pen smiled. "So there we were with some filter papers in which, we hoped, the tiny particles of selenium were trapped. The filters were stained bright green by the shampoo. I brought one to show you." She whisked off to the kitchen and returned carrying a tray with two glasses on it. One glass contained pieces of green-stained coffee filter lying in what looked like oil, and the second glass contained only a corked upright test tube, with a dark half inch of solution at the bottom.

"One of my friends in the lab knows about horses," Pen said, "and he reckoned that racehorses are used to the taste of linseed oil, which is often given them in their feed as a laxative. So we got some linseed oil and soaked the filter in it, and the selenium floated out of the filter into the oil." She pointed to the first glass.

"Neat," I said.

"Yes. Then we poured the result into this test tube, waited twenty-four hours, and the selenium particles slowly settled to the bottom. We poured off the surplus oil, and now we have concentrated selenium." She picked the tube out and showed me the shadowy liquid. "It is selenium. We checked."

"You're marvelous."

"Brilliant," she agreed. "We also calculated that that particular shampoo was almost ten percent selenium. And we all agree that this much selenium, in the test tube, is enough to cause deformity in a foal—or any other species. We also agree that it's the *time* when the mare ingests the selenium that's crucial; you'd have to give it every day for three or four days, starting two or three days after conception."

I slowly nodded. "That's the same as Oliver's time scale. And Pen, there were a lot of *different* deformities."

"Oh sure. It could affect any developing cell, regardless."

I picked up the test tube. "I suppose all you'd have to do would be stir this into a cupful of oats."

"That's right."

"Or . . . could you enclose it in a capsule?"

"Yes, if you had the makings."

"Mm. . . . Calder could do it, I suppose?"

"Calder Jackson? Why, yes, I guess he could." She remembered something. "He's on television tomorrow night, incidentally. He's going to be a guest on Mickey Bonwith's talk show."

"That's transmitted live, isn't it?" I asked thoughtfully.

"Yes, that's right." She looked at me with slight puzzlement. "What's going on in that computer brain?"

"A slight calculation of risk. Tell me, if I found myself again in Calder's surgery, what should I look for, to bring out?"

She stared at me with her mouth open. Then she said, "You can't mean *Calder?*"

"Well," I said soberly. "It seems to me, sad though it is to admit, that if you tie in Dissdale's offer for Sandcastle with someone deliberately poisoning the mares, and then add Calder's expertise with herbs, you do at least get a *question mark*. You do want to know for sure, don't you think, whether or not Calder and Dissdale set out deliberately to debase Sandcastle's worth so that they could buy him for peanuts. So that Calder could perform a well-publicized 'miracle cure' of some sort on Sandcastle, who would thereafter always sire perfect foals."

"But they couldn't. I mean, we *know* them."

She fell silent, staring at me in a troubled way, and I said, "There's one other thing. The first time I went to Calder's place he had a lad there who reminded me of the boy at Ascot."

"You mean Ricky Barnet," Pen said, nodding.

"Yes. I can't remember Calder's lad's name, but at Oliver's I saw another lad, called Shane, who *also* reminded me of Ricky. I've no idea whether Shane and Calder's lad are one and the same, but *if* Shane did once work for Calder, he might *still* have been working for him, feeding selenium to Oliver's mares."

Pen took her time and at last said, "*Someone* would have had to be there on the spot to do the feeding, and it certainly couldn't have been Calder or Dissdale. But couldn't it have been that manager, Nigel? It would have been easy for him."

I shook my head. "I thought of that. But there's one reason why it probably wasn't: besides Oliver, only Nigel knew that one of the mares down for Diarist was actually covered by Sandcastle." I explained about Oliver's impulse mating. "And that foal is perfect. It might not have been if it was Nigel doing the feeding."

"Not conclusive," Pen said slowly.

"No."

She stirred. "Did you tell the police all this?"

"I meant to, but it's all so insubstantial. Such a lot of guesses, maybe wrong conclusions. And a lad I saw for only half a minute eighteen months ago . . . I thought I'd better come up with something definite before I went back to Wyfold."

"Can't you take another good look at this Shane?"

I shook my head. "Shane has left Oliver's, and Oliver doesn't know where he went. I think we *might* find him if we were to photograph Ricky Barnet and ask around on racetracks."

She smiled. "It might be worth a try."

My mind drifted back to something else worth a try, and it seemed that hers followed. "You don't really mean to break into Calder's surgery, do you?" she said.

"Pick the lock," I said. "Yes."

"But . . ."

"Time's running out, Pen, and Oliver's future with it."

June

THE next day, Friday, June 1, I took up a long-offered invitation and went to lunch with the board of a security firm to whom we had loaned money for launching a new burglar alarm. I was there to ask a favor, and with some amusement they gave me three keys that would unlock almost anything, and also a concentrated course on how to use them.

"Those pickers are strictly for opening doors in emergencies," one of the board members said, smiling. "If you end up in jail, we don't know you."

"If I end up in jail, send me another set in a fruitcake."

I thanked them and left, and practiced discreetly on the office doors in the bank, with remarkable results. Going home, I let myself in my own front door with them. Then I put on a dark turtleneck jersey over my shirt and tie and drove to Newmarket.

I left my car at the side of the road some distance from Calder's house and finished the journey on foot, walking quietly into his yard, checking against my watch that it was almost ten o'clock, the hour of Mickey Bonwith's television show.

The yard was dark and peaceful, all lads long gone. I came to the surgery and fitted one of the lock pickers into the keyhole. The tumblers turned without protest, and I pushed the door open and went in.

There were no windows to worry about, so I closed the door, switched on the light and immediately began the search for which I'd come: to find selenium in homemade capsules, or in a filtering device, or in bottles of shampoo.

The locked cabinets at both ends of the surgery opened easily with the picks, but the contents were a puzzle, as only a few of the jars and boxes were properly labeled. These seemed mostly to be the herbs Calder had talked of: sarsaparilla, comfrey, fo-ti-tieng, myrrh, garlic.

I had taken with me a polyethylene bag that had a zipper across the top. Into that I systematically put two or three capsules from each bottle, and two or three pills of each sort. Pen, I thought, was going to have a fine old time sorting them all out. With the bag almost half full, I carefully locked the cabinets again and turned to the refrigerator. Inside, there were no bottles of shampoo. No coffee filters. No linseed oil. There were simply the large plastic containers of Calder's cure-all tonic.

I thought I might as well take some of that too, and rooted around till I found some empty medicine bottles in a cupboard below the workbench. I poured some tonic into a bottle and returned the plastic container to the fridge. I stood the medicine bottle on the workbench ready to take away, and turned to the drawers where Calder kept things like hops.

With mounting disappointment I went through every drawer. Bags of seeds: sesame, pumpkin, sunflower. Bags of dried herbs: raspberry leaves, alfalfa. All as before. In the bottom drawer were the plastic sacks of hops. Moving one slightly, I saw that under it lay a brown leather case.

I hauled it out onto the workbench and opened it with a pick. In it I found no bottles of dog shampoo, but other things that turned me slowly to a state of stone.

The contents looked as if the case belonged to a doctor: stethoscope, penlight, metal instruments, several tubes of antibiotic ointment. A large bottle containing a few white pills was labeled DIURETIC. And a pad of prescription forms. It was the name and address stamped on the forms, and the gold initials embossed on the leather case that stunned me totally.

I.A.P. on the case.

IAN A. PARGETTER, VETERINARY SURGEON, on the prescriptions. His case had vanished the night he died. This case.

With fingers beginning to shake, I took one of the tubes of antibiotics and some of the diuretic pills and added them to my other spoils, and then checked that everything was in place.

I felt as much as heard the surgery door open. I turned, thinking one of Calder's lads had come in and wondering how I could explain my presence; and I saw that no explanation at all would do. It was Calder himself crossing the threshold. Calder, with the light on his curly halo; Calder, who should have been a hundred miles away talking to the nation on the tube.

His first expression of surprise turned immediately to grim assessment, his gaze traveling from the medicine bottle of tonic on the workbench to the veterinary case lying open. In his shock, disbelief and fury he acted with such speed that even if I'd guessed what he would do, I could hardly have dodged.

His right arm swung in an arc, pulling from the wall bracket that held it a slim scarlet fire extinguisher. The swing seemed to me continuous. The end of the fire extinguisher in a split second filled my vision and connected with a crash against my forehead, and consciousness ceased within a blink.

THE world came back with the same sort of on-off switch. One second I was unaware, the next, awake lying on some smelly straw in an electrically lit horse box with a brown horse peering at me suspiciously from six feet above.

For a minute I couldn't remember how I got there. Then in a snap, I had total recall of the evening.

Calder. I was in a box in Calder's yard. I was there because, presumably, Calder had put me there. Pending what? I wondered.

I made a move to stand up, but found that though consciousness was total, recovery was not. A whirling dizziness set the walls tilting; cursing slightly, I made it only to one elbow.

The top half of the stable door abruptly opened and Calder's head appeared, his face showing shock and dismay.

"I thought," he said, "that you'd be unconscious. I hit you so hard. You're supposed to be out." He was looking at me almost with apology. "I'm sorry, Tim. I'm sorry you came."

"Ian Pargetter," I said. "Did *you* kill him?"

Calder produced an apple and fed it to the horse. "I'm sorry, Tim. He was so stubborn." He patted the horse's neck. "He wouldn't do what I wanted. Said it was over, he'd had enough. Said he'd stop me, you know."

I tried again to stand up, but the whirling was still there.

"Ginnie," I said. "Say it wasn't you who hit Ginnie."

He simply looked at me, and didn't say it. He said merely, and with clear regret, "I wish I'd hit you harder, but it seemed enough." He moved a step backward, and while I was still struggling to my knees he closed the top of the half door and bolted it, and from outside switched off the light.

The sudden darkness made it even harder to stand up, but at last I found myself leaning against a wall, more or less upright, brain settling into equilibrium.

A gray oblong of window gradually detached itself from the blackness. Window . . . way out.

I slithered around the walls to the window and found it barred on the inside. To keep horses from breaking the glass, I supposed. Five strong bars were set in concrete top and bottom, as secure as any prison cell.

Through the dusty windowpanes I had a sideways view across the yard to the surgery, and' while I stood there and watched, Calder went busily in and out of the lighted doorway, carrying things to his car. I saw what I was sure was Ian Pargetter's case go into the trunk, and an armful of the jars that contained unlabeled capsules. Calder was obliterating his tracks.

I yelled at him, but he didn't even turn his head. The only result was startled movement in the horse behind me, a stamping of hoofs and a restless swinging around the box.

"All right, steady down," I said soothingly, and through the window I watched Calder lock the surgery door, get into his car and start out of his driveway. The lights of his car passed briefly over the trees as he turned out through the gates, and then were gone. I felt suddenly very alone.

From the dim light of the sky I could see the outlines within the box: walls, manger, horse. The big dark creature didn't like my being there, but I could think of no way to relieve him of my presence. It looked most annoyingly as if I were going to stay where I was until Calder came back. And then . . . what? If he'd intended to kill me, why hadn't he already made sure of it? I thought of Ian Pargetter, dead from one blow of his own brass lamp. Calder must have killed him on a moment's ungovernable impulse, for not . . . What had he said? For not wanting to go on, for wanting to stop Calder.

Calder had struck at me with the same sort of speed, swinging the fire extinguisher ruthlessly at the man who had saved his life. Saved Calder's life. Why ever did I do it? After that day, he had killed Ian Pargetter, killed Ginnie; if I hadn't saved him, they would both have lived.

The despair of that thought filled me utterly.

THE horse became more restive and began to paw the ground.

I looked at my watch, the digital figures bright in the darkness: it was twenty minutes or thereabouts since Calder had left. The horse swung around suddenly in the gloom with unwelcome vigor, bumping against me with his rump.

"Calm down now, boy," I said soothingly. "Go to sleep."

The horse's reply was the equivalent of unprintable: the crash of a steel-clad hoof against a wall.

Perhaps he didn't like me talking, I thought, or indeed even moving about. His head swung around, then reared up violently, and with a foreleg he lashed forward at the wall.

Not funny, I thought. Horrific to have been in the firing line of that slashing hoof. At that time I was standing with my back to the door, so that to the horse I must have been totally in shadow; but he would sense my presence. If he could see me too, would it be better?

I took a tentative step toward the window and had a clear, sharp and swiftly terrifying view of one of his eyes. That eye was stretched wide, staring as if blind, glaring wildly at nothing at all.

The black nostrils looked huge. The lips as I watched were drawing back from the teeth. The ears had gone flat to the head and there was froth forming in the mouth. It was the face, I thought incredulously, not of alarm but of madness.

The horse backed suddenly away, crashing his hindquarters into the rear wall and rocking forward again, but this time advancing with both forelegs off the ground, the gleams from thrashing hoofs curving in silvery streaks in the gloom, the feet hitting the wall below the window with sickening intent.

In panic I pressed into a corner, but it gave no real protection. The manger, I thought. Get into the manger.

The manger was a metal trough built diagonally across one of the box's rear corners, with a sturdy wooden support. As a shelter it was pathetic, but at least I would be off the ground.

In the next few seconds the horse seemed to go utterly berserk. He whirled and kicked and hurled his bulk against the walls, and I was knocked over by one of his flailing feet.

I didn't realize at that point that he'd broken one of my arms, because the whole thing felt numb. I made it to the manger, got one foot in . . . sat on the edge . . . tried to raise my other foot . . . and couldn't do it fast enough. Another direct hit crunched on my ankle and I knew this time that there was damage.

The air about my head seemed to hiss with hoofs and the horse was beginning a high, bubbling whinny. Surely someone, I thought, would hear the crashing and banging and come.

I could see him in flashes against the window, a rearing, bucking, rocketing nightmare. He came wheeling around, walking on his hind legs, the forelegs thrashing, and he knocked me off my precarious perch with a swiping punch in the chest that had half a ton of weight behind it.

I fell onto the straw, trying to curl my head away from those lethal feet. A crushing thud landed on the back of my shoulder and jarred like a hammer through every bone, and I could feel a scream forming somewhere inside me, a wrenching cry for mercy, for escape, for an end to battering.

His mania grew worse, and it was he who was finally screaming, not me. The noise bounced off the walls, stunning, mind-blowing, the roaring of furies.

He somehow got one hoof inside my rolled body and tumbled me fast over, and I could see him arching above me, his forelegs so high that he was hitting the ceiling. This is death, I thought. This is dreadful, pulverizing extinction.

Before I'd even finished the thought his forelegs came crashing down, with a hoof so close it brushed my hair; and then again he reared dementedly, the skull meeting the ceiling with the force of a ram. The whole building shook with the impact, and the horse, his voice cut off, collapsed in a huge mass across my legs, spasms shuddering through his body, muscles jerking in stiff kicks.

He was dying in stages, the head already inert on the straw. An age passed before it was done. The heavy body went flaccid and lay in perpetual silence, pinning me beneath.

THE RELIEF OF FINDING HIM DEAD and myself alive lasted quite a long time, but then simple gratitude for existence progressed to discontent that things weren't better. His bulk lay across my legs from my knees down, and getting out from under him was proving an impossibility.

The left ankle protested screechingly at any attempted movement. I couldn't lift my left arm for the same reason. There was acute soreness in my chest, making breathing painful.

The physical discomfort shut out much in the way of thought, but eventually I began to ask questions, and the biggest was, What would Calder do when he came back and found me alive? He wouldn't expect it. No one could expect anyone to survive being locked in with a mad horse.

I remembered him giving the horse an apple while I'd struggled to stand up within the spinning walls, and I remembered him saying on my first visit that he gave his remedies to horses in hollowed-out apples. This time, though, it had been no remedy. It had been a drug to madden, to turn a normal steel-shod horse into a killing machine. But the horse hadn't completed his task. When Calder returned he would make good the deficit.

On that thought I tried again to slide my legs out. I was unprepared, however, for the onslaught of so much pain all at once: it brought actual tears into my eyes.

The oblong of window began to lighten toward the new day—Saturday, June 2. Calder would come back and finish the job, and he would say, "I didn't know Tim was coming to see me. I was in London. I've no idea how he came to shut himself into one of the boxes. The whole thing's a terrible accident, and I'm shattered. . . ." And anyone looking at the horse would conclude I'd been pretty unintelligent and also unlucky, and too bad.

The sun rose and shone slantingly through the bars. The horse and I lay in intimate silence, dead and half dead—waiting.

A car drove up fast outside and doors slammed. There were voices calling to each other. Female and male. But not Calder's.

Hope surged back, and I called out myself, saying, "Here. Come here," but it was only a croak, inaudible beyond the door. Suppose they were looking for Calder, and when they didn't find him, drove away.

The top half of the door swung outward and a voice yelled

incredulously, "He's in *here*." The bolt on the lower half clattered and three figures appeared, coming forward, speaking with anxiety and joy. Judith and Gordon and Pen.

"Thank God," Gordon said. "Thank God."

Judith was gulping and so was I. "Are you all right?" she said.

"Not really. But everything's relative."

"If we put our arms under your shoulders," Gordon said, surveying the problem, "we should be able to pull you out."

"Don't do that," I said. "Get a knacker."

"My dear Tim," he said, puzzled.

"They'll come with a winch. Their job is dead horses."

"And an ambulance," Pen said. "I should think."

I smiled at them with much love. I asked why they'd come, and they explained that they'd been worried because Calder's television program had been canceled.

"Mickey Bonwith was taken ill," Pen said. "They announced that there would be no live Mickey Bonwith show, just an old tape, and to expect Calder Jackson at a later date."

"Then Pen telephoned us and told us where you were going, and why," Judith said.

"We've been awake all night," Gordon said. "We grew more and more worried when we couldn't reach you, so we came."

You couldn't ask for better friends. I said, "Calder will come back."

"Tim," Pen said with decision. "If he's coming, did you get what you came for? Did you get a chance to take any samples?"

I nodded weakly. "Yes. They're here."

"Here? But didn't he search you?"

"I don't know. But he didn't find the pills."

"Then where *are* they?"

"I learned from Ginnie about keeping your hands free," I said. "They're in a plastic bag, inside my pants."

They stared incredulously and then they laughed, and Judith, with tears in her eyes, said, "Do you mean . . . all the time . . ."

"All the time," I agreed. And we all laughed together.

SOME things would be best forgotten but are impossible to forget, and one could put the next half hour into that category. At the end of it I lay on a stretcher in the open air, two ambulance men near me, and my deadweight pal was half up the ramp of the knacker's van.

Gordon was telling the knacker's men that it was essential to remove a blood sample from the horse. Judith and Pen were both yawning. I wearily watched some birds wheeling high in the fair blue sky and wished I were up there with them, and into this riveting tableau drove Calder. As he came striding from his car his mouth formed an oval of apprehension and shock.

He looked at the dead horse on the ramp, and from there toward the horse's box, where the door stood wide open.

From there he turned and saw with horror the bag Pen held tightly, the transparent plastic bag with the capsules, pills and other assorted treasures showing clearly inside.

"Where did you get that?" Calder said, staring at the bag as if his eyes would burn it.

"Tim had it," she said. Her gaze went to me, and Calder seemed finally to realize that my stillness was not that of death. He walked to the stretcher and saw me alive, awake, aware.

Neither of us spoke. His eyes seemed to retreat in their sockets, and the shape of his jaw stood out starkly. I saw in him the realization that my survival meant his ruin. He looked at me with a searing intensity, and then turned abruptly away and walked with jerky steps back to his car.

"We should get the police," Gordon said, watching him go.

I showed no enthusiasm for that boring ritual. Britain was a small island, and Calder too well known to go far.

Pen looked at the plastic bag in her hands and without comment put it inside her handbag. She glanced at me and I nodded, relieved that she and her friends would unravel the capsules themselves.

AT TWO that afternoon a family of picnickers came across a car parked out of sight of any road behind some bushes. The engine was running, and they saw a man slumped on the back seat with a tube in his mouth. They knew him because of his curly hair and his beard.

Tributes to Calder's miracle working appeared on television that evening. It seemed ironic that the master who had known so much about drugs should have chosen to gas his way out.

By the time I heard all this, I was lying in a hospital room, half covered in plaster of paris. On Monday evening Pen came up from London to report on the laboratory findings. She put a bunch of roses in my drinking-water jug and said they were from Gordon and Judith's garden.

"They both send their love," she said chattily. "You look exhausted."

"Tiring place, hospital."

"Yes. Well." She pulled the visitor's chair closer to the bed. "Tim, you have really, as they say, hit the jackpot."

"Do you mean it!" I exclaimed.

She grinned cheerfully. "It's no wonder Calder killed himself after seeing you alive and knowing you had taken all those things from his surgery." She opened a slim black briefcase on her knees and produced several typewritten pages.

"First, I must tell you that the Equine Research Establishment reported on the telephone this morning that the dead horse had been given ethylisobutrazine."

"You don't say."

Her eyes gleamed. "It's a drug used as a tranquilizer for dogs, but it has an absolutely manic effect on horses. The research people said that any horse given enough ethylisobutrazine would go utterly berserk and literally try to climb the walls."

"That's just what he did," I said soberly.

"And now listen to this, dearest Tim. When we found what Calder had been doing words simply failed us. You remember," she went on, "when we went to Calder's yard that time at Easter, we saw a horse that had blood in its urine. Crystalluria was what he called it."

"Yes. He cured several horses who had that."

"Mm. And they had been previously treated by Ian Pargetter."

I thought back. "Some of them, certainly."

"Well, you told me before they carted you off in the ambulance that you found some capsules in Calder's surgery labeled only with letters like a plus w, b plus w and c plus s. Three of the capsules with one transparent and one blue end *did* contain c and s. Vitamin C and sulfanilamide. Well, separately they are relatively harmless, *but together they can cause a nasty case of crystalluria.*"

I stared at her.

"Calder used those capsules to *cause the horse's illness*. Then his miracle cure was simply to stop giving them."

"No!" I said. "He *couldn't*."

She nodded. "It means, you see, that Ian Pargetter almost certainly *knew*. Because it was he who would have given the horse's owner the capsules to dole out every day. And they were precisely what was making the horse ill."

"Pen!"

"I'll explain just a little. If you give sulfa drugs to anyone— horse or person—who doesn't need them, you won't do much harm, because urine is normally slightly alkaline or only slightly acid, and you'll get rid of the sulfa safely. But vitamin C is citric acid, and the acid works with sulfa drugs to form crystals, which cause pain and bleeding . . . like powdered glass."

"It's diabolical," I said.

"Yes," she said. "Once Calder had the horse in his yard, he could give him bicarbonate of soda, which would make the urine alkaline again and also dissolve the crystals, and with plenty of water to drink, the horse would be well in no time. Miraculously fast, in fact." She paused and smiled, and went on. "We found three more homemade capsules, with pale green ends this time, and we reckon that they were your a plus w."

"Go on, then," I said. "What's a and what's w?"

"A is antibiotic and w is warfarin, a drug used in humans for reducing the clotting ability of the blood."

"That pink pill you found on the surgery floor," I said.

"Oh, I'd forgotten that. Well, if you give certain antibiotics *with* warfarin, you increase the effect of the warfarin to the extent that blood will hardly clot at all, and then you get severe bleeding from even a small broken blood vessel."

"Every time I went to see Calder, there was a bleeder there."

She nodded. "Warfarin acts by reducing the effect of vitamin K, which is needed for clotting. So all Calder had to do to reverse things was feed lots of vitamin K, which is found in alfalfa."

I blinked. "It's incredible."

"You see," she continued. "Putting two drugs in one capsule was brilliant, because no one would think they were giving a horse two drugs, but just one. Pargetter could have put Calder's

249

capsules into any bottle, and the horse's owner would think he was giving the horse just what it said on the label. And there's more. How about all those poor animals who were so weak they could hardly walk?"

I swallowed. "How about them?"

"You said you found a large bottle labeled 'diuretic,' or in other words, pills designed to increase the passing of urine. Well, we identified them as thiazide diuretic pills. If you gave them over a long period, you would cause *exactly* the sort of general progressive debility shown by those horses."

I was past speech.

"And to cure the debility," she said, "you just stop the diuretics and provide good food and water. And hey presto!" She was enjoying her revelations. "We come now to the horses with non-healing ulcers and sores."

Always those, too, in the yard, I thought.

"Ulcers and sores are usually cleared up by applications of antibiotic cream. We took that tube of antibotic cream you found in Ian Pargetter's case, and we tested it. And lo and behold, it didn't contain antibiotic cream at all."

"What, then?"

"Cortisone cream." She smiled at my noncomprehension. "Cortisone cream is fine for eczema and allergies, but *not* for general healing. In fact if you scratched a horse and smeared dirt into the wound to infect it and then applied cortisone cream twice a day, you'd get an ulcer that would never heal. Until you sent your horse to Calder, who would lay his hands upon your precious . . . and apply real antibiotics, to let healing begin."

"Dear God in heaven."

We sat for a while and pondered.

"It does answer an awful lot of questions," I said finally.

"Such as?"

"Such as why Calder killed Ian Pargetter," I said. "Ian Pargetter said he'd had enough. He said that he would stop Calder, too, which must have been his death warrant."

"I wonder," Pen said, "why Ian Pargetter wanted to stop? The two of them must have had a nice, steady income going."

"Selenium," I said. "Making horses ill in order to cure them wasn't risking much permanent damage, if any. But selenium is forever. The foals would be deformed. I'd guess that when Calder suggested it the idea sickened Ian Pargetter."

"And Calder wanted to go on with it all. Enough to kill."

I nodded. "Calder would have had his sights on a fortune as well as an income. And if Ginnie hadn't somehow got hold of that shampoo, he would very likely have achieved it."

"I wonder how she did," Pen said.

"Mm." I shifted uncomfortably. "I've remembered the name of the lad Calder had who looked like Ricky Barnet. It was Jason."

"What about him?" Pen said.

"I remember Calder saying he gave herb pills to Jason for him to give to the horses. But with Ian Pargetter gone, Calder would have needed someone else to give those double-edged capsules to horses, because he still had horses in his yard with those same troubles long after Pargetter was dead."

"So he did," she said. "Except . . . when we got to his yard last Saturday there weren't many horses there."

"I think that was because Jason had been busy working at Oliver's farm, feeding selenium in apples."

A visual memory had flashed in my brain. *Apples.* Shane, the stable lad, walking across the yard, swinging a bucket and eating an apple. Shane, Jason: one and the same.

"What is it?" Pen said.

"I need photos of Ricky Barnet. As soon as I get out of here. They say I can leave tomorrow, though everything still hurts. There's some problem with ligaments or tendons or something, in addition to the broken bones."

"*Tim.*" She gave an eyes-to-heaven laugh. "I brought you a present from my shop." She dug into her handbag. "Here you are, with my love."

I took the small white box she offered, and looked at the label on its side. It said COMFREY.

She grinned. "You might as well try it. Comfrey does contain allantoin, which helps to knit bones. And you never know. Calder really was an expert with all sorts of drugs."

ON TUESDAY, June 5, Oliver Knowles collected me from the hospital to drive me on some errands and then take me to his home. I hadn't told him how I had been injured, and he said dryly when he saw me that on the telephone I had referred to a "crack or two" and not to half an acre of plaster.

The nurse who wheeled me to his car handed Oliver a slip of paper. "There's a place along the road where you can hire wheelchairs." To me she said, "Get a comfortable one that lets your leg lie straight out, like this one."

She helped me into the car with friendly competence, and then Oliver and I did as she advised, storing the resulting cushioned and chromium comfort in the trunk of his car.

"Now," I said, "the next thing to do is buy a good Polaroid camera and a lot of film."

Oliver found a shop and bought the camera while I sat in the car. "Where next?" he said, coming back with the parcels.

"Cambridge. An engineering firm. Here's the address." I handed him the paper on which I'd written Ricky Barnet's directions. "We're meeting him when he comes out of work."

"Who?" Oliver said. "Who are we meeting?"

"You'll see."

We parked across the road from the firm's gate and waited, and at four thirty on the dot Ricky Barnet came out. Beside me I heard Oliver stir and say, "But that's Shane," and then add doubtfully, "No, it isn't."

"No, it isn't." I leaned out the open window and called to the boy. "Ricky. Over here."

He crossed to us. "Been in an accident?" he said, looking in. "Sort of."

He climbed into the back of the car. He hadn't been too keen to have his photograph taken for the purpose I'd outlined, but he was in no great position to refuse.

Oliver drove off and stopped where I asked, at a suitably neutral background—a gray-painted factory wall—and Ricky got out of the car and stood in front of the wall. Oliver took the first picture, and we waited for it to develop.

Oliver looked at it, adjusted the light meter and tried again.

"This one's all right," he said, watching the colors emerge. "Looks like Shane. Quite amazing."

With a faint shade of sullenness, Ricky posed for as long as it took to shoot four boxes of film. "That's fine," I said when the films were finished. "Thank you, Ricky. By the way, do you remember, when Indian Silk got so ill with debility, which vet was treating him?"

"Yeah, sure, that fellow that was murdered. Him and his partners. The best, Dad said."

I nodded, and we drove him back to his company, where I cheered him up with payment for his time and trouble. Then he roared off on his motorbike.

"What now?" Oliver asked.

"Newmarket," I said. "I'm meeting Ursula Young."

He gave me a bewildered glance but drove without protest, pulling into the parking lot where Ursula had said to meet her.

We arrived there first, and Oliver finally gave voice to a long-restrained question.

"Just what," he said, "are the photographs *for?*"

"For finding Shane."

"But why?"

"Because I think he gave the selenium to your mares."

"Do you think he killed Ginnie?"

"I don't know," I said after a pause. "I don't know."

Ursula arrived soon after we did. Like Oliver and Ricky she looked taken aback at my plaster, but rallied in her usual no-nonsense fashion and climbed into the back of Oliver's car.

I passed her thirty of the forty pictures of Ricky, whom of course she knew immediately. "Ricky looks like a lad who worked for Oliver," I said, "and it's *that* lad, who may go by the name of Shane or Jason, that we want to find." I explained why, and added, "Also, if you find anyone who employed him in the past, ask if by any chance a horse he looked after fell ill."

"Well, all right," she said briskly. "I'll start spreading the pictures about at once, tonight, and call you with the results."

"Ursula," I said. "If you find where he is now, make sure he isn't frightened off. We don't want to lose him."

"I'll do my best." She smiled and patted my shoulder.

THAT evening, bit by bit, I told Oliver about Pen's report and of the drug-induced illnesses of Calder's patients. I told him that Calder had killed Ian Pargetter and why, and I explained how the idea of first discrediting, then buying and rebuilding Sandcastle had followed the pattern of Indian Silk.

"Dissdale withdrew his offer for Sandcastle the same night Calder died," Oliver said when I finished.

"What exactly did he say?"

"He was very upset. Said he'd lost his closest friend, and that without Calder to work his miracles there was no point in buying Sandcastle."

I frowned. "Do you think it was genuine?"

"His distress? Yes, certainly."

I wondered if it was possible that Dissdale was an innocent and duped accomplice. His pride in knowing the great man had been obvious at Ascot, and perhaps he had been flattered and foolish but not wicked after all.

Oliver asked how I'd found out about the drug-induced illnesses and Ian Pargetter's murder, and I told him.

He sat staring at me, his gaze on the plaster. "You're lucky to be in a wheelchair and not a coffin," he said, and poured us both brandy. "I'm almost beginning to believe that somehow I'll still be here next year, even if I do have to sell Sandcastle."

I sipped my drink. "Tomorrow we'll make a plan contingent upon Sandcastle's being reinstated in the eyes of the world. Look at the figures, see what the final damage may be, draw up a time scale for recovery. If the bank gets all its money in the end, it'll most likely be flexible about when."

"Good of you," Oliver said, hiding his emotion.

"Frankly," I said, "you're more use to us salvaged than bust."

He smiled wryly. "A banker to the last drop of blood."

BECAUSE stairs were difficult for me, I slept on the sofa that night, where Ginnie had dozed on her last afternoon, and I dreamed of her walking up a path toward me looking happy. Not a significant dream, but an awakening of fresh regret.

The next evening Ursula telephoned with triumph in her voice. "You won't believe it," she said, "but I've already found three racing stables in Newmarket where he worked last summer and autumn, and in *every case* a horse in the yard fell sick!"

I asked what sort of sickness.

"They all had crystalluria, but all three were sent to Calder Jackson, and he cured them straightaway."

"Was the lad called Shane?" I asked.

"No. Bret. Bret Williams. The same in all three places."

She dictated the addresses of the stables and the dates (approximate) when Shane-Jason-Bret had been in their yards.

"You're marvelous," I said.

"But *Calder* . . . The implications are unbelievable."

"Believe them. Shane worked for Calder," I said. "All the time. Permanently. Wherever he went, it was to manufacture patients for Calder."

She was silent so long that in the end I said, "Ursula?"

"I'm here. Do you want me to go on with the photos?"

"Yes, if you would. To find him."

"Hanging's too good for him," she said grimly.

The next morning Oliver called Detective Chief Inspector Wyfold and asked him to come to the farm. Wyfold reluctantly agreed, and later, as we told him what had been happening, his impatience dissipated and his natural sharpness took over.

We gave him copies of Pen's analyses, the names of "Bret Williams'" recent employers and the last ten photographs of Ricky. He said, "We interviewed this groom, but—"

"No, you didn't," Oliver said. "The photo is of a boy who looks like him. We think Williams may have killed Ginnie."

Wyfold pursed his lips but nodded. "We will certainly redirect our inquiries," he said.

He put his best muscle into the search, and it took him only two weeks to find Shane, who was arrested on leaving a pub in the racing village of Malton, Yorkshire.

Oliver telephoned me with the news at the office, where I'd returned via a new wheelchair ramp up the front steps. "He's calling himself Tarquin now," Oliver said. "Tarquin Williams. The police are transferring him here, and Wyfold wants you to come to police headquarters to identify him as the man called Jason at Calder's yard."

I said I would, and went in a chauffeur-driven hired car, a luxury I seemed to have spent half my salary on since leaving Oliver's house.

I arrived at the police station at the same time as Oliver, who pushed me along a corridor to an interview room. It contained a table, three chairs, Wyfold, a policeman . . . and Shane.

He looked cocky, not cowed, and when he saw Oliver he

tilted his head jauntily. On me he looked with only a flickering glance, not knowing me from our two very brief meetings.

"Hello, Jason," I said.

His head snapped around immediately.

"I met you at Calder Jackson's yard," I said.

"You never did."

"You were giving sunlamp treatment to a horse, and Calder Jackson told you to put on your sunglasses."

He made no more effort to deny it. "What of it, then?"

"Conclusive evidence of your link with the place," I said.

Oliver turned to Wyfold and in half-controlled bitterness said, "Now prove he killed my daughter."

"*What!*" Shane had risen in panic to his feet, losing in an instant the smart-alecky assurance. "I never did," he said.

We all watched him with interest, and his gaze traveled from one face to another. "I didn't kill her. It was him. He did it."

"Who?" I said.

"Calder. Mr. Jackson. He did it. It was him, not me."

Wyfold began telling him in a flat voice that he had a right to remain silent and that anything he said might be used in evidence, but Shane wasn't clever and fright had too firm a hold. I found myself believing every word he said.

"We didn't know she was there, see, listening. And while I was carrying the stuff back to my room Calder saw her moving, so he hit her. I didn't see him do it, but when I got back, there she was on the ground, and I said she was the boss's daughter, and he said all the worse, because she must have heard us and was on her way to tell everybody."

The words came tumbling out, and the policeman, now sitting behind Shane, was writing at speed in a notebook.

Wyfold said, "What did he hit her with?"

"With a fire extinguisher," Shane said. "He kept it in his car, see. He was real fussy about fire always. Would never let anyone smoke anywhere near the stables."

"Fire extinguisher . . ." Wyfold spoke doubtfully.

"Yeah, one of them red things," Shane said urgently. "He was holding it by the nozzle, and Ginnie was lying flat on the ground. I said, 'What have you done?' and he said she'd been listening. We'd been talking about the stuff, see."

"The shampoo?"

"Yeah." He seemed to feel only the slightest alarm at the mention of it. "I'd told him, see, that the stuff really worked, because there'd been a foal born that morning with half a leg, and Mr. Jackson said great, because there hadn't been a murmur in the papers and he was getting worried he hadn't got the dose right. So he said this was probably the last lot I'd have to do, just do the six bottles he'd brought, and then take off."

Oliver looked very pale, with sweat along his hairline and his mouth rigidly closed with the effort of self-control.

"I thought I took the six bottles off to my room, see, but when I got there I'd only got five, so I went back to look for the one I'd dropped. But I forgot it when I saw him standing there over Ginnie and him saying she'd heard us talking, and then he said for me to get in his car and he'd drop me at a pub where the other lads were, so it would seem like I couldn't have been back home killing the boss's daughter, see? When we were on our way to the village I remembered about the bottle I'd dropped but didn't think it would matter much, because no one would know what it was for, it was just dog shampoo."

Wyfold said, "And did you walk back from the village later with the other grooms, knowing what you would find?"

"Well, yeah. Only Dave and Sammy, see, they'd got there first, and when the rest of us got back, an ambulance was there and I just kept in the background."

"What did you do with the other five bottles of shampoo?" Wyfold asked. "We didn't find any in the rooms."

"I took them down the road a ways and threw them in a ditch. After they'd all gone off to the hospital."

"You could show me the ditch?" Wyfold said.

"Yeah, I could."

"And I'll need to know what you did with the shampoo—how you prepared it and gave it to the mares."

"Oh." An echo of the cockiness came back. "It was dead easy, see. Mr. Jackson showed me how. I just had to put a coffee filter in a washbasin and pour the shampoo through it down the drain, and there was that stuff left on the paper. Then I turned the coffee filter inside out and soaked it in a little jar of linseed oil, and then I'd stir a quarter of it into the feed, if it was

for a mare I was looking after anyway. Or scrape up a teaspoon-
ful and put it in an apple for the others. Dead easy."

Wyfold asked, "How often did Mr. Jackson bring you bottles
of shampoo?"

"He didn't. I mean, I had a case of it under my bed. Brought it
with me when I moved in, see. But then I ran out, so I rang him
up from the village one night, and he said he'd meet me at the
back gate at nine on Sunday."

Wyfold said it would be best if Shane made a formal statement
now, and gestured to Oliver and me to leave. Oliver, in undiluted
grimness, silently pushed me out of the room, then pushed me
outside, where I found myself making an unscheduled turn into
a small public garden. He sat on a bench beside me, his eyelids
slightly reddened but his manner calm.

"She died happy," I said. "It's better than nothing."

"How do you mean?"

"She heard what they were doing, she picked up the shampoo
Shane had dropped, and she was coming to tell you that there
was nothing wrong with Sandcastle and you wouldn't lose the
farm. At the moment she died she must have been full of joy."

Oliver raised his face to the pale summer sky.

"Do you think so?"

"Yes, I do."

"Then I'll believe it," he said.

October

GORDON was coming up to sixty, the age at which everyone
retired from Ekaterin's, like it or not. He had his regrets, but
they seemed to be balanced by a sense of relief. He said he was
looking forward to his leisure and that he and Judith would go
on a celebratory journey as soon as possible. Before that, however, he was to have a day of medical tests in hospital.

"They want to make these checks before we travel," he said.

"Very sensible," I said. "Where will you go?"

He smiled with enthusiasm. "I've always wanted to see Australia. Never been there."

At work we continued in the accord we had felt for so many
years. I would miss him badly, I thought, and even more be-

cause I would no longer have news and contact with Judith. The days galloped by and my spirits grew heavy as his lightened.

Oliver's plight had been extensively aired by Alec in *What's Going On Where It Shouldn't*, thanks to comprehensive leaks from one of Ekaterin's directors—to wit, me. And the paper had let everyone know that Sandcastle himself was a rock-solid investment. The article said:

> As for the mares covered this year, breeders are advised to let their mares go to term, because there is roughly a fifty percent chance that the foal will be perfect. Breeders of mares who produce deformed or imperfect foals will, we understand, have their stallion fees refunded.
>
> Meanwhile, fear not. Sandcastle is fully reinstated. Apply without delay for a place in next year's program.

As a result of this miracle-working column, Oliver thankfully reported that confidence in both his stallion and his stud farm was creeping back. Two thirds of the nominations for next year were filled already.

From the bank's point of view, too, Oliver's affairs were no longer in turmoil. The board had agreed to extend his loan for three extra years, and Val, Gordon and I worked out rates at which Oliver could repay without crippling himself. All finally rested on Sandcastle: if his progeny inherited his speed, Oliver would reach the prosperity and prestige for which he had aimed.

Gordon came to the office one Monday, saying he had met Dissdale the day before at lunch. "I had quite a talk with him," Gordon said. "He really didn't know that Calder was a fake. He says he can hardly believe, even now, that the cures weren't cures or that Calder killed two people."

"Dissdale," I said dryly, "still wants to believe in his hero."

Gordon nodded. "Another thing Dissdale said was that Calder was as stunned as he was himself to find it was Ekaterin's who had loaned the money for Sandcastle. Dissdale thinks Calder was feeling remorse at hammering Ekaterin's, after an Ekaterin had saved his life. He said Calder had liked you very much."

Liked me, and apologized, and tried to kill me—that too.

Movement had slowly returned to my shoulder and arm now that the plaster was off, and via exercise and massage normal strength had returned. Things weren't quite so good in the ankle department: after more than four months I still wore a brace. But I had rented a flat that had an elevator to take me aloft and a garage in the basement, and on the day I drove out of there in a car with an automatic gearshift, no work for the left foot, I reckoned life had become reasonable again.

ONE Thursday Gordon mentioned that Judith was coming to collect him from the bank after work to take him to the hospital. He was to spend the night there, resting for his day of tests on Friday. I said, "When she has settled you in, would she like me to give her some dinner?"

"I should think she would love it. I'll ask her."

He telephoned Judith, then told me she was pleased, and we arranged that when she left him in the hospital she would come to join me in a nearby restaurant. And she came, with a glowing face, eyes sparkling, wearing a blue full-skirted dress.

I don't remember what we ate. I was brimming over with the intoxication of having her there to myself, and I wished she were my own wife so fiercely that my muscles ached.

"When are you going to Australia?" I asked.

She hesitated. "We leave in three weeks."

"So soon!"

We drank wine and coffee and told each other much without saying a word. Not until we were nearly leaving did she say tentatively, "We'll be away for months, you know."

My feelings must have shown. "Months. How many?"

"We don't know. We're going to potter. India, Singapore, Bali, then Australia, New Zealand, Tahiti, Fiji, Hawaii, America." She fell silent, her eyes not laughing now but full of sadness.

The restaurant had emptied around us and the waiters hovered with polite faces. I fetched Judith's coat and we went outside to my car. She got in beside me and I drove all the way to Clapham without consciously seeing the road.

Gordon's house behind the big gates lay quiet and dark. Judith looked at me, and I leaned across in the car, put my arms around her and kissed her. She kissed me back with a feeling and a need that seemed as intense as my own.

As if of one mind we each at the same time drew back. I

looked ahead through the windshield, seeing trees against the stars—seeing nothing. A long time passed.

"We can't," I said eventually.

"No."

After another long minute she opened the door beside her, and I opened mine.

"Don't get out," she said, "because of your ankle."

I stood up, however, on the driveway, and she walked around the car toward me. We hugged each other for a long, hungry minute of commitment and farewell.

She walked over to the front door and unlocked it, and looked back briefly, once, and then went in, putting the walls between us in final, mutual, painful decision.

December

I FELT alone and also lonely, and I telephoned to Pen one Sunday in December and suggested lunch. She said to come early, and I arrived at eleven thirty to find coffee percolating richly and Pen trying to unravel the string of the Christmas kite.

"I found it when I was looking for some books," she said. "It's so pretty. When we've had coffee, let's go out and fly it."

We took it onto the common, and she let the string out gradually until the dragon was high on the wind, circling, darting, fluttering its frilly tail. It drew us slowly across the grass, and Pen glanced at me. "Is this too far for your ankle? Or too fast?"

"No and no," I said.

We had just reached a spot near Gordon and Judith's house when a gust of wind took the kite suddenly higher. The string snapped, and the dazzling wings soared away free, disappearing to a shape, to a black dot, to nothing.

"What a pity," Pen said, and then paused, seeing where my gaze had traveled to the tall, cream gates, firmly shut.

"Let her go," Pen said soberly. "Like the kite."

"She'll come back."

"Take out some other girl," she urged.

I smiled lopsidedly. "I'm out of practice."

"You can't spend your whole life—" She stopped. "Parkinson's disease isn't fatal. Gordon could live to be eighty."

"I wouldn't want him dead," I protested.

"Then what?"

"Just to go on, I suppose, as we are."

She took my arm. "Let her go, Tim, for your own sake."

As we went silently back to her house I thought of all that had happened since the day Gordon stood in the fountain. Thought of Ginnie and Oliver and Calder, and of all the gateways I'd gone through to grief and pain and the knowledge of death.

"You're a child of the light," Pen said contentedly. "Both you and Judith. You always take sunshine with you. So carry the sunlight to a new young girl who isn't married to Gordon and doesn't break your heart. That's good advice, so take it."

"Yes, doctor," I said, and knew I couldn't.

ON CHRISTMAS EVE, just as I was leaving to go to friends in the country, the telephone rang.

"Hello," I said.

There was a series of clicks and hums, and then a breathless voice said, "Tim . . ."

"Judith?" I said incredulously.

"Yes. Listen, just listen. I don't know who else to ask. Gordon's ill and I'm alone and I don't know, I don't know . . ."

"Where are you?"

"India. He's in hospital. They're very good, very kind, but he's so ill—unconscious. They say cerebral hemorrhage. I'm so afraid, I do so love him." She was crying. "It's so much to ask, but I need . . . help."

"Tell me where," I said. "I'll come at once."

She told me where. I was already packed, and I went. But because of the season and the off-track destination there were delays, and it took forty hours to get there. Gordon died before I reached her, on the day after Christmas, like her mother.

Dick Francis was born in Tenby, Wales, in 1920, and left school at fifteen "because all I ever wanted to do was ride horses." He was well on his way as a professional rider when World War II intervened, and he joined the Royal Air Force. At the war's end he resumed his racing career.

Dick Francis

In ten years, from 1948 to 1957, he rode 2305 mounts, had 345 wins, 285 places and 240 shows, and was one of Britain's leading steeplechase jockeys. He was forced to retire from the track with a damaged spleen—having survived a battery of other serious injuries. A steeplechase rider, he explains, expects to take more falls than a flat-race jockey: on the average he takes a spill in one out of every ten races, hitting the ground at about thirty miles an hour.

Francis' outstanding record as a jockey has been equaled, if not surpassed, by his literary career. Beginning as a racing columnist for London's *Sunday Express*, he soon switched to books. So far he has written twenty-one novels, which have been published in eighteen languages and have sold millions of copies.

"Thank God for Mary," Francis says of his wife. She types his manuscripts, proofreads, and does the extensive research his books require. To research one, she became a professional photographer; for another, a pilot. For *Banker*, she delved into the world of London merchant banking.

The pharmacological background of *Banker* had an accidental origin. A professor at the University of California wrote Francis asking if he would autograph a book for him. "Of course I said yes," Francis says, "and he turned up one day at our London flat with two big suitcases packed with everything I had ever written. We invited him in, and while I was busy signing, he got talking about his work—pharmacology. It was all so fascinating, I asked him if Mary and I could come to visit him in the States sometime. We did, and that was how *Banker* began."